TRIAL BY DARKNESS

Also by Charles Gorham

The Gilded Hearse
The Future Mr. Dolan
Trial by Darkness
Martha Crane
The Gold of Their Bodies
Wine of Life
McCaffery
Carlotta McBride
The Lion of Judah

TRIAL BY DARKNESS

CHARLES GORHAM

CUTTING EDGE

ISBN-13: 978-1-962896-21-4

Published by
Cutting Edge Books
PO Box 8212
Calabasas, CA 91372
www.cuttingedgebooks.com

To Ethel with firmest love

PART 1
THE PATH OF A POINT

CHAPTER ONE

"CONNECTICUT," as an old, famous governor of the state once was obliged to caution his son, who was thinking of becoming a painter, "Connecticut is not Athens."

There have been no significant Attic improvements since Governor Trumbull's day, and perhaps Avery Hollister's father would have done him a service had he offered the same advice, a century and a half later. But Avery's father had no way of knowing that his son had been born with a nostalgia for heaven, or that in the end he would turn out to be the first Hollister in nine generations to desert the Connecticut Valley. Had he known, he would not have been pleased.

Besides, Avery was his mother's boy, at least in the beginning. Then he became his father's, and later on nobody's boy or man either, until finally he became his own.

But that is getting ahead of the story.

Avery began his life in a pattern that had suited the Hollisters for a long long time. The pattern was broken and things were changed, partly because of the war, and partly because of his mother, and his English cousin who came to visit in a war summer, but mostly because in Avery himself there was some ingredient that wasn't in the others.

When he was a little boy, Avery adored his mother. Later of course he simply loved her, but when he was four and five and six, in flannel shorts and striped jerseys, he adored her. His universe was his mother's domain—her studio, the gardens, her pretty bedroom and her pink immaculate bathroom, with its jars and bottles and long mirror, that was big enough to reflect them together when they emerged steaming from the marble tub.

In this setting, with his mother, he passed the first five years of his life, hardly aware that there were other people in the world aside from himself, his mother, and Annie McBain, who had once been his mother's maid and was now her housekeeper. His father was a giant who smelled of tobacco and sometimes confused him by asking questions he did not understand, and who was, occasionally, to be seen on a horse. His brother Morgan was a monster to be avoided, who sometimes for no reason slapped him or twisted his arm until it hurt.

They were left much more to themselves than the average mother and youngest child. They had something out of the ordinary in common. They had been present together at tragedy, and the others, Avery's father and brother, Morgan, took it for granted that the tragedy had drawn them together, and somewhat removed them from the rest of the world, as people who have survived certain generally fatal illnesses are afterward to a degree separated from others, and objects of awe.

The Christmas season Avery was three, he and his mother had gone to visit his mother's parents in Rhode Island. Morgan and his father had remained at home. On Christmas Eve, during the drive back to Connecticut, the heavy Pierce Arrow car had gone out of control on the icy road and both the old people had been killed.

Avery's recollection of the accident was vague.

He remembered the windows of the car, coated with ice that looked like lace, and thought he remembered the old man, who wore a coat with a mink collar, leaning forward in the driver's seat to wipe the glass with the back of his glove, just before the car began to slide. There was a crash as the car hit the fence, and another crash as it struck a tree and turned over. Avery was thrown into the darkness, and felt the snow on his cheek like a knife. He cried "Mother! Mother!" but there was no answer. It was black dark, and he heard nothing but the hissing of the snow and the sound of his own teeth chattering. He felt the numbing cold in his lips and understood that he was dying.

When he woke up, his mother was with him. There was a white bandage on her head. He was not in his own room, but in a strange green room that smelled funny. His chest ached and he could not breathe. His mouth felt burnt. Near him was a machine with two orange-painted tanks. His mother bent over him, touching his cheek. Behind her were a nurse and a man in a white coat, with a stethoscope hanging from his neck.

"Sleep, darling," his mother said. "Just sleep."

He had pneumonia, in both lungs, and nearly died, since the year was 1931, and there were no miracle drugs. It was not until almost a year later, when there was another Christmas, that he learned his grandfather and grandmother were dead and that he would never again be taken to visit the big house in Providence.

He was told then, though he didn't understand, that his grandfather had loved him, and in order to demonstrate that love had set up a trust fund for him—money he would get later on, when he was grown up.

He was not told that his mother had insisted the car continue on the dangerous road, though his grandfather had wanted to stop, because she knew that in Hull Avery's father and brother were waiting and could not bear to disappoint them, and that she therefore believed herself responsible for the death of her parents and the dangerous illness of her son.

Avery wept for his grandparents when informed of their new residence in heaven, but he was not really concerned. He hardly remembered the old people, and he had his mother, his pretty mother. She nursed him through the bitter illness, sleeping on a cot in his hospital room, and through the long convalescence, when he was weak and not allowed to play outdoors as much as his father thought suitable for a growing boy.

He thought his mother was beautiful, and everyone else agreed with him. She was never described with any adjective other than beautiful. It is not a word uttered comfortably in New England, except in deference to scenery, and the ladies of Hull, describing her thus, managed to incorporate reprimand with the compliment. "Of course Nancy's beautiful," they would say, "and she does have nice clothes, at least they must be, for what they cost. But she looks sort of, well, *frail*."

What they meant and would not say, was that her beauty was old fashioned. It was the beauty of another era, another climate, another landscape. She was a well-dressed woman with a smart contemporary surface, yet the subtle observer always understood that the flesh beneath the Carnegie suit was the softer flesh of antebellum beauty, the flesh of a woman who fainted when the press was too great, who rode sidesaddle in heavy melton skirts, whose passions were deep, private and concealed. None of this was overly stated in terms of appearance or behavior. It was nuance, aroma, like the trace of perfume that sometimes lingers in the drawer of an antique chest, having seeped into the pores of the wood—the perfume, the breath, of another era, another world.

Such people, with the flavor of the past about them, are romantic, and Avery's mother was romantic—the kind of New England woman who might have run off with a Confederate cavalry leader, and been deserted for the gaming tables, to expire with exquisite sadness of some nondisfiguring, attractive weakness of the lungs. She was not at all the right wife for Avery's father, John Hollister of Hull, and in order to answer the demands of her acquired duties she must have drawn heavily upon resources she did not really possess, always a dangerous and exhausting tactic, and perhaps it was this in the end that consumed her, like a Fourth of July rocket, the fire gone, the hot intensity obscured, the beauty left there in the sky, nothing remaining but a charred cardboard cartridge that drops soundlessly on the clipped fresh grass.

She was a pale Pre-Raphaelite blonde, and everyone said she looked like the best portraits of Christina Rossetti. Though she admired the French painters, she was not the woman a Frenchman would have painted, except for money. Her face, her whole being, had a literary quality—a touching, sad beauty, inferential and poetic. Her life since marriage had been devoted to the construction of a private world, delicate, ordered and tasteful, and in which for a time she was able to move with confidence and love. When that world was smashed, of course, she was smashed with it. There were those who regarded her as frustrating, because she was screened from the world, and others who thought her absurd. To Avery, when he finally understood her, she seemed tragic; the world had touched her only to wreck her; she had not been supplied at birth with the ingredients for survival.

She was no longer much at ease, when he was a child, among the people the Hollisters knew. She had begun to withdraw, and the death of her parents and Avery's illness offered a pattern for withdrawal too attractive to resist.

When he was little they would sit for hours, mother and son, in his mother's whitewashed studio, while she painted and he watched the bright trite landscapes take shape on the canvas, sometimes passing an afternoon in silence, sometimes talking about the city of Paris, which she loved.

She made Paris seem enormously romantic.

She had been a student there in the way well-off American girls are art students in Paris, living with a friend and the friend's aunt in a respectable part of the city, going each day to an atelier where there were bearded, faintly dangerous characters, and sometimes even to disreputable cellars on the other side of the river where actual cutthroats might be seen with their women.

It had been antiseptic adventure; she had been a virgin and almost unkissed when she married Avery's father.

She had a great map of Paris, printed in tones of gray and pink, bright green geometrics indicating boulevards and parks. She would spread this map on the studio floor and she and Avery would kneel over it like a couple of generals planning an attack. He memorized the foreign names and began to learn the French language. When he was four and five and six he must have known the city almost as well as a Parisian taxi driver.

He was happy when he was little. He loved his mother and he loved the house in which he had been born. His people had lived in that house for two hundred years and though it had grown from a simple house to something resembling an estate, the Hollisters never forgot the fact that colonial timbers continued to support the central part of the structure. It was a big white clapboard house, placed well back from the hard road and protected by a gathering of beautiful elms. The spirit of its origins had been preserved, and people who compiled illustrated books on old New England architecture generally included a photograph of it.

The grounds were enclosed and beautiful. There was an acre of lawn that his father said was as good as any in East Anglia. In summer, while his mother lived, there were masses of flowers and items of shrewdly placed autonomous shrubbery that was always expertly pruned.

His father called the place a farm, though of course it wasn't really a farm but simply a gentleman's house, with a model barn for horses and another for his father's herd of matched Guernsey cows. His father had built the tennis courts and the long concrete pool in which he was later taught to swim.

Inside, there was a quantity of old and valuable furniture— Windsor and slatback and Sheraton chairs, Staffordshire brought out from England, handsome American Empire pieces of walnut and cherry with satinwood inlays. The house had grown with time, and did not have the museum aspect of some old places in Hull and Avon and Wethersfield, bought by New Yorkers or airplane people and "restored." It was an accumulation, a setting created by accretion and the blending of various tastes, softened, in that generation, and touched with art, by Avery's mother.

There were, when Avery was young, five servants in the house—the housekeeper, McBain, a cook, a pair of maids whose faces changed but whose uniforms remained the same, and a scullery girl who came and went by the day. It did not occur to him that this manner of life was unusual. Once, when some clothes he had outgrown were taken from his closet by McBain, he asked what was going to be done with them.

Annie turned, her arms filled with frayed sweaters and shorts that chafed. She was a forthright, redhaired woman, then just past forty, and came from a misty highland village where people had fierce respect for the past.

"They'll go to the puir children, lad," she said.

"What are the poor children, Annie?"

"People whose fathers haven't the money to buy them new things," she explained, her voice touched with a soft burr.

"Is my father rich, then?" he asked.

"Your father's a gentleman," she said. "Among other things, he has sufficient money."

She went out of the room with her armful of clothes; Avery wept for the poor children he had never seen, who would wear clothes too tight in the crotch because their fathers were not gentlemen.

It was an unreal life. It ignored the world. For a long time, Avery assumed that everyone lived as he did, aside from the pathetic, unseen poor to whom his old clothes were sent, and no one troubled to explain to him that this was not the case. He was a small child in the Thirties, and beyond the fieldstone gates of his father's place, the world that had produced that place, the world that had produced his father, was breaking up. The times were precarious and hungry, but at the farm they were not much affected. Avery's father was concerned, for he was aware of his responsibilities, but his own money was secure; the depression actually improved his position.

Avery's father was an anachronism, a vestigial Yankee aristocrat. He was a man who believed that he placed his trust in the old virtues. He had faith in England and in New England. He believed in a kind of symbolic austerity, especially for youth. He did not impose an austere existence upon his sons, as the English are reported to do, with hard beds and cold baths and dreary food, on the theory that character will thus be improved. But he insisted on rigid allowances, careful treatment of clothing, attention to formal discipline. His sons addressed him as "sir," and this did not embarrass him.

He could not bear the sight of wasted food.

It was an obsession.

He had curbed his own prejudices and expected others to do likewise.

"All the peas, Morgan," he would say to Avery's older brother, "all the peas, or no dessert."

He was decent about it. If Avery hated a certain vegetable, he got only a token portion, but that symbolic mite must be eaten, down to the last segment of bean or blob of mashed turnip.

He was not a Puritan, for along the way the Hollisters had become Episcopalians, but he was the descendant of Puritans and in New England the Puritan conscience is engaged with the air, if one has a certain kind of breathing apparatus. There was, somewhere in his past and faintly in the atmosphere about him, an army of unalterable law that he apprehended and thought he lived by, but was seldom inclined to state in any definite terms. He would not, for example, have called himself an aristocrat or member of the upper class, though he certainly believed he was one or the other or both. He did not necessarily feel that he was better than anyone else, but he thought he had been provided

with certain endowments that obliged him to be more responsible in his conduct than most people. Therefore, he felt, he and
his family and the people they knew were especially qualified for
disinterested political leadership and the scrupulous stewardship
of money. He lived, not in reference to a code, but rather to a kind
of social and economic compost heap of schools, money, clothes,
clubs, social connections. If it had been suggested to him that
his values had proven inadequate to the times, or that he did not
really live by them at all but only thought he did, he would not
have understood what was meant.

He had a strong, graceful body and a long, unmistakably
British head. He wore suits and shirts made for him in London
that gave him sartorial authority. He had elegance, and controlled
charm. He had commanded a platoon of British infantry when
he was eighteen and a company of American infantry when he
was twenty, having gone out from Yale in 1915 to join the King's
Royal Rifle Corps. He was thirty-two when Avery was born, in
1928, and looked younger than he was, resembling certain early
steel engravings of Alexander Hamilton, with the same clean-
lined face and precisely defined mouth.

Later, after he broke with his father, Avery for a long time
saw nothing but his defects. It was unfair; his father had virtues
as well as faults. He did what he took to be his duty, and did it
according to the standards he had inherited and believed in.

As a father he was not absolutely desirable.

Youth in itself had no real charm for him. His sons were to
be turned into young gentlemen as much like himself as possible. There are fathers who regard their sons as a kind of second
chance, who are greedy to be surpassed. There are others who see
in their sons only imperfect copies of themselves, to be brought
as closely as possible into alignment with the model. Avery's
father was the second kind; he felt that if his sons measured up
to his own performance, neither he nor they would have cause to
complain.

The boys would grow up, go to Colborn School, where he had gone, and to Yale, and finally marry, living in houses that would be modest approximations of this one. Even if they went away, to become journalists or lawyers or soldiers, they would really remain here in Hull, and just be absent on visits.

The Hollisters were people with the deepest roots it is possible to have in America and they believed these roots went undersea to England, so that they were proud of their English connections and proud of their exchange privileges with the best London clubs. Avery's father, and his father's friends, would have resented the suggestion that they were artificial British colonials, for they were American patriots, often going into politics and always going to wars. Nevertheless, Avery's father actually had said one day, "I do not think that I should care to live in a world in which there was no England."

The Hollisters had an actual English connection, though none of them as yet had ever seen him. That was Avery's cousin, David Fearing, who was an orphan. His father had been a British regular officer, killed on the Somme six months before David was born. His mother, who had been a Hollister, had died giving birth to him, and David had remained in England, brought up by his father's family.

"We must have him here one of these days," Avery's father often said. "If his mother had lived she'd have brought him here and he would have grown up in this house the way you boys have."

But until the war came and changed things, David Fearing was not seen at Hull. He remained a mysterious, rather romantic figure, almost a myth, the English cousin, who was now at Eton and now at Cambridge and now somewhere in the south of France with the uncle who had undertaken to rear him.

Avery's father moved about Hull with the confidence of a young squire. He was the town's first citizen. But he was also a

Hartford man, for the source of his income was Hartford and his greater prestige was there too.

Hartford is a city that clings to the Yankee virtues. It has no Ritz Hotel and has never had a Mrs. Jack Gardner. The old families have not been dispossessed as they have been elsewhere, and there is about Hartford an air of complacent repose that strikes a visitor from, say, Detroit, as almost antiquarian. Hartford has no desire to be New York or Boston or New Haven. It is satisfied with itself, and this leads to a stability of attitude unusual in America. This Hartford attitude—it would be unkind to call it smug—Avery's father epitomized. He believed in Hartford, in himself, and in the virtues that resided in his name.

Being Anglophile, he also believed that men are by nature more important than women, and for a boy this is an idea hard to resist. When he was small and guarded by his illness and the tragedy that linked him to his mother, Avery avoided his father. He wanted nothing to do with him. He preferred his mother's world, the pale sweet world in which he felt happy and quite safe. But of course his father could not permit him to remain in that world. He was a boy, even though only a second son; there were things he must learn from men and from older boys. He had been his mother's child too long. When he was five it was time for him to undergo a second, more disturbing weaning.

CHAPTER TWO

ONE morning, the summer he was five, he woke up in what seemed the middle of the night, aware of someone moving in the dark outside his door. He got out of bed to see who it was and met his father, dressed in boots and a bright red shirt, unshaven and romantic looking. He grinned at Avery and said, "Hi, young fella. What are you doing up?"

"I just woke up," Avery said. "Where you going?"

"Fishing," his father said. "We're going to Turpin's Pond."

It was a pond on the farm property, a mile or so from the house.

"Can I come?" Avery asked.

"Think you can make it?" his father said.

Avery nodded. Morgan was going, he knew, and he suddenly wanted to go too.

"Well, get your clothes on, then. Wear your blue jeans and boots."

It all had the character of an expedition. Downstairs, in the dining room, coffee boiled over an alcohol flame. His father and Morgan, in their woods clothes that smelled of gun oil and marsh, talked in conspiratorial whispers.

They crept out of the house into the gray morning, closing the screen door carefully. They crossed the meadow through the high wet grass and entered the wood, following an old lumberman's road, the trees closing in to form a tunnel of leaves that hung over the rotted corduroy and shut out the rising sun. The air was cool, and sweet with the smell of the forest floor and of tiny flowers, bright as dabs of pure zinc white, that broke through the damp crust of rotted leaves and pine needles. Far ahead, through the leaf passage, was a sharp, exciting splash of sunlight, toward which they were heading.

In the lead, Avery's father took the rise in slow steady fashion, not breaking his pace. Behind him, Morgan kept in step. Avery tumbled after them, slipping on a section of corduroy that was slimy with rot, so that he lost his balance and fell, smearing his hand and forearm with slime and mud.

Avery's father called back, not stopping. "Get the rhythm, Avery. That's all there is to climbing. A slow, steady pace, and never hurry, never break your rhythm. Then you'll never feel it. Keep your stride, and you can climb all day."

His chest was covered with damp leaves and he had been shaken up by the fall. He held back the tears and brushed the leaves away. He ran a little, catching up with Morgan, who turned and grinned.

"Get the rhythm, kid," said Morgan. "Take it easy."

He was six years older than Avery, and had a kind of associational orthodoxy, an atmosphere of rightness about him, that Avery did not have. Avery watched him climb, repeating the rhythm of his father's stride. "Get the rhythm," he counseled himself. "Get the rhythm."

He was to hear it again and again: get the rhythm, keep your eye on the ball, squeeze the trigger, squeeze it, don't jerk, post, Avery, post, use your knees, you have to ride *him*, not let him ride you, get the rhythm, son, the rhythm, keep your head down, Down, DOWN!

He followed his father and brother. They paused, for a few minutes, on a rock shelf beneath which was a sheer, dangerous drop of perhaps a hundred feet. Avery caught his breath. From far away came the ingratiating sound of falling water. The mood of the forest was insistent and there was a sense of detachment from the world, though the main motor road to Hartford was half a mile away. During those few minutes, while they stood on the ledge like alpinists, the privacy of the forest gave him a feeling of unity with the others. He felt excited and good, eager to please his father and Morgan, and to impress them. Then Morgan scaled a stone out over the treetops and it struck something with a peremptory sound, breaking the hushed mood. They went downhill to the pond, egg-shaped, lovely, edged by trees.

When his father and Morgan began to fish, Avery found a flat rock and dozed in the sun. He fell into a dead sleep, exhausted by the long climb. When he woke up, the sun had moved and his rock was in shadow. He felt cold and for a moment lost, for his father and brother had worked around the shore line and were out of sight. Then he heard their voices.

"We'll have to get Avery a rod next year," his father was saying. "The kind you had when you were his age. It's time he learned to cast."

"He's a good kid," Morgan said, "but sometimes he seems like an awful sissy."

"It's not his fault," his father said. "Your mother spoiled him when he was little. Kept him in the house too much."

Avery got up, tears in his eyes. He didn't want to be a sissy, and he knew it was wrong to prefer being indoors with his mother to being here in the woods with his father and Morgan. He climbed down from the rock and walked to the edge of the pond, where he picked up a sharp stone shaped like an Indian dagger. A causeway of rough stone ran out into the water for twenty or thirty feet, ending in a flat boulder that was in the sun. He navigated this, holding the stone dagger in his hand, and stretched out on the big rock, his face toward the water.

Far beneath the surface he saw a great fish that swam moodily, seeming almost to tread water, remaining in one position with hardly any movement of its tail. He had the idea that if he could inch down quietly he could spear the fish with his stone knife, as he had heard the Indians did. He eased down until his nose touched the water, stalking the enormous phlegmatic fish. Then he raised his arm and struck. He lost his balance and plunged into the pond, sinking far down, his lungs stabbed by the icy water. He felt the slime of the weeds at the bottom, then came to the surface for an instant. He must have screamed before he went down again, for his father reached him in time to pull him out before he drowned.

He had the sensation of being strangled in sleep, then came to and saw his father's face, close to his own. His father straddled his body, and his father's hands were on his chest, pressing, relaxing, pressing, relaxing, pressing, relaxing. His mouth was filled with the taste of vomit, and the pressure on his chest hurt, but he felt strangely at peace. Then his father got up. He was soaked, and water ran from his hair and clothes.

"What were you trying to do, Avery?" he asked, not angrily.

"What were you trying to do?" asked Morgan. "You almost drowned."

Avery lay on his back, aware now of the rough ground that hurt his flesh. "I was trying to catch a fish," he said. "A big fish."

His father laughed, shaking his head. "You'll never catch one that way, son. You have to be born in the South Seas to catch fish with your bare hands." He caught Avery's hand and pulled him to his feet. "How do you feel? Think you can walk home?"

"Sure. Sure I can," he said.

But he couldn't. Before they had gone a quarter of a mile he stumbled and fell, feeling sick at his stomach. His father slung him to his shoulder and carried him, uphill, then down, not stopping to rest. When they reached the meadow and could see the house, he said, "I'm all right now, sir. I can walk."

His father shook his head. "I carried you this far. Might as well carry you the rest of the way." He was not going to be deprived of credit for carrying Avery home.

Morgan ran on ahead, yelling so that they could hear him at the house. "Avery fell into Turpin's Pond and almost drowned.

Dad saved his life. Avery fell into Turpin's Pond and almost drowned. Dad saved his life."

There was an interlude of crisis.

He was rubbed with witch hazel until his skin was red, and fed a tablespoonful of whiskey. He felt warm and confident and filled with love for humanity, especially for his father, who had saved his life and who now sat on the edge of his bed, touching his cheek with a rough hand and saying, "You're all right, fella. You're fine. You've got plenty of guts."

Even Morgan couldn't spoil it when he came into Avery's room and said, "I bet you did it on purpose, stinker, just because you don't know how to fish."

His father *had* saved his life, no matter how he had actually got into the water, and in some way, to Avery, this seemed to constitute formal recognition of him as a human being. That night at dinner he studied his father, watching the strong square hands manipulate the knife and fork, and watching the long line of muscle that ran under his father's jaw. He loved him. The fear inspired for six years was turned into love and awe and respect. His father was strong and he was on his side; he had even saved his life.

Later that summer he saw him perform an act of courage so extraordinary that it seemed to him his father must be the bravest man alive, a man who simply didn't know the meaning of the word fear, like the hero of a book he had started to read.

Near the farm was a public beach and picnic ground, used mostly by town kids and city people who drove out in cars. Sometimes when Morgan was bored he would go there and take Avery with him. There was a shack where they bought hot dogs and vicious chemical pop, run by an irritable pasty-faced man who hated Morgan because he thought Morgan was too big for his breeches. He was the kind of defeated man who hates all fortunate people, and Morgan liked to get him mad. One day when

Morgan said, "Come on, will you please, my good man," using a fake English accent, he lost his temper. He slapped Morgan hard on the cheek, making a loud noise and sending Morgan reeling backward.

"Yuh little snot-nose," he said. "You just wait 'til I git *ready* to serve yuh. I don't give a durn who y'are."

Morgan was eleven and not big enough to take on the man himself. Avery watched him standing there, his lip trembling from the pain. "Come on, kid," he said. "Let's get out of here."

They went to the forest rangers' station, where there was a phone, and Morgan called Hartford, collect. When he hung up he grinned and said, "Dad's coming out. Right away."

They went outside, paying no attention to the crowd of town kids who stared at them, and waited until their father's car rolled powerfully over the dirt road, bigger and more expensive than any of the cars in the parking space, and impressive because of its high polish and the tin tag on the license plate that said: LEGISLATURE.

Their father walked between them into the hot-dog stand, where the man stood behind his griddle. "This boy says you slapped his face," he said. "Did you?"

The man didn't answer. Avery's father moved toward him, and then the man did a foolish thing. He took a revolver from the cash register and pointed it at the three Hollisters.

"Don't you touch me, you big bastard," he said nervously. "Don't you come near me, or I'll kill you, hear?"

Avery's father made a sudden movement and knocked the gun from his hand, then pulled him from behind the counter and slapped him hard across the face.

"Don't you ever touch one of these boys again, do you hear?" he said. "If you do, I'll beat you so bad you won't be able to hit anyone."

Avery looked at his father, and then at the hot-dog man, who was so frightened and enraged he had started to cry.

There was a commotion at the door and a state trooper entered the shack, his hand on his gun. He recognized Avery's father and touched the brim of his hat. "Something wrong, Mr. Hollister?" he asked respectfully.

Avery's father smiled and said, "I think it's all taken care of, officer. Unless Mr. Podwosjki here, or whatever his name is, wants to press charges against me for assault. I hit him."

Avery's eyes were on the revolver that now lay forgotten on the floor. He had to know whether or not it was loaded with real bullets and moved toward it, fascinated and afraid. His father stepped ahead of him and picked it up. He broke it open and pushed out five dirty cartridges that fell like nuts on the oilcloth counter, then held the barrel to the light and squinted down it. He handed the gun to the man, saying, "You don't keep your gun much cleaner than you keep your place, do you?" He turned to the trooper and asked, "Is this shack under state license, officer?"

"Yes, sir," the trooper said. "Park Commission."

His father nodded. Then he turned, and the boys followed him out of the place. He stood beside the car and looked critically at Morgan.

"What did you say to that Polack, to make him mad enough to hit you?" he asked.

Morgan lowered his eyes.

"I was pretty snotty to him, Pa," he said.

His father looked at Morgan until Morgan's eyes came up. Then he said, "Morgan, I won't have anyone hitting you. But you have got to remember that you're a gentleman, and a gentleman doesn't take advantage of his position. Do you understand?"

Morgan nodded. "Yes, sir," he said. "I'm sorry."

They watched the big car drive away. Morgan shook his head. "Did you see him knock that gun out of the guy's hand? Right out of his hand? It was loaded all right, too."

"Do you think he was scared, Morg?" asked Avery.

"Scared? Pa? Don't be a dope."

They went back to the hot-dog stand, where the man served them sullenly. The next week, he was replaced by a white-haired Irishman from Hartford who knew their names and asked them about their father.

On the beach that day a farmer's son, two years older than Morgan, put his hand against Morgan's chest and pushed him. "You must think your old man owns the place, jerk. Well, he don't, see? It's public."

Morgan picked himself up and advanced, as he had been taught at school, hitting the bigger boy on the jaw, then brutally in the stomach, so that the boy dropped his hands and was sick.

"You mind your own business, townie," Morgan said, turning away. "And don't ever mention my father's name again."

What remained in Avery's mind was the way the dirty bullets plopped out of the cylinder onto the dirty oilcloth. It was those bullets, compact and lethal, that proved to him that the whole performance was not a fake and that his father was really fearless.

After the incident, for some-time, he was fascinated by guns, and would go out to the skeet range and watch his father and Morgan smash clay pigeons around the clock, admiring the beautiful chased Belgian guns, and gathering up the pasteboard shells to keep for souvenirs. He was nearly six, but for some reason his father did not suggest that he try to shoot the twenty-two. When he asked about it his father told him that his mother wanted him to wait until he was a little older and stronger. For the first time in his six years of life, he was conscious of specific resentment of his mother.

"What does she know?" he said. "Women don't know about guns."

"Well, that's true, son. But we don't want to get her upset, do we?"

"Well, no, sir. I guess not." He frowned. "But Morgan did, when he was six."

His father shook his head. "Better wait, son," he said. "Wait until you're a little older."

That September Morgan taught him the fundamentals of football, so he would have a jump on the others a few weeks later when he entered Sturgis Manor School and went out for the midget team, made up of six and seven-year-olds. It did not occur to anyone, even to his mother, that he would not play on the midget team, and then with the juniors and seniors, and finally with the school team; or that he would not go on to Colborn, where Morgan was going this fall, and play there, and finally to New Haven, to play there, as his father had done, and his grandfather.

He wore an old uniform of Morgan's, and a new scarlet and yellow helmet, and stiff new cleated shoes that the Sturgis Manor catalogue advised parents to buy for their boys before they sent them to the school. It was a school that believed in compulsory sports, and that started football a few years earlier than most American schools.

Beyond the horse barn, on a cleared space, a pair of goal posts had been erected, and forty yards of football field marked off with a tennis liner. For three weeks that September, Avery smashed into his brother, learning to *drive, drive, drive,* the way Morgan said to do, to fall on the ball, to block, and to cut out of the line. Morgan was patient with him and only once or twice was irritated enough to hurt him. Sometimes his father joined them, but then he and Morgan would pass to one another, and he would sit on the bench, forgotten.

That fall, too, just after Avery's sixth birthday, his father had occasion to impress upon him the importance of telling the truth, and to make clear to him the sheer uselessness of falsehood.

In his study, his father had a French clock with open works protected by a glass dome. The clock had always fascinated Avery, and one afternoon, alone in the house, he climbed to a chair and attempted to take it down. The glass dome slipped from his hands and the clock fell to the floor, the bright brass wheels bent and twisted on the polished floor, amid the splintered glass. He got down quickly, terrified, and ran from the room, remaining away from the house until time for dinner.

During dinner, nothing was said, but when the meal was finished his father asked him to come into his study. The ruined clock was where it had fallen and the shattered glass gleamed up at him accusingly. His father pointed to the wreckage.

"Did you break that clock, Avery?"

Avery ordinarily preferred the truth, but something, on this occasion, prompted him to lie. "No, sir. I didn't," he said, holding his ground, his mouth firm, his head up, his eyes remaining steadily fixed on a point just above his father's stomach. His father sat back in his chair, the oiled springs making a pleasant sound.

"Do you know what a lie is, Avery?" he asked.

"Why, yes, sir."

"Well, then, what is a lie?"

"Well, sir, something that isn't the truth."

"That's right, Avery. A lie is something that isn't the truth. And a lie is what you are telling me, when you say you didn't break the clock, isn't that so?"

He shook his head. "No, sir."

His father sighed and leaned forward.

"Avery, suppose I tell you I can prove you broke the clock?" he said gently. "What would you say then?"

Avery looked steadily at his father. No one had seen him, his mind protested. The house had been empty. No one had seen him. It might have been a cat that had broken the clock, or one of the maids, or even a burglar. It was simply his father's word against his. He couldn't prove it, because no one had seen.

But he did prove it. At least he proved it to Avery's satisfaction, and his own.

He took a stamp pad from his desk and a sheet of crisp white paper, then motioned Avery to his side. "Give me your hand, son," he said. He was disarming, and Avery obeyed, fascinated and a little excited. His father rolled his fingers across the pad, one by one, then transferred the prints to the paper, until there were five black prints in a row, then let go of his hand and picked up the largest piece of glass, a side of the dome. He blew on the glass and held it to the light, then blew again, nodding. He rose and touched Avery's shoulder.

"Now, Avery," he said, "those are your fingerprints, there on the paper. They are unique. Do you know what that means?"

"No, sir."

He kept a large globe in his study, that could be lighted from the inside so the colors of the countries glowed. He lighted the globe and spun it, making the colors blend, then stopped it suddenly with his finger.

"Frenchmen," he said, pointing to France, "Germans, Russians, Chinese. Up here, Eskimos. Down here, Patagonians. All kinds of people, all over the world. Billions of them. But only one of them could make those marks on that bit of paper, Avery. And that one is you."

He took Avery's smudged hand, turned it over and looked at it, then let go, and picked up the piece of glass.

"You can't see the prints properly," he said. "You need powder for that. But you *can* see them." He blew on the glass and showed Avery a smudge that might have been anything. "Do you see?"

Avery nodded.

"Now, of course, I'm an amateur at this. But I'm willing to bet that if we took this piece of glass and that piece of paper over to the State Police Barracks, where they have an expert, that he'd find the prints on the paper and the glass were made by the same fingers. Your fingers."

His father smiled at him, absolutely no malice in his face, or cruelty, only a certain pardonable satisfaction with himself for having adroitly carried off what he believed to be a valuable demonstration of the inevitability of truth. Avery looked at him, the meaning of his father's performance becoming clear in his mind, and terrifying.

"It was an accident," he said finally. "I wanted to look at it, and it fell."

His father nodded, bending to lift the twisted clockwork from the floor. "It can be fixed," he said. "I'm sure it can be fixed."

Avery was not relieved by this opinion. He felt that he had been tricked, not so much by his father, as by the fingers of his own hand.

"You must learn to tell the truth, Avery," his father said. "Gentlemen don't tell lies." He smiled. "Except, perhaps, to ladies, on special occasions. But you're too young for that."

Avery hung his head.

"Go along, now. Go straight to bed."

He went into the living room, where a small fire burned. He stared at the flame for a long time, his logical, small child's brain turning over what had occurred in the study. Then he thrust his hand into the fire, with some idea that he could burn away the marks on his fingers that had betrayed him. But the pain was too much. He screamed, and his mother ran from the other room.

"What on earth have you done, darling?"

"Nothing," he said. "I was just trying to fix the fire."

She took him upstairs to her bathroom and rubbed cream on his fingers, then helped him undress and get into bed. She turned out the light and sat on the edge of his bed, holding his hand.

"I don't want to go to school," he said. "Why do I have to? I can read. You taught me to read."

"Oh, darling, school's fun. You'll love school." She bent and kissed him.

"I don't want to go," he said.

He had formed an idea of school. It was a place populated by dozens of Morgans, and dozens of men like his father, where he would be made to play games he did not want to play.

He was not far wrong.

"Darling, you must grow up," said his mother, suddenly quite serious. "I've babied you too much, you know. You're a big boy now."

"Yes, mother."

He rolled away, closing his eyes. After a while his mother got up and went out of the room, leaving him alone in the dark, where he could not sleep because his fingers smarted from the taste of the fire. He had a premonition of failure, and a sense that he was being moved toward a slavery, the nature of which he felt rather than understood.

There was a sound at his door and he looked up to see his father's figure, outlined by the glow of the hall light. He had a moment of sheer terror. Not long before, he had seen his father smash the heads of three female puppies, from a litter that had turned out badly, breaking their necks expertly with one terrible movement of his arm. As his father came toward him in the darkness, he thought for a moment that he was to be killed as the puppies had been, and he moved away convulsively, toward the wall, so that he bumped his head.

But his father sat down gently on his bed, the springs giving under his weight, and rumpled his hair.

"I didn't mean to scare you, son," he said. "I just wanted to make you understand that you must tell the truth. It was for your own good."

"I understand, sir," he said.

"If you do something wrong, Avery," his father said, "the thing to do is to tell the truth. Tell the truth and take your medicine. Then everything will always turn out all right."

"You mean, no matter what you do?" he asked.

"That's right," his father said. "No matter what you do, the best thing is to tell the truth and take your medicine."

"Suppose you killed somebody?" he said, trembling.

His father laughed.

"Even then," he said. "But you're not going to kill anybody. Unless there's a war. And then you have the right to kill them. The enemy, I mean."

His father rumpled his hair again, then leaned over and kissed him. It was a rare thing, and the effect on Avery was almost one of shock. He felt his father's beard against his cheek, and the smell of his father's tobacco and clothes. He put his arms around his father's neck and held him for a moment.

"Are you mad, Daddy, about the clock?" he asked.

"Not any more," his father said, disengaging himself. "Not now that we've got it straightened out." He put a big hand on his shoulder and squeezed. "We understand one another, Avery, don't we?" he asked.

"Yes, sir," Avery said. "You bet."

His father got up and went out of the room.

He rolled in the bed, filled with a happiness that was kinetic, almost purely physical.

It was a miracle.

He had been forgiven.

And his father loved him. He understood this with wonderment and enormous gratitude.

CHAPTER THREE

I T WAS his father who took him to school, on the first day, driving him there in his big car. They turned into the school road, and the colony of white clapboard buildings came into sight, bright white buildings with green blinds, the land dipping beyond the buildings, where the playing fields rolled toward the river. Hanging from the doorway of the Main Building, that was called Wilderness Hall, was a vivid scarlet and yellow sign that said: STURGIS MANOR SCHOOL for BOYS, *Founded* 1874, the words arranged around a coat of arms with a Latin motto. It was a small boys' boarding school and most of the students lived in the dormitory buildings on the other side of the football field. Avery was to be a day boy, as Morgan had been, going and coming in the school bus.

His father stopped the car.

"Now, son, your first day of school is important. You want to make a good impression, you know."

"Yes, sir," he said. He was dressed in his new school suit, a gray jacket with the school coat of arms sewn to the left breast, and a little round cap, with the letters SMS embroidered in gold on the front. He was apprehensive and self-conscious, but the presence of his father reassured him somewhat.

"Morgan did very well here," his father said. "He played for the school for two years, and was captain of football his last year. That will do you a lot of good, you know. He's sort of paved the way for you."

"I understand," he said.

It was always MorganMorganMorgan. He wished that his father, just for today, would forget Morgan.

"Well, then, come along," his father said.

They went into the office, a pine-paneled room with pictures on the wall, and a big man, bigger even than his father, came out of a little office, smiling.

"Well, John," he said, shaking hands with his father. "This is Hollister, Minor, eh? Fine-looking boy."

"Mr. Foresby, Avery. The headmaster."

He shook hands with Mr. Foresby, and said, "Hello, sir." Then for some reason that was beyond him, he made an absurd French bow, and said loudly, "Comment-alley-voo?"

The gentlemen laughed.

"Speaks French already, does he?" Mr. Foresby asked, putting his hand on Avery's head.

"His mother taught him a few words," his father said. "She taught him to read, too. I hope you don't have to unteach him."

"I don't think so," Mr. Foresby said. He knelt beside Avery and felt his shoulders and the muscles of his legs, the way a groom or horse-buyer might feel an animal. "Good solid lad," he said. "Good pair of legs. Nice shoulders." He looked straight into his eyes. "Going to play for us, son, when you get the weight?"

"Yes, sir," Avery said, obediently.

Mr. Foresby stood up. He put a hand on his father's shoulder. "You know, I played against your Dad," he said. "Twice. You'll have to go some to be the competitor he was. He was rugged. A really rugged tackle. The kind you don't see very much any more."

"Oh, well," his father said. "That was a long time ago. A long time ago."

But he was pleased. He slapped Avery on the back and said, "Well, son, I'll leave you now. You're in good hands."

After his father had gone, the headmaster took him across the green to Vicksburg Hall, and introduced him to Mr. Cobble, who taught the pre-prime boys to read and write and add and take away, during such time as the boys could spare from their efforts on the white-striped fields that could be seen from Vicksburg's opened windows. Mr. Cobble was a gentle Princetonian, who had hoped to be headmaster of the school and been disappointed. He had fine hair, white as paper, and smooth pink cheeks.

Avery liked him.

He rapped with his pointer, and the class came to order.

"Will those boys who know how to read please raise their hands," he said.

There were twenty boys in the class. Four hands went up, then a fifth. Avery did not raise his; he had a dread of calling attention to himself.

Mr. Cobble looked at him and said mildly, "Hollister, you can read, can't you?"

Avery stood up.

"Well, sir..."

"Can you read or not?" the master asked.

"Yes, sir," he said. "I can read."

"Well, then, sit down and put up your hand, boy. If you can read you must go in the Red Group, and use the other book."

Avery sat down and put up his hand. Years later, whenever he had occasion to think of Sturgis Manor School, where he passed the next six years of his life, he always remembered, with a flush of hot embarrassment, that first morning, when he had been ordered to put up his hand to show that he could read.

Then the books were passed out and Avery opened his eagerly. It was mint new, with stiff bright pages and smelled of paste and printers' ink, a romantic, exciting smell, an invitation and reassurance that he was the first, the very first, to look upon these pages. It was like walking on new snow, where no one had ever walked before. He read the first page and the second, a little disappointed because he was able to read the whole book during the ten minutes that Mr. Cobble devoted to distributing the simpler books to the Blue Group, the members of which could read nothing and write nothing, even their own names—a fact that seemed incredible to Avery.

The pointer was rapped and Mr. Cobble said, "Red boys, do the first two pages. Blue boys, your attention, please."

He produced a card that said CAT in enormous letters and had a picture of a cat beneath the word. The Blue boys said CAT in unison, then DOG, then BOY, then GIRL, which made them giggle.

Avery, for the second time, went rapidly through his reader, then went through it a third time, before Mr. Cobble turned his attention to the Red Group.

His school life had begun.

What he thought of, as he stared through the windows of Vicksburg Hall, at the immaculate playing fields beyond, was his father's observation about Morgan's having sort of paved the way for him. *I can do as well as Morgan, he thought. I can do better. Much better.*

It was an idea so daring as to be almost sacrilegious, and he marveled at the audacity of his own imagination. But the idea remained with him; it was the central idea of his life as long as he was at Sturgis Manor, and longer, much longer.

CHAPTER FOUR

H E PLAYED on the midget team and the junior team and the senior team—never quite as well as Morgan, but well enough to gain the approval of his father and Mr. Foresby. Because his mother had taught him French, and because he liked arithmetic, he did a little too well in his studies and had to be skipped to the form above, twice. This worried his father, who had a fear of oddness, but Mr. Foresby reassured him.

"He's a sound lad, John," Mr. Foresby said. "It isn't as if he didn't get out there and drive too. He's a good little back. Lots of spirit."

Avery had a fear of oddness too. He tried to make up for being bright by playing football over his head.

Between his sixth and twelfth birthdays, he learned all they could teach him at Sturgis. Being a day boy and living at home, he also learned what his father could teach him. He learned to ride a horse, rather than having the horse ride him, and to shoot with a rifle or shotgun, squeezing the trigger, squeezing it. He learned to play tennis the way his father did, a good long smashing game. His father taught him to play squash, and advised him to favor it over his tennis.

"Get some kind of exercise every day," his father advised. "Make it a habit, the way you brush your teeth and comb your hair. Half an hour, an hour, every day. You'll never regret it."

He did as they told him.

He conformed.

He had obligation to the past and future, to himself and to his family, and especially to his father. He was the product of some forty generations of careful breeding, and the face he turned toward the world might be said to have originated at the Battle of Hastings. The centuries showed. They were recognized by other people and by Avery himself, who saw them not so much in the mirror as in the similar face of his father.

He looked like his father.

His hair was sandy and his eyes gray-blue, a little less blue than his father's. He had a long head and a pleasant mouth, and he smiled easily. He had the clear good coloring one associates with the well-born. Unlike most New Englanders, he tanned readily, and in the summer he was brown, his hair lightened several shades by the sun, giving him a nearly Scandinavian appearance. He was tall for his age, with able shoulders and long, rather light legs ... a good-looking boy, not remarkably different in appearance from several thousand other boys of his age born to families of the sheltered class along the eastern seaboard. He inspired confidence, and if he was proud of his family and his heritage, there was nothing priggish about him.

In his last year at Sturgis, he seemed to have met every requirement imposed by his family or school. He should have been perfectly satisfied with himself.

There was just one thing wrong.

He never quite believed in himself, except when he was within the privacy of a book or a problem in mathematics. He often felt he was playing a part, that he was in some way a fake. And he felt, nearly always, that he was different from the others, that his mind and spirit were not quite in tune with theirs, or with his father's or brother's. He was ashamed of his own seriousness, and sometimes impatient with his tendency to question what everyone else seemed to take for granted.

Everyone else admired Mr. Foresby, and Avery pretended to admire him too. Afterward, when he had left the school, he realized he had loathed him.

"Fellows," Mr. Foresby would say, "we're not trying to make athletes out of you. Or Einsteins either. We just want to help you do the most with what you've got. With what God gave you."

Then he would smash his big fist into his big palm and bellow, "Hit 'em hard, fellows! Hard!"

And the boys would roar back, "Hit 'em again, hard! Hard! Hit 'em again, hard! Hard!"

Mr. Foresby believed in sport, and he seemed to regard the war in Europe, that had just begun, as the historical branch of sport. Each week, during the spring of Avery's last year at Sturgis, the spring of 1940, he gave a talk on the war situation, using maps and little flags.

One day that spring, an officer of the RAF, who had only one arm, made them a speech and told them that their school was quite like his own private school in Norfolk.

"Except," as he said, "that your food is a jolly sight better than ours, and you get more pocket money. A bob a week was our lot."

He looked alertly around the room, his sandy mustaches brushed out stiff, the bright wings on the breast of his tunic gleaming above the purple and white diagonals of his medal ribbon.

"Not many of you chaps could manage on that, what?"

The day after the Flight Lieutenant spoke, two Sixth Form boys ran off to Canada and tried to enlist in the RCAF. Mr. Foresby was so delighted with them that he managed to make his reprimand sound like a citation for gallantry. For several days the boys carried with them the aroma of adventure.

The following week, Kurt von Klemperer, whose father was a German Embassy official, packed his bags. He was called for by a long black car that flew a swastika flag on the mudguard, and departed forever without saying good-bye to his friends, his small Teutonic chin held high as the limousine turned its continental back on the white New England buildings and the close-cropped playing fields.

Avery watched the German boy drive off. The French mistress watched too, standing beside him. "A regular little boche, eh?" she said. "He wants his uniform."

Avery laughed.

He was fond of Mademoiselle, and she liked him, because he made progress with her language. She had a pleasant, cynical accent, and smoked cigarettes in the French manner, holding them in the corner of her mouth, whenever she thought she would not be seen by Mr. Foresby or his wife. She was underpaid and overworked and not very happy—an applecheeked woman in her early thirties with fine hands and a sober French mouth.

"You too, Avery?" she asked. "Would you like your soldier suit?"

She was half joking with him. He smiled and shook his head. "No." He glanced at his gray flannel jacket. "I'll get along with this."

She touched the lapel of his coat and said, "One hopes so, Avery. One hopes so very much."

He was fond of her; she was his one real friend at the school. She seemed to understand him, and to understand a lot of the things that went on in his head and confused him.

CHAPTER FIVE

THE school gave a prom, late in April, and Morgan, home from Colborn, came to dance with the Farmington girls that had been imported for big brothers and alumni boys. He wore his dinner jacket, and the unfamiliar clothing made him look foreign and much older. He picked out the prettiest Farmington girl, one with a loose red mouth and rich black hair.

Avery watched him dancing with her, envious of the casual way his brother seemed to operate, the way he talked to the pretty girl and held his cheek close to hers. He didn't like to dance much, and anyway, he got stuck with somebody's kid sister, who smelled of talcum and starch and sweat and who panted a little whenever he missed a step and bumped against her incipient organdy-clad breasts.

After a while he escaped and went out into the romantic night, sweating a little from dancing and grateful for the cool night air.

He walked down toward the football field. A hundred cars were parked there and the moonlight glistened on their paint. The music, coming through the doorway, sounded pleasanter outdoors than it had inside. It was a heavy, aching night, filled with promise and with danger.

He walked the length of the football field, then climbed the rise on the south side, so that he was a few feet above the level of the playing surface. He walked along aimlessly with the moonlight on his face.

Then he stopped, for in the stillness he heard the sound of heavy breathing and a psychic awareness of danger touched him. A little way off he saw a splash of white, and he moved forward, fascinated. He saw a dark male back, moving in avaricious rhythm, and the turned white face of a girl beneath it, her dress pulled up so he saw a section of thigh white as marble. He stood still as a frightened rabbit, the blood pounding in his temples, wanting to run, knowing he was being a heel to watch, but held there by what he saw, the movement and the girl's stricken face, and the bare raw flesh of her thigh. At the center of his reaction, overriding fear and disgust, was a terrible, cold, clinical curiosity. It was almost as if he watched a film, or a laboratory demonstration.

Then he heard a harsh, ugly word. The movement stopped, and the man rolled away from the girl, his face clear in the moonlight. It was Morgan. He saw Avery just as Avery saw him, and leapt to his feet, shaking his fist. "Get away!" he said. "Get away!"

Avery couldn't move for a moment. *Jesus,* he said to himself, *it's Morg. Jesus Christ, it's Morgan.* Then he turned and broke into a run, pulling up when he saw the lights of the school. His father and mother were in the doorway. The band was playing "Good Night Ladies," and the Farmington station wagon stood on the driveway with its motor running. The mistress who had chaperoned the girls called impatiently, "Hurry along, Miss Sampson's girls! Hurry along!" He thought of the dark girl with Morgan and wondered what they would do to her if she didn't get back to school with the others. Then his mother saw him and he moved into the light. "You're all out of breath," she said. "You've been running."

He was a senior prefect and among other things obliged to keep the younger boys in line. "Aw, some kids sneaked out of the dorm, and we had to chase 'em," he said.

They drove home without Morgan. "He's got a lift," his father said. "We'll go along."

"But it's after twelve!" his mother said.

"And he's nearly eighteen. You can't treat him like a baby, Nancy."

At home there were sandwiches waiting and a thermos jug of coffee, but the idea of food made Avery sick. He went straight upstairs. He undressed and put on his bathrobe, then sat in the dark waiting for his brother, staring at the hands of his alarm clock, that glowed implacably and seemed not to move. He was filled with awe of his brother, remembering the time Morgan had made him inspect the first hair that grew on his body, and the time he had made him look one morning, when he awakened with proof of his new manhood demonstrated.

It was after two when Morgan arrived. Avery heard his door close, then walked down the hall to his room. He was frightened, but could not resist the demand to see his brother.

"Morgan?" he called. "It's me. Avery."

Morgan opened the door, looking strange in his dress shirt, with his coat off, the black tie hanging from the collar making him appear dissolute in an oddly antiquated way, the trace of fatigue on his healthy athlete's face suggesting drink, and gambling hells, and fast women.

"You still up?" he said indifferently. "How come?"

"Can I come in for a minute?"

"Well, sure, I guess so," Morgan said, looking at the watch on his wrist. "Better be quiet, though."

His room was always neat, but Morgan's was like a dormitory rat's nest—clothes flung carelessly on chairs, neckties hanging from the chandelier, various items of athletic equip-ment strewn about, in confusion probably as well thought out as the careful wrinkle in Morgan's collars and pseudocareless knot of his tie, or the used look of Morgan's beautifully unpressed flannels. There was a banner nailed to the wall, a traffic stanchion, and a blue and white porcelain sign taken from the lavatory of a New York, New Haven and Hartford coach. Thumb-tacked above Morgan's work table were a dozen snapshots of girls and a few of other boys, dressed in football clothes.

He could not understand the evaporation of Morgan's anger and thought he had better make sure of it immediately. "Gee, Morgan," he said, "I'm sorry about what happened. Don't be sore, will you?"

Morgan looked puzzled for a moment, then laughed. "That's all right," he said. "You were just doing your job. If you will get yourself made a prefect, I suppose you have to go around prying like the usherette in a New Haven movie."

Avery understood that Morgan thought he had been assigned to patrol the field and realized that this made his snooping seem less childish and less contemptible.

"How about the girl?" he asked. "Was she sore?"

Morgan laughed. "Don't worry about that little tramp," he said. "She's been caught at better schools than Sturgis. I think she got a bang out of it—having somebody watching her. She's a pig."

"She's an awful good-looking girl," Avery said.

"Everybody's girl," Morgan said. "She is stacked, though. And she knows how to operate."

Avery took a deep breath.

"Morgan," he began tentatively, "were you really, were you doing it to her?"

"Well, kid, I sure wasn't playing parchesi with her," Morgan said. He threw himself on the bed, his black, striped legs stretched out. "We sure weren't playing marbles."

"Gee, Morgan, did you ever do it before?"

"Sure. Lots of times. Only I keep away from the pigs in football season."

"Why is that?"

"Takes all your drive away, sonny."

Avery stared at his brother, fascinated as a new soldier is impressed by an old campaigner. Morgan had been his big brother, his rival, the immediate, present human being Avery was assigned to outmaneuver and eventually outstrip. Tonight he had become something else. He was the guy who had been there; the one who knew.

"Morgan," he said suddenly, "how do you know, when a girl's that way?"

"You'll know, kiddo. When the time comes."

"But how?"

Morgan shrugged. "You'll just know, that's all. You can always tell, if there's something doing."

He got up, slipping the black suspenders from his shoulders. He looked at Avery and seemed to brood for a moment, then said, "You want to know something, kid?"

"What?"

"Will you keep it to yourself?"

"Sure, Morg. Sure."

"I flew a plane the other day, a Cub."

"No kidding?"

Morgan nodded. "I landed it myself," he said. "The guy said I could learn easy. He said I've got the touch for it, the feel."

"Was it fun?"

"Fun?" His brother looked at him. "It's the best God damn fun you can imagine." He stretched his arms, and yawned. "Now get out of here, will you, and let me get some sleep? I'm beat."

"Good night, Morg."

Morgan overestimated him. There are those who know, when the time comes, the way birds know which way to fly, and there are those who don't and must find out, and who sometimes devote terrible lifetimes to the inquiry. Avery belonged to the second group and somehow, with torturing foresight, he apprehended this as he lay in bed, bright flashing lantern slides of the girl's white thigh and agonized face passing across his vision in the dark, all somehow mixed up with an instant on the dance floor when his chest had touched the breasts of his partner. His body chafed and he was crowded by awareness of sin. He was nearly twelve and beginning to change, and the boys in his form were two and three years older than he, so that for a year or two now he had been steeped in schoolboy sex. He knew everything and he knew nothing. He lay in his bed and fretted, then suddenly sat up straight. There was a remedy, he remembered. "When you get ideas like that, fellows," Mr. Foresby had advised the Sixth Form, "just hop into a cold shower. That'll get rid of it for you."

He couldn't take a cold shower now because the noise would wake everyone up, but he got out of bed and went down the hall to the bathroom, sponging his body with a washrag that he held under the cold tap.

It didn't work.

The next day he was restless, attacked by memory of the night before. It was the time of spring when people are subject to rebellious urges. Instead of going to the gym, when his classes were finished, he went for a walk, by himself, along a back road.

After a while, ahead of him, he heard voices.

It was Mademoiselle, out for a walk with the pre-prime boys, herding them like a group of sheep: "*Vite:Vite:Vite!*"

Walking the youngsters was one of her assignments, and she liked it no better than the rest of her chores. She hated the job, and hated this country, with its lush, disorderly timber-land, unregulated streams, wooden houses, wooden bridges—a landscape barbaric and untidy to an eye that was used to the orderly forests and disciplined farms of the Seine-et-Oise.

"*Bon jour, Mamzelle!*" he called.

"*Bon jour, Hollister.*"

She turned, a cigarette held in the corner of her mouth. "Come and walk with me for a bit," she said. "Keep me company."

He fell into step beside her; the six-year-olds ran on ahead.

"You are better off walking with me," she said, "than hitting a silly ball with a stick."

"I don't play baseball," Avery said. "I was just going to run for a while."

"Where must you go in such a hurry that it is necessary to run?" She glanced at him sideways, the cigarette at an angle, making her look faintly dangerous, like an Apache girl in a movie.

"Oh, you know. Just on the track. For practice."

"I know, Hollister," she laughed. "I just make fun of you. Or at least, not of you, but your Anglo-American mania for exercise, this weird belief you all have that a man gets virtue by enlarging his heart, or exhausting himself, running around a track that goes nowhere, or moving a ball from one part of a field to another, or chasing a fox that he does not want and would not eat, or getting into a little enclosure and smashing the face of an acquaintance until a bell commands him to stop, whereupon he shakes hands with the smashed face." She shook her head, making the ash fall from her cigarette. "It is a bad myth, this one."

He laughed. "Don't the French play games?" he asked.

"Oh, yes. When they are children."

He kicked the mustard-colored dust. "Well, in a way, we're still children," he said.

"Yes, you are children in a way," she said. "But you do not play like children. In the classroom you are children, always larking when you should be *grave*—serious—but when you play you are like men. It is all serious then. Like a battle. A war."

What she said was logical and in one sense true, but he didn't like to accept it. "Well, of course, we do like to win," he said. "But it isn't the way you say it is. It's, well, sport."

"*Alors!* You boys play football the way men make war. It is not a sport." She paused, then smiled, and went on. "Suppose, one afternoon when you were playing Storm King, the other side decided to be really serious, to bring knives and blackjacks and broken bottles. Suppose they decided that since this was a serious business, upon which sums of money are expended, to be really serious. What then?"

"But that's against the rules. The referee would stop it."

Mademoiselle laughed, and there was a bite in her laughter that made him uncomfortable. "Well," she said, "perhaps the side with the broken bottles would change the rules, and bring their own referee."

He knew that what she said was wrong. But somewhere in her concept lurked a core of truth, and this coexistence of truth and falsehood, in amalgam, was baffling.

"You don't understand," he said. "The referee has to come from a neutral school. It's the rule."

He realized that he sounded pompous, but he could not find the real flaw in her argument, that he knew must be there. She was too clever for him, and he sensed that she talked only partly to him and partly to try the sound of some speculations that had been pursuing her. She stopped, turning, and touched his cheek, a swift, elegant gesture, full of affection.

"Avery, forgive me," she said. "I talk politics, in silly terms, and just confuse you. And they are French politics, at that."

They stood for a moment, facing each other. The cigarette had burned down to a tiny butt that seemed glued to her lip. She let it drop to the ground and stamped out the spark with her heel.

"Run along now," she said. "Go and run really fast, so that you can feel you have a right to your dinner."

She began to walk.

He kept pace beside her, dissatisfied.

"You've got it all wrong, you know," he said. "I don't know just why, but you're wrong."

She stopped again, and put a hand on his shoulder. He could smell her breath, heavy with tobacco smoke, and a whisper of the perfume she used. The hand on his shoulder was curiously possessive. The gray, troubled eyes looked into his.

"Avery, you will be all right," she said. "I have a feeling you will be all right. You will survive."

"Well, I should hope so," he said, not understanding.

"It is not so simple, to survive," she said. "Even in a physical sense, these days, it is not so simple. Other ways——" Her hand came off his shoulder and she made a gesture in the air. "That is almost impossible. There are too many murderers. Too many shell holes into which one may fall."

He started to speak, but Mademoiselle put a hand on his mouth.

"Go now, Avery," she said. "Before I corrupt you further. I am in a dirty mood, really."

He hesitated, then realized that she really wanted him to go. He turned and walked back the way he had come. What disturbed him was the tone of the encounter, rather than the things Mademoiselle had said. She had seemed filled with friendship toward him, almost with love; yet underneath there had been something that was related to enmity. They had been like two enemy soldiers, enjoying a brief, invented truce.

The next day she was gone. She had driven off during the night in her little English car and there were dozens of rumors to account for her departure, most of them variations of the theory that she had been made pregnant by one of the masters, perhaps by Mr. Foresby himself, and sent away from the school in disgrace, with a purse full of American money. He knew the rumors weren't true, even before he got the postcard from her, with printing on it in French and German, and a round Wehrmacht censorship stamp.

"*Dear Avery,*" she wrote, "*I am taking my exercise too, now. Everyday. Running around a little road that doesn't go anywhere. Be a good boy and have a good long life.*"

He didn't learn until some time later that she was dead a few weeks after she got home to France, tortured by Gestapo agents who declined to shoot her immediately because they believed she had worked for the underground while she had been in America. A news magazine printed the story, describing in deadpan prose the things that had been done to her before at last she was killed. He read it with dull unbelief, remembering the cigarette sticking to her lip, and her argument that had been wrong, but stated in such oblique, foreign fashion he had not been able to refute it, though his fundamentals had been challenged.

CHAPTER SIX

THAT spring he had occasion to challenge Mr. Cobble's fundamentals, and almost got into trouble. The point at issue was inarguable and concerned the Divinity of Christ.

In Mr. Cobble's Bible Class they had learnt how the world was made, and he had already caused a crisis. One day, on the nature walk, when the science master had shown them a rock he said was two million years old, he had interrupted the man.

"But, sir, that's impossible isn't it?"

"Why do you say that, Hollister?" The master was a weary, kind man who wanted nothing so much as peace.

"Well, sir," Avery had said, "in Bible Class Mr. Cobble told us the world was 6,938 years old."

He was certain of the figure, for he had written it down, and later attempted to compute the number of ancestors that stood in direct majestic line between his own Yankee body and the body of Adam, writhing in the tortured delights of Original Sin. The reckoning was Bishop Ussher's, and perhaps Mr. Cobble had intended the boys to take it symbolically; nevertheless, he had announced it, and the idea that the world had a definite age had appealed to Avery.

The science master stared at the rock, which certainly looked two million years old. "Well, Hollister," he said finally, "of course that's religion. This is science. Geology." He turned and moved his pointer to a safer object, a maple sapling everyone knew wasn't more than three years old. Avery wasn't satisfied.

"But, sir," he said, "if it's true in religion, doesn't it have to be true in science too?"

"Well, Hollister," the master explained, "one is a matter of Faith, the other of Knowledge. We take the Bible as a matter of Faith, and geology as a matter of Knowledge. Do you see? Now this tree——"

He let it go.

But he wasn't satisfied, and later, when they studied the Resurrection, he had his difference with old Mr. Cobble.

His mother had explained the Resurrection to him when he was little, and made it seem perfectly simple, showing him copies of famous paintings by Italians and Spaniards in which the phenomenon itself was depicted. It had seemed believable then, and quite beautiful. But when he read the lesson in Bible Class he remembered the two million year old rock, and his mind was clouded by doubt. "You mean, sir," he asked, "that He was dead for three days and then rose up and went to heaven, body and all?"

"Why, yes, Hollister," Mr. Cobble said mildly. "That's right."

"But, sir, that's impossible."

The master smiled sadly and observed, "I think it's been generally accepted for about two thousand years, Hollister. Perhaps humanity has been wrong all this time, but it seems to me that two thousand years give humanity something of an advantage over your eleven." He took up his pointer and turned back to the sand-colored map that hung over the blackboard.

"This is Galilee," he announced, pointing. "This, where you see the star, is Bethlehem."

Avery heard no more.

He laughed out loud in Bible Class, and the sound shocked him, almost as much as Mr. Cobble.

"Yes, Hollister?" the master said. "You are amused?"

Avery stood up, blushing, dreading the notoriety he knew would follow, but unable not to stand his ground.

"No, sir," he said, gripping the back of the chair in front of him. "That is, I just thought of something."

"Yes, Hollister?" There was a warning in the master's voice. "What was it you thought of?"

Mr. Cobble was righteous and indignant. The sacred documents under his nose made him sure of his ground as a Baptist lay preacher in the red mud country.

"Well, sir," Avery said, "I thought of the Lamb upon His throne, sir." He paused. "And it's just that, well, sir, we have some lambs on the farm, that we feed up all summer and kill in the fall, and I just thought of one of them on a throne, and it made me laugh, sir."

This was pure fabrication; he had thought no such thing. The words had supplied themselves, and been offered, as if some bad spirit within him wanted to make Mr. Cobble ridiculous.

Mr. Cobble's pink face turned the color of a red-hot stove, and his hand closed around the pointer.

"Hollister, I think you'd better be excused," he said, his displeasure barely under control. "I think you're ill."

"Oh, no sir! I'm all right."

The master took the pointer in both hands and held it so tightly that his knuckles showed white.

"Go!" he cried. "Will you please, please go?"

There was a note of hysteria in the voice, nearly a sob, and it was embarrassing. Avery walked down the center aisle, his heels making a defiant sound in the silence that had followed Mr. Cobble's outburst. He knew that what he had done to the master was unforgivable. He had made Mr. Cobble step out of character, drop the armor of his technique, and speak to a schoolboy as a human being, exposing his weakness and weariness, permitting the thin edge of advantage to pass to him for an instant. For a master in a boys' school, this is fatal as the fighter pilot's split-second error, that puts his aircraft in the other's guns. He walked away, ashamed of having hurt Mr. Cobble, but unrepentant of blasphemy. He was absolutely certain that if Jesus Christ had died on the Cross, He had rotted like anyone else, and that there had been no ascent to heaven.

When the headmaster sent for him, the next day, he expected to be expelled or at least deprived of his prefect's badge. But all Mr. Foresby did was explain that it wasn't gentlemanly to raise religious questions. "You know, Avery," he said, "it's the easiest thing in the world to get the reputation for being odd It may get you a little attention for the moment, but in the end it always does you harm. Be better than the others, but be better in the same way, understand?"

"Yes, sir."

"All right then. This is wiped out. It never happened. Forget it."

He went out of Foresby's office, knowing he had been given a break. He had missed a class and had half an hour to wait before the next one. He walked across the green and down the slope. He wondered whether he was not already a bit odd. The possibility troubled him, for he wanted passionately to be like himself, and also to be like all the others, or at least to occupy, in the school and afterward, the precise position that a person of his particular family background would be expected naturally to occupy... the position that Morgan occupied, and his father, and grandfather, and that they had occupied, all the way back in time to the dim dust cloud that rose over the heads of the archers at Hastings. He didn't want to be odd, to break the mold, to disappoint either time or his father. But he didn't want to pretend to believe in things his mind told him could not be true.

He wanted to please. He burned to excel, and he burned to please. It was something inside him that intervened, and made unacceptable ideas rise in his mind. Maybe, he thought, it was the Devil.

Most of all, at that time, he wanted to please his father. He had forgotten the giant in the nursery, or drawn a screen across the memory. There existed only the Hero—the man who could drive, ride, shoot, fight, laugh at revolvers handled by inferiors, the man of the men, Himself, who could do anything, and would defend him, or Morgan, or his mother, against those who sought to do them harm.

That night, after dinner, he went to the study, where his father sat at his carved desk, orderly piles of papers making a fence between the door and his chair. The papers were insurance policies his father must sign, as president of the company, thick, folded wads of paper that looked like money, and did not acquire meaning until his father had signed them.

He coughed politely and his father looked up.

"Son?"

"Sir, do you believe in the Resurrection?"

"Do I *what?*"

"Do you believe in the Resurrection, sir? About Christ being crucified, and raised from the dead?"

His father was caught off guard.

"The Resurrection," he said contemplatively, as if finding it difficult to recall precisely what it was the word meant. "Why, yes, Avery. I suppose I do."

"But if He was dead, Dad, how could He be raised up? People aren't raised up. If it was His soul I could understand. You know, His spirit. But I don't see how His Body could be raised up."

His father puffed seriously at his pipe and said, "Well, there's a Literal way of looking at it and a Symbolical." He uttered these words with relief, as if he had searched his memory for them and found them just where they were supposed to be.

"You mean Faith and Knowledge," Avery said, recalling the advice of the science master.

"Well, yes, that's another way of putting it," his father said. He had taken a course in Comparative Religion, because it was a subject no member of the varsity football team had ever failed.

He scraped his memory and turned up phrases, explaining the idea of myth, as he had been taught to understand it.

As he listened, Avery understood that his father neither believed nor disbelieved, but accepted. He was sorry he had asked the question.

"Does that clear it up for you, son?" his father said.

"Well yes, sir," he said. "I guess it does. Thank you." He started to go out, but his father called him back, and handed him a sheaf of papers protected by a heavy envelope.

"There's something you won't hold in your hand every day," he said. "That's a policy for a million dollars. The biggest we've ever written."

Avery looked at the bank-note paper. It was the first time his father had ever discussed money with him, except to explain how his allowance worked. The insurance business was a mystery to him, though it was assumed that he and Morgan would go into it when they grew up, and follow along after their father. He felt proud, even though he understood that his father had shown him the policy to make up for the fact that he neither believed nor disbelieved in the Divinity of Jesus Christ. "Is it on a man?" he asked. "A person?"

His father nodded. "One man. A very rich man in Texas." He looked at the policy, then explained how his firm had gotten it after the oil man had been turned down by two big companies and was preparing to go to Lloyds. It was Avery's father who had talked with the Texan and understood that his motive was not a fraud in the future, but simply part of his character, like his big hat and unusual belt with diamonds set into the leather. It had been a shrewd item of judgment and his father was proud of it.

"He just wanted to have the biggest policy in that part of Texas," he explained to Avery. "The same way he has the biggest car and the biggest hat and the biggest ranch and the biggest wife. He's not the kind of fellow you'd want to have to dinner, but he's not a crook."

He grinned at Avery and picked up his pen that had a band around the top like an old fashioned wedding ring. He signed his name and blotted it and put the policy into his drawer.

" 'Night, son," he said.

Avery went out of the room with his heart singing. To hell with the Resurrection. His father seemed to him to be the greatest man in the world, and the fact that he wasn't President of the United States, instead of the man that was President now, that they said was crazy and part Jewish, was something he couldn't understand.

At this time he was engaged in a fanatical study of his father. There was nothing about his father that didn't interest him, nothing trivial. He hoarded information about him, and even totems that attached to him: an old tie, a broken pipe, a scuffed, discarded wallet, a fishing hat he had worn, with a trout fly pinned to the band.

He did not, as Morgan had done, take him for a model. Morgan wanted actually to *be* his father; Avery wanted to be himself, and his father's son. He wanted to please his father. More than anything on earth or in heaven, he wanted his father's constant, reliable, invariable approval.

CHAPTER SEVEN

NOT long after this, his father took him to a session of the State Legislature in Hartford. His father had been a member for ten years and his grandfather for thirty. Morgan, who would inherit the seat, had been taken to a session when he was about Avery's age.

"You'll be bored," his father warned him. "But I guess it's a good idea for you to see the thing in session. It may help you understand why the country's going to the devil."

He was not bored. He was fascinated, from the moment they entered the Capitol until the session was over.

In the marble hall outside the chamber, little groups of men foregathered and exchanged confidential information, like men at a prize fight or the stock judging ring at a county fair. Here and there among the men were political, horse-faced country women. As he and his father entered the hall, a young, good-looking city woman was lecturing to a tolerant group of leather-faced tobacco farmers. She wore a gay hat with a feather and a sleek fashionable dress. In the crowd of men in wrinkled suits she looked out of place, like a dime-store ring on a farm wife's finger.

"You will admit that a hundred years is a long time," she was saying. "You've controlled the Legislature for a hundred years—a century, mind you—but you think a third term for the President will bring down the Wrath of God, and that's only a matter of twelve."

The long-faced Yankees laughed indulgently, the way men will laugh with a pretty woman. Avery's father touched his arm.

"Democrat," he said. "Woman from New York who bought a big farm over in the western part of the state."

Avery stared, trying to distinguish a quality of difference in the Democrat's appearance, but all he saw was a well-dressed woman with a vivid mouth and blonde hair that trembled when she laughed. He knew that in the South respectable people were Democrats, but that was because of the Civil War. In Hull the Democrats were poor people, or people who had once been poor and not yet forgotten it. He stared at the Lady Democrat and she smiled at him.

"Hi there!" she called to his father. "Is that your boy?"

"One of them," his father said. "Say hello to Mrs. Calder, Avery. Ivy Calder."

"I suppose you're a Black Republican," she said, shaking hands with him. "Just like your father."

His father laughed. "Ivy, why don't you go home and enjoy your money?" he said. "Come along, son. You'll be corrupted."

Ivy Calder smiled at his father, and he had the sense that something passed between them, something elliptical and strange, and filled with danger. He took an immediate, irrational attitude of antagonism toward the New York woman, though he was fascinated by her, too.

"Why is she a Democrat, sir?" he asked. "I mean, I thought people like that, with money enough and everything, would be in the same party with everybody else."

"Oh, hell, Avery," his father said. "She's a woman who's had three husbands, a forty-foot sailboat, an airplane, a couple of children, a big place in New York, a big place in the Florida Keys, and a ranch in Wyoming. Now she's got a herd of Black Angus, and she's a Democrat because that's the best way to attract attention."

They passed through the leather-covered doors with oval windows and entered the Legislative Chamber. He followed his father down the aisle, to the seat and desk marked HULL. Mr. Sweeney, the other representative from Hull, was already in his place, a thin man in a blue serge suit, dangerous looking as a scalpel, who owned the Hull Supply Company and drove a long, pale-blue Buick. In politics, and socially, he deferred to Avery's father.

"Brought your boy, eh?" he said, getting up. "Hi, sonny."

"Hello, sir," Avery said, not liking to be called sonny by a man who often waited on trade in the store, when the clerks were busy.

A minister from Haddam, in a black serge suit, read a prayer, then a red-faced priest from New Haven, in broadcloth, read another. The gavel sounded and the session began.

"Gonna be some action this after," Mr. Sweeney said. "They're gonna bring up that fool Convention thing again."

Avery's father nodded. He looked across the Chamber at Mrs. Calder's bright hair, that stood out against the men's dark clothes. She turned and waved and he waved back. "They haven't got the votes," he said. "They just haven't got the votes."

At noon the session adjourned and they went to lunch in a restaurant near Pearl Street, where he ate oysters and a slab of pink roast beef, and his father drank sweet-smelling beer that came in a foreign bottle. The restaurant was dark and ancient, half a story below the street, and crowded with well-dressed men. It was older, his father told him, than the grill room on Cedar Street in New York, where he ate lunch when he went there on business. There was a comforting hum of voices that made him feel safe and included, but did not mar the intimacy between him and his father or disturb their conversation. There were no women; his father explained that at lunch time the room was reserved for men. He felt a sense of his own masculinity that warmed him like an open fire. He was a man among men.

They finished lunch and walked back uphill to the Capitol.

The afternoon session began in low gear, the legislators filled with food and moribund. But at about four o'clock, the Lady Democrat from Litchfield County rose to a point of personal privilege and managed to hold the floor. Avery didn't understand her argument, but the excitement in her voice, the tension boiling inside of her, he felt with his skin, the way he sometimes felt the warning stages of a violent summer storm.

"Sit down, Ivy, for the love of Pete!" someone called from the gallery. "You haven't got the votes."

She went on talking, though no one except Avery and his father seemed to be listening to her. His father watched her, smiling a little, estimating her in the same way Avery had seen him judge an animal he had just bought or contemplated buying.

"You'd think a man could break that woman," he said. "The way he'd break a horse."

Mr. Sweeney laughed. "Not thinking of trying it, are you, John?" he asked.

"No," Avery's father said. "No, I'm not. I don't break horses any more, either. There comes a time in life."

But as they watched Ivy Calder, Avery felt the excitement that ran through his father's body. His father was like a boy on the edge of a fight, filled with curiosity, and the thirst for conquest, anticipant and a little scared. "Why does she talk, Dad, when no one's listening?" he asked.

"She's talking for the papers, son," he explained. "Those fellows down there." He pointed to the press table, where a battery of reporters worked. "She's talking for them."

When she sat down, Ivy Calder looked across the hall at his father and smiled. She was panting a little and her breast heaved. She looked provocative and filled with sex. He understood what his father had meant when he said a man might try to break her, like a horse. She was a woman who wanted taming, who seemed to invite the process. There was something reckless about her, and destructive. He hated her, as he watched her challenging his father, but he could not take his eyes away.

The gavel sounded and his father got to his feet, looking around the big room that was filled with his friends and partisans. He was sure of himself as a Tenth Viscount, rising to address the assembled Lords on a matter about which everyone present had been in agreement for several centuries. When he spoke, his voice was stronger and harsher than usual, filled with authority, and a kind of professional wit, informed with something related to cruelty. At the sound of his voice, that he knew and did not know, Avery felt a thrill of pride and fear.

"I am all for chivalry," his father began, "and respect for ladies is something I think we all feel. But when the Honorable Lady from Litchfield," he paused, "and Miami, and Key West, and West 52nd Street, and Reno, Nevada—" he paused here, to wait for his laugh, got it, and went on—"when this Honorable Lady takes up nearly half an hour of this body's time, that should be spent dealing with schools and roads and other such petty matters, to inform us of the history of a state she's lived in for only three years—well, I think she's come to the wrong place. I understand there's an establishment not far from here where the lady could get her hair fixed and her nails manicured, and her skin covered with expensive mud, and be listened to by the mud-packer and the hair-fixer and the manicurist, and they'd all be getting paid for listening to her, because that's part of their job. I'd like to suggest that when the Honorable Lady is minded to disemburden herself of her thoughts on the antiquity of the Connecticut Constitution—of which we're all darned proud, incidentally—and on the beauty of the Connecticut hills, that some of us were lucky enough to be born in the sight of, well, I'd like to suggest that she take herself off to the beauty parlor, where she'll be sure of being listened to."

He sat down. From the rear of the hall, someone called, "You said a mouthful, John!" From the gallery, someone shouted, "Dirty fascist!" Then there was a lot of applause. Avery looked at Mrs. Calder; she was laughing and then he saw her stick her tongue out at his father. It seemed to him very unladylike, but his father just laughed. "Can't faze Ivy," he said. "Say that for her."

Mr. Sweeney laughed. "Changed your mind, have you John?" he asked.

Avery's father shook his head. "No," he said. "I haven't."

"Your Pa could run this show if he felt like it," Mr. Sweeney said. "Way he went after Ivy Calder, I thought maybe he wanted to."

"You're wrong, Joe," his father said. "I don't want it."

"Lookin' for something bigger, eh?" Mr. Sweeney said. "Case we get into the war?"

"Maybe." He looked down at Avery and smiled. "Just talk, son," he said. "Political talk."

It was nearly midnight when the session adjourned. The air outside smelled cool and fresh after the animal warren reek of the chamber. From the high hill, the city of Hartford looked like a great illuminated map of red, green and golden lights. A halo of amber floated above the city. The high light in The Traveler's Tower showed like a beacon. Behind them, the golden dome of the capitol was floodlit, a gigantic gilded breast aspiring to the stars.

Avery was exhausted and happy.

They said good night to Mr. Sweeney and watched him get into his vulgar car, then walked down the graceful drive that rose from the street to the portico of the capitol. Avery waited in the dark while his father unlocked the car. A state trooper flashed his light in his face, then trained it on his father. "Oh, it's Mr. Hollister, sir," he said. "Excuse me."

"Good evening, Lawford," his father said, shaking hands with the trooper, who hesitated, switching his light on and off, then said, "The boys sure appreciate what you did for them, sir. They won't forget it. You made a lot of friends."

"Glad to do it, Lawford," said his father. "Glad to."

Avery had once watched a state policeman beat the head of a drunken man with a pair of chromium handcuffs; he was impressed by the fact that a man in the same uniform behaved like a servant toward his father. "What did you do for that policeman, Dad?" he asked, when they were clear of city traffic and on the main road home.

"I got their hours changed a little, son, that's all," his father said.

He didn't want to talk. He kept his eyes on the road and drove fast, as he often did when he was tense, keeping the big car steady at sixty, seventy miles an hour. Avery guessed he was thinking about Ivy Calder. He wanted to ask about her, but by this time he had developed enough respect for his father's moods to understand that sometimes he didn't like to be bothered.

When they got home they sat in the kitchen and drank milk, his father's glass laced with a couple of ounces of bourbon whiskey that curled in the milk like vanilla.

"Well, son," his father said, "what do you think of politics? Dull, eh?"

"It was interesting," he said politely. He hesitated, then said, "That woman, Mrs. Calder. How old is she, Dad?"

His father looked at the charged milk. "Ivy?" he said. "I don't know. Twenty-eight. Nine, maybe."

Avery knew his mother's age and mentally computed the difference. His father yawned and finished his milk. "Good night, son," he said. "Sleep tight."

"Good night, sir," Avery said. "And thanks. Thanks an awful lot."

In his bed, he decided he hadn't learned much about politics, beyond the fact that Democrats, when they were well off, were not very dependable people. But he had learned something about his father. He had seen the power his father possessed and the respect it prompted in others—Mr. Sweeney, the policeman, the men who cheered and applauded him and ostentatiously called him John. He had caught the quick breath of his father's affairs: the dark comfortable manly restaurant, the legislature, the exciting world of manhood, his father's world, that had nothing to do with the farm or his mother. The day had been a promise, a foretaste of manhood. But just before he fell asleep, he remembered the bright red tongue that Ivy Calder had stuck out at his father.

"Damn whore," he said to the darkness. "Dirty damn New York whore."

In Avery's mind she was established as the archetypal bad woman, the bad woman from the big city, who was probably out to trap his father with whiskey, perfume and satin pajamas, and maybe even doped cigarettes.

He saw her again, during the summer, in a restaurant where he and his mother had gone for lunch. She was with his father, at a small table, their heads together, faces strange in the candlelight, for it was a fake quaint restaurant, with a lot of pine and flintlock muskets. On the way out, he and his mother had stopped for a moment, and he saw that his father was embarrassed, like a schoolboy caught breaking a rule. Something was said about the fact that his father and Mrs. Calder were on the Governor's civil defense committee, and his mother had smiled and said, "Of course, the war. It makes demands."

In the car going home, he said, "That woman, Mrs. Calder. She's a representative."

"Is she, dear?" his mother asked. "Representative of what?"

"You know. State representative. She's a Democrat."

"Well, dear," his mother said. "Perhaps your father is trying to make her see the error of her ways." She laughed, but he turned and saw the tears in her eyes. "Dirty whore," he muttered to himself. "Dirty damn New York whore."

CHAPTER EIGHT

IS mother feared and hated the war that was closing in and making itself felt, even though the United States wasn't in it yet. That summer she was conscripted into the Women's Volunteer Corps. She dreaded the meetings and loathed the mannish slate-colored uniform, although the color was becoming to her.

"I will simply not wear this hideous thing," she told Annie McBain one day when Avery was in the house. "I feel like a fool, getting dressed up like a female soldier, to go have tea with Mrs. Whipple. And it's so fearfully ugly."

"Thank God it's you that's wearing the soldier's kit," said Annie, "and none of the laddies. They wouldn't be going to tea with the Whipples. They'd be going to tea with Jerry, and it's a rotten brew he serves up. Worse than anything you'll be likely to get at the Whipples."

Avery was standing in the doorway. "It doesn't look bad, mother," he said. "And don't forget, you might get a medal, like Mrs. Whipple got from the other war."

He was joking with her, but it made her cry, intemperate, anguished crying, as if she were in pain. It frightened him, and he stepped forward, into the room.

"Now, now, none of that," Annie said. She turned to Avery. "Ye'd best run along, laddie. Your mother's not feeling well."

"No Avery!" his mother called. "Don't go. Stay with me."

There was a frantic note in her voice that was unfamiliar; it was almost as if she had uttered a cry for help. He stepped quickly to her side, and Annie retreated. It was one of those moments when a servant, who has for twenty years been almost a member of the family, is made to realize that in certain situations she is still a stranger, casual as the anonymous boy who comes to mow the lawn. Annie turned and closed the door behind her. He put his arms around his mother, feeling the shuddering of her body.

"Mother," he said. "What is it? What's the matter?"

He took a handkerchief from his pocket and gave it to her. She cried into that, dropping helplessly into her little satin chair by the window, from which she had a view of the garden, reaching off toward the farm buildings, beautifully tended and foreign looking, as she had made it after years of care. "I'm so lonely," she said. "So lonely." She looked through the window at her garden. "It has all gone bad. It has turned to s——."

The word struck him like a blow in the face. She never swore. His father's modest "hells" and "damns" always made her uncomfortable. She had shocked herself too, for the trembling ceased, and she cried quietly for a few minutes, while he sat on the pale rug at her feet, holding her hand.

Then she said, "Forgive me, darling. It's not fair. Don't be angry with me. Please?"

"Of course not," he said. "Everybody says things like that sometimes."

She looked at him, perplexed, seeming to be unaware that she had used the word, now that the hysteria had passed. "It's this war," she said. "This brutal war." She touched his cheek, then took his chin in her hand. The day was hot, but her hand felt cold as ice. "People change," she said. "Their blood quickens. You think they've grown up, and learned to be men, but the war shows you that you're wrong. They go looking for things they should have put away, outgrown. The war makes them look for adventure. It reminds them of it."

He knew she was talking about his father, and probably about Ivy Calder, but he didn't quite understand. He began to speak, but outside, on the driveway, there was the sound of gravel flying under the wheels of the car. Then a horn blew impatiently. His mother got up quickly. "Run down and tell them I'll be right there, will you like a dear?" she said. "And hurry, sweetheart. They're very impatient ladies."

The impatient one was Mrs. Whipple, who sat in the front seat of the station wagon, that had red crosses painted on it to make it look like an ambulance. She grunted when Avery told her his mother would be right down, but Mrs. Choate, who was driving, winked at him and smiled. She was young and pretty and her husband was in the British navy. He got a whiff of her perfume. Then his mother came out of the house, smiling, the pain drawn back into some private corner.

The car drove off and he went into the house, to the kitchen, where he found Annie, bristling at him a little because she had been sent away. But he knew Annie; she was his second mother.

"Can I have some tea, please?" he asked.

"If you like."

She gave him a cup of weak tea, and stood leaning against the sink, watching him drink it. The cook was having her half holiday, and the two farm girls dressed as maids were at work in another part of the house, so that he and Annie were alone in the kitchen. He understood Annie well enough to know that if he said nothing her resentment would be overcome by her desire to talk. After a few minutes she said, "Your mother's not well, laddie, you know."

"You mean she's sick? She *got* something?"

Annie shook her head. "It's what she *hasn't* got that's givin' her trouble. I've seen it before, in the other war. There's those that are worse hurt at home, away safe from the bombs an' the bullets, than many a soldier that fought through Flanders. I've seen lads that were four years in France, with the Black Watch, living in the muck and slime with the rats, killing the Germans, and watching their friends die all around them, and they came home, pretty as you please, with their kilts swinging and their bonnets at the slant, filled up with a load of beer, tearing the Clydeside apart, takin' possession of Glasgow, spendin' up their demob pay as if they'd been off on holidays and picked up a few quid on the races, then going back to their wee towns in the hills, none the worse for what they'd been through. And I've seen women that never heard a gun, except for the one some hunter shot off in the hills, seen them just breathe in the air of war like poison gas, until it took hold of their nerves, and they cracked into a thousand pieces, like a china plate that you drop on the floor."

"But, Annie," he said. "Mother doesn't know anybody in the war."

"It's in the air, lad," she said. "Nothing you can put your finger on, just something in the air, like mist."

She stared moodily at the row of polished copper pots.

"I feel it myself, when I listen to the radio, or look at the papers. But I'm tough, laddie. An' I went through it all once before, waitin' for a chappie that never came back, with the other chaps, from Flanders."

She turned away, making herself busy with the dishes that were displayed on an open-front pine cupboard. Avery regarded her broad back, clad in clean blue chambray, the white bands of her apron crossed in back, like a soldier's belts. He had heard the story from his mother—of how Annie McBain had lost her young man in the war and emigrated because she couldn't bear the pain of being alone with her own people, in the midst of familiar scenes and within the sound of familiar voices.

He got up and walked down the dirt road toward the highway, confused, remembering the astonishing word that had flown from his mother's lips, like a vicious chip from a log of wood, when the ax strikes it a glancing blow.

To him the war was being fought in another country, far away, another world, dim and distant. There was Mademoiselle, who had died in the war, and the English pilot who had told them at Sturgis about his private school, but he was glamorous and unreal, and Mademoiselle had disappeared into the gray mist of morning, so that news of her death was anticlimactic, unnecessary to her oblivion.

He understood the war to be a matter of bombed and occupied cities, for Mr. Foresby had explained this to them with his maps and photographs and little colored flags.

He had seen movies of the war, and pictures in the paper.

But he didn't feel it that way.

What he felt when he thought war was a green plain, flat as a stage, with armies drawn up in rank and file, one side scarlet, the other blue, firing disciplined volleys, rank by rank. That was the way his father had set up Morgan's lead soldiers, once, and explained the Battle of Fontenoy, telling Avery, as he moved the gay miniscule men, that war was like chess, and that a good commander thought out his moves like an expert chess-player.

He turned back toward the house, bored, with nothing to do, and all the summer before him, now that school was over with, and he was finished with Sturgis Manor. He almost wished that it were fall already, and that he was at boarding school, though he dreaded the thought of going away, and was afraid that he wouldn't like Colborn, or, perhaps, afraid that Colborn would find him "odd" and not like him.

That summer, Morgan really learned to fly, under a government training scheme. Every fine day, he put on a white duck helmet and drove out to the Hartford airport in the old farm car he was allowed to use. On bad days he stayed in his room and worked navigation problems on large mysterious-looking charts. He was the first of his group to solo, and from that day he was a pilot, impatient to be old enough to join the Air Force as a cadet.

He was secretive about his flying, perhaps because it was the first adventure he had chosen for himself.

"Could I go with you sometime, Morg?" Avery asked one day. "I'd like to see your plane."

"There's nothing to see," Morgan said. "It's just an airplane."

"Why don't you take him?" his mother asked. "It would be exciting for him."

"Oh, Ma, it's no place for a kid," said Morgan, "he'd just be in the way. And he might get hurt. He might get hit by a prop, or something. We had a crack-up, just the other day. Tuesday. A guy spun in from a thousand feet, right into the deck."

He made gestures with his palms, simulating an airplane.

"Morgan!" his mother said. "Was the boy hurt?"

Morgan looked at her, wondering if he'd heard her correctly. "Hurt?" he said. "Well he was killed, naturally."

Avery's mother gasped, and looked at Morgan, then at him.

"What's the matter with you, Morgan?" he asked angrily. "You ought to know better than that."

He looked at his brother, bitter toward him for upsetting his mother, but with awe too, because Morgan had actually seen the other boy die.

Morgan rose, putting on his white helmet, looking at his mother and at Avery with contempt.

"Shut up, Avery," he said. "What do you know about it?" He turned to his mother. "There are people getting killed every day," he said. "Every single day. Besides, that guy was a darned poor pilot. He should have gotten out of it. He had plenty of time. Plenty. I would have gotten out of it. So would anybody else who really *was* a pilot."

There was an intense, reckless drive in Morgan's voice, that Avery understood was partly pose, partly assumed professionalism. But part of it was real. He had changed since he started flying. He was more removed from the family, more of a stranger.

Avery had always had an ambivalent attitude toward him, of resentment and admiration, and he had regarded Avery with a mixture of contempt and tolerant affection. Now it was almost all contempt, and Avery had the feeling that this was Morgan's attitude toward all people who were not pilots. They would meet in the hall, and Morgan would come straight on, not giving way, so that Avery had to press against the wall like a track-walker, until he passed.

He sometimes behaved as if Avery did not exist.

His attitude toward his mother was courteous, but there was the kind of tension between them one sometimes senses between lovers who are breaking up, and who give attention to certain forms, through habit, half resentful that the forms no longer inspire the same responses or the same closeness. In actual fact, Morgan *was* breaking with his mother that summer, and the break was definite as divorce, or death, though unstated and unacknowledged. Morgan, Avery knew, had never been in love with his mother, as Avery himself was, at least not beyond the time when he needed her physical warmth for protection.

Brooding over it, after Morgan had left for the airfield, and his mother had gone upstairs to her room, he remembered something Morgan had said to him a year earlier, one afternoon in summer.

They had been off somewhere on the farm together, and something, perhaps the extraordinary clarity of the summer day, had given them a rare sense of identity with each other, so that they were unusually frank and a little sentimental. The differences of age and temperament were reduced in importance by the queer sense of continuity and alliance they felt. They threw themselves down on the sweet-smelling grass to rest, and Morgan chewed a straw, mashing the tender stalk to a pulp with his teeth, then drawing the wet stump along his arm. They were sunburnt and dressed in Tee-shirts and blue jeans. They looked more than usually alike.

There was a patch of shade where they rested, and the drowsy afternoon was like an ocean around them, so that they seemed to be on an island at sea, cut off from the rest of humanity. They felt pledged together, by blood, place, and custom.

"What do you think is the matter with mother?" Morgan had asked.

"What do you mean?" he said.

"Well, she's not very old. Not really. Younger than Dad. But she seems old. She seems, well, almost like an invalid, somehow."

He made no comment. His brother went on, picking up another straw and drawing it through his fingers. "She always liked you better than me," he said. "Always."

"Aw, Morgan, you're crazy," he had said, knowing that what his brother had said was true in one way and false in another. "She likes us both the same."

"No," Morgan had said stubbornly. "As soon as you were born she decided I was second best. Maybe because you are the baby. Maybe because you were sick when you were little. Maybe because the other kid died, that was born after me. I don't know."

He had moved closer to his brother. Both of them were on their bellies, the sweet-sour, sexual smell of the grass and earth close to their faces.

"I guess she loves Dad best," he said. "Better than us, anyway."

"That's different," Morgan had said. "Anyway, he's different. He does what he pleases. Just exactly what he God damn pleases."

That was the end of the fraternal interlude.

Morgan had leapt to his feet and they had raced downhill, through the meadow, the tall grass flicking their faces like a horse's tail. Not far from the house Morgan had pulled up and waited. They were both a little out of breath, and stood in the sun for a few minutes, panting, the light breeze chilling the sweat on their bodies.

"What do you mean, he does what he pleases?" Avery had asked.

Morgan had kicked at the grass. "Well, gee, he's a *man,* isn't he?" he had said. "He doesn't have to ask *any*body about anything. He just does what he wants to. Everybody else has to fit in—you, me, Ma, the whole family. He's just like a king."

As he sat in the breakfast room, after his mother and Morgan were gone, this conversation came rushing back to him, intact, with the smell of the crushed grass fresh in his memory, and the exact sound of his brother's voice reproduced in his mind.

"That's what he thinks he's doing now, the bastard," he said aloud. "He thinks he's doing just what he God damn pleases. He thinks he's a man."

"What's that, Avery?" Annie asked, beginning to clear the breakfast dishes. "What were you swearing to yourself about?"

"Oh, nothing!" he said irritably. "Nothing."

The summer was queer, and out of time, with Morgan busy flying, and his father more in the city than usual, and his mother gone strange so that more and more it was difficult to depend on her responses.

He seemed to have outgrown the things that had once filled his summers, and to have found nothing new to replace them; he was eleven, almost twelve, and he belonged to nothing, or to no one.

Sometimes, that August, he would stretch out on the lawn, oppressed by the heat, nearly suffocating, yet unable to find the energy or the will to go swimming. He took to loafing in the kitchen, watching the maids at work, or the cook. One afternoon he wandered down to the work barn, where a farm hand in a torn undershirt, his sweaty shoulders marked with grease, tinkered with the engine of a tractor. He watched for a while, then asked, "What are you doing?"

The farmhand was a high school boy, perhaps seventeen years old. He looked at him with contempt and said, "Changin' the oil filter, can't you *see?*"

"Show me how, will you?"

The boy straightened up, the dirty filter in his hand, and drew a greasy finger across his face, making a black mark.

"Why would you want to learn a mucking job like this?" he said. "When you will always be able to hire some poor slob like me to do it for you?"

"Gee, I only asked—"

"Get the hell out of here, will you?" the boy said angrily. "It's too damned hot."

Avery turned away.

The following week he was twelve years old and his father gave him a steel wrist watch with his name engraved on the back. His mother gave him a bag that was stamped *Avery Hollister, Colborn School,* and Morgan gave him ten dollars, because he had been too busy flying to have time to get him anything.

CHAPTER NINE

E WENT up to school by himself, a little frightened at the idea of living in a cubicle alone instead of at home in his own room, but not really doubtful of his ability to succeed at Colborn.

He had almost been there already, because his father and grandfather had gone there, and Morgan, and he had heard about it all his life. The class he entered was typical. There were two Ellsworths, an Alsop, a Coventry, a Coolidge, the Pitcher twins, and dozens of others whose names sounded familiar to him. There was Roger Bell, with whom he was later to share a study, and who quickly asked for help with his work. There was a boy named Dennis McCoy, instantly picked as the form's outsider.

"He doesn't belong here," said Bell. "His father's a mick politician in New York. Practically a crook."

"New policy," someone said. "New blood."

At this moment the new blood was crossing the Colborn Green, a good-looking, dark Irish boy who grinned cheerfully at Bell and Avery and the others. Bell turned his back, and so did Alsop and Ellsworth. Avery saw McCoy's bewilderment, then saw his jaw harden. He called out, "Hi, McCoy," and McCoy nodded.

"We're giving him the treatment," Bell said. "Better pass him up."

"Is that a rule?" Avery asked.

"No," said Bell. "But it's a good idea to stay along with your own crowd."

After that Avery made it a point to speak to McCoy, more because he knew it annoyed Bell than for any other reason. He had no real interest in Dennis McCoy, or in Dennis McCoy's mick father, who, as he later learned, might be practically a crook, but who also was sometimes asked to stay overnight at the White House. He was occupied with his own job, which was filling the place prepared for him by his brother, his father and his grandfather.

He made a good beginning, and managed to wipe out the disadvantage of being two years younger than the others. He came back for his second year, assured of a place in the top third of the Fourth Form.

The war, of course, changed things.

In December of his second year at Colborn, there was Pearl Harbor, and the boys prayed in their beautiful chapel and went to class the next day, astonished and a little irritated by the fact that school had not been put aside, but seemed to go on just as before, untouched by the bloody fact.

He telephoned his father and was rather hurt when his father seemed unimpressed by his agitation, his eagerness to do something, anything, to show that he understood his duty.

"Just carry on as you have been, Avery," his father's voice, made tinny by the phone, advised him. "There'll be plenty to do, later on. The thing to do now is sit tight and carry on."

"Yes, sir," he said. "What will you do, sir?" He had some idea his father might spring to arms like a minuteman, perhaps even appear at school, dressed in uniform, to say goodbye.

"I don't know," his father answered. "I haven't decided. But you just carry on with your work, son."

"I see, sir."

He came out of the booth, struck with anticlimax. There had been no more change in Hull than here at school. The war might as well have involved another country altogether, for all the effect it had on him, or the people around him.

CHAPTER TEN

I T DID not have much personal effect until a year later.

Then, in February of 1943, Morgan left college and went into the Air Force as a cadet. Avery's mother called the school, and he was sent home to see his brother, before Morgan went to Maxwell Field.

This was a mistake.

Morgan didn't want to see him, or anyone else, except a girl he knew in New Haven, and his flight line instructor in Primary School, whom he did not know and had never seen, but already understood.

At dinner the night before he left, Morgan was in a mood of forced gaiety, trying to amuse his father and disarm his mother. Avery, naturally, was ignored, and became rather sullen as the meal progressed, resentful because he had been called home on a week end when he wasn't wanted.

After dinner, his father took Morgan into his study. When he saw the maid pass with the brandy, two glasses on the tray, he understood that his brother was being offered his first parentally approved drink.

They were in the study for a long time, while he and his mother sat by the fire, not saying anything, both conscious of being excluded. When they came back into the living room, Morgan's eyes were bright, and his father's hand was on his shoulder. They were absurdly alike, resembling a father and son advertisement.

"Here's your soldier, Nancy," Avery's father said.

He looked up at them, suddenly reminded of a poem Mr. Cobble had read, two years ago, at Sturgis:

Where are you going, young fellow my lad,
   On this glittering morn of May?
I'm going to join the colors, Dad,
   They're looking for men, they say.

Morgan looked self-consciously gallant, trying to please his father, to behave as he knew his father would expect a new volunteer to look. Avery realized that he was the only one who knew that Morgan simply wanted to fly, not especially to kill Germans, or Japanese, but simply to fly. The idea that patriotism was a less powerful lure than a 3,000 H.P. engine would have been repugnant to his father; to him, Morgan was a young man answering his country's call. His father gave Morgan's shoulder a squeeze, then pushed him toward his mother. Somehow the idea was conveyed that he had taken absolute possession of Morgan, now that Morgan had been sworn in, and was just loaning him to his mother. Morgan bent to kiss her, then looked for a chair near the fire. Avery did not move until his father's voice cut in.

"Let Morgan sit there, Avery. You'll have lots of time to sit by the fire."

He got up quickly, trying not to betray resentment. "Sure, Morgan," he said. "Sit down."

Morgan hesitated, looking at the chair, then decided that his father had been right, and sat down, stretching his legs. The effect of the unfamiliar brandy was to make him behave as if he had a slight, exhilarating fever. "This is the life," he said, as if just returned from a hard campaign. "I'll bet it's not like this in the cadets."

"Four fellows from Colborn went," Avery said, the untrue words supplying themselves in response to his need for attention. "One of them was the only good halfback on the team."

There was a silence of the kind that follows a sneeze in church. Then his mother said, "Aren't the Colborn boys a little young?"

"They're not so young," he said stubbornly. "This fellow, the halfback, is nineteen."

Morgan snorted. "He must be a dumb cluck then. Nineteen and still in school."

"Avery," his father said, gently, but in the tone he used when he wanted Avery to leave the room. "I'm sure Morgan's interested in what goes on at Colborn. But perhaps he'd like to talk to your mother for a bit, do you see?" He smiled. "After all, a man doesn't go to war every day."

"Oh, for Christ's sake, Dad! I'm not going to war, I'm going to Alabama."

"Morgan, I won't have that kind of language in the house. Apologize to your mother."

"I'm sorry," Morgan said sulkily. "And as far as Avery's concerned, let him talk. I haven't got anything to say."

Their mother leaned forward. "Boys, please!" Her hands fluttered. "Let's all *love* one another."

Avery got up and stared into the fire, three apple logs that burned implacably and gave off a fruity aroma. "May I be excused?" he asked. "I have some work to do."

His mother nodded and he turned away. He went into the main hall, but instead of going upstairs to his room, took a windbreaker and slipped out of the house into the bright cold night. The sky looked like an astronomer's map, densely black, and filled with stars unusually definitive and brilliant, so that the winter's-night sense of mystery was heightened. It was a clear, New England night, ascetic and beautiful, the kind that seems meant to dignify the transcendentalist soul.

He walked toward the horse barn, his feet breaking the ice crust on the snow. The rhythms of Mr. Cobble's poem would not leave his mind, but remained with him like vibration communicated, the words chasing one another through his memory like toy trains on a track:

> But you're only a boy, young fellow my lad,
> You're not required to go
> I'm seventeen and a quarter, Dad,
> And ever so strong, you know.

He paused, his ankles deep in the snow, so that the cold came through his socks, and made a deliberate, physical effort to thrust the rhythm out of his body. It was a sensation like that of swimming under water; the held breath exploded from his mouth in the same way, the breath seeming to carry with it the plaguing words and rhyme scheme. Far off a horse neighed, sending the frantic sound across the snow. He walked on to the barn, and opened the half-door, looking at the horses, their cryptic faces seeming to resent the chill night that came through the door. He was sorry he had caused the scene by his bid for attention. It had not been fair, Morgan *was* going away, he might even be killed. He was entitled to indulgence, like a fellow on his birthday. He felt a pang of sadness at Morgan's going, and regret for the fact that he and Morgan had never really been friends.

The animals moved on the concrete floor, making a noise of steel, and somewhere, down the barn, a horse kicked the side of his stall. He closed the door and walked back toward the house, following the tracks he had made coming out. In the starlight, he saw his brother.

"Avery!" Morgan called quietly. "Come here."

They moved together, across the snow, like enemy outposts fraternizing in the darkness.

"The brandy made me dopey," Morgan said. "I thought a little air would clear my head."

Avery looked up at the house and saw that the light in his room was on, though he had left it turned off. He understood that his brother had gone there and not found him, and come out into the dark to look for him.

They fell into step, trudging through the snow.

"They don't understand," Morgan said, turning his head toward the house. "They don't understand anything."

They stopped and stood facing one another, the starlight on their faces.

"You know I don't like the college," Morgan said. "I'm not going back, when the war's over." He paused, looking toward the house again. "But don't tell him that."

"No," Avery said. "No, I won't."

"He——" Morgan fought for his words. "He's, well, he's the greatest guy in the world, no kidding. He's swell. But he just doesn't seem to understand what goes on in my head any more."

Avery looked at his brother, feeling for the first time affection uncontaminated by jealousy, or fear, or resentment of Morgan's primogeniture.

"I didn't mean to be snotty to you, Avery, before," Morgan said. "It's just that, I can't talk to them. I was putting on an act. Don't be sore, will you?"

"Sure, Morgan," he said. "I know how it is. You know how they want you to act, and so you act that way, even though you don't feel that way, and it makes you feel as if you were telling a lie."

"That's right," Morgan said. "Dad gave me a brandy, in there, and talked to me about women, and about being an officer, and a gentleman, and about the British army. Gee! What we talk about, the fellows, I mean, is how soon we'll get to fly fighters, and what kind of ships they'll have by then, when we graduate. You know."

"Sure. I know."

Morgan put a hand on his shoulder, then clenched his fist and pretended to hit him on the jaw. "Anyhow, Avery, I'm sorry. No kidding."

It was the only time, in all their lives, that Morgan ever told him he was sorry, without being ordered to do so.

They walked back to the house together and went into the kitchen. There was a wan light from the hall, and the copper pots, hanging from hooks, looked like heads hanging on a line. There was the smell of the stove, and food, and of brass polish and soap. Morgan switched on the light and hopped up onto the table, swinging his legs. "Make us some cocoa, eh, kid?" he said. He looked cheerful again, like a college boy on holiday.

Avery got a pot and the cocoa can and stood with a hand on the stove, watching the water simmer and boil. There was a bowl of whipped cream in the refrigerator, and he put a spoonful in each cup. They sat down in the servants' chairs, sipping the hot, sweet cocoa, feeling very close, very much in alliance. He looked at his brother and grinned. "Don't get yourself killed, Morgan," he said.

Morgan laughed. "Not me. I'm cautious, not bold. There are old pilots, kid, and there are bold pilots, but there are no old, bold pilots."

"You be careful, anyway, Morg," he said.

They finished their cocoa and went upstairs to bed. In the dark, Avery kept seeing his brother's face, with the starlight on it, telling him that he was sorry he had been snotty to him.

He felt love for Morgan, and felt that it was strange and rather sad that he and his brother until tonight had not been able to meet one another with their visors up, to trust one another as human beings, rather than merely as sons of the same father; sad, because now it was too late. He understood that after the war Morgan would not come back to this house or this life. He was not just going away to Maxwell Field or to the war. He was going away for good, and now that he was going, Avery felt he had hardly known him at all.

CHAPTER ELEVEN

LATE in May, Avery went home, in response to a letter from his mother that said:

> ... *please, darling, please please please do arrange to come home for the week end. All sorts of things have happened. Your father's off to Washington and Morgan's off to his last flying school and your cousin David is coming for the summer; to get over some dreadful wound he got in the fighting in Africa.*
>
> *Love love love love...*

He did not understand the part about his father, and did not remember his cousin David, except as a photograph in an album. The tense tone of the letter upset him.

When he got home he found that his father was not going to Washington on a trip, as he had supposed, but to live, at least most of the time, until the war was over. He had been appointed to the War Department by the President he had always hated.

"It's just a gesture," he explained, "but I can't refuse, and maybe I can help save some of the country's money, so we won't all be bankrupt when the war's over."

The idea of Hull without his father was beyond his imagination. Hull, the farm, the Hollister place, the whole thing was his father. His father had always been the center of it.

"It means you and your mother will be alone," his father said. "And I'm sorry for that."

"Well, there will be this fellow Fearing," he said. "He'll be here, part of the time."

"Few weeks," his father nodded. "Maybe a month. Of course, I've asked him to stay as long as he likes. It's the least I can do. For one thing, he's my sister's boy. And for another, he's been through hell." He looked at Avery and smiled. "Look after him, will you, son?"

Avery nodded. "Yes, sir," he promised. "I will."

"You'll be the man of the house," his father said. "It will be up to you. He'll probably want to fish. Most Englishmen like to fish. And he'll want to ride. There's Ginger, he can have. Or Lady. You'll find plenty to do."

"Sure we will," he said.

His father stared at the wall, looking troubled, then frowned and said, "I don't like to say this to you, Avery, but you're nearly fifteen, and—well, frankly, I'm worried about your mother. I thought about it, when the President asked me to take this job. But there wasn't any way to refuse." He paused, then said, "Damn it!" and slapped his desk with his palm, making the papers flutter. "How could I refuse?"

He seemed to be asking for approval and Avery said, "I don't see how you could, sir. If they need you in the Government, you have to go."

His father looked at him gratefully.

"Your mother's not happy about it. She seems to have the notion that I'm really going to war, to fight, instead of to a desk in Washington. She's not well, Avery. Not well at all. This war has taken the life out of her. She's not herself. Oh, I know she never cared much about going out. She liked it better at home. But she used to enjoy the garden, and she hasn't touched it this spring. She used to like to fool around with her painting, but she's given it up. She doesn't seem to care about anything, except you, and Morgan, and maybe me. She's afraid. The doctor says it's her nerves. But that covers a lot of territory. She's—she's morbid."

He refused to understand what his father was trying to tell him. It seemed disloyal, and unfair. But when they went in to dinner, he found himself watching his mother, studying her, listening to her voice in a new way.

She didn't seem morbid. She seemed gay, but there was something strange in the way her eyes were never still, and there was a subtle altering of the pitch of her voice, so that sometimes it sounded like a stretched wire, stretched too tightly, threatening to part. He thought it was a rotten break for her to have a stranger coming to visit, just when his father was going away. He took a dislike to David Fearing, whom he had never seen, and wished his cousin had stayed in England to do his convalescing. He didn't want to have his summer vacation spoiled by an outsider.

CHAPTER TWELVE

HE CHANGED his mind when David arrived. He had expected a British officer straight out of a Hollywood film, with a trick mustache and a chin-up manner, who would want pans of hot water in his room and perhaps want the newspaper ironed in the morning.

David wasn't like that. He looked disconcertingly like Morgan and was easier to get along with than anyone Avery had ever known. Avery liked him, and so did his mother, which surprised Avery. She didn't care for strangers and hated having people stay in the house, but something about David Fearing put her at ease with him—perhaps the fact that he looked like Morgan, ten years older, perhaps because he seemed to understand her from the first.

"You know," he said, the day she and Avery met him on the station platform in Hartford, "I had expected an aunty-looking aunt. I can't call you aunt. You don't look like anyone's aunt."

"Well, I'm not your aunt really," she said, smiling at him. "I'm only your aunt-in-law. So perhaps you'd better call me Nancy."

He stood there looking at her, then, suddenly, they shook hands, though they had just done so. "Right," he said. "Nancy it is."

There had been, between them, instant awareness of communication, empathic and direct, and Avery shared it. Sometimes, on a bus or in the street, you will see a face, or the eyes of a face, and in that instant there is more communication than can be drawn from a dozen years' association with a person who generates on another wave length. It is the instantaneous contact that matters: swift and palpable as electric charges, certain as electric shock. All the questions are asked and answered, and you seem to start from a point never reached with most people.

This direct communication passed between David and Avery's mother, and between David and himself. They felt comfortable together, from the first, and David turned the summer into an adventure for Avery and his mother.

He was like the perfect older brother for Avery. Avery could like him and admire him, without ever being in competition with him. He almost made up for the absence of Morgan and his father, playing tennis with him and swimming in the pool, doing the things he used to do with his father and brother, before the war.

For his mother, David was like the first breath of foreign air that excites the disembarking traveler. He quickened the sense of life in her, that seemed to have died. He had lived in Paris, and he reminded her of youth, and seemed to make a bridge for her with a happier part of the past. He was a challenge to her and inspired daring innovations. She hadn't played tennis for years, but when he asked her to she played with them, and Avery discovered that she liked the game. David persuaded her to ride. She looked reckless and slim waisted in breeches and a white shirt. When they came back, and the horses had been led away, she took the cigarette David offered her and bent her head to the match he held, looking oddly dissolute.

"Mother, you don't smoke," said Avery, who had been nervous, riding beside her.

She raised her head and smiled at him. "Oh, Avery darling, I do all sorts of wicked things. Secretly, you know."

He laughed. He didn't know whether he liked the sophisticated way she looked when she smoked or not; but he did like the new way she laughed, a low, thrilling laugh with an element of danger in it, and he liked the way she joined him and David, turning things into a threesome, raising his status.

His mother slept late, and in the morning he and David were always together. David taught him to fence. He bought foils in Hartford and a pair of white jerkins with scarlet hearts sewn to the breasts. They fenced in the open, on the cleared space where Morgan had taught him to play football, the ancient phrases of the sport glamorous and exciting to Avery.

"*En Garde!*"

"*Touché!*"

They swam when they finished fencing, then lay on the grass until lunch time, sometimes reading, sometimes just staring at the sky and the high white clouds that drifted across it. They talked; at least David did most of the talking, while Avery listened. He liked to listen. David was orthodox, his bona fides had been checked, for he belonged to the same regiment his father had belonged to and had the same decoration—the D.S.O.—the actual medal of which was kept in a box in his father's study, and yet David was not like anyone Avery had known, at school or here in Hull. David appealed to the part of him he had always been a little afraid of, the part he felt made him somewhat odd— the serious part he kept hidden.

He drew experience from David, taking it in first as entertainment, then making the chemical change, so that what he heard became experience—vicarious, like experience gained from books and plays and quick intuitive apprehensions of the minds of strangers—but quite real. He was a bright boy, and he had been at schools that didn't approve of bright boys, schools that wanted the all around man, and where intense interest in nonathletic pursuits was regarded as odd and undesirable. He yearned for experience and intellectual variety, and that summer he felt the ranging power of his mind for the first time.

David was good for him, but he placed him in a moral predicament. Sometimes he asked questions Avery had avoided asking himself. David had gone to Eton, and then to Cambridge. He asked about Colborn and Avery said, "It's just a school, a boarding school."

"But what's it like?" David asked. "I mean what are the boys like, the masters?"

"Would you like to meet one of the fellows?" he said. "A friend of mine, the fellow I room with has a place down on Cape Ann and he asked me to come down in August. I told him I'd ask you." He hesitated. "His name's Bell," he said. "Roger Bell. He says there's sailing. He has a sloop."

"Oh, I would like that," said David. "I like to sail."

"I'll write to him," Avery said. When Bell had asked him, up at school, he had put him off because he didn't know what his cousin would be like; now he wanted to show him off, and he hoped David would wear his uniform, with all the bright ribbons on it.

"I hated school," David said. "Sometimes I felt like telling them all to go to the devil. Do you ever feel that way?"

It was the fatal idea; just stating it made him flinch. "I don't know," he said. "I guess I have, sometimes." He stared at the grass. "You know, Dad went there to school, and Grandpa, and Morgan. And I like it, most of the time. It's just that sometimes it seems to be a lot of crap. For instance, Collamore, he's the headmaster, always tells the new kids, 'There's only one rule in this school, boys. Be a gentleman!' Well, that's crap. They have a million rules, and you can never break a single one of them and still not be a gentleman."

David laughed and said, "Who in the bloody hell wants to be a gentleman? Temporary or otherwise?"

"Well, gee," said Avery. "I do. You do."

He was near the age of moral choice, bewildered by his inability to reconcile what he had been asked to believe with what he saw around him. He was confused by the presence of good in evil and evil in good, and until he met David no one had suggested to him that the one was necessary to the other.

David told about an officer in Africa who had hidden in a hole, during a battle in which three of his men had been killed. "He was really comic, you know, this chap, hiding in the sand the way an ostrich is supposed to do but doesn't. He simply wouldn't come out."

"Did they shoot him?" Avery asked, having heard from his father that cowardly officers were shot in the other war.

"Oh, Christ no," said David. "He was all right, after a bit. He wasn't a bad sort, really. He simply had no temperament for war. It must have been awkward for him to find that out in the desert. He was a bloody great athlete and so on, at Oxford."

"But if he was yellow ... " Avery said.

"Hell, Avery, you can't shoot everybody who gets scared," said David. "There wouldn't be any army."

One night at dinner David mentioned a woman he had known in France, a famous and beautiful woman who had enjoyed a number of publicized romances.

"Do you know *her*?" his mother asked. "Tell me about her."

David thought for a moment, then said, "I think she is the most honorable woman I've ever met. She is absolutely honest. Impeccably honest."

His mother nodded. "I've always envied her," she said.

Avery looked across the table at her and saw that she was serious. He was astonished. Once Morgan had been reprimanded for mentioning this woman's name in his mother's presence, as if he had used a dirty word. He and Morgan had talked about her, and he had a powerful and terrible vision of her, nude and wanton on the white French beach, In bed that night he tried to understand how such a woman could be honorable. Honorable women, he knew, never submitted to lust with pleasure, and in any event never to more than one man and to him only with the sanction of the church. Carnal love between people old enough to be his parents he thrust from his mind as loathsome; when such ideas intruded at all and he tried to envision his father in the throes of sexual depravity, his partner was never his mother, but always someone else, usually Ivy Calder, the New York whore.

"Your mother's wonderful, isn't she?" David said to him one day. "She's—there's an enchantment about her. Something strange and elusive." He paused, then said, "You know, I've never had a mother. I suppose in a way I've been looking for one all my life."

Avery was used to familiar attitudes toward his mother— his own, his father's, Morgan's, Annie's—all benevolent, all protective. David made him see a part of her he didn't know at all—the part that his father had fallen in love with, years ago, and that had been buried for a long time, under the weight of personal sorrow and a dreadful fear of invasion by the world.

David was wonderful with her. He had a way with her, not flirting with her, exactly, but displaying a kind of old-fashioned gallantry women seemed to like in young men. He read to her, and persuaded her to play the piano, which she hadn't touched for years because Avery's father disliked music. They looked attractive together and natural, sometimes like brother and sister, sometimes like romantic lovers, occasionally, in certain moods, like mother and son.

There were moments of discomfort.

One evening after dinner they sat on the flagstoned terrace that led into the garden, half of it in the open, half under cover and joining the house. David and his mother had tall drinks made with white wine and soda and he had ginger ale in a glass like theirs, so that his drink looked the same, and this gave him a pleasant adult sense of fraternity with them.

A thunderstorm was making up, and they felt the tension in the superheated air. They sat in the hot twilight around a white iron table, a furled umbrella erupting through it like a stricken tent, phallic and immobile, casting a shadow across the table and the lawn. The storm pressed down but would not break. The dead air was cosmic, preternatural, so that they moved cautiously, as if making a sudden sound might cause the world to explode. Avery had a sense of danger, and the shadow of the umbrella, grotesquely suggestive, was like a warning sword on the grass, that was yellow in the fading light. The silence was unbearable; it called for a catastrophic, expressionist scream. They all felt it. After a while David let out his breath sharply and said, "Do you mind if I turn on the radio?"

"Please do," Avery's mother said. "I feel as though I were being strangled."

David went into the roofed part of the terrace and got a station in New York that was playing self-confident dance music, then turned and said, "Would you like to dance? Or is it too hot?"

Avery looked at his mother. She got up, touching her hair, then ran her hands over her hips, smoothing her dress. He felt a pang of jealousy as she took David's arm and walked with him into the covered terrace, where the flags were cemented together. For an instant they stood in silhouette, in a classic, formalized attitude of courtship, then moved together and began to dance. The evening light and the charged air were seductive, filled with sex. Avery was conscious of his mother's breasts tight against David's chest, nothing between their naked bodies but the thin silk of her dress and the thin mesh of his polo shirt. The music that directed their movement flowed through his body like blood, insinuating music that aroused him. He was confused by the statements of his body, and tortured by surges of guilt and jealous desire.

Then the storm broke and a peal of thunder rolled up through the valley like artillery. The static snarled in the radio, above the music, which had changed character, so that wilder, franker African rhythms came from the loud speaker. The lightning flashed and showed his mother's face, then David's, close to it, and the awful, sexual fact of the dance was brutally stated, inescapable. Avery moved under cover as the rain poured down, carrying a silk scarf his mother had left on her chair. He stood in shadow near the wall of the house, twisting the scarf in his hands, watching his mother and David.

The music stopped and they drew apart. They walked to the edge of the terrace and looked out across the flat lawn, watching the furious summer storm, lightning splitting the mottled sky that was like a fierce Spanish painting.

"Avery, come and see the storm," said David.

He moved forward and stood beside them. The triangle was in order again. On the round white table the three glasses sat, filled to the brim with rain, great drops splashing in them. The umbrella hung like a wet flag, impotent, its meaning destroyed.

His mother drew back, laughing. "It's blowing in," she said. "Let's not get wet."

The living room seemed brilliant after the darkness that came with the storm. He handed the scarf to his mother and she smoothed it out, shaking it. It was a thin scarf from Paris, beautifully printed, showing a dozen ballet dancers in various familiar positions. "Isn't it pretty?" she said, showing it to David. "It's from Paris."

As he bent to admire it the storm cut the power line and the lights went out. The room was black and the lightning flashed at the windows. "Get some candles!" his mother said. "I hate the dark." He heard her sob. He and David lighted the candles and then he moved toward her, embarrassed for her, and ashamed. "Please mother, don't," he said.

"It's the storm," David said. "It gets to your nerves."

"I'm sorry," she said. She lifted the scarf and laughed. "It's silly to cry over a French scarf that I didn't buy in France at all, but in Hartford, just because the lights went out."

"You can cry over anything," David said. "I used to cry in the desert sometimes because the smell of engine exhaust reminded me of a street in London."

Avery understood this; sometimes in his bed he had cried for nothing at all, and sometimes he couldn't cry when he should have been able to. He watched David, close to his mother, bend quickly and kiss her cheek. It gave him a strange feeling. He had never seen a man kiss his mother, unless you called Morgan a man. His father never kissed her, when anyone could see, though it hadn't occurred to him until now that there was anything unusual about that.

"Sometimes I feel as if I were made out of jelly," his mother said. "Calf's foot jelly, that they put in those baskets you send to ships. And sometimes I feel as if I were made of thin plaster. Hollow. So if someone tapped me with a hammer I'd break into a thousand pieces."

"I know," David said. "They call it battle fatigue, if anyone's had a shot at you. Of course, it hasn't got anything to do with battle." He walked across the room to the cabinet where the liquor was kept. "You need a drink," he said. "A good strong drink without any water."

He poured a glass of whiskey and handed it to her. "But I don't drink whiskey," she said.

"Drink it."

She looked up at him and smiled. "Orders, Captain?"

"Orders."

She drank the whiskey and made a face. After a little her eyes brightened. David poured a drink for himself and held the glass in his hand as if unable to make up his mind to drink it. Then the lights came on, startling them. He raised the glass and threw back his head, an ugly, familiar gesture. He licked his lips and threw the glass in the air, catching it like a ball. "Drink has its uses," he said. "Just the thing, at certain times. Blurs the edges nicely. Makes old scenery look like new. Turns real worry into romantic concern. Causes fear to resemble adventure. Makes an ugly girl indifferent, an indifferent one pretty, a pretty girl beautiful." He looked gratefully at the glass, then tossed it again and caught it. "Oh yes. It can be a fine thing, drink."

He was playing the charming wastrel out of an old drawing room comedy, clowning with her and doing it well enough to make her laugh, and to make Avery laugh too.

The storm passed and they went outside, looking across the fresh wet lawn at the sky, that was streaked with orange and violet. The heat had broken and the air was washed and cool. The tension had passed. Avery put an arm around his mother and she rested her head on his shoulder. David looked at the sunset and said. "Fine day tomorrow, eh?"

"It should be," he said, "after the storm. It should be a good day."

A few days later, when he came in from swimming, he found Annie in his room, putting away his laundry. "Well, laddie," she said cheerfully. "Swimming again, eh?"

He glanced down at his trunks and said, "That's rather obvious, isn't it?"

"Been with Captain Fearing, I suppose?"

"Well, what if I have?"

Annie was his old friend, but he had not reached the stage of development where one friend need not be reduced in grade to make room for another.

"Oh, don't be narky about it," she said, closing the drawer, then turning to look at him. "You've got quite a crush on the captain, haven't you?"

He tasted salt in his mouth. "That's a God damn insolent thing for you to say, McBain," he said. McBain was what his father called her, when he was irritated with her.

She smiled. "I'm sorry, Avery laddie. I didn't mean to make you mad. It's just that I'd think you'd want to be with some boys your own age. Girls too, for that matter."

He was sorry he had been rude. "Those kids," he said. "They hang around the Twin Oaks all day, or around the beach, drinking cokes and listening to the jukebox. I don't call that fun."

She kissed him on the cheek and went out of the room, her arms filled with his dirty shirts.

She was right.

He had a crush on David, and so had his mother.

She had given up going to parties in Hull, but now she went because people asked David, and she found that she enjoyed it.

"Do you know," she said one night, when they came home from a party given for David. "I never in my life thought I'd have a good time at the Whipples'. I've loathed that woman for years. But it was fun!"

David laughed. They were all in the kitchen eating sandwiches Annie had set out for them. "You should have seen your mother tonight," he said. "She had old Major Horsepistol or whatever his name is, in positive rut."

"David," his mother said. "It's bad enough to shock Mrs. Whipple. You musn't shock Avery too."

"I'm sorry," David said, his mouth full of sandwich. "But he was in a flap."

She laughed. They all sat down at the kitchen table and the pleasant triangular feeling returned. Avery was rather pleased with his mother. It didn't occur to him that coming out of prison might endanger her. He had no idea what was happening, to her, or to David. He simply saw two people who had fun together, and it made him happy to be with them.

CHAPTER THIRTEEN

IS mother had almost given up painting, but that summer, because it amused her, she tried a portrait of David. The portrait was to be a kind of joke, and he posed for her in his dress tunic, wearing his actual medals.

"I feel like a damn fool in this," he said. "I've hardly worn it. We used to put them on sometimes, when we were in the training battalion and went to Rosa Lewis' hotel. It amused Rosa."

She nodded. "Well you're to please me now, and not Mrs. Lewis. Sit still! Be an apple! That's what Cézanne told his sitters. Be an apple. Does an apple move?"

"I feel more like a boiled fowl."

"Be an apple," she insisted. "That's what Cézanne said, and he must have known."

At first, painting seemed good for her. She seemed happy and relaxed about it. But after a dozen sittings she put down her palette one morning, thrusting her brush into the turpentine bath. "I can't go on with this," she said. "It's not fun any longer. I was right to stop when I did, and it's no good trying to go back. The past is gone."

David got down from the model stand and looked at the canvas. Avery joined him. She had finished one side of the head and a section of the neck and shoulders, very careful, precise painting, expert-amateur, not at all like the self-consciously free style she used in her landscapes. The effect was disturbing. The likeness was photographic as far as it went, pathetically lifelike. Half-finished, it suggested a man stricken by some corrosive disease that had eaten away the flesh from a part of his face—one side firmly painted and suggesting living tissue, the other roughed in over the charcoal drawing, in grisaille, totally lifeless, dead as rust. It was as if in the process of painting she had seen something in David, beneath the surface, that frightened her. He sensed it too, looking at the portrait. "Dr. Jekyll and Mr. Hyde," he said. "You'd better finish it, or it will haunt me in my sleep."

"I'm sorry, David. I simply can't." She smiled and said, "Go and swim, you two, or fight with swords. Do something." She looked at the half-finished canvas, then around the studio. She was like a trapped bird. "There's a car," she said impatiently. "There's gas. You don't have to stay here, as if the house were a prison. Go. Go out."

"Will you come with us?" David asked.

"No. No. You two go."

She seemed desperate to have them go. Avery looked at her, worried. When she was moody, he understood her. He could appreciate the sadness. It had always been part of her—a suggestion of end of summer about her, or of a dying fall in music. It was part of her beauty. But the violent shifting of mood alarmed him. He didn't like to leave her alone. But she pushed his shoulder gently and said, "Go along, Avery darling. You and David go."

They drove to the coast, where it was cooler, and watched the boats on the Sound, but after an hour Avery said, "Let's go back to the house, shall we?" He had a kind of premonition, and it frightened him.

When they entered the house it seemed cool, after the heat of the road, and emphatically empty. "Mother!" he called. "We're back."

They found her in the studio. She didn't turn when they entered, and looked still as death. Avery called to her and she turned. "I've finished your portrait, David," she said, her voice vibrant with an undercurrent of panic. "I've done the left side from memory. I'm afraid it looks a bit mechanical. Rather like a hand-colored photograph. But it *is* finished."

The wet oil color gleamed in the light. It was true that the face looked machine made, yet it looked like David too. Technically, it was one of the best pictures she had ever painted, with a good deal of bravura and self-assurance. It was the last painting she attempted, while she was well.

"Do you know," she said quietly, "I think that if I'd left that picture unfinished, or scraped the canvas, or torn it to bits, that I should have gone mad? Stark, raving mad?"

Avery felt a stab of fear. He looked at the painting again and said, "It's good, mother. Quite good."

"Is it?" she asked. "I didn't like doing it."

She looked at an unframed canvas that hung on the wall. It was like scores of paintings she had done, faintly like Renoir, loose and voluptuous and rankly amateur, extravagant with color, all pink and rosy, a section of garden with some grass and a large, imagined nude. "I enjoyed doing that," she said. "And it's worthless. David's portrait is quite valuable."

It was true. The portrait was as competent, and antihuman, as the Trustees' portraits that hung in the Refectory at Col-born, for which adequate sums had been paid. He squinted at the picture. "It's good," he said. "Damned good."

"Is it, Avery?" his mother asked. "Surely not good enough to make you forget your language."

"Sorry, mother."

"That's all right, dear. But please be careful."

It was as if she had said, 'Pick up your toys, though, darling, after this,' or 'Please, darling, do remember to scrub your knees with a brush.'

"Your mother is a survivor from another, better age, my lad," said David, "when people had more quality than they have today."

"Don't make me sound antique," she protested.

"It's not a matter of antiquity," he said. "Only of quality." He smiled at Avery. "You have quality too, young Avery," he said. "Your mother is the survivor of another, better age, and you are the survivor of a newer, better age that we haven't entered yet."

"And you, David? How about you?" asked Avery's mother.

"Oh, I'm nothing," he said. "A pastiche. Twentieth century man in a cellophane wrapper. Made of plastic with a thin layer of genuine gold electronically applied, gold that gleams and won't tarnish but that's so thin it can be sold in Wool-worth's and that unfortunately *will* rub off."

"And now we know," she said.

"And now we know," said David.

They went into dinner and David managed to keep her amused, so that her mood passed, and she became quite cheerful after drinking two glasses of wine. They were going out, and Avery rather wished they wouldn't.

He waited up until quite late, sitting in a chair in the living room, but he fell asleep there, and when he woke up it was past one. He stumbled up the stairs, groggy, and went to bed. He didn't hear them come in at all.

David had a cable from England, giving him a month's extension of leave, because there was no posting for him; he stayed on. Early in August, he spoke at the Legion war bond rally in Hull. He wore his uniform, starched khaki that Annie McBain ironed for him, his medal ribbons sewn to the tunic. Avery and his mother sat on the platform, under a hot canvas awning, while a band played and a legionnaire, sweating in a suit made of blue felt, made a long patriotic address.

The rally was held on the Common in Hull and the platform faced the World War tank and the statue of the Civil War soldier. The grass was still fresh and green and the trees were thick with leaves. There were farmers in the crowd, with wrinkled shirts and stiff straw hats that looked like baskets. A state trooper in a pith helmet stood beside his patrol car. There were some soldiers in rumpled cottons and one sailor in impeccable white.

David spoke exceedingly well, in a voice that wasn't quite his own and reminded Avery of a famous voice he could not quite place. He realized, after a few minutes, that David was taking off the voice as well as the sentiments of the British Prime Minister. He made reference to the American Revolution, "in which you chaps gave us a darned good licking." He spoke of the war in the desert, of the air raids on Britain, of the brave people on Malta. He was a great success. When he finished there was a burst of applause and cheers and the Post Commander shook his hand.

"Was I all right?" he asked, sitting down beside Avery and wiping his forehead with a khaki handkerchief. "Do you think they really liked it, or were they just being polite?"

"You were fine," Avery said. "You sounded different."

David laughed. "Oh, well. You know. On parade, on parade, off parade, off parade. Must give the troops what they want."

When the speeches were over, the band played the "Star Spangled Banner" and "God Save The King." David stood at attention, his hand raised to his cap. Then the Legionnaires crowded around him, shaking his hand and slapping his back. "You were great, kid. Great," one of them said. "I was with the Limeys in the last war, see?" He pointed at the ribbons on his chest and David nodded. "Old Pip, Squeak and Wilfred," he said, shaking the man's hand.

Avery and his mother stood in the background, feeling awkward and out of place. Then David turned and said, "Do you mind if I go along with these chaps? They want me to see their headquarters." He smiled apologetically. "I don't like to refuse."

Avery's mother touched his cheek; for a moment, their eyes met. Then she said, "You should go. It will do you good to get a bit beery with them."

He went off with the Legionnaires, leaving Avery and his mother alone. They drove back to the farm and had dinner together, feeling a sense of incompleteness because David wasn't there. They had gotten used to him, and hadn't realized how dependent on him they were to liven things up. After dinner they sat on the lawn until the sun went down, not talking, but just sitting and admiring the garden in the dying light. Then it got cool and Avery's mother rose, her pale dress ghostly in the evening light. "Good night, darling," she said. "Don't stay up too late."

"I'll be in soon, mother," he said.

But he didn't feel like going to bed. He sat for a couple of hours in the light of the summer moon that made long liquid shadows across the lawn, brooding, enjoying the cool air. Then he heard a car in the driveway, and a screeching of brakes. He heard David, beerily singing:

Bless 'em all, Bless 'em all
The long and the short and the tall

A car door opened and shut, then David called, "G'night, Bill, old blanket. 'Night, Larry. Jimmy. Thanks, chaps. Thanks."

Avery remained still, in the shadows. A few minutes later a bright patch of light appeared on the dark flank of the house, in David's room. Then David came to the window, naked, rubbing his chest. Through the screen, Avery heard him humming the song he had been singing. After a bit the light went off.

Avery walked across the lawn to his mother's garden. The voluptuous smell of the flowers affected him like the presence of a pretty girl. He felt restless and lonely, missing something. After a while he turned and went into the house, closing the door quietly after him. He went down the hall to David's room and saw that the door was open. But the room was empty. The bed had been turned back neatly, but David wasn't in it. He turned away and started back to his own room. As he passed his mother's door, he heard a sound and stopped, suddenly aware of the pounding of his heart.

"Nancy, you're beautiful," he heard David say, his voice muffled, coming through the door. "You're lovely."

He stood in the hall, paralyzed, confused.

"David sweetheart, you mustn't," he heard his mother say. "You simply mustn't."

Then David spoke, but he couldn't understand the words, and his mother laughed lightly, and said, "No, darling. No."

"Nancy, Nancy…"

He stood motionless as a frightened deer, his breathing stopped, his ears straining until the blood seemed almost to burst from them. What he heard then was conclusive and crude—the sound of the bed and of sexual breathing, his mother's cry that was half pain and half joy, David's voice, hoarse and terrifying, making love to his mother.

He swayed, then steadied himself. He had a desperate urge to burst through the door and encounter them. But he couldn't. He stood for a moment, hearing the bed and hearing his mother say: *David, David,* then turned and went to his room.

He was in panic, shocked by the fact itself but even more by the terrible fact that he knew it. What came clearly through his agony was the knowledge that he must not tell, must not ever tell. The habit of protecting his mother had been formed early. He must never tell. He must keep what he knew in his own heart, and he understood that the shame he felt and the inexplicable personal guilt, would always be with him.

He had not seen, he had heard, but the visual rose in imagination and made him sick at his stomach. He tried to thrust it from his mind. He didn't want it. It was his mother, and he knew his mother, so that the truth could not be true. He could not blame his mother; she seemed a victim, an innocent, a violated saint. He blamed himself.

"You'll be more or less head of the house," his father had told him. "Take care of things. Look after your mother."

"Yes, sir," he had said. "You can depend on me, Dad."

He tried to install himself in his father's position, to deduce what his father would have done, had his father stood in the hall just now instead of himself.

What would his father have done?

What would Morgan have done?

Avery didn't know.

He lay in bed, half waiting for his mother's door to open, and tried to decide what he should do, since he stood in his father's place. It could not be his mother's fault. His mother had never, in all his life, ever been to blame for anything. It was David, the bastard. What should he do about David? Challenge him, drive him out of the house? Shoot him? Try to fight him with his fists?

He didn't have the equipment; he was a boy, not fifteen.

Then he remembered with a flood of relief that in ten days he and David were going to Roger Bell's place; that would get David out of the house. Until then he didn't know what there was that he could do.

He fell into torturous sleep. He did not hear the door open. He slept erratically, and dreamed, and through his agony there ran an admixture of despicable jealousy, of David and of his mother, and both of them together.

In the dark he came full awake. It was four o'clock in the morning. He got out of bed and went down the hall to David's room, where David slept on his bed, naked, the sheet thrown off. Avery looked down at his body, at the scar that ran across his chest, then down at the vulgar maleness, in the moonlight coming through the window. It would be easy to kill him. He could go downstairs and get his father's revolver and shoot him while he slept. It would be easy, and it would be right.

But he didn't.

He stared at his cousin, disgusted by the gross male body and the sour smell of beer on his breath, and felt helpless and bewildered. He could not regard what he knew to be true as operative fact. His mother was simply not capable of committing physical sin.

Yet she had done it.

He went out of the room and stopped in front of his mother's door. "Mother," he said softly. "Mother. ... "

"Avery?" she called. "What is it, dear? Are you all right?"

The sound of her voice made him tremble.

"Yes, mother, I'm all right. Just going down the hall," he said.

He heard her turn in her bed, then went back to his own room and sat beside his window. He had a sick awareness of doom, and the hour of night made it seem irrevocable. At last he went to sleep again, turning and tossing on his damp mattress.

The next day, when he saw them in the clear morning light, with the smell of coffee in the air, what he knew was true seemed fantastic. He saw David brushed and shaved, dressed in a clean white shirt, and his mother fresh and serene as a flower, kissing him gently on the cheek, and he could not believe it. He could not.

But as he watched them smile at each other and saw their hands touch as his mother handed David a cup, he read things into these simple exchanges that would yesterday have seemed incredible. He watched them, the next few days, feeling guilty as he did it, and ashamed of himself for spying. He saw nothing he hadn't seen pass between them since the night of the storm, when David had danced with his mother, but now everything had a rotten meaning.

Things were wrong, and he knew it was his job to put them right, but he didn't know how to go about it. Once, when David made a joke, he forgot himself and laughed, as he always had before, and his mother smiled and said, "Well, Avery, you're cheerful again. You've been so broody lately, I thought you were bored with us."

"Leave the boy alone, Nancy," David said good naturedly, "he has the weight of youth to carry, and that's a terrible load these days."

Avery could have killed him. He got up and walked away, wandering down the dirt road toward the highway. But before he'd gone very far he turned and almost ran back to the house.

He didn't intend to leave them alone.

That much he could do, until it was time for him and David to go down to Cape Ann.

CHAPTER FOURTEEN

THAT week end his father flew home from Washington, without letting anyone know.

"I hitch-hiked," he explained. "On an army bomber going up to Boston. It was too good a chance to miss."

He looked tired, but he was filled with the breath of affairs. The excitement of the high-level war clung to him like a perfume. He looked important, stronger and tougher and more important than David, beside whom he stood in the living room, having a drink before dinner.

The dinner was tense. The mere presence of four people at the table instead of three formalized the arrangement, with his father and mother in their usual places, he and David facing one another. He felt degraded. He found himself staring at David and feeling hatred he couldn't contain. The adult conversation made his fuse burn shorter. It seemed intolerable to him that David was allowed to remain in the house, making innocent, polite conversation with his father, when he should at the least have been beaten bloody, and perhaps even beaten to death.

They were discussing the President, and his father was saying, "Of course he can be elected as often as he pleases. Everybody works for him. He signs everybody's pay check."

"Well, John," his mother said slyly, "he signs yours, and of course you won't vote for him."

His father laughed. "Mine's only for a dollar a year. My vote comes a little higher than that."

"They like him in England, you know," said David. "He has an appeal."

His father nodded. "His charm has been exaggerated. But he's a clever man."

"Roger Bell's father says he's got paranoia," Avery said, the words coming to the surface of his mind like weed, uttered without thought. "Roger Bell says his mother—"

"Oh, now, Avery, you don't believe that," David said. "That's just another story."

Avery lost control. "I don't see what you know about it," he said. "You're a foreigner. Bell's father is an officer too. And he says—"

"Avery!"

His father's voice was like a great black whip, hurtling down the length of the table, snapping right in front of his nose.

"Sir?"

"Apologize to your cousin."

Avery stared at his plate. His mouth was numb as in a dentist's chair. The seconds passed, and the crackling of his father's will and anger was nearly audible. His father waited, as if he held a stop watch in his hand, then said, as the sweep hand passed the mark, "Avery, leave the table."

"John, please!" his mother said.

Avery got up, put his napkin on the table, then picked it up and folded it into the shape given by the iron.

"Please don't do this on my account," said David.

Avery's father looked steadily at him. Avery turned and left the room. As he passed through the door he heard his mother make a hurt sound and cry, "John, why did you?" He paused in the next room, standing still as a piece of furniture, listening to the silence that came from the dining room. Then there was a burst of voices, and the sound of David's courteous laughter. He ran to the staircase and up to his room, throwing himself on his bed.

He was furious with himself for having behaved like a fool, and with his father for treating him like a child. It would serve his father God damn right if he found out what a louse David was.

But in the morning, when he met his father in the hall, he didn't have any weapons. For a few seconds he held his ground, looking straight into his father's eyes. Then he surrendered.

"I'm sorry, sir," he said. "I didn't mean to be rude."

His father nodded. Avery felt as far from him as he had ever felt in his life.

"Better tell David you're sorry too," his father said. "It was a darn rude thing to do."

"Yes, sir."

"Right," said his father. He touched his shoulder, then grazed his chin with his fist. "We'll forget it, shall we?"

"Right," said Avery.

He stood in the hallway, watching his father go away.

He had not seen his father for almost three months and he had missed him. He wanted to be with him, but as it turned out, he hardly saw him during the whole of his father's visit.

In the afternoon the house was filled with people, the way it had been on week ends in peacetime. There were eighteen guests for dinner and he ate in the kitchen with Annie McBain.

Sunday morning, they all went to church, where he watched David take Communion though he had no right to do so. He stood in church beside the three adults, watching the well-dressed people rise and kneel and seem both to understand and believe what was revealed to them by the service. He envied them. He had the wish to believe, and be saved. And the brave atheism of broad daylight seemed crude, here in the church. But this ambivalent piety passed off as he came out of the church into the bright sunlight.

They were all hypocrites, he knew—capable of smiling at people they loathed, drinking the whiskey they warned you against, smoking the poisonous cigarettes, dancing until three A.M. when you'd heard them swear they hated to dance, going to bed together in dark rooms and doing things they punished you for asking questions about. It was a tremendous, transparent, organized fraud, a hoax they worked on themselves and one another, and most of all, on you. It was a joke, an enormous joke, and since he had not been admitted to the joke, Avery hated and feared it.

Before he went back to Washington, his father took him aside and explained that David Fearing was a hero and had been through desperate experience in the desert, that he was here to rest and could hardly be expected to devote all his time to an adolescent boy, that Avery was being unfair and self-centered in addition to being rude, and probably being unpatriotic. "It doesn't make any difference what you feel about him," his father said. "He's your guest and you're his host. It may not be convenient for you to have him here, but that can't be helped. The point is, you're to be courteous, do you understand?"

"Yes, sir," Avery nodded. "It's just that, well, you know. He's an Englishman and all that."

He stood in his father's study, looking down at the objects on the desk, feeling the need to say something, unable to produce the truth, or even a substitute for it. He was seized by a kind of antilogie.

"Anyway, he drinks," he said.

"Well so do I," his father said. "So does your mother."

"I mean he gets drunk," Avery said.

His father's face changed, like the face of a schoolmaster who has made up his mind. "Let's not discuss it any further, Avery," he said. "You've apparently taken a dislike to your cousin, and that's too bad. But it doesn't alter your responsibility. There is a war on, you know. I told you I was depending on you to carry on here."

"Yes, sir," Avery said.

"All right then." His father got up and smiled at him, then reached across the desk and touched his shoulder. "Let's forget it, shall we?"

They went out onto the lawn together. It was a cool August night, and the fireflies browsed like night-flying aircraft.

"I may go into the army, son," his father said, looking off at the low hills. "It's not certain, but I may."

"To fight, you mean?" he asked.

"No. We'll leave the fighting to Morgan, in this war. It would just be so I could do my job better."

Avery nodded.

"We won't say anything to your mother, though," his father said. "There wouldn't be any point in worrying her."

They walked down the slope of the lawn together, reaching the flower border. "Dad . . . " Avery said.

"Yes, son?"

"I—" Avery looked at the neat edge of brick that guarded the border from the lawn. He had nothing to say. There was nothing to say that he had the vocabulary for. "How long do you think the war will last?" he asked, finally.

"I don't know," his father said. "A year at least. Maybe two. And then there will be the Japs."

They walked back to the house and his father went upstairs to pack his bag. He had a seat on an army bomber taking off at Hartford, and Avery's mother drove him to the field.

Avery didn't go. He and David remained at the house, sitting on the lawn, waiting for Avery's mother to return. David stretched lazily and said, "Do you really want to go to your friend's place, in Massachusetts?"

Avery stiffened. "Of course I want to go," he said. "It's all arranged. They expect us."

David didn't argue. The next day he and Avery went down to Cape Ann on the train.

CHAPTER FIFTEEN

BELL'S people had a big house on a point of land that reached out into the Bay, and Roger had an eighteen-foot sloop. Roger's father was in the navy, but his mother was there, and Avery didn't like her. Her mouth was painted a deep sticky red. Her hair was black and polished and close to the head. She radiated a kind of high-fashion sex, spurious as altered coffee. Roger called her Doria, an affectation that troubled Avery. She had chafed through a man-less summer, irritable and deprived of her function, which was to be admired and waited on by her husband and her husband's friends, who were now all gone to war. She regarded David, in his soldier suit and on best behavior, as a legitimate object of prey.

Avery sensed this, standing in the sun on the private dock with Roger and his mother, staring at Doria's painted nails on David's khaki sleeve.

"You'll bunk with me, Ave," Roger said. "Just like at school. Your cousin can have the bedroom in the corner."

There were spare bedrooms, and Avery would have liked it better by himself, but he couldn't tell Roger this. Roger teemed with energy and command. He took Avery upstairs and helped him unpack.

"Have any fun, this summer?" he asked. "What'd you do?"

"Oh, you know. Swam. Fished."

"Meet any women?"

"Well, sure."

Roger moved closer to him, lowering his voice. "Listen, Ave, you know what? I lost it."

Avery looked at him, not quite believing him.

But Roger grinned confidently. "I knew I would, for sure, this summer," he said.

Bell's father had been a classmate of his own father. Bell was, by natural assumption, leader of the Form. He was one of those boys who become leaders automatically, who don't have to play football or fight or bully the smaller boys or study in order to achieve prominence. Roger simply radiated prominence. He was a sixteen-year-old man of distinction, with a good head and pleasant, clean-looking features. He had a smile that seemed to inform you, "Look here, I'm really a good fellow, even if I am a bit better than you." It was this qualified priggishness, plus superb, instinctive political art, that made him arbiter of the class, so that at school, the room he and Avery shared was a place to which others came for help and advice, as people go to the headquarters of a district leader.

Avery had contempt for Roger, but he envied his ability to control almost any situation in which he was likely to find himself. There were a dozen approximate Roger Bells at Col-born School, and hundreds, thousands, of approximate approximations of him in preparatory schools and high schools all over the country. He was fortune's favorite, the kind of person concocted exactly according to the recipe, nothing left out, nothing added, no skim milk, no garlic. It was impossible to find fault with him, yet he was worthless and potentially worthless. And Avery knew it; he disliked his roommate.

"What about you?" Roger asked. "Did you get any?"

"Well sure," said Avery. "What do you think?"

"Swell!" said Roger. "Now we both know the score, eh?"

They sailed all day, Roger and Avery, then had a party on the beach attended by Roger's summer friends, the boys confident and very brown, understanding boats, the girls sleek and indifferent, with short sunburnt hair that blew in the wind like hair in advertising photographs. They looked so much alike it was hard to tell them apart. They were a crowd, and naturally ignored Avery, behaving as if he were not there at all. They were polite to David, calling him Sir, and impressed by his British knowledge of sailing.

"It's a good thing you brought him," Roger said. "He can get Doria off my neck. She's been going nuts all summer, by herself."

Avery looked at Bell's mother, sitting with her legs drawn up under her chin, showing a lot of thigh, talking to David. "Sure," he nodded. "I see what you mean."

"Give us a chance to have some fun," said Roger.

The fun was a pair of Portuguese girls they picked up in an inlet down the shore a couple of days later. They were dark girls with beautiful, jet-black hair. One was called Rita, the other Maria Cruz. The one called Rita had old-country earrings in her pierced ears. They spoke in down east voices, subtly altered by the voluptuous language they used at home.

Roger sailed along shore, then turned into a small still cove, where they dropped anchor and broke out the lunch the Bells' cook had prepared for them. He turned on the radio, then whispered to Avery, "That one you've got, Rita, she's a cinch. All you got to do is play your cards."

They danced to the radio; Avery was aware of the musty smell of Rita's hair, and the slightly acrid smell of her flesh.

"How about a swim?" Roger said.

He stood up and dropped his khaki shorts to the deck, standing nude for a moment while both girls screamed and pretended to put their hands over their eyes. Then he dived accurately, swimming out for a few yards, and turned, treading water. "Come on, stinkers. Come on in," he yelled.

The girls laughed and took off their clothes, their brown bodies beautiful in the sun. Avery undressed, his back to the girls. They swam for a while, then Roger and Maria Cruz clung to the anchor chain. He heard them laugh, then heard the girl say, "Roger! You bad boy!"

Rita swam back to the boat and climbed aboard, pulling her clothes over her wet body. Avery followed her and dressed quickly. They watched Roger and Maria Cruz swim toward shore, then saw them climb across the rocks and disappear into a thicket. Rita regarded them philosophically.

"They're gonna have a wrestling match in them woods," she said.

Avery stared at her.

"If you got any ideas, jerk, forgit 'em," she said. "For one thing, yer oney a kid, see. An' fer another, I don't do that," she nodded toward the beach. "I don't mind a little mooching around, but I'm still the way God made me, see? That Mary, she's crazy."

She wore a religious medal on a chain. She took it in her hand for a moment and looked at it, then stuffed it into her shirt. She went on talking about Maria Cruz, and the trouble that lay in her path, using language that was brutal and direct. "She's gonna get knocked up, that Mary. Knocked up higher'n a kite."

"You shouldn't talk that way," he said, the language making him uncomfortable.

"Who the hell are you to tell me how I should talk?" she said. "You little snot." She went forward, sitting on the anchor bitts. Avery moved into the shade of the furled sail. After a while he got up and walked to the bow, standing beside her. "I'm sorry," he said. "I didn't mean to make you mad."

"Who me?" She looked at him indifferently. "I'm not mad. Don't mind me. I'm liable to tell off the Pope, if he talks to me cockeyed."

She put her hand on his neck and pulled his face down to her own. "Come on, kid. Kiss and make up."

He bent and she kissed him, her mouth tasting of salt from her swim, then pushed him away. "That's all there is," she said. "There ain't no more."

He moved away from her, ashamed of himself for not knowing how to get what Roger had told him was there. After a while

Roger and his girl swam back to the boat and they got under way, sailing back to the inlet where the girls lived. There was a gray weather-board shack and a line of washing that hung between a corner of the shack and a tree. It was desolate. Roger held the sloop in close and they leapt ashore. Maria Cruz called, "So long, wolf!" Then he eased her off, and they sailed toward the house. "How'd you make out?" he asked, his eye on the head of the sail.

Avery was ashamed to tell the truth. "Oh, fine," he said, making a sign with his thumb and finger. "A cinch."

"Mine was a dud," Roger said. "She used to be okay, but she reformed."

Avery regretted the unnecessary lie. The musty smell of Rita's hair was still in his nostrils. He felt dirty, and wanted a bath.

When they reached the house it was nearly dark. They walked up the path from the dock without speaking, their rubber soles making no sound. As they neared the porch, they heard David say, in a voice that struck Avery like a hammer, "Doria, you are lovely." Then he saw them, close together in a hammock, and Roger coughed. His mother called lazily, "Roger, darling, if you're starved there's food in the kitchen. Help yourself, will you?"

In the kitchen, Roger cut chunks from a cold ham and balanced them on jagged sections of bread. They ate these sandwiches and drank milk, saying nothing, both of them aware of what they had interrupted, on the porch, between David and Roger's mother. After a while, his mouth full, Roger said, "I guess Doria really goes for your cousin, eh kid?"

"For God's sake, Bell," Avery said, his voice trembling, "will you stop calling her Doria? She's your mother. Can't you call her mother?"

In the kitchen doorway, Mrs. Bell laughed cheerfully at him. "He calls me Doria, dear, because that's my name, and because I happen not to like being called mother."

Avery turned red. "Gee, I'm sorry, Mrs. Bell," he said. "Honest I didn't mean anything."

"That's all right, Avery," she said. "I just wanted to explain why Roger calls me Doria." She paused. "Has he given you enough to eat? Would you like something else?" She glanced at the crude sandwich in his hand, then said, "It looks inelegant, but nourishing."

"No. No, this is fine," he mumbled.

She had managed to put him in the wrong. He hated her, he hated Roger, he hated David, and the Portuguese girls. He hated the whole human race, except, illogically, his mother, whom he wanted passionately at that moment as an infant craves the breast. But his mother wasn't there. He was alone with strangers.

When he got into bed, monstrous accusations took shape in the darkness as he lay there, unable to sleep, the sound of the sea coming through the open window. His world was dispersed, and not useful to him. His pride was hurt and his small capsule of love was already split, so the contents were unprotected.

"Well then, Hollister, are you a pessimist?" one of the masters at Colborn had asked, after reading a paper of Avery's.

"No, sir," Avery had answered. "I'm an optimist."

"Well, what do you believe in?"

"Well, sir, I believe in my mother and father, and in, well, in America. And I guess I believe in, well, the future."

"And yourself, Hollister? Do you believe in yourself?"

"Yes, sir," Avery had replied without hesitation. "I believe in myself."

The master had paused, his pointer in his hand. "I see you've left out God," he said. Avery had not answered, and the master had smiled. "Doesn't it leave quite a hole?" he had asked.

"Well, sir, you see—" Avery had begun.

"Oh, yes. I see," the master had said. "None of our better students believes in God these days. It's not the fashion."

Avery recalled this interchange, as he lay under a strange roof, on a strange mattress, the awful breathing of his host now making a noise like an imperfectly functioning ventilating machine.

He was confronted with a problem. The question that plagued him, dredged up by his confusion, was how there could be good without God, and how evil without good, and how life without good and evil. He was listening to the mutterings of Greece, and he was too old to put the questions off and too young to think them less important than the winning of wars or girls or dollars. He was at an age that demands statement, requires a testament; it was no good saying *you will know later, understand later*—or that these things will matter less when the meat on your bones is tougher.

And he was besieged by the powerful, contradictory fact of sex, and the symbols of sex that infiltrated the world around him. He was terrified of his writhing body, and of the imagined, contestant bodies of the people he saw in daylight. People were nothing but animals, no better than the cows in the barn.

He had not been able to tolerate the picture of David embracing his mother, but he saw David that night, in undulating, awful embrace with Roger Bell's mother. What kind of a son-of-a-bitch was David, anyway? he asked himself. It made his own mother somehow seem more innocent, to have seen David with Roger's mother.

It was a dark night of the soul; he arose on his elbow and looked across the room at Roger, whose sleeping face was immune, and detested him.

In the morning, when he saw them all, David refreshed and accurately shaved, Doria in fresh denims without the hammock wrinkles, Roger filled with innocent good manners, he was astonished. It seemed incredible that they had not been somehow involved in his own catastrophic night.

"Good morning, young Roger," David said, morning-clean in his white shorts and fresh blue shirt. "Any chance of a sail with you two? I'm excellent crew, you know."

Roger looked at him candidly, then said, "Why not?"

"I've got a headache," Avery said. "I think I'll just hang around."

"Suit yourself," Roger said.

He sat on the dock, watching the water. He was apprehensive, aware of foreboding. When Doria Bell called him from the house and told him long distance was on the wire for him, he knew it was disaster. It was Annie McBain, in a firm Scots voice, to tell him his brother had been killed in Texas and that they needed him at home.

"Hold on to yourself, laddie," she said. "Don't let it smash you up."

"No," he said. "I won't."

He put the phone back on the hook and went upstairs to pack his things. He was half finished when David tapped on the door and came into Roger's room.

"You had a call from home," said David. "Is anything wrong?"

"Morgan was killed," Avery said. "This morning." He didn't turn around. David moved toward him and touched his arm.

"I'm sorry, Avery," he said. "I'll get packed up and go with you."

"I'd rather go alone," said Avery.

"Oh?"

David had the good sense not to argue with him. "I suppose you're right. It's not the time you want strangers around," he said tentatively.

"No. It isn't," Avery said.

There was a pause, then David said, "I'll go down to New York, then. I'l be at the Ritz Hotel, if you want me."

"Do as you like," Avery said.

He picked up his bag, stepping past his cousin, and went out of the house without saying good-bye to Roger or Roger's mother.

CHAPTER SIXTEEN

I T WAS dark when he reached the house.

The lower floor was lighted and a faint glow showed at his mother's window when his taxi stopped in the driveway. He wondered if his father was already home, then realized that he couldn't be. He carried his bag up the steps and reached for the knob, just as Annie opened the door.

"Avery, lad." She kissed his cheek. He had never been so glad to see her or grateful for her familiar smell. She peered behind him. "Isn't the Captain with you? Did you come alone?"

"He's in New York," said Avery.

"You must be tired out, laddie. Are you hungry?"

"No. No, thanks." He put down his bag. "Where's mother?"

"She's upstairs, laddie," Annie said. She hesitated, then touched Avery's wrist. "She took it pretty bad, Avery. She's resting right now. The doctor gave her something."

"Can I go up?"

"In a little while," Annie said. "Have something to eat first."

"I'm not hungry, Mac," he said. "Really."

She fed him anyway, cocoa and a neat sandwich made of sliced chicken, the crusts trimmed from the bread. He found that the sight of food made him hungry; when he finished the sandwich he asked for another. He sat watching Annie make it, feeling strange. He had been gone only five days, but the house seemed changed.

"He was a fine lad, Morgan," Annie said, placing the sandwich in front of Avery. "A fine boy."

Avery nodded; "He was okay," he said, slowly. "Morgan was okay."

He ate the second sandwich, then asked, "Can I see mother now?"

"I guess so, Avery," said McBain. "The doctor left about an hour ago." She paused. "She may be asleep."

He tapped gently on his mother's door, then opened it quietly. She lay on her bed, her head framed by the pillow, her face lighted from one side by the table lamp. You could not accuse her of anything. She was incompetent, beyond accusation. She looked like some grotesque approximation of his mother they had placed there in order to deceive him. She resembled a medieval German *pietá*, fashioned of crumbling, painted plaster, the colors softened by time. He tiptoed to her bedside and stood, looking down into the murdered face.

"Mother—" His voice was thick. "Mother, it's Avery."

She stirred in the morphinic sleep and her eyes opened slowly, unwillingly.

"Morgan," she said. "It's Morgan."

She attempted to raise her drugged arms to embrace him, but could not. They fell back to the bed. Her eyes closed. He stood numbly wanting to shout, 'It's me, mother. It's me, me, me.' But he didn't. After a few minutes he turned and went downstairs.

The living room was abnormally still, as if something was missing, and he looked inquiringly about. Then he realized that the clocks had stopped.

"Your mother stopped them," Annie said. "She wanted to cover them with cloths, but then the doctor came."

"Mother did?"

Annie nodded. Avery shook his head. It was the kind of thing, done by a friend, that would have made his mother uncomfortable. He realized that she had been mortally hurt, and dimly understood the catastrophic fact that the hurt would not be healed, by time, or the doctor's morphia. He went to the

French doors and stared across the brooding lawn. "Somehow I feel to blame. As if it was all my fault," he said.

Annie nodded. "People always feel that way," she said. "They feel guilty because they're alive, and glad to be alive."

He nodded. It was not what he had meant, but he was grateful to Annie, nevertheless.

At dawn his father arrived, gray and unshaven. Avery heard the car in the drive and ran to the door to meet him. His father entered the house reluctantly, as though he felt he could put off the fact for a few seconds longer. Then he shook hands with Avery and said, "Good morning, son. How is your mother?"

"She's upstairs, Dad. The doctor was here. He gave her something."

His father nodded. "I know. I talked to Parks on the phone."

He sat in a big chair, staring at the cold fireplace. The grief that Avery saw looked genuine. His father looked just as a man should look who had just lost his eldest son, and namesake.

"How did it happen, Dad?" he asked.

His father shook his head. "They were trying to get through to Texas for me, but I couldn't wait. There'll be a letter. They'll tell in the letter."

"I'm sorry, Dad," he said. He remembered Morgan, saying to him *"A pilot would have gotten out of it. Anybody that was a pilot would have gotten out of it."*

His father rose and walked to the fireplace, taking up his familiar position, one elbow on the mantel. "Yes. Yes, it's a damned shame," he said. "That's war, Avery. That's what happens in war." He took out his pipe and looked at it as if it were a strange object that had gotten into his pocket by mistake. "I think I'll go up and see your mother, son." He glanced at Avery. "Have you been awake all night?"

"Well, sir, I—"

"I know," his father said. "You'd better get a bath and some rest. There'll be lots to do, later on." He paused, then said, "Where's David? Is he upstairs?"

"He didn't come, sir. He went to New York. He thought it would be better."

His father nodded. "Didn't want to intrude, I suppose. It was thoughtful of him." He hesitated, looking at his pipe. "I'd have liked for him to have been at the funeral, though," he said. Then he touched Avery's shoulder. "Get some rest, son."

"Yes, sir."

He went upstairs, Avery watched the familiar back, feeling guilty, and aware of the secret in his heart. Morgan's death, almost from the moment Annie had called him, had seemed symbolic and retributive; he linked it directly to betrayal of the house, during a time when he had been serving as his father's stand-in. He felt that he was to blame, that his failure was in some way attached to the fact that his brother, his big brother, was smashed and dead on the alien desert, two thousand miles away. He took Morgan's death directly, almost as a sign from God.

He went out of the house, sick at heart.

It was gray dawn, pink just beginning to show. He stood in the cool morning air, then walked around the house to the east side. The lawn stretched away, and beyond it, meadow. Through a break in the hills the new day was forming up, an exciting band of brilliant sun showing strong against the hills, beneath the rose-colored light cloud. He watched the sun come up, and the sight contained the same offer it has made for many centuries—it has been bad in the night, but this is morning, here is the earth's turning again, reminder of the second chance, the third, or fourth, or four millionth … the dependable, axiomatic light after dark, that makes denial of God inappropriate in the morning. He felt the sun on his face and it lightened his heart a little, dulling the rumor his soul had started, the whispering insistence that his failure was in some way the cause of the tragedy that had entered the house.

He went back to the house by the kitchen door, smelling fresh coffee on the stove, and bacon frying in a pan, and the black tea that Annie drank in the morning. Home is a place—we all know that. He was home, and the strangers were gone. The thing to do now was to keep them gone. He was at home: The soft Scotch voice he listened to was the first voice that had ever addressed him, years ago—before he had heard his mother's voice or his father's or Morgan's.

"Poor bairnie," Annie said. "Poor lad."

She shook her head and raised the heavy kitchen cup to her lips: the Scots woman grieving with her English sister over the ways of the Widow Maker—something nostalgic in her pose— and in the fragrance of the strong tea—an echo of Wipers and Loos and Vimy and Arras, and all the strong-points in Flanders, where the British army had paused to rest during its four years' walk to the Rhine.

"Avery!" she called. "Wake up laddie!"

He had fallen asleep, with his head on his hand.

"Come along wi' ye, boy. I'll go up to your bed wi' ye."

She tucked him into his bed, as though he were four and not nearly fifteen; consequently, he slept.

CHAPTER SEVENTEEN

THE officer who brought Morgan Hollister home was not a pilot, since all these were busy with the war, but he was a captain and a graduate of Princeton, details due to the thoughtfulness of Morgan's commanding officer, who had derived from Morgan's record the fact that Morgan was a gentleman.

The captain—his name was Coatsworth—took charge of the military arrangements, while Mrs. Whipple and the Volunteer ladies managed the civilian side of things—discussing hymns with the minister and warning friends not to send flowers of delicate hue that might be inappropriate for a military funeral. Mrs. Choate, the young one who drove, touched Avery's cheek with a hand that smelled of perfume. "I'm sorry, Avery," she said. "I remember Morgan. He was a swell guy." It was the first natural thing anyone had said to him, and it made him feel better. "Thanks," he said. "He *was* a swell guy, Morg. It's a dam shame."

Mrs. Choate agreed with him and moved on.

He sat in the living room and tried to feel a sense of loss. His brother was a swell guy, and he was dead, and he felt rotten about it. But he could not develop what he understood to be the grief of the proper appearance—a kind of slow respectful sorrow, informed with dignity. He knew that he should feel an emotion like the one produced when he looked at a marble memorial statue—a sense of death clothed in the dignity of stone, clarified into established fact that everyone accepts and is sad about.

He didn't feel anything like that. He felt an occasional pang of fear at the vision of his brother's bloody head, the slow imagined descent of the plane, the instant, vindictive fire as it crashed. He felt the finality of Morgan's death, in overwhelming, sickening waves, and the objections that came into his mind were phrased in dirty street words, not dignified at all, shockingly unrelated to the temperate sorrow the others displayed as they filed past the closed coffin.

In a corner of the room, beyond the crowd, his father talked with Captain Coatsworth. Upstairs, his mother rested in an euphoric region the doctor maintained by giving her morphine every four hours, and as he sat in the living room, waiting until it was time to go, his mind kept drifting back to the instant in the hall, when he had heard her voice, and David's voice and heard David making love to her. He could not visualize what he had heard, any more than he could imagine his mother dancing the cancan or his father drunk with a chorus girl. It was impossible, and because it was impossible, he could not blame his mother, though it might have been easier for him to have blamed and then forgiven her.

After a while his father came to him and touched him on the shoulder. "Time to go, son," he said. "Time to go to the church."

The Hollisters were buried in a shady section of the cemetery, several generations resting together, those rebellions over and forgotten. Morgan was carried there from the church on a caisson sticky with new olive drab paint, followed by a squad of combat engineers conscripted for the ceremony. The incantations were offered, the volley fired, the flag folded and offered with a salute to Avery's father. What stood out in Avery's mind was the sound of the rifle bolts, the acid smell of the powder smoke, and the accurate way in which two soldiers folded the flag into a neat package of bunting.

He sat beside his father in the church, and stood beside him at the grave, and saw the tears in his father's eyes and the trembling of his father's lips. On the way home his father was silent for a long time, staring at the countryside through the slick half-window of the car. Then he said, "It's too bad he didn't get his commission before it happened."

Avery nodded.

His father had held the King's Commission, and one signed by the President of the United States, and understood the importance of such things. Avery looked at him, trying to read the expression on the face that was both strange and familiar; what he saw baffled him. It was not quite grief and not quite pride, but something compounded of the two. It would not be accurate to say that Avery's father took pleasure in Morgan's death, but it would be denying the truth to refrain from saying that he was spiritually enriched by it. It was the great sacrifice, the symbolic one, and Avery's father was dignified by it, as no doubt the Lord had been. He turned to Avery and said quietly, "Well, son?"

It was not really a question.

Avery made no answer.

They got out of the car at the house and his father thanked the blank-faced driver.

For a week his father remained at home, phoning Washington twice a day. The doctor came morning and afternoon, and his mother improved sufficiently to sit near the window of her bedroom and tell his father that he would not be doing right to resign, as he offered to do, and that of course they must all go on. His father refrained from telling her that, for him, going on meant taking the brigadier's star he had been offered and again wearing the uniform. He understood that the thought of him in uniform would add to her pain.

He was able to control his pride and it is to his credit.

But he did tell Avery, and showed him the letter that began *Dear John* and ended with the famous signature, and that told his father in such a friendly, almost jocular way, that his job could be done *so* much better if only he had the rank to go with it. The letter made the offer sound like a prank on the military, but also made it sound important. It was a very shrewd, very flattering letter.

To be a general in the army, even without a brigade to command, was to achieve the greatest military eminence so far reached by the Hollisters in the thousand years since the Norman conquest. There had been captains and majors and colonels. There had been an ensign under Miles Standish, in the days when that was a military rank. But none of them had ever worn the bright star of a general officer, and Avery's father was justified in being proud of the honor, even though it came from a Democratic president, who had selected this method of removing a Republican from what had become a politically sensitive post.

His father was proud, and filled with a high sense of duty. Both these emotions were confused by the death of his son, the illness of his wife, and the complications of his personal affairs in Washington, where he sometimes shared the bed of Mrs. Ivy Calder, Avery's New York whore.

It was not the time to provide him with problems that had no solutions. Avery didn't intend to. He respected his father and himself, and he was trying to do his duty.

"Will it be okay if I send David's stuff to him, Dad?" he asked. "I mean his clothes and all? He's at the Ritz Hotel in New York."

His father didn't understand. "Why would you want to do that?" he asked. "He's coming back here. I talked to him on the phone."

Avery stared at a corner of his father's study desk; he was in dangerous territory, and he knew it. He felt his mouth go dry.

"I don't think he should come back here, sir," he said, finally.

His father's head came up sharply.

"I thought we'd settled that, Avery," he said.

"It's not that, sir," Avery said. "It's—"

"What are you trying to say, Avery?" his father asked, striving to keep his temper. "What's on your mind?"

"Well, sir, it's mother," Avery said. "He bothers her. He gets her upset."

"Nonsense," his father said. "Your mother likes him."

Avery stood, his scalp prickling. He groped for a way of indicting David that would not compromise his mother. He suddenly remembered a master at Colborn who had been sent away in disgrace at night, and remembered the terrible accusation that had burnt through the school in the morning, when the master was gone and the school porter had packed his trunk and carried it to the railroad station. As his mind turned over, his father waited.

"Well, Avery?" His voice conveyed impatience; Avery looked up.

"Anyway," he said. "He's no good. He's queer."

"He's what?" his father asked, not comprehending.

"He's queer," said Avery. "He's a fairy."

His father leaned forward, the muscles of his jaw tense.

"That's the God damnedest thing I ever heard," he said, after a moment. He looked at Avery. "Do you know that David has a D.S.O. and bar? Do you know that he killed fourteen Germans, personally, with a Sten gun?"

Avery didn't know this, and as he stood in front of his father, the blood rising to his head, a vision of the fourteen mutilated Germans rose in his imagination, making him a little sick. "Anyway," he said stubbornly, "he made a pass at Roger Bell, down at Cape Ann."

"Avery, that's a damned lie," his father said dispassionately.

"No, sir," he insisted. "It's the truth."

There was a moment of silence. Then his father picked up the phone on his desk and dialed the operator. "I'd like to get Roger Williams Bell's place, please. It's at Rockport, Mass. Yes, I'll wait."

Avery leapt to his feet. "Don't do that!" he said. "Do you have to prove everything? Can't you take my word for it?"

His father hung up the phone. "No," he said. "I can't." He got up, leaning across his desk. "You've always had a lying streak. You lied the time you broke that clock. Remember?" He pointed at the French clock, his finger trembling. "Didn't you?" he shouted. "Didn't you?"

Avery mumbled, "Yes, sir." He was afraid, physically afraid, afraid of being smashed to death.

"And you're lying now," his father said. "You're telling a God damned lie."

His fist was raised and his anger reverberated in the small room. Avery backed away.

"What is it?" his mother cried from the doorway. "Why are you shouting? It's wicked of you both. So wicked."

She stood like a ghost in her light summer nightgown. Then she swayed, and his father moved quickly around his desk and caught her as she fell. He carried her to a chair, then turned. "See what you've done," he said. "See what you've done. You may have killed your mother."

The telephone rang neurotically and his father picked it up. "No," he said. "Cancel the call. I don't want to speak to them now." He dropped the phone brutally back to its cradle and looked across the room at Avery. "You little bastard," he said. "Don't you think there's enough trouble, without having you make it worse?" He turned to Avery's mother, and Avery ran from the room in terror, away from the accusative, enemy voice.

He felt pursued. He had a sense that a conspiracy was meeting against him, arranging events so they led to his doom. And he could not get it through his head that his father had called him a bastard and a liar; it was like being rejected by God, for Avery's father in many ways was more God than God the Father. It had always been Avery's father. Always. He had been the center, the judge, the jury and the court of appeals, fountain of strength, wisdom and law.

We'll have to ask your father, dear. He'll know about that.

That'll be for your dad to decide, an' not me, laddo.

You little crum, leave my stuff alone, or I'll tell Dad and you'll see!

I don't intend to tell your father about this, Avery. He wouldn't like it.

Gee, Hollister, ask your old man, will you? He'll let you.

Hollister, you'll have to have this signed by your father.

Father, may I?

Father, can I?

Father, is it true that—?

Dad, the fellows at school say—

Dad, how big is Texas?

Dad, where did Lindbergh start from?

Dad, what is Hitler, anyway?

Sir, is it true that the best thing is to shoot yourself?

Why, Daddy?

Why, Father?

Why, Dad?

Sir, why?

CHAPTER EIGHTEEN

H E STOOD in his blue suit, his wet collar tight around his neck, so that it choked off his air. He looked desperately about him, furtive as a black escaped prisoner in Georgia flushed into the open by the hounds. The sun that had reassured him yesterday would not come up tomorrow. It would never come up again. He looked behind him at the peaceful house, bathed in soft afternoon light, and turned from it in fear, running again.

There was a railway cutting in the rock, a mile from the farm, through the fields and across the rough. When he reached it, he stopped running and threw himself on the ground, careless of his clothes and of his hands, which were now cut by thorns and brush. He lay with his head near the ledge, panting and exhausted. Below, in the secrecy of the gorge, the bright tracks lay like jewelry, shining against the cinder roadbed. The smell of the railway, of hot metal and steam and soft coal and cinders and tarry wood, came up from the gorge, an alien smell.

His cheek was hard against the rock. After a while he raised his head and realized that his face was cut and that he was bleeding. He drew his hand across his cheek and stared at the bright smear of blood, fresh as paint on his smudged hand. He stood up, and a train whistled, far off down the track, then came into sight, racing toward him. He stood on the counter of the railway gorge, the inviting, bright tracks below him, steel and orderly and implacably honest. He was determined to leap, and tightened his muscles for the effort as the train rushed closer. But it passed, with a whipping, arrogant sound, and he did not leap, perhaps because there was no one to see, or perhaps because, through the defeat came the argument of his soul—an insistent assertion that he had the right and need to live, as the burdensome Spartan cripple must have felt, when all logic was on the side of his dying. There is a bright golden thread that runs through the fabric of man's history, and that can be a sign to him of hope. Perhaps it was this golden thread, spun thinner and finer than ever, in this dark year of war, but still gold, that formed a barrier between Avery and the pool of air that filled the railway gorge. He stepped back from the brink of the cliff.

The awareness of time returned. He blinked his eyes, half surprised at where he found himself, concerned by the sight of the blood on his hand. The hour that had passed since he ran from the house had the character of an episode half dreamed, half imagined, rather than reality. But fear of the house was still there, the real fear that had made him run. He stared at the empty tracks and the blank rock walls that were serrated by marks of the dynamite drill. He would not go home, where they thought he was a bastard and a liar.

He walked back across the field through which he had run, and down a slope overgrown with tough sooty grass, emerging from the field to the concrete highway, and fell into step with himself, keeping to the right on the shoulder of the road, the white, hypnotic center line like an infinite tape that led him toward the west. When he had walked for about an hour the sun was gone, and the passing cars began to show their parking lights. A truck drew up beside him and the driver called from the cab, "Want a ride, Bud?"

He nodded.

"Well, climb on up, then," the man said. "I'm not gonna come down and help you."

The cab of the truck was cozy, and authoritative as the wheelhouse of a ship. The driver wore a cap on the back of his head, the band adorned with union buttons. "Beats walkin', don't it?" he asked.

Avery looked at him, and felt better. "Yes," he said. "I was tired."

He was tired, he realized now. He was exhausted. There had been the sleepless night, when he had waited up for his father, and then the funeral, and the idiot run through the fields to the railway, and the hour's walk on the highway.

"Yeah. You look pooped," the driver said. "That's why I stopped for you. Goin' far?"

Since he had no idea how far he was going or where, he didn't answer.

"I said, you *goin'* far?" the man asked again. "I'm only goin' to N'york."

"That's where I'm going," Avery said.

He didn't care where he went, provided it was away from Hull, away from the State of Connecticut.

The driver hesitated, glancing at his clothes. "Your folks live in New York, do they?"

Avery nodded. "That's right," he said. "West side."

"Well, you'll be home tonight," the driver said. "This ain't the New Haven Railroad, but she gets there, just the same."

They drove through the night, the road opening before them like a tunnel, cut by the long beams of the truck's headlights, the heavy mysterious rhythm of the engine lulling and reassuring.

"Hungry?" the driver asked. "Have a sandwich." He reached under the seat and produced a package, which he handed to Avery. "Open it up," he said. "Go ahead."

There were four sandwiches. Avery unwrapped one, handing it to the man, who ate it with one hand on the wheel, guiding the heavy truck as easily as a nursemaid pushing a go-cart. "Go on," he said. "Have one."

"I can't take your food," said Avery.

"Go on. Go on," the man said. "Don't be a jerk. Eat it. That's what it was made for."

Avery ate a sandwich, heavy with meat and cheese between fresh spongy bread, and said, "Thank you."

"That's all right," the man said.

He gave him coffee from a thermos and forced a second sandwich on him. He was eating his own second when they approached a curve; he took the wheel with both hands, the sandwich held in his mouth, looking so comical that Avery laughed.

"All kinds of tricks in this business," the man said, when the truck was straightened out. "You learn to have eyes like a cat."

Far off the lights of the city glowed against the sky. They passed through abandoned uptown streets, between rows of out-lying warehouses, then rows of jerry-built five story apartment buildings. Soon they were in the heart of the city.

"Where do you want to get off, kid?" the truck driver asked.

They had stopped for a traffic light; the truck shuddered under the idling engine. The lonely sidewalks looked worn out, after the day's heat and the pounding of feet. The city slept restlessly.

"Anywhere. Anywhere at all," Avery said.

The man looked at him suspiciously. "Say, kid, are you on the lam?" he asked. "Are you running away from something?"

Avery hesitated, then nodded. "I guess so," he said. "I guess I am."

"Jesus, you kids!" the driver said. "Maybe you ought to go back, huh?"

"No. Not now," Avery said, looking at the red traffic light.

The driver put the truck in gear and they rolled slowly down-town. "You got any money, kid?" he asked.

Avery shook his head. The man dug into one of his pockets and gave him a dollar. "Probably I ought to tell you to go home," he said. "But I guess it's your own business."

Avery took the money. "Thanks," he said. "Thanks a lot." When he got out of the truck he shook hands with the driver and said, "Gee, you've been swell. Thanks."

The man laughed. "Forget it. I been on the bum myself. I know what it's like." He moved the levers of the truck and gunned the engine. "Take care of yourself, now," he said. "So long."

"So long," Avery called.

The truck moved slowly away in the darkness, its dimensions picked out like a needlepoint pattern in green and red and amber buttons of light, so that it looked like an enormous, mobile Christmas tree. Avery's arm rose from his side and he waved at the vanishing lights. He had made a friend, and parted from him. The wrinkled dollar was in his left hand and he stared at it for a moment, then turned and began to walk through the city until he came to a lighted place, an all-night cafeteria.

He drank black iodinic coffee and stared at the columns of figures on the check that had been delivered to him by a machine that rang. He had come away from the house in panic, without money or clothes, and without plan, and the absurdity of his position began to impress him as his panic thawed. The first thing to do was to get some money. He turned over in his mind the names of boys he knew at school who lived in New York, and rejected them all, because their families either knew his own, or were linked to it by social chain of command. Then he remembered Dennis McCoy, whose father was supposed to be some kind of political boss here in New York. He didn't really know McCoy, but he had broken the school tabu and treated McCoy civilly. The chances were that McCoy would give him twenty dollars or so.

He got up and riffled through the phone book, then dialed the number. After a while a voice answered, a low, controlled voice that had power: "Tip McCoy speaking."

"I'd like to speak to McCoy, please," Avery said. "Dennis McCoy."

"Dennis isn't here right now," he was told. "Who are you?"

"I'm a friend of his. Avery Hollister."

"Oh yes," the man said. "Avery Hollister. What's the matter? Are you in some kind of a jam?"

"I don't know," said Avery.

"Where are you?"

"In a restaurant. I don't know just where."

"Well find out, and tell me. I'll hold the phone."

When he came back and gave the address, the man said, "Order something and sit right there. I'll be along as soon as I can get dressed."

He went back to the table. About twenty minutes passed. The cashier looked suspiciously at him and he looked away. Then a man in a white silk suit that his father would not have worn walked into the restaurant, glanced around him, and came straight toward him. "I'm Tip McCoy," he said. "You must be Dennis' friend. He's up in the country for the summer. Maine."

"Gee, Mr. McCoy," said Avery. "I'm sorry to be so much trouble. It's just that, well, I was supposed to see some people, and Mac, I mean, Dennis, is a friend of mine from school."

"Forget it," Tip McCoy said. "If you're one of Dinny's friends, you don't have to explain anything. Forget it."

They drove across the city in a powerful black car and pulled up in front of an apartment house on Central Park West. Avery followed Mr. McCoy through the lobby and they went up in the elevator to an apartment that was furnished in the impersonal, modern manner—clean sheer walls and low, antiseptic furniture, with rugs that looked like enormous towels. It was an apartment that seemed to have been designed to conceal a dangerous or assertive personal taste. There had been money paid, and the place had been delivered, complete. Avery had the conviction that every item of furniture had been purchased at exactly the same time. Everything was of the same age. This living room had been born at a certain instant; one day movers would appear in ticking aprons, and it would die at another certain instant, simply cease to exist.

But over the brass-faced fireplace was a painting that made his heart leap. It seemed almost to have been placed there as a decorator's joke, to expose the meaninglessness of the room. It was the portrait of a young girl with polished, tawny skin and an attenuated face exquisitely painted, arabesque in line, impeccable, so groomed it made the onlooker feel shabby and unpressed.

"Italian painter," Mr. Coy confided. "Modigliani."

Avery washed in the modern bathroom, sponging the caked blood from his cheek and combing his hair. When he came back to the living room, a colored maid was setting out a plate of ham and eggs. Mr. McCoy had disappeared. "Here's your food," the maid said, in a bland, snobbish West Indian voice.

"You shouldn't have done that," Avery said. "You didn't have to get up."

"I get paid for it," she said impassively, and withdrew.

Mr. McCoy came back, wearing a cream-colored dressing gown. He looked like the photographs of him Avery had seen in the papers; he might have been a worldly Catholic archbishop, an Irish leader during the Trouble, a chief inspector of police, a tough Hollywood director or, as in fact he was, a powerful metropolitan political boss. He glanced at the ham and eggs and said, "Better eat. Do you good." He sat down and watched Avery eat. When Avery finished, he leaned forward and said, "You're John Hollister's boy, aren't you? You look like him. A lot like him."

"Do you know my father?" Avery said. He was surprised.

Mr. McCoy shook his head. "I've met him in Washington," he said. "I wouldn't say he was a friend of mine. We, uh, differ politically."

The West Indian maid appeared and took away the plate. Then she made a drink for Mr. McCoy. There was no human contact with her. She was detached as the busy signal on the telephone. Avery's eyes followed her as she went out of the room. Mr. McCoy laughed. "Does she give you the creeps?" he asked. "A lot of people don't like her. But I like her. I don't like the ones who talk. When I want a drink or something to eat, I want that, not conversation. Conversation is for barbers. With them you have to expect it. But not in the house."

Avery looked at Mr. McCoy and the man smiled at him.

"Look," he said, "Dennis told me you did him a favor. Maybe we do you one. What are you doing down here in town with a cut on your face, instead of up in Hull, where you belong?"

"I don't know," he said.

"I'm not a policeman," Mr. McCoy said. "You don't have to tell me anything. But if you want to talk, go ahead."

"My brother was killed," Avery said. "In the army. He was in an AT6. He spun in, from five hundred feet, and burned." He repeated the phrases that the captain had offered his father. Then he said, "I ran away."

Mr. McCoy took a pull from his drink.

"Look, son," he said. "This is none of my business. You're a friend of my boy's, and you have a bed here. If you need some money, you have that too. If you're in trouble with the police, smashed up a car or something, perhaps we can take care of it." He paused, seeming to consult his glass. "If you want to talk about it, fine. If you don't, fine too."

Avery nodded.

"Do you know what I am?" Mr. McCoy asked.

Avery reddened. At school, one of the boys had found a newspaper story on the McCoy machine and everyone in the Form had read it. It was in a Republican paper, and unfriendly to Avery's host.

"Well," he said awkwardly, "I—"

"They call me a boss," Mr. McCoy said. "I'm not that. I'm a listener. A professional listener. And what I hear, I don't repeat." He smiled. "If I have any influence, with the Boss, it's because I know how to listen, and keep quiet afterward. It sounds simple, but it's really quite an art"

Avery smiled and the man smiled back. The smile told a lot about the power and the myth. It was a smile that transformed the face. It inspired trust.

"When you talk to me, you talk to Tip McCoy, and not to anyone else," Mr. McCoy said. "It's like talking to the wall, except that I can hear, and I answer questions, when they're asked." His eyes surveyed the room, then came to rest on the rim of his glass. "Lots of people come up here just to tell me their troubles. I listen. And I never repeat what they tell me. So, if you want to get anything off your chest, don't be afraid to talk."

Avery sat for several minutes, looking first at Mr. McCoy then at the exquisite painting on the wall, then at the toes of Mr. McCoy's handmade shoes.

Then he did a strange thing.

He began to talk rapidly, almost monotonously, without inflection, and without plan. Perhaps it was the clinical impersonality of the room, perhaps the hypnotic effect of fatigue, perhaps the fact that for some reason he had believed the assurance that when he talked to Tip McCoy that he talked to no one else, as a Catholic believes in the sanctity of the confessional.

He talked.

He had tried to talk to his father and got nothing but his father's rage, when he had needed his father's love.

Now he talked and got love from a man almost as different from his father as a man could possibly be—an immigrant Irish politician, who spoke in the accents of a city that his father regarded as a vulgar slum with a gilded center. He said things he had said to himself in Hull, and other things he would never say, in Hull, or anywhere outside of this flat-faced room.

When he finished, Mr. McCoy nodded. He got up and made himself a drink, then returned to his chair. "What were you running away from?" he asked. "Your father? Or your mother?"

"I don't know," Avery said. "Everything, I guess. He got me confused, the way he yelled at me. I didn't mean to say anything. But he got me confused, and then he called me a God damn liar." He paused, then looked up defiantly. "He had no right to call me a liar. I'm not a liar."

"No," said Mr. McCoy. "But it was a lie, wasn't it? What you told him, I mean. At least, it wasn't true."

Avery stared at the floor and thought, then said, "Yes, it was a lie. But he wouldn't have believed me, even if it had been true. He wouldn't have taken my word for it."

"No," Mr. McCoy agreed. "I don't suppose he would have."

"It wasn't exactly true," said Avery. "But it was true in a way." He hesitated. "I mean it was true that David is really a son of a bitch no matter how many Germans he killed. My father should have believed me anyway. He should have taken my word for it." He paused, thinking, then went on. "It's all his fault. The whole thing. It was all his idea."

"The war, you mean?" Mr. McCoy asked gently.

"Well, no, not the war. I mean—"

But he meant the war, and his mother's sadness, and his cousin, and his brother's absence and his father's, and the way the family had been broken up. He blamed his father for all of it, in his heart. And what had happened between his mother and David he blamed on his father too, for the simple reason that he could not blame his mother, and his father was next in line. To have blamed his mother would have been like blaming his own blood. She had been blameless too long. She had been protected too long. She could only be the victim of a kind of rape that involved subornation of the emotions. David had drugged her with companionship, and taken advantage of her.

It was his father. It was his father's God damned fault, for not being there when he was needed. He looked up at the serene painting that smiled down and seemed to taunt him. "I don't know," he said. "I just feel as if everything had gone to hell."

"It has," Mr. McCoy said. "And not just in Connecticut, either." He looked at Avery. "What are you going to do?" he asked.

Avery got up and walked to the window, a flank of casements that composed most of one wall of the room. He parted the curtains and looked out into the city. The dark Park was spread beneath him, reaching east and north and south, the motor drives traced out in lights. Beyond the park a section of the city forged eastward, toward the river. Far below on the street, a car crept along with its headlights showing, then somewhere, far away, the siren of an ambulance or police car wept to the night and sent a thrill of fear through him, then a pang of remorse at the thought of his mother, and of his brother's body, in its new, muddy grave, the ground near it littered with brass cartridge cases. He let the curtain drop, and turned into the room. "I suppose I ought to go back," he said. "When I went away, this afternoon, I didn't know where I was going. I just ran, away from the house, away from my father. Then, when I came to the railroad, and the train was coming, I thought I would kill myself. And then I started to walk, and the man in the truck brought me to New York." He looked at Mr. McCoy, and demanded, "Why is it strangers are nice to you? Why should they do things for you, when they don't have to, like the truck driver, like you, and your own people are bastards to you?"

"I've often wondered," Mr. McCoy said. He stood up. "How about getting some sleep?" he said. "Then in the morning you can duck back home. Do you want to call your people? Let them know where you are?"

He shook his head. "No, I won't phone," he said. "I'll just go back tomorrow."

He slept in Dennis McCoy's bed, in a room furnished like the rest of the apartment. On the wall was a felt banner that said: COLBORN SCHOOL. The banner and the school photographs on the desk surprised him. McCoy had been rejected by the school, and responded with contempt, pretending not to give a damn what the school thought of him.

Yet the school must mean a lot to McCoy, he realized, and suddenly felt sorry he hadn't done more than just speak to McCoy. He found himself wondering about McCoy, and remembering his face, and he was curious about him. On the neat blond wood desk was a row of books between glass bricks; the titles were strange to him: *Rerum Novarum, Apologia Pro Vita Sua, The Confessions of St. Augustine.* Over the bed was a crucifix, with a figure of Christ and the letters I.N.R.I. He stood in the strange room, amid the contradictory objects, contemplating the image of the Catholic God, the Latin words forming themselves involuntarily upon his lips: *Iesus Nazarenus, Rex Iudaeorum.* "Jesus of Nazareth, King of the Jews," he said aloud. He removed the cross from its hook and placed it carefully on the desk, then took off his clothes and got into bed.

The next day a chauffeur drove him back to Hull. He did not see Mr. McCoy again. He sat beside the silent driver, who looked like a bodyguard. As they approached Hull, the larger questions of truth and falsehood, belief and disbelief, were brushed aside by the practical question of what his father would do to him. He was filled with acute physical fear of his father, and expected to be beaten, perhaps beaten to death. He had a vision of his father's face, with murder in it, glaring at him from behind the desk, a moment before his mother had come into the study.

He was terrified, and afraid for his mother, too.

When the man let him out at the door, he stood in the drive-way for a few seconds, hesitant, afraid to encounter his father. He walked around the house to the kitchen door. Annie looked up and made a clucking sound with her tongue. "You're a fine one," she said. "Running off."

"Are they mad?" he asked. "Are they mad at me?"

She laughed,

"Avery, you're the lucky one, you know. Your father left yesterday, late afternoon. And the doctor's had your mother asleep for hours with that needle of his. They don't even know you've been gone." She paused, smiling at him. "To tell you the truth, I wouldn't have known myself, I've been that busy, except that this morning a gentleman called and said you were in New York and would be back this afternoon."

The anticlimax was too much.

"I could have been dead!" he cried. "I could have had an accident, and been killed. Nobody cares. Nobody gives a damn. Nobody gives a God damn."

Annie caught him by the shoulder of his coat and shook him like a child.

"Avery Hollister, stop that swearing in my kitchen. If you must swear, go down to the barn. That's the proper place for swearing. Not the house."

He threw off her hand and ran out of the kitchen, up the stairs and into his room. He was bursting with volatile, desperate hatred of his father, of Annie, of the entire household, hatred, actually, of the blood that ran through his veins. He sat on the edge of his bed, until the boiling chemical action of the rage had run itself out. When he stopped trembling and got up from the bed a change had taken place in him—the change that had begun almost exactly twenty-four hours earlier, when he had run from his father's study, and pulled up only when he reached the railroad cutting and the invitation of the tracks in the gorge. He felt a hardness of soul so definite it shocked him, and he touched his body and stared at his hands, as if he expected to see stigmata appear on the palms. He walked to the window and looked out across the fields at the late summer landscape, withering trees and browning grass. His fist touched the window sill and a strange, almost exultant feeling of independence rose in his chest.

"The bastard," he said quietly. "The dirty bastard."

"Avery!" his mother called. "Avery, darling, is that you?" He squared his shoulders and walked to the door.

"Just a minute, mother. I'm changing."

He put on a pair of flannel trousers and a white tee-shirt, then walked into his mother's room. She sat in her little French love seat, near the window, her face sad, her eyes distant. He bent over her, kissing her cheek, momentarily repelled by the sickening medical odor that rose from her body and mingled with the nostalgic odor of her perfume. She took his hand; her palm felt hot and dry.

"Where have you been all morning, darling? Off somewhere? Enjoying yourself?"

The strange, painted, plaster face looked up at him with a sad smile; he understood that he would go through such hopeless passages with her again and again, and again and again, for this was his mother, and he was her son. He sat down beside her and gently withdrew his hand. When he did this his mother's hands flew suddenly in the air and for an instant seemed to hang there, fluttering like birds.

"Have you been with David?" she asked. "Swimming? Playing with swords?"

"He's not here, mother," he said. "He's gone to New York. Pretty soon, I suppose, he'll go back to Europe."

His mother looked sadly at him and nodded.

"I keep forgetting. Of course. David's gone. And Morgan's gone. And your father. Your father didn't want to go," she said. "But Dr. Parks made him. Of course he had to go, he had to return to his regiment. That's a man's place in the war, isn't it, Avery?" She looked at him, smiling. "With his regiment?" she said.

He nodded.

"But of course, you're not a man yet. You're only a boy," she said. "Just a child. My child. My Avery."

She threw her arms around him and pulled his head close to her breast, so that he had the sensation of suffocation, and the medical smell made him dizzy. As he sat there in his mother's embrace, that was like a clutch, the rhythm of a rhyme nattered in his brain, without words; the frustration was enraging. Then the words came, with a flood of relief: 'You're only a boy, young fellow my lad, you're not required to go. I'm seventeen and a quarter, Dad, and ever so strong, you know.'

She released him, finally, and he stood up. He looked around the familiar room, that had always contained for him an element of magic, so that merely being in it had been a kind of adventure. It seemed to him now a rather silly room, pathetic and old fashioned; the glamorous furniture looked worn, the romantic colors faded.

"Yes, of course, I am a child," he said, ironically conscious of his theatricality. "I'm only a boy, young fellow my lad, and I'm not required to go."

"What, Avery?"

"Nothing, mother," he said. "It's just a poem we learned at school."

Her eyes filled with great tears.

"Avery, you make me unhappy," she said. "Go away."

He went downstairs to the living room and dropped into a big chair, wondering what he was to do with the three weeks that faced him before his return to school.

He had always been glad to get back to school when holidays were finished. But now the prospect of a year at Colborn was tasteless, even repellent. It meant going back to a room with Roger Bell, to the football team, with its *drive,drive,drive,* back to being a dormitory prefect, back to acceptance of demands on his time that deprived him of things he wanted to do. There seemed no point in it. He had done well at school, because it had been expected of him, because his father had expected it of him. It no longer seemed worth while. The only thing he really cared about at school was school itself, the text books and the things you studied. The rest of it was crap.

He got up from his chair, feeling better because he had decided not to room with Roger Bell, not to play on the football team, and not to care about the fact that his father would be displeased.

"I'm just as good as he is," he said aloud. "Maybe better."

He went into his father's study, where he was not supposed to go except on invitation, and sat down in the leather chair that was shaped to his father's body. He picked up the phone and put in a call for Captain Fearing, at the Ritz Hotel in New York, and waited while the connection was made, hearing the operators' voices: *Hartford, Connecticut, calling Captain David Fearing. Hartford, Connecticut, calling Captain Fearing.*

"Fearing, here," came David's voice.

"This is Avery," he said. "I am sending your things down to New York by express."

There was a pause, and the wires hummed, then David said, "Well, all right, Avery, if you say so. I was going to come up, just for a day or two, you know."

Avery spoke very calmly.

"If you come into this house, you bastard, I'll blow your head off with a shotgun."

"What the devil are you talking about!"

"You heard me," Avery said.

After a moment he heard David's breath being let out. Then David said, "All right, Avery, if you feel that way. But let me give you a piece of advice, will you?"

"I don't want your advice."

"I'll give it to you anyway," David said. "Don't try to judge people, Avery. Don't try to play God."

"Go to hell," Avery said. "Go straight to bloody hell."

He hung up the phone, and swiveled around in his father's chair, looking through the window. There was a salt taste like blood in his mouth.

But he felt better.

He had crossed his father's will on a fundamental issue, and the reward was a sense of liberation from obligation to his father's pattern. "To hell with him," he said. "To hell with him."

CHAPTER NINETEEN

H E WENT back to school for his last year in a mood of controlled defiance, and proceeded to destroy the prestige he had acquired during his first three years there.

A few days after school started, he looked up Dennis McCoy, who lived in a small single room in the entry next to his. McCoy was a dark Irish boy, eighteen months older than Avery. His face had a potent Celtic intensity that called to mind the more romantic Irish martyrs—Kevin Barry and Michael Collins and the young Lord Mayor of Cork, who starved to death in his cell. When Avery knocked and entered his room, McCoy looked up, surprised.

"Hello, Hollister," he said. "Slumming?"

McCoy had been at Colborn for three years, but hadn't contracted the school accent.

Avery sat down on the bed. "Look, McCoy," he said. "I don't know whether your father mentioned it or not, but last summer I tried to get hold of you in New York, to borrow ten bucks from you. I was in a jam, and your father let me stay overnight at your place."

"Oh?" said McCoy.

"Did he tell you about it?" Avery asked.

McCoy shook his head. "He told me you called up," he said. "But he didn't say anything about your staying at the place."

"Well, I did," Avery said. "I was in a jam. I hope you don't mind."

"Hell no," McCoy said. "Why should I mind?"

"Your father was damned nice," Avery said. "He was swell." He looked at McCoy and saw part of McCoy's father in the thin, serious face. He had a memory of the antiseptic room, and the painting over the fireplace, and of Mr. McCoy's voice, saying, "When you talk to me, you talk to Tip McCoy and not to any-body else. It's like talking to the wall, except that I can hear, and answer questions." He was a little ashamed that he had come here to make sure McCoy's father had really meant what he said. He looked away, then said, "Going to eat, Dennis?"

It was Thursday night, and they were allowed to sit where they pleased in the refectory, instead of at their assigned tables.

"Well, sure," McCoy said. "I was just going down."

As they crossed the Green, they met a group of Sixth Formers, who did a double-take, surprised at seeing McCoy with Avery, or with anyone else for that matter. For three years, McCoy had been the Form's outsider. Only Avery and a few others had spo-ken to him at all, and no one had been his friend. At a school like Colborn, where everyone is secretly aware of his own failure to approximate the mythical, ideal Colborn boy, it is necessary to have at least one person on whom the others can look down, in order to reassure themselves ... a boy so completely un-Colborn that he makes the others feel sure of themselves. McCoy had been assigned this role the day he arrived at school. He was Irish and Catholic, the son of an immigrant, more interested in books than sport, unwilling to take on the school's sartorial and verbal conceits—all in all, the perfect tenant of the Sixth Form's slum.

After the other boys had passed, he said to Avery, "I don't think your roommate is going to like the idea of your eating with me. He has his position to think of."

"I'm living by myself this year," said Avery. "And anyway, I don't give a damn what Bell thinks about anything I do."

He didn't explain anything more and McCoy didn't ask him. They had dinner, not talking much, feeling one another out, and afterward went into town on the bus and saw the early movie, taking advantage of their brand-new privilege of staying out until ten o'clock. There was a guard between them, because for three years Avery had belonged to the group that owned the school, but they liked one another, and after a while the guard came down.

The school permitted Avery to relinquish his status without much protest. The headmaster tried to persuade him to patch things up with Bell, but Avery told him there was nothing to patch up.

"I haven't got anything against Bell, sir," he said. "I just want to live by myself, that's all."

"I don't like it, Hollister," Mr. Collamore said. "I don't like to have boys living by themselves. Makes them moody." He looked up. He was a ruddy ex-athlete, dressed in expensive oatmeal tweed. "Sure you won't change your mind, and go on with Bell?"

"I'd rather not, sir," Avery said.

"Very well, Hollister," the headmaster sighed. "You may do as you wish."

"Thank you, sir," said Avery.

He turned and went out of Collamore's office and on the way out of Charter Hall ran into Roger Bell. Since school started, he had avoided Bell, and brushed past him now, but Bell called after him.

"Einstein, for Christ's sake! Wait a minute."

Avery turned. Einstein was the name Roger had given him in Third Form year, when he had gotten 100 in algebra. He hated it, but had suffered in silence, to avoid being baited. Now he said, "My name is Hollister, Bell. Just call me that, will you?"

"Okay, okay," Roger said. "But what's the matter with you? How come you didn't let me know you were going to turn hermit? I could have written to some of the fellows."

"I'm sorry about that," Avery said. "But I didn't know what I was going to do, last summer."

He didn't want a fight with Bell. He merely wanted Bell to leave him alone. He turned and started to walk away, but Bell caught his arm and said, "Wait a minute, Hollie. Don't be in such a rush."

Avery stopped. Bell looked at him for a moment, then said confidentially, "Look, Ave, this is none of my business. But you're one of the best men in the school. Your family has good standing here, and you've done all right on the football team. Then of course, you get good marks too."

Avery waited.

"I mean, I don't give a damn if you don't want to room with me. But why waste your time with that bog-trotter McCoy?"

Avery laughed. "For God's sake, Bell," he said, "I'll bet you'd call Yeats a mick, if you met him."

"Who?" asked Roger, thinking Avery must have referred to someone in the form below.

"William Butler Yeats," said Avery, a little smugly, because he knew how to pronounce the poet's name. "A writer."

"Oh," said Roger. "Well, I don't know about that. It's just that I wondered why you'd want to get mixed up with a guy who really doesn't belong here at all. It seems to me you'd be better off with your own crowd."

"I think you hit it on the nose, Roger, when you said it was none of your business," Avery said.

"Okay," said Roger, with the virtuous air of a man who has tried to do his duty and failed. "Go ahead. Read Yeats or whatever his name is with your Papish friend. But you'll be sorry for it all your life."

"Well, Roger dodger old boy, it's my God damn life," said Avery. "You let me run it, will you?"

"Okay," said Roger. "Suits."

He went into Charter Hall and Avery walked away.

"Yeets," he said. "The dumb slob. Yeets."

After that, Roger and Roger's crowd made it a point to treat Avery with formal politeness, addressing him always by his last name and nodding woodenly to him when they passed him on the Green. Avery persuaded himself that he didn't give a damn. He dug into his schoolwork, and talked books with McCoy. He passed a good deal of his time in McCoy's little room, where McCoy had illegal caches of food and a portable phonograph. The friendship developed rapidly, but it was always under control; they were rather like cellmates, arbitrarily placed in mutual isolation.

Avery found himself agreeing that Colborn was really a second-rate school and that there was no real challenge in the work they did for their courses.

"God, I hope I get a chance to learn something when I get to college," McCoy said, one day. "There are so damn many things I want to know."

"Where are you going?" Avery asked.

"I don't know," McCoy said. "My father wants me to go to Princeton. He's got an idea that things are easier, if you go to the right places. He never went to school at all, except for a few years in Ireland. He's a funny guy. In most things, he's practical, but he has some screwy ideas about education. Do you know what he said, when he found he could get me into this place? He said, 'Get your passport stamped, Dinny. Get it on the record.' "

"Did you want to come here?" Avery asked.

"Did you?"

Avery flushed. "Well, I didn't have much choice," he said. "All my people went here. My father. My brother. My grandfather."

Until this year, it had never occurred to him to wonder whether he had wanted to come to Colborn, any more than to wonder whether he had wanted to be born in Hull. It had been taken for granted that he would come here. His name had been entered on the Colborn lists the week after he was born. Meat and potatoes, soap and water, bread and butter, Colborn and Yale—it hadn't ever entered his mind, until this minute, that there were really any other places he could go to school.

"I know," Dennis said. "With you, it's different. You come from one of the better Colborn families." He looked out the window, then turned back. "No," he said, "I didn't want to come here. I'd rather have gone to a parochial school in the toughest part of New York. I came here to please my old man. But I stayed to please myself. I was damned if I'd let a guy like Bell, for instance, drive me out of any place."

Avery found himself making excuses for the others.

"They don't mean to be bastards," he said. "It's just that they follow one another, that's all."

"Yeah," McCoy said moodily, "that's all. Of course, that's all the Nazis do, too. They just follow one another. All good buddy buddies." He paused for a moment and his face went hard. Then he said, "I don't give a damn. I'm used to it. I don't give a damn whether they like me or not."

This was not quite true.

McCoy pretended to be indifferent to his exclusion, but sometimes the hurt showed.

One day he and Avery were in McCoy's little room, and a dozen boys on the Green were singing:

> To the tables down at Morey's
>   To the place where Looie dwells,
> To the dear old Temple Bar
>   We loved so well....

McCoy gazed down at them, listening to the sentimental song, his face trying to express contempt, but failing and revealing pain instead.

"Jesus!" he said. "Sometimes I hate every single bastard on the face of the earth. Including myself, just for being born."

There were tears in his eyes and he turned away, closing the window, but the voices could still be heard, dully:

Gentlemen rankers, out on a spree....

"Hell, Dennis, they were only singing," Avery said. "Just some snotty guys singing, making believe they're in New Haven already."

McCoy turned on him.

"Get out of here, will you? Get the hell out of this room. This isn't your room. This is my room."

Avery went out. He stood in the hall for a moment, outside McCoy's door, and heard Dennis throw himself on the bed, then heard the sound of his voice: *Ave Maria, gratia plena, Dominus Tecum.... Sancta Maria, Mater Dei, ora pro nobis peccatoribus....*

The alien prayers frightened him and awed his Protestant soul. He tiptoed away and went slowly down the stairs. He did not understand McCoy's religion or McCoy's attitude toward it. Sometimes Dennis sneered at the Church and at the moon-faced priest in town to whom he regularly made his confession. And sometimes he seemed almost desperate in his need to believe, to believe with absolute faith.

It was not a subject you could discuss.

It was the thing about Dennis that made him really strange to Avery—strange, and frightening, and appealing. Dennis, Irish, Catholic, and metropolitan, was the symbol of everything opposed to what Avery's father believed in; Dennis was part of the other world, from which Hull defended itself.

CHAPTER TWENTY

EVERY third week end, he went home to see his mother. She had improved, as the doctor had promised. She no longer wanted sedatives during the day, and took most of her meals downstairs. When she talked about things that had happened before Morgan was killed, she often seemed perfectly all right, and her memory was not especially unclear. She sometimes confused the Wehrmacht with the Kaiser's army, but so, he reminded himself, had distinguished British generals and certain members of the American State Department.

Even now, he couldn't blame her. He couldn't feel that she was anything but a victim. He loved her, and he wanted her back.

Her appearance was disturbing. She looked younger than before Morgan's death, but in an antique way. The clothes were the same and the face somewhat the same, but there had been subtle changes in the carriage of the head, certain modifications of characteristic gestures that suggested her lack of contact with the present, her almost contrived withdrawal into the past.

David had carried her into the past, back to Paris when she had been young, and now she went back behind that time. She was obsessed with the early struggles of the modern French painters, with their integrity and devotion to purpose, and talked endlessly of Cézanne and Manet, Pissarro, Degas and the others, everything she had read about them coming back in a flood, so that she sometimes seemed to move in that world, of Paris, and Provence, and Fontainebleau, in the earlier century.

One evening in mid-November, when Avery was home for the week end, they sat before the fire in the living room and she rambled on about old Cézanne, painting in the rain, so intent on his motif he did not realize he was soaked to the skin, and how this had given him the chill that killed him.

"Think of it, Avery," she said. "The belief that old man must have had in his talent, the belief in art, the sureness of himself. Doesn't it inspire you?"

"Of course, mother," he said absently.

At that time he had no love for painting, and Cézanne's struggle as an artist meant nothing to him. But the old Provençal's fight with his father spoke directly to him; he listened, fascinated, as his mother told how Cézanne had been so afraid of his father that he had not married until long after his first son had been born.

"Do you know what he was always afraid of, Avery? He was afraid they would get their hooks into him, their *grappin*. After a while he got so he couldn't bear to have anyone touch him. He was suspicious of everyone. He had almost no one he could trust, and he thought his best friend had betrayed him."

This made a kind of sense to Avery that the colored reproductions of apples and pines and rocks did not. After his mother had gone to bed, he took down her *Life of Cézanne* and read it, sitting before the fire, appalled by the dreadful, unstated power the painter's father had enjoyed. The tough old phrase, "I won't let them get their hooks into me," remained in his mind and became one of his own bulwarks, part of his ammunition. He liked the sound of it, and sometimes, in the night, repeated it to himself: *On ne me mettrait pas le grappin dessus.* In the foreign language, he made the words sound like a positive declaration of faith.

CHAPTER TWENTY-ONE

A T CHRISTMAS time his father was home for three days' leave. Avery had talked with him twice on the telephone and had one letter from him, but had not seen him face to face since the black afternoon in the study. He was ready for a row, but there was no row. There was tension, but the presence of his mother made them keep it out of sight. They were both gentlemen, after all, and aware that gentlemen concealed what they felt in the interest of courtesy to ladies. Besides, his father was in uniform, with medal ribbons and gold chevrons sewn to his blouse and stars on his shoulders; a family row would not have suited the dignity of his rank.

His father was prepared, apparently, to accept part of his rebellion. At dinner on Christmas night there were mashed turnips in a silver dish, as on Christmas there had always been, and that he always had eaten and loathed. This year he said politely, "I don't care for any turnips, thank you, sir."

His father glanced at him and hesitated, the heavy Georgian spoon in his hand. "Very well, Avery," he said. He paused, the spoon held like a silver baton, then served himself an exceptionally large portion of turnips.

Avery watched him, impressed by his brass and the color on his chest, trying to figure out for himself what went on in his father's head. He couldn't do it, for he was fifteen, and his father was more than thirty years older.

His father was uncomfortable at home. The pressure of his duty was great, for one thing, and he should not have taken leave. For another, he had no equipment with which to deal with his wife's illness. For years he had accepted her presence and respected her privacy, without much thinking about his need for her as a silent source of approval, or of the importance that approval had assumed in his day to day living. He missed something. He was like a man who had lost his wrist watch, and carries, because he must know the time, his father's old gold pocket watch, always looking first at his wrist, then remembering with a flash of irritation and dredging the old watch from the awkward and unfamiliar pocket. He could not get used to the change in his wife. He had, for example, been used to calling her on the telephone and immediately establishing his identity, his authority and his security, the sound of her answering voice being a symbol of everything he was anchored to—house, farm, town, fortune, pride, past, present, future. This is not to say she had been much in the forefront of his mind; he was not a romantic man or a reflective one, but a man of precedent, good manners and habit. He had once loved his wife's body—the way she laughed and moved across the room. He had been enchanted by her quality of unreality, an exaggeration of which now was the expression of her illness. She had once inspired him to considerable physical abandon, and on occasion to certain heights of romantic utterance. All that was gone, of course, and it seemed appropriate to him that it should be; he had contrived the usual apologies for his own remaining predatory vigor. What had been left between them, before Morgan's death, had been habit, familiar and unquestioned as the evening brandy or morning coffee—habit, and the keen, nearly thematic respect with which such men regard their wives.

Now the habit had been spoilt, the pattern destroyed. When he called her on the telephone from Washington, she seemed uncertain of where he was, or what was the year, or the time of year.

He understood that there was nothing to do but wait.

Parks, the Hartford people, the man in Washington who had refused to send a bill, they all said, "Give her time." He could do nothing but accept their judgment. After all, they were doctors. It was their business to know about such things as shock on entering the menopause.

Time, Time, Time.

He was besieged by time. He was at the age when a man is most of all conscious of time, of ages recorded in obituary notices, of achievement by juniors, of his own station in the ranks of his contemporaries—so that reading of the death of a man only a few years older than himself can depress him for days, as can the knowledge that the new senator from that western state is five years younger than he. He was at the time of life when men tot up the years that are left, and wonder where time has gone, try to remember their fathers, at this precise period in life, getting out old photographs and doing sums on the backs of old envelopes. An aged general snarling defiance from some island in the Pacific, or a prime minister who might have been his chronological father, gives a thrill of hope to such a man, while the accomplishments of a thirty-year-old aviation general make him feel the age in his bones, the time grip on his heart. During this time of life, a man's days fall away like the dead leaves in autumn, and he questions the validity of the short run ahead. Of course, this preoccupation passes—again TIME—and may, like toothache or gonorrhea, amuse the unafflicted, but it is a true agony while it persists.

It was not the moment for him to deal with the problems that beset him.

But he had been briefed.

He knew his duty.

When she took her eyes from the turkey on her plate and looked wistfully at the red candles, saying, "Isn't it a pity Morgan can't be home for Christmas? This war. This terrible war," he did not show bad temper. He nodded politely and agreed that it was indeed a pity.

When the meal was finished and he read the obligatory Dickens to her and to Avery and the standing servants, her mind seemed to have cleared, the way a pool that has been muddied clears. When they sang the usual Christmas songs, around the piano, she played nicely, and her tears were those of respectable feminine sentimentality, not of madness.

"Merry Christmas, Avery!" she called, blowing him a kiss from her seat at the piano.

He smiled and said, "Merry Christmas, mother."

Her smile was the old familiar one that he knew, and brought back the past, so that tears rose in his eyes. His father saw this, and put a hand on his shoulder.

"Makes you sentimental, doesn't it, son? The singing and the tree and the lights on the snow."

Avery nodded, a lump in his throat, unable to control the emotion conditioned by fifteen years of association. "Yes," he agreed. "I guess it does."

He turned away. His father's face fell, and the pressure of the hand on Avery's shoulder increased for a moment, then the hand was removed and they drew apart. Avery stared at the heavy log burning in the fireplace. He wants me as a stand-in for Morgan, he thought. He thinks he can push me around, and then because he misses Morgan, act as if nothing had happened. But he was not going to be used. He took the chair near the fire, that he had once been asked to relinquish in honor of Morgan's departure for the war, and listened to his father talking to Annie, who stood with her hands folded, about the war, and the President, and the Chief-of-Staff. He hated the war, and hated his father's uniform and medals, though he envied them too.

The next day, before he departed, his father talked with him in his study. He had apparently decided to ignore what had happened during the summer, to behave as if it had never happened, and Avery understood that this was intended to be a kind of pardon by his father. He said nothing to his father about the fact that he had given up football, and nothing about having broken up with Roger Bell.

"Getting on all right?" his father asked. "Everything going well?"

"Certainly."

There was a pause.

"Well then," his father said, "I guess there's not much to say."

"No, sir."

He needed his father and he wanted him, and both of them knew that this was the time to make some sign that would put things right. But they came of undemonstrative stock; they had no language of conciliation. They dealt with each other in terms of symbols, and now that the symbols were spoilt, there was no communication at all.

His father got up, ready to go. Avery did not volunteer to drive to the airport with him, so he went alone, driven by a boy from the farm, hesitating for a moment on the driveway, then getting into the car beside the boy, who was already at the wheel. Avery smiled. He knew that his father detested riding in a car driven by anyone but himself, but that the dignity of his rank confused him. He watched the car turn out of the driveway, then went back into the house. He felt let down and rather sorry his father hadn't picked up the fight where it had stopped when he ran from the study, across the fields and into New York.

CHAPTER TWENTY-TWO

O NCE during the late spring he went to look at Morgan's grave. Seed grass covered the wounded earth, delicate light green blades like hairs on the raw soil. He read the carving on the granite stone that had been set in place after the funeral and that he had never seen.

> Aviation Cadet
> John Morgan van Ameringe Hollister
> United States Army Air Forces
> —On Active Service—
> 1922—1943

> *Ὦ ξεῖν, ἀγγέλλειν Λακεδαιμονίοις ὅτι τῇδε*
> *κείμεθα τοῖς κείνων ῥήμασι πειθόμενοι.*

The lines of Greek, he guessed, had been a suggestion of the minister, who had been led back to his Amherst Greek by the fact that his church was a kind of clapboard Parthenon. He read what was carved on the stone and stared at the foetal grass on the grave, trying to feel what everything he had read and been told informed him he should feel. He felt nothing but vague embarrassment at the sight of his brother's name in the granite. The stone did not suit the mood in which Morgan had actually gone to war, and that Avery had understood on that winter's night when they had met in the snow. He could not read the Greek phrases and was moved by a desire to know what they meant. He copied them onto the back of an envelope, then stood with paper and pencil in his hand, staring moodily at the grave.

He could not persuade himself that Morgan's body actually was here, rotting in the ground beneath his feet. He was unable to find grief in the sight of the grave or satisfaction either—but only lack of meaning.

When he got back to school he asked the classics master to translate the Greek lines for him. The man studied the paper for a few seconds, troubled by Avery's poor transcription. Then his face brightened and he read off the glorious syllables. He paused, then looked up and said in English: "Tell Sparta, Passerby, That here obedient to her commands we lie."

The turning of the centuries was too much, even for Avery's new cynicism. Tears came to his eyes and he dabbed at them with his handkerchief.

The master handed him the envelope. "We gave Greek here, you know, until just a few years ago," he said. He hesitated, then said, "Sometimes I think we'd be better off with less science and more Greek. Do you know what Dr. Johnson said, Hollister? He said Greek was like lace. A man got as much of it as he could."

Avery rose. He understood that the master was pleased to have been asked. "Thank you, sir," he said. "I just saw this somewhere, and wondered what it meant."

"Not at all," the master said. "Thank you."

Avery hesitated, then said, "Would you write it out for me, sir? The English, I mean?"

"Of course."

The master took a stiff sheet of paper with the school arms embossed on it, the kind used for writing to parents, and inscribed the Greek with a thin sharp pen, then wrote the English words beneath it. "There you are, Hollister," he said. "Tell Sparta ... " he paused, looking up. "Do you know where it's from?"

"No, sir."

"It's by Simonides. It's on the monument to the Spartan dead, at Thermopylae."

"I see, sir."

Outside, under the trees, Avery read what the master had written, then folded the paper, and slipped it into his wallet. He kept it there as a kind of totem; even after he had learned Greek for himself and memorized the phrase in a better translation, he did not throw the bit of paper away. The words were not associated with his brother. They were an expression of the sense of the past, a sudden, and nearly dramatic reassurance of the fact that men had lived through time before him, that he did not get from his history courses. It was emphatic. Sometimes in a great gallery, wandering amid the transported past, a marble face seems suddenly illumined with present life, and the gentle stone smile is as real as the smile of the lover just left, or at one's side, and warmth generated twenty centuries ago, in Athens, descends from the marble and touches the beholder. Simonides' salute to the Spartan dead touched Avery in this way, with the touch of art.

Not much later, he was touched by a relative of art.

One afternoon in May, Ledyard, who taught him mathematics, took him aside and asked, "What are your plans, Hollister? What are you going to do with yourself, in college, and afterward?"

Ledyard had been his best teacher; he had given meaning to algebra the others hadn't managed to give to language or history or literature.

"I don't know, sir," he said. "Science of some kind. I don't know what." He had thought of engineering, and sometimes of architecture, but he hadn't made a decision. Until this year his father had made all the decisions for him.

"You have a good head, Avery," Ledyard said. "A good clear brain and a nice sense of mathematics. You may have a talent for it." He took a book from the shelves behind him and handed it across the desk. "Why don't you look this over, when you have an hour or two to kill? I think it will interest you."

"Thank you," Avery said. He looked at the title: *Elements of Analysis.*

"Keep it," Ledyard said. "Don't bother to return it."

That night he went through the book Ledyard had given him. It was a dense tough book, but a revolution was embalmed in it. As Avery leafed through the pages he got a sense of this. His eye was struck by a paragraph heading: PATH OF A MOVING POINT. The phrase sent a thrill through him, and he read the paragraph below, his attention held by the concluding lines:

Unfortunately, in practice, the equation is very seldom given in advance; it is usually necessary, as a first step, to derive the equation from a geometric definition of some kind. This problem will occupy the present chapter.

He read the paragraph again. Being unacquainted with the danger that inhabits this tendency, he found it filled with transcendent meaning. He got up from his bed and copied the words from the page. There it was, he decided. In Chapter Two, before the summer and David's visit, the equation had always been given in advance. But now he was in Chapter Three, where it was seldom given, but usually had to be derived. He put the paper on which he had copied the words into his wallet, with the scrap of Greek from his brother's grave. Then he went back to the book, excited with his flight of philosophy as some great Teutonic brain on the verge of discovering the secret of light. He read on through the chapter headings, and the general argument of the book seemed to confirm the personal inference he had drawn from the section on the Path of a Moving Point. Such ideas can be almost voluptuous; after he switched off his light, he lay in bed for a long time, vividly awake, spinning out the application to himself and his own life he thought he had found in a branch of mathematics about which, actually, he knew little more than the name of its inventor. A boy doesn't lead his class for a number of years with his humility intact; Avery was pleased with himself. He was a point, moving on a path, that he intended to derive from an equation somewhere en route to be found. His mind bubbled with excitement, and he felt enormous, gathering power within himself.

At last he slept, and dreamed of his father in the dark midst of battle.

It was a kind of premonition. The next day Annie called him and told him his father was overseas.

"He might have let us know," said Avery. "He might have called us, or something."

"Avery, laddie, he couldn't do that," she said reasonably. 'He'd've been breaking security."

Annie had been through the other war, and knew all about such things as security. She was right and Avery knew it. Nevertheless, he couldn't help feeling that his father could have let them know if he'd wanted to. A few days later he had a letter from an APO address and learned that his father was in England. The cabalistic SHAEF meant nothing to him, or anyone else beyond the secret perimeter of high-level war, but he understood that his father was not going into actual battle, but was only going to fight from a desk.

The New York newspapers mentioned his father's name, and *Life* Magazine had a photograph. One day Mr. Collamore stopped him on the Green and said, "Well, Hollister, how does it feel to have a father who is actually making history, instead of just teaching or studying it?"

Avery did not answer the headmaster's smile. "I don't know about that, sir," he said. "I am not in the general's confidence."

The statement, with its undertone of private meaning, seemed clever to Avery, and he did not regret the hurt expression that appeared on Collamore's face.

"Oh, well, naturally not, in military affairs," the headmaster said. "Naturally not." He smiled apologetically and passed on. Avery went on to his room and sat down to his work. He was preparing for final exams, working harder than he ever had before. He had been impresed by Ledyard's suggestion that he might have a talent for mathematics. He had won school prizes and been praised as a bright boy, but no one had ever told him before that he might have a talent for something. A talent was something different. And this talent was one that his father never had; his father couldn't add in his head and had always regarded arithmetic with a kind of good-natured, athlete's bafflement. He smiled, a little grimly. The fact that his father hated mathematics made the subject more attractive to him, and more challenging.

At the end of the term, he led the school with 980 points out of a possible 1000.

"You have a right to be proud of yourself, Hollister," the headmaster told him, having called him into his office for the purpose. "It's a fine record. Your parents will be pleased."

"Yes, sir," Avery said, utilizing his discovery that an adult can contend with defiance, depression, ebullience or rebellion, but not with indifference. "I'm sure they will."

"Aren't *you* pleased?" Mr. Collamore asked. "You must have worked darned hard."

"Well, yes, sir, I suppose I am," Avery said placidly.

Mr. Collamore inspected Avery and did not understand what he saw. He associated high marks with boys who masturbated and had bad skins. He was always faintly suspicious of a boy who made more than 900 points out of the year-end 1000. Perhaps because he had himself made a four-year score of 901, he regarded this as the highest really respectable average. Anything higher meant you were dealing with a boy who might give trouble, if not here then later on, at New Haven or Cambridge or Williamstown or Hanover, usually with a boy who was not the Colborn type at all, and who should have been sent to one of those new-style schools in Vermont, where everyone lived in a remodeled barn and classes were held in the cow pasture. He could recognize such boys, and knew how to deal with them, but this lad Hollister didn't fit the pattern. For one thing, he was properly clothed in unpressed flannels and a jacket from the right shop. His shoes were white and quite dirty. His sandy hair was recently cut. He could easily have been picked out by *Life* Magazine for the cover story they had prepared but never used—"Typical Colborn Sixth Former is Avery Hollister of Hull, son and grandson of old boys, etc., etc., etc."

Hollister's father was a trustee and the school had sent his brother to Yale.

But there was something wrong.

Something very wrong.

Mr. Collamore took up a printed form from his desk and glanced at it. "I thought you were going to New Haven, Hollister," he said. "What made you change your plans?"

"I don't know exactly sir," Avery said a little tensely, afraid Collamore might interfere, maybe even write his father. "For one thing, I thought I'd like to go to college in a bigger city."

"Why not Harvard then? Or Princeton? It's close to New York. Why Columbia? I don't think we've ever sent a boy to Columbia. In fact, I'm sure we haven't."

"You'll be sending two this year, sir," Avery said. "McCoy's going to Columbia."

"Ah, yes," Mr. Collamore sighed. "McCoy. I see." He looked up. "Have you discussed this with your father, Avery?" he asked, altering his tone. "I see that your mother has signed the application."

"My father's overseas, you know," Avery said. "I don't think it would be right to bother him at the moment."

Mr. Collamore looked at him, wondering for a few seconds, perhaps, how far he was morally entitled to go, in the absence of the boy's father. He decided not to interfere.

"Very well, Hollister," he said pleasantly. "After all, I suppose in the end it's your own affair." He paused. "Is your mother coming over for graduation?"

Avery shook his head. "No, sir. She's been ill, and hasn't been going out very much."

Mr. Collamore nodded sympathetically, then stood up and shook Avery's hand. He must have been troubled by the fact that somehow Colborn had failed to turn Avery into the kind of boy the school was in business to produce. Avery understood this, and could not help being amused by the headmaster's bewilderment.

The next day he graduated while Annie McBain looked on, and in addition to his diploma, which was made of genuine parchment, he was given the bronze medallion that was the Headmaster's Prize.

CHAPTER TWENTY-THREE

H E FACED the idle months ahead of him with impatience, and wished he were sixteen and old enough to enter college in July, the way Dennis McCoy was doing, instead of waiting until fall.

There was nothing to do.

He had wanted to ask Dennis to come and stay for a week or two, but he hadn't because he didn't want Dennis to see his mother when she wasn't well.

One afternoon he went to the Twin Oaks Pavilion, outside of Hull, where teen-age town kids danced to the music of a juke box. The vacant-faced girls and self-confident boys reminded him of the crowd at Roger Bell's place. The idiot music bounced back from the low raftered ceiling. There was the smell of pop and cosmetics. He turned away, depressed and a little hurt because no one had nodded to him, or spoken. They were town kids; he knew them all by sight and name, and yet knew none of them. He had been separated from them always, by schools and custom and his father's prestige.

At the end of his first week at home, he took out the book Ledyard had given him, intending to see how far he could get with the subject, on his own. He began to read through the sections, casually at first, merely as diversion, then with rising excitement, until suddenly he broke through the plodding words of the text to the subject itself, and understood that he had found his metier—his problem and his world.

It was the Damascene vision.

As the architecture of Descartes' thought took shape in his mind, he felt a surge of excitement pass through his blood, the emotion of discovery. He rose from his desk and went to the window, feeling giddy and filled with a sense of triumph.

Here was the pure world he sought, not fixed to the ground like a rock, but moving, placed exultantly in space. Here were eternal truths, independent of a world in which men and women had bodies that were soiled at birth—truths that had been true before the first man drew breath, and that would remain true, off in space, when the last man had expired and the planet was cold. He looked out into the twilit air, toward the thin line of haze on the horizon. He could almost see, in the New England heavens, the perfect point without mass, that moved in accordance with beautiful law—law that he could learn and that would be his passport to a world in which there could be no disappointment, no betrayal, because the essence of that world was perfection itself. He went back to his desk and ran quickly through the book, the bold-face phrases that marked the numbered sections impinging on his mind with lyric clarity, tumbling through his imagination like stars tumbling through a forming universe. He gripped the arms of his chair, to assure himself that he was real. In all his life, nothing had ever seemed to address him as directly as the words, the ideas, in this book, with their intimations of immortality and of infinite authority. He experienced a moment of burning happiness, then switched on his gooseneck lamp, drew the block of graph paper toward him, and bent his head over the book. All that he wanted now was time—time, and to be left alone by a world he thought was unfit to live in.

So Avery, that gifted June, listened to the music of the spheres almost at the instant that in Normandy tough-fisted parachute infantry of the Eighty-second Airborne Division were being dropped into circles marked on maps, far from the coast, on the

Cherbourg Peninsula. There was blood on the water, as Annie had predicted; blood and pain too. The world held its breath, until it seemed that the earth itself had interrupted its axial turn until the boats were on the beaches and the troops had dug like land crabs into the pock-marked littoral of France.

Annie and his mother went to church, to pray with a hundred million other women. He listened to the radio, choked with fear for his father, though he tried to tell himself that his father was not in the battle or near it, but safe at a desk in Grosvenor Square. He listened to the bulletins that seemed merely to duplicate one another and tried to picture the assault waves clawing into the Norman beaches and to picture the dead men floating on the water. It was appalling, and the imagination left him drained and stunned.

When his mother came back from church it was late afternoon and the sun slanting through the French doors made shadows on the floor like prison bars. She had taken to carrying a parasol when she went out at midday and she turned in the sun, looking at the shadow her body and the parasol made. "Just like the *Grande Jatte*," she said. "Isn't it pretty, Avery? Isn't it lovely?"

He looked at the shadow and nodded. "Yes, mother. Very pretty."

He had formed the habit of offering tentative answers, until he determined the part of the past she was living in; it disturbed and confused her if he made a mistake, the way a child is disturbed when an adult ignores his invented world, or declines to converse with his imaginary friend. He wanted to be kind; or at least wanted not to be cruel, and this meant playing perpetual charades with his mother. What she felt, inside, he had given up trying to imagine. He did not know whether her fantasies were like scenes in a play, with tragic, lucid entre-actes, or dissolved one into the other, like scenes on film. She turned to him now, pointing with her parasol. "Avery, there's been an invasion," she said.

"Yes, mother."

"It's all my fault, you know," she said. "Cézanne's mother hid him in the attic when the soldiers came to take him away. That's what I should have done with Morgan and your father. I should have hidden them in the attic."

He nodded. "Yes, mother. Perhaps that would have been best."

She looked at him wonderingly, as though she did not understand what had been said, then turned and went out of the room, twirling her parasol like a cane. In the next room, Annie met her and said, "Come along up for your nap now, Miss. It's time for your rest."

Annie treated her like a child queen, going on walks and gardening with her, dealing out the sedative pills when she could not sleep at night, keeping the record of her behavior the doctor had asked her to keep.

Once a week, Dr. Parks came in person; two or three times a week he telephoned. One day Avery cornered him.

"How is my mother, Dr. Parks," he asked.

"Oh, holding her own," said the doctor. "Holding her own." He stared down at his black bag that was scuffed and battered like an old woman's shoe. He had always been the Hollisters' doctor; he had delivered Avery and Morgan. "She's holding her own, Avery," he repeated wearily.

"Against time, doctor?" Avery asked. "You said time was the answer, remember? You said she only needed time."

"Of course," said the doctor. "That's all she needs."

"She'll never get over it, will she doctor? She'll get worse, won't she?" he said.

"Of course she'll get better, Avery," said the doctor. "I think she shows a very definite improvement."

Avery thought Parks was a fool.

"Do you think we should get another doctor?" he asked Annie, after Parks had gone.

She shook her head. "I wouldn't. These things—I don't think the best of them knows much. This one probably knows as much as the next. They all read the same books you know, lad. They follow one another like sheep." She paused. "You know what the truth of the matter is," she said. "Your mother doesn't really want to get well, quite yet. So what good would it do to have a lot of strangers overrunning the place, tapping the poor thing with their rubber hammers and flashing their lights in her poor eyes, the way the ones from Hartford did? She's just hiding out, you might say. When she decides it's safe to come out, she'll come out, and there's no doctor going to persuade her, so there's no use having her troubled at all."

He agreed. He saw no hope for his mother, and certainly did not want to assume responsibility for relieving Parks and calling in another corporal's guard of specialists from Hartford or New York. He thought there was a good deal in what Annie said about his mother's merely hiding away, and sometimes he couldn't help feeling that this indicated a flaw in her character, a lack of will, though when he reasoned with himself he knew he was not being fair.

CHAPTER TWENTY-FOUR

IN AUGUST he had a letter from his father, in answer to one he had written nearly two months earlier. *"I don't believe you will be happy in New York,"* his father wrote. *"The people are not our kind, and you will be an outsider there. However, you are at liberty to discover this for yourself. I've written Hawkenson at the bank, and he will take care of your funds for the fall, on the same scale we had set for New Haven. Please look after your mother and let me know if there is any change. I hear from Parks regularly, and he is encouraging."*

He wasn't sure whether he was relieved or disappointed. He had expected opposition, perhaps a threat, perhaps an operative disinheritance. He had not expected indifference. He had, of course, no way of knowing that his father had written first a reprimand, then a plea, and finally this letter of consent, or that his father had been without sleep for three days, under fire and in ardent danger. For his father was in France, with a division, instead of at a desk in Grosvenor Square, but he didn't learn this until later.

He put the letter away and went into the bathroom to shave. There had been no one to teach him how to go about it, and he had taught himself, using one of his grandfather's straight razors, that were kept in his father's bathroom. There were seven of them, one for each day of the week, so the steel could have a rest, as his father had explained. They were kept in a padded box with his grandfather's name on the lid, and each razor had the name of its day set into the handle in silver.

He cut himself and when he came downstairs with a band-aid on his cheek his mother cried, "What have you done to your face!" When he explained that he had cut himself with a razor, she began to cry softly, then looked at him accusingly and said, "But Avery, sweetie, you don't shave."

"No, mother," he agreed. "Not very well, at any rate." His face was sore and the lotion he had found in his father's bathroom made his cheeks smart. The familiar odor, near his nose, made him uncomfortable, sharpening the sense of his father he had got from the letter he had just read. He was troubled and uneasy, filled with a sharp sense of the past, of guilt and of betrayal and of something lost that he could not isolate, but associated with time that was gone. It was his childhood that was lost, the part of him that had hoped his father would forbid him to go his own way. But he didn't recognize what was missing, that made his heart ache.

After dinner he and his mother walked across the lawn to her neglected garden. She did not seem mad or melancholic, but only detached, and her face in the flattering evening light, was young looking and lovely, but empty of meaning, almost vapid. He stared at her, something in the light reminding him of the summer before, and of David, and the moment in the hall when he had listened to her and David making love in the bedroom where he had played as a child. He tried to bring the known truth into focus with reality, to feel contempt or loathing, or hatred or forgiveness. He couldn't. She was not guilty by reason of incompetence. You could not indict her or make her stand trial. He was unable to feel anything but pity and a sense of loss, of waste. Yet a phrase his father had once used flashed through his mind, carried in the tones of his father's actual voice. "Ignorance of the law is no excuse, son," his father had said.

But it was.

He touched his mother's shoulder, then was swept by nostalgia and shuddered. "Avery, you're cold," she said. "But it's so warm."

"I'm not cold, mother," he said. "Someone walked over my grave, that's all."

"Don't say that!" she cried. "You mustn't say that." She gripped his arm. "You have a good long life, Avery," she said. "A good long life. It doesn't matter what your father says, or that Morgan's dead because he tried to please him. You mustn't mind him. He belongs to the past. You must follow your own star, and not mind the others." She touched his cheek. "They don't know what you and I know, son, do they? How can they know? We are different, you and I."

He felt the tears blurring his eyes. This was his own mother speaking, as if she had emerged from the tomb to help him. He took her in his arms and kissed her, holding her close, feeling rich love for her that wasn't qualified by anything. When he let her go she smiled and said, "It's so lonely for you, Avery. I'm ill so much of the time, and your father's gone, and Morgan. You shouldn't be here alone like this, with just me and the servants. It's not healthy."

"It's all right, mother," he said.

They walked down to the garden, that hadn't been properly tended for weeks because they were short handed at the farm, and that she had ignored until now. She looked at the weeds and the shabby edges. "My garden," she said. "My pretty flowers. They've let them choke."

She sank to her knees, ignoring her dress and her unprotected hands, pulling at the weeds until her fingers bled. The sun dropped and they could hardly see. Avery knelt beside her, taking the weeds from her as she tore at them with fury, with bitter, personal hatred. "So much neglect," she said. "So much neglect." She was like a person who has just emerged from anesthesia, some fixed idea leaping into his consciousness. He watched her, in the evening gloom, wondering if time was actually working and the illness had begun to pass.

It was too much for her. In the morning Annie shook her head and said, "Poor thing, she had an awful night, Avery. A terrible night. And the pills that man keeps leaving seem to do no good any more. No good at all."

There was nothing in time; he should have known it. He felt a wave of sick disappointment pass over him. "What will you do this fall, when I'm gone?" he asked.

"We'll manage," Annie said. "Don't you worry yourself. We'll get on, your mother and I." They were in the kitchen, where he had his breakfast. She turned away from the stove and caught his hand. "Avery, laddie," she said, her voice intense with feeling, her Highland accent stronger than usual, "I've known you since the moment you were born. If you were my own boy, my own blood, I couldn't love you more. Don't destroy yourself fighting God's will. You have a life to live, and to live at all these days, you must toughen your heart. Your mother will be all right with me. I love her. You must go off to the university, as you've planned. You've missed the war, praise God, and you've got to live."

He turned away. He almost wished his mother had not come out of her grave last night, but had remained buried and harmless. When she was in her other world, there was nothing he could do. If she was going to be well again, to come back to real life, she would need him, she would need him as much as she needed air, because he was all that was left.

Annie was right. He was young, and he had to live. He had a whole life to live. But his mother's face kept emerging blurrily from the blue-squared paper on his work table, and he couldn't concentrate. It wasn't exactly true that Morgan was dead because he had tried to please his father, and yet it was true in a way, as what he had said to his father about David had been true in a way but not exactly true. He forced his mind back to his work, back to pursuit of the perfect world, in which the essence and appearance of things would be identical.

CHAPTER TWENTY-FIVE

TOWARD the end of August he found himself tired and quite stale. He had finished the book Ledyard had given him, and read most of a calf-bound copy of Newton he'd found on the library shelves downstairs. He broke off work and began to loaf, reading until noon, and going for long aimless walks across the farm, coming back to the house for his swim before it was time to get ready for dinner.

One afternoon he went east and climbed a low hill just beyond the border of his father's property, from which he had a view of the valley, with bright glimpes of the river. It was hot, but there was a sense of summer's end in the air. When he stopped and threw himself on the ground, he felt a slow, brooding summer breeze that chilled the sweat on his body. He was stripped to the waist, wearing shorts. He lay on the ground, panting from his climb, and allowed the breeze to cool him, then sat up and took his book from his pocket. It was a thin English copy of *Marius,* and as he read, the portentous syllables seemed to be absorbed by his blood. He gazed off over the valley, trying, as Pater suggested, to isolate the precise instant, to fix his eye on a particular patch of violet shadow on the hillside beyond the river, and in the instant to become that shadow. But he could not do it. He wanted to *be* the landscape, to exist not just in it, but with it, as part of it. He concentrated, until he was startled by a voice behind him.

"Hello there!"

He got to his feet. It was Mrs. Choate, who drove the Volunteer Corps car, but in shorts and halter she looked quite different from the way she had in the ugly uniform.

"Why it's Avery Hollister," she said. "What are you doing up here?"

"Oh, nothing," he said. "I just come up here, sometimes." He stood looking at her, his throat tight. She was a woman his mother knew, but she looked like someone Morgan would have made a pass at. She was twenty-eight or thirty, a pretty woman with tawny skin and blonde hair that gleamed in the sun as though brilliantine had been brushed into it, and a bright mouth that emphasized her tan.

"So do I," she said, smiling at him. She took a silver case from the hip pocket of her shorts and lighted a cigarette. There was a faint coating of sweat on her lip and it glinted in the light. She tossed back her head and ran a hand through her hair, the cigarette in her mouth. When she did this, she looked like a movie actress.

"Have you had a decent summer?" she asked. "I suppose you spend all your time at the Pavilion, dancing with the pretty girls."

He shook his head. "I don't go there. It's dull."

She laughed and said, "It certainly doesn't sound dull. It sounds like a madhouse when you pass it in a car." She sat down, her knees drawn up under her chin, so that her long thighs pulled at her shorts and the outline of her body was displayed. He looked at her, then looked away, embarrassed by what he felt. She patted the ground and said, "Sit down and talk to me, Avery. I'm lonely."

He sat near her, aware of her smell and the moist red curve of her lips. She took the book from his hand and leafed through the pages, then raised her eyebrows and said, "Nothing like a little light reading for a summer afternoon. Why on earth are you reading this?"

"Oh, you know, for school," he said, ashamed to admit he read it for pleasure.

"You'd better watch out," she said. "If you study too hard your brain will blow up." She tossed her head and her hair grazed Avery's bare shoulder and he moved quickly, and she laughed. "Tickle?" she said, "I'm sorry." She rubbed his arm, then leaned back, stretched out at full length beside him. Under the halter her breasts looked enormous. He felt the urge to flee, together with a desperate, urgent need to stay. He could not take his eyes away from the place where the halter fell away, and he could see the white skin that had been protected from the sun. She moved lazily and made a purring noise like a satisfied cat. "Ummm, it's heavenly up here, isn't it?" she said.

"Yes," he said thickly. "Yes it is."

"Light me a cigarette, will you, like a dear?" she said. "I'm much too comfortable to move."

He looked down at the hip pocket where her cigarette case was, then reached for it, feeling the weight of her body on his hand. He managed to light a cigarette, his hands trembling a little. As he leaned over her his eyes were on her thick glossy lips that were slightly parted, giving her face a slack, intensely sexual appearance. He kissed her, astonished by the glandular softness of her mouth. She put an arm around his neck, pulling him down, moving her tongue against his mouth, then pushed him away and looked up into his face. "Why Avery Hollister," she said. "How do you do?"

He put out the cigarette and bent over to kiss her again. He felt a rush of blood to his head. *This is it,* his mind told him. *This is what Morgan was talking about. This is what Morgan was doing, to that Farmington girl. This was what you knew how to do, when the time came.*

It wasn't. When he moved his hand over her body, down toward her hips, she stopped him and pulled the hand up to her breasts. She opened the halter and moved his head down, so that his lips touched her breast and he felt the beating of her heart like an engine under water. He tried to touch her thighs again but her nails bit into his shoulder and hurt him. "No," she said. "Don't do that."

After a while, panting and confused, he rolled away. She sat up and pulled the halter tight again. His mouth felt dry and his body ached. "I'm sorry, Avery," she said. "I shouldn't have let you kiss me. But you look so young and sweet."

"That's all right," he said sullenly. "It doesn't matter." He was filled with dull rage at her and at himself. He was certain that anyone else, anyone at all, Morgan for instance, or Roger Bell, would have had what he wanted from her. She was married, he argued. She must have known what she was doing. She was married and had a kid. She wasn't just some girl at a dance, where you knew there was really nothing doing and just went through the motions because it was the thing to do.

"Avery, look up," she said.

She caught his head between her hands and kissed him quickly then pushed him away. She took a handkerchief from her pocket and doubled it tightly over her fingers, dabbing roughly at his mouth, the way his mother used to dab when he had a smudge on his cheek. "You're a sweet boy, Avery," she said. "Don't be mad at a poor widow woman."

"Widow?" he asked.

"Well no," she said. "Not really. But I might just as well be, you know. I guess this damned war is going on forever."

She caught his hand and he swung to his feet, then she turned and went off downhill. He stood there alone, frustrated and despising himself. "Bitch!" he muttered. "Dirty bitch!"

He sat down and picked up the little book, but the long sentences filled him with disgust and he threw it away. It caught in a tree, the pages fluttering in the breeze, and seemed to be laughing at him. He got up and flung himself down the slope toward home, loathing himself and the human race and the filthy body that had betrayed him and caused him to make a fool of himself.

Nevertheless, the next afternoon, he climbed the same hill, this time without a book, but with a package of cigarettes he had walked into town to get. He waited for an hour, but she did not appear, that day or the next. He was as furious with her as if she had failed to keep a rendezvous. Morgan would have made it, he knew. Roger would have made it. He could see Morgan, in his imagination, bending over Mrs. Choate the way he had bent over the black-haired girl from Farming-ton, knowing just what to say and do to make her laugh, to put her in the mood. He was nearly sixteen and he had hardly kissed a girl, except for somebody's sister at a dance, and somebody else's sister at a party. The first one had been like kissing a beach ball, and the second had scared him. Then there had been the Portuguese girl on Roger Bell's boat, who had smelled like a burlap bag and told him he was a jerk kid. He yearned for experience of the kind that young men had in books, but he had a suspicion that he was incompetent and the interlude with Mrs. Choate seemed to confirm this.

He saw her again in Hull, just before he went away to college. She was at the wheel of a big car and wore a bright print dress. Beside her sat a four-year-old girl, wearing a dress of the same print. She waved a white net hand at him and called, "Hi, Avery!"

He grunted something and turned away. He heard the little girl ask, "Who man, mummy? Who that man?" and heard Mrs. Choate say, "Why that's Avery Hollister, dear. Nancy Hollister's boy." The car purred and moved off; he stared after it. "Why the old hag," he muttered. "She's nothing but an old hag."

What he could not understand was why she had let him kiss her in the first place. He wondered what she had got out of it that he had not.

She had added considerably to his confusion.

Once when he had been ill, before his fever was gone, he had attempted to fit into a frame the parts of half a dozen jigsaw puzzles that had been broken up and discarded and thrown into a box they brought him by mistake. The box top showed a completed puzzle—View of Delft by Vermeer—and all day as he lay with his fever he had tried to construct the View of Delft from the bits and pieces of other puzzles, and in the end had been so confused he had thought he was going mad. It had been a desperate adventure in illogic, or antilogic, and when he thought of madness and the forms of madness, he always remembered the jigsaw puzzle that couldn't be made to fit.

He felt a related, idiot confusion when he tried to figure out Mrs. Choate, and the curious behavior of respectable adults, the contradictory gulf between what was said and what was done in the developed adult world. They were hypocrites, all of them, and not to be trusted. They had made a rotten world that was full of deliberate malicious lies. His father had lied when he promised him that everything always would be all right if he simply did his duty. His mother had lied when she promised never to desert him. Mr. Collamore had lied when he told the school he believed in freedom and then turned the Sixth Form into a kind of secret police. Mrs. Choate had lied when she kissed him that way and then backed out, and lied again just now, when she waved at him as if nothing had happened. McCoy's church was a lie, and so was the stone church in Hull. The history book was a lie, and so was the devil in his flesh. Even experience itself was a lie, for he couldn't depend on experience to sustain his independence of his father, but often had to stoke the fire.

They were all liars.

The only thing he had encountered that wasn't a lie, and that by its nature could never be a lie, was the bright clear world of analytic geometry, in the forms of which, as he plotted them out, he saw other forms in his mind, austere and beautiful as sculpture.

A few days later, packing for college, he was vaguely uneasy, until it occurred to him that this was because he was getting ready to leave the house without the collaboration of his mother. In other years she had been in his room when he packed for school, overseeing his laundry tapes and examining flannels for spots. This year, as he got ready, she was busy with her garden. At the end of summer, when most things had already been killed by a vicious early frost, she had remembered her flowers again, and now fanatically attacked the weeds and the slovenly edges, trimming the wasted grass with shears. It was pathetic to see her kneeling at the borders, using a hand cultivator that looked like a claw at the end of her arm. "Mother, it's too late," he had said. "No, no!" she had insisted. "There's been too much neglect. Too much. It's wicked."

He had turned away, filled with a mixture of pity and disgust. He had read somewhere that nurses who work with mental patients sometimes themselves become deranged, as if there were contagion or attraction in the madness, seducing the normal brain from reality, into the self-ruled psychopathic world. The idea came to his mind now, as he stood in front of his trunk, packing shirts into the drawers. He wondered whether he might not have been infected by the empty house, the loneliness, and by his mother's irrational aura, that pervaded the house like a scent. He was glad to be going away, away from Hull, away from Connecticut and New England, away from the world of which his father regarded himself as a curator. "It's not as if you were going to your father's college," Annie had said, "where people would know your name and look after you." "No, it's not," he had agreed. "It's not the same thing at all."

CHAPTER TWENTY-SIX

O F COURSE it wasn't the same thing, and probably wouldn't have been the same at New Haven either. The year was 1944, and the war had changed the colleges.

Dennis McCoy met him at Grand Central Station and they rode uptown in a cab to Morningside Heights. It was a clear late October day and the city looked exciting. There were pretty girls on the streets and purposeful-looking young men, and thousands upon thousands of troops in all kinds of uniforms. Avery looked out the window of the cab, feeling an attractive mixture of fear and anticipation. "What's it like?" he asked Dennis. "How do you like it?"

"You won't like it," Dennis said. "Maybe you should have gone to Yale."

"What's the matter with it?" Avery asked.

"It's not a college," Dennis said. "It's a naval base. The navy has everything. They've got the dorms and the dining halls, the whole damn set-up. You and I, my friend, are civilians and right now civilians are kind of in the way at Columbia College. And everywhere else, I guess." He looked at Avery and grinned, then said, "Do you know where we're living? We're living with a bunch of future Bible-bangers in the Theological School dormitory."

"How come?" said Avery.

"Navy," said Dennis. "The navy is in the regular dorms." He looked ungratefully at Central Park, and said, "If I go in the service it will be the army, buddy, and not the God damn navy."

"But what about the school," said Avery. "I mean, the classes and all that?"

Dennis shrugged. "The classes are all right," he said. "If you like classes."

They got out of the cab in front of the Theological School dormitory and Dennis helped Avery put his things away. Then he said, "Let's go and eat, shall we? We generally go to Angelo's. They don't have a liquor license, so the officers from the V7 school pretty much pass it up. But you can get wine."

"Whatever you say," Avery said.

Angelo's Spaghetti House was a narrow restaurant on Amsterdam Avenue, with red checked cloths and a tin ceiling stamped to look like plaster work. Dennis led the way to a round table in the back of the room, at which three young men were seated. One was a sandy blond with a broad forehead and pleasant gray eyes, dressed in a flannel shirt and an old tweed jacket, looking rather like a campus Communist. Another was thin and metropolitan looking, with dark brown, brooding eyes and an ingenuous, friendly grin. The third was a florid German type, with brass-colored hair that looked marceled and a pink butcher boy's face, wearing an expensive business suit and a bond salesman's dickey bosom shirt. Dennis introduced them.

"Angus Cotton," he said, nodding at the boy in the flannel shirt. "Herb Klein. Freddie Breitbart." They nodded and said "Hello Hollister," and Avery shook hands with them. Then Breitbart said, "Not another Colborn boy? The tone of this place is improving." Breitbart was the one in the dickey bosom shirt; he was a little older than the others, and seemed amused by his surroundings, and considerably amused by Avery and Avery's standard Colborn clothes.

"Hollister is the real article," Dennis said. "Not an ersatz product like me. His father and grandfather went there too."

"What brings you rich to Columbia?" Breitbart asked. "Is it just so you can be closer to Brooks Brothers' Mother Church?"

There was an undercurrent of challenge under Breitbart's banter that Avery didn't like. "I'm not rich," he said. "And it didn't say on the application that you had to come from a slum school."

"I thought all Colborn boys were rich," Angus Cotton said, grinning. "I thought you had to bring your old man's bank statement, along with your pedigree."

Dennis picked up a table knife and held it like a dagger. "Lay off my pal, see?" he said, in a movie gangster's voice. "Or I'll cut your heart out, see?"

They shared an Italian rubber pie, then ate bowls of steaming spaghetti lathered with rich tomato sauce and chunks of crusty Italian bread that was good without butter. The food was good, and very cheap. "Beats the Refectory at school, anyway," Avery said.

Cotton looked up sharply. "Oh, quite, old boy," he said, imitating Avery's accent. "Quite."

When they got back to the dormitory, Avery said to Dennis, "What's the matter with those guys, anyway? They seem to have a hell of a chip on their shoulders."

Dennis laughed. "You can't blame them, kid," he said. "To them a Colborn boy is a jerk like Roger Bell, a snotty rich kid with a phoney tie, who is going to high-hat them because they went to the local high school, and who will probably do them out of a job some day, or a good hospital appointment." He paused, then said, "You don't understand these guys, Avery. They're poor. I mean poor. Klein's old man is a tailor up in the East Bronx. Cotton's old man is a labor organizer. He was in the can for six months, for leading a strike, out in Toledo. Breitbart's people have dough, but they're immigrants, and they were once poor. They're bound to be suspicious of a guy who comes from what they figure is a snob school." He grinned and rumpled Avery's hair. "Hell, I'd be suspicious of you myself, if I didn't know you," he said.

"I see what you mean," Avery said. "But what the hell—"

"Forget it," Dennis advised. "They worked over you, and that's all there will be to it. You'll see. It'll be all right the next time. They're good guys."

Avery stood up and looked around the little room. There were two narrow cots, two battered work tables, and two uncomfortable-looking chairs. The walls were darkened by the soot of the city and there were patches that looked like scabs, where the last tenants had hung their pictures. It looked not at all like a college room in a movie, or like the suite in New Haven in which Morgan had lived. *"You will be an outsider there,"* his father had written. *"The people are not our kind."* He took off his coat and loosened his tie. "Oh, the hell with it," he said. "I didn't come down here to be a social success. I came down here to learn some math." He glanced at the beds, then said, "Which is yours, Dennis? Left or right?"

"Left," said Dennis.

Avery glanced at the head of the bed. At school and in his room at home, Dennis had always hung a little cross over the head of his bed, but there was no cross here. Dennis looked at him, then looked away. "Is there anything the matter with you, Dinny?" Avery said. "You look as if you hated the whole damn world."

Dennis laughed. "Well, hell, Ave, I've always done that." He stood up and stretched. "No, there's nothing wrong," he said. "Nothing at all. Nothing a bullet in the brain wouldn't take care of, anyway." He walked to the window and looked out, then turned and said, "Come on, let's turn in. You've got a million forms to fill out in the morning."

In the dark, in his bed, Avery lay awake and listened to the sound of the city outside. He could feel it, and he could feel the presence of millions upon millions of people, pressing in on the university and on this little room, that looked like a room in some railroad Y.M.C.A., but that was half his, and the rent for which had been paid with the first check he had ever written. To hell with the navy, he thought, and to hell with Breitbart and his snotty remarks. He was on his own. Coming here to Columbia was the first really free step of his life taken without consultation and against the instincts of others. He thought of Bell at New Haven and of Alsop and Ellsworth at Harvard, and he was glad he was here, even in a dormitory with a crowd of incipient circuit riders.

CHAPTER TWENTY-SEVEN

A PIECE of luck got him started well in the subject he had come to college to learn.

At the end of the first week, they had a quiz in mathematics, and the next day his instructor, a young graduate student named Willcox, asked him to stop by at his office, a little cubicle furnished with a desk, a glass-doored bookcase, and a curiously shaped piece of sculpture that Avery looked at aggressively, making Willcox laugh.

"If you're wondering what that is," he said, "it's a statue of water."

"A what, sir?" Avery asked.

"A statue of water," Willcox repeated. "And for God's sake, don't call me sir. It makes me nervous." He grinned, then said, "Sit down."

Avery sat.

Willcox filled his pipe and lit it, then said, "Have you been to college somewhere before, Hollister?"

Avery shook his head. "Why no, sir. I came straight from school."

"What school?"

Avery told him and Willcox smiled. "Colborn, eh? What brings you here amongst us proletarians?"

"I don't know," said Avery. "New York, I guess." He was getting sick of being tagged as queer, simply because he had gone to Colborn. But Willcox just smiled and said, "Half the English faculty of this place are here simply because they like to go to the theater." He took up a paper and glanced at it, then said, "But to get back to you, Hollister. When did they start to teach college math at Colborn?"

Avery explained that he had done the course on his own, and Willcox nodded, impressed, but not quite as impressed as Avery had expected him to be. He rummaged in a drawer of his desk, and took out a printed examination paper. "Look, Hollister, take this with you," he said. "It's last year's final. See what you can do with it. Maybe we can save you some time."

Avery stood up, looking at the plaster cast of the statue that Clerk Maxwell had made for his friend Willard Gibbs, at Yale. He reached out and touched it, running his fingers over the strange lined surface. It was a mountainous, atavistic shape, austere, and quite beautiful. "Water," he said. "A statue of water."

That night he went through the examination paper, and the next day returned it to Willcox, who looked at his work sheets and answers, then nodded approvingly.

"You'll probably have to take a formal achievement test, Hollister," he said. "But I think we can arrange to get you into Professor Douminoff's calculus section. That will be more fun for you than listening to me give out on a subject you seem to know pretty well." He puffed at his pipe, looking at Avery, sizing him up, then said, "I think you'll enjoy it. Douminoff's quite a boy. We think a lot of him around here."

"This is darn nice of you," Avery said. "I—" He wanted to thank Willcox for treating him like a man, but he didn't know how to put what he felt into words without sounding foolish.

"Forget it," Willcox said. "Pull up a chair, and I'll try to bring you up to date on what they've covered in calculus."

Avery sat beside the instructor and they both bent over the book. When he joined the calculus section on Monday, he was abreast of the class, as far as the actual work was concerned, but his first hour under Douminoff was a revelation to him, for it showed him what mathematics could be, in the hands of a man who loved it.

Douminoff was thin and gray, with a head like an imperial eagle. He paced the long dais like a tiger, holding the hundred-odd boys' attention effectively as an actor. He seemed to lecture not just on the subject, but on the whole of life. As he strode up and down the platform, pausing now and then to make a notation on the blackboard, he seemed to Avery to be illuminating the whole range of human thinking. He was exactly what Avery had expected to find here on Morningside Heights; he was what Avery had come here to find. Douminoff's bearing, his quick, nervous, clear speech, the tigerish stride, the emphatic, mannered gestures with the chalk, gave his lecture the effect of a recruiting speech for science. "Gentlemen," he said, looking out at the rows of young men in the theater-like lecture room, "Gentlemen, the essence of mathematics is its freedom. It was freedom that made it possible for Newton to accomplish a leap of the mind. Newton was a man. He lived and died. But he behaved like an immortal. He assumed that all the numbers had been counted, and he proved that finite man is capable of infinite thought. It was the first great break in the Aristotelian wall."

As Avery listened, his heart quickened. This was it, he understood. This was what he had come to college to discover.

When the hour was over, Douminoff stood at the lectern, putting his papers into an old brief case with a foreign-looking combination lock, oblivious of the class, his gray head bent, his eyes down. But as Avery passed, he looked up suddenly and called, "Mr. Hollister?"

Avery turned quickly, startled, surprised that Douminoff knew his name.

"Sir?"

"Do you think you'll be able to manage this?" the professor asked, his gray eyes estimating Avery.

"Yes, sir," Avery said. "I understood everything."

Douminoff laughed. "I've been at this for forty years," he said, "and I still don't understand everything that was in my lecture today." He paused, smiling. "But you could follow along all right, eh?"

"Yes, sir."

"Fine! Fine! If there's anything you don't get, ask. I'm in my office Tuesdays and Thursdays, four to five, right?"

Avery looked up. There was a passage of understanding. He felt that Douminoff liked him and didn't care whether he had gone to Colborn or to the State Reform School.

"Right, sir," he said.

Douminoff closed his brief case and leaped from the dais, then sprinted across the room, light on his feet as an athlete, expressing the energy of a steel spring. Avery walked out of the building and stood in the sun, beside the statue of a French miner. What had happened to him in the lecture room had been conclusive as an initiation. Douminoff had made a convert, or at least, recognized one.

Avery walked across the campus, suddenly in love with the place. The rigid, metropolitan arrangement of buildings did not seem depressing, as it had on first view. Here was a place for work, for business—an academic factory, stripped of nonessentials. It gave him a feeling of importance. It was real, he told himself. This enormous, impassive, unimpressed university was real, and in touch with the real world. Douminoff was real, in a way no one at Colborn ever dreamed of being, in a way his father never dreamed of being.

CHAPTER TWENTY-EIGHT

URING his first three years at Columbia, Douminoff was the central fact of Avery's intellectual life. There were others, but Douminoff was the heart of the adventure.

McCoy and Cotton complained of their professors, but Avery was satisfied. And he was satisfied with the life. It was tough, and hard and unrelieved, but he liked it.

He liked the work, and the rhythm of the life, and he liked the sessions at Angelo's, where he and Dennis usually ate.

Dennis had been right about Klein and Cotton and Breitbart and the others. After they had given him a trial run, they seemed prepared to accept him as a member of what they called Angelo Petroni's Four F and Infant Prodigy Club.

He liked them.

He had met only two Jews in his life, a boy named Berns at Sturgis Manor, and Claude Bloch, at Colborn, and Bloch, being a Rothschild, was not really a Jew at all. Klein was the first Jewish Jew he had met, and he was both suspicious of him and fascinated by him.

The accreted layers of prejudice did not fall away with ease. He was sometimes ashamed of the fact that if Klein beat him in argument, or kidded with him a little too sharply, or wore a tie that he would not have worn himself, that he was apt to think, in a smug, blazing flash: *That's a Jew for you.* Jews were vulgar, loud, clever, tricky, rich, and they smelled. Klein met none of these specifications, being soft spoken and Talmudic in manner, and possessing a systematic, almost plodding mind, rather than a clever one, and being both quite poor and scrupulously clean.

One night Klein fell to talking about the Jews, and suddenly broke off, holding his water glass in his hand, so that the light hit the surface of the water.

"You know," he said reflectively, "until I was fourteen years old, I went to Hebrew School?"

"You mean they taught in Hebrew?" Avery asked.

Klein laughed. "Oh, I went to a regular school too," he said. "P.S. 139, in the Bronx. But afternoons, twice a week, I went to Hebrew School." He smiled, shaking his head, and uttered a few words in the strange language. His face was clouded with memory. The strange, exotic words sent a thrill through Avery, the kind of thrill the Greek words from his brother's grave had produced, when he heard them from the master at Colborn.

"I didn't mind learning the language," said Klein. "It's something to know, like anything else. But the religion. That was another thing." He looked at McCoy and smiled. "You have he Prince of Peace and the Sainted Virgin. We had the God of Wrath. He used to terrify me. The teacher was an old man with a beard, who wore a fur-lined overcoat in the classroom and carried a long pointer. If you made a mistake, he rapped you on the knuckles, good and hard. We had the classes in the basement of an old synagogue, and it was cold as a sewer. It ruined religion for me. Whenever I hear the word Yahweh, I think of that cellar in the Bronx, with the damp cement walls, and the stink of that old man, who made me so sick I couldn't eat my dinner."

When Klein had finished, Avery and the others sat silently, a little embarrassed by the self-revelation. Then Klein laughed and said, "I quit going, as soon as I started high school. My old man raised hell about it."

"It's a funny thing," Cotton said. "Most kids are forced to go to Sunday School and whatnot. But when I was a kid, ten years old, eleven, there was nothing I wanted to do as much as I wanted to go to Sunday School with the other kids. My Dad wouldn't let me. I agree with him now, about the church, but I don't know whether he was right, then, or not. All the other kids went, and they thought my sister and I were queer, because we weren't allowed to go."

Avery told about the time at Sturgis he had made a scene in Bible Class, and the others were amused, so he went on to tell about Sacred Studies at Colborn. Dennis listened and said nothing, but as Avery talked and the others laughed, his face tightened, and all at once he got up from the table and went out of the restaurant without saying anything. The others watched him go, then Cotton said, "Why the bastard didn't even pay for his dinner."

Avery picked up the check.

"I'll pay for his," he said.

"What's the matter with him?" said Angus. "He acted as if somebody spoke out of turn."

"He's a Catholic," Avery said. "Or at least he's trying to be."

"Oh?" said Cotton.

That night Dennis slept at home, and the next evening, at dinner time, he did not appear. Avery didn't see him until after eleven, when he was already in bed. When Dennis came into the room, he seemed cheerful, and his eyes were bright. As he passed the bed, Avery caught a swift, dangerous scent of whiskey.

"Did I say anything last night to make you sore?" he asked.

Dennis shook his head. "No. Hell, no. I just got in a mood." He grinned. "Hell, I'm Irish, ain't I? The Irish have a right to have black Irish moods."

He sat at the window and began to sing, quietly, in a thin, artificial voice, with a brogue:

The priest's at home boy, and may be seen
'Tis easy speakin' with Father Green;
But you must wait 'til I go an' see,
If the holy father alone may be.

It was a sad, plaintive tune. Dennis dropped a shoe to the floor, and then went on with it:

> The youth knelt down to tell his sins,
>   *Nomine Dei,* the youth begins
> *Mea Culpa,* he beats his breast,
>   And in broken murmur repeats the rest.

He hummed the rest, taking off his clothes, until he came to the end of the song, when he sang the words, raising his voice:

> 'Twas at Dungannon this young man died,
>   At Geneva Barracks his body lies.
> And all good Christians, as you pass by,
>   Say a prayer, shed a tear, for the Croppy Boy.

He got into bed and switched off the light. "The Croppy Boy," he said heartily, his voice a little thick with whiskey. "Another martyr for Old Ireland. Another murder for the Crown. Up the Rebels. Down with the Yeoman Cavalry."

"Go to sleep, Dinny," said Avery. "You've got a class in the morning. Go to sleep."

"Yes, sor!" Dennis said. "Whatever your worship pleases, sor! Will you be wantin' the horses in the mar-nin, sor?"

Avery laughed. "Go to sleep, you drunken mick, or I'll throw a shoe at you."

Dennis laughed pleasantly and said, "Righto, Avery. Good night."

"Good night, Dennis."

Dennis rolled over and went to sleep, making the narrow bed creak. The next morning, he was fine. He even remembered to pay Avery for his dinner.

"Don't ever mind me," he said. "I think I'm a little touched."

That night at Angelo's, he argued books with Angus Cotton, making his points cleverly and displaying quantities of charm and wit. Only Avery understood that he was overplaying it a bit. Dennis was bitter and unhappy, and a few weeks later, after the abbreviated Christmas vacation, Avery stirred up the black Irish pool again, without really meaning to.

One afternoon in January, when Dennis was out, Avery was called on by three young men who looked like Colborn dormitory prefects. They wore expensive flannel trousers and intensely clean soft white shirts. They looked like members of the same family, and Avery realized, with something of a shock, that he looked like a member of the same family.

"Hollister?" one of them said. "I'm Elliot, Jim Elliot, from The Hall. St. Mac's."

"Oh?" said Avery.

He knew about The Hall. It was the little club of Columbia rich that lived in discreet privacy in a fine old house west of the campus. Most fraternities were closed for the duration, and none of the others was serving meals, but The Hall carried on, and The Hall, unlike most of Columbia, was impressed by the fact that Avery came from Hull and had gone to Colborn School.

"This is Bill Joyce," Elliot said. "And Sandy Rutherford." He smiled, offering Avery his hand, and said, "Can you give us a few minutes' time, old man? We'd like to talk to you."

Avery stepped back and they came into the room. Pinned to each immaculate shirt was an enormous jeweled pin in the form of the Greek letter Mu. Joyce looked down at his pin, following Avery's eyes, then smiled and said, "That's so one St. Mac's man can recognize another across the room, even when both of them are a bit foxed."

The other boys laughed. They filled the small room, and Avery had a sense of entrapment, as if he were a criminal finally caught, or a schoolboy being visited by a disciplinary party of upper formers. The splendid complexions, the familiar clothing, familiar accents, familiar faces, seemed to imply: *You don't really want to get away, you know. Not really.*

He wanted to be British and superior, but he was outnumbered, and disarmed by the casual, self-confident manners of his visitors. Elliot glanced at the books on his table, then said in a man-to-man voice, "Hope you don't plan to grind away much longer, old man. We've come to take you to dinner with us, at The Hall."

Avery looked at him and regained some of his composure. "By force?" he said, glancing from one boy to the other.

Elliot laughed. "Not exactly," he said. "But seriously, Hollister, we'd like very much to have you come." He paused, looking at Avery, his eyes quite guileless. "We don't do any rushing, you know, in the ordinary sense. We have three or four legacies a year, and aside from those, there aren't more than five men in each class we're interested in. Frankly, we think you may be one of them."

Avery went with them.

He didn't know exactly why he went, though certainly one reason was that he could think of no way of refusing without being deliberately rude. But there were other reasons, beyond civility and curiosity, and having to do with the fact that he had not really changed as much as he believed, with the fact that he was, in spite of himself, a Colborn boy, with the Col-born drive toward conformity in his blood.

The Hall was a handsomely furnished house, inhabited by a well-groomed quiet that seemed out of place in New York, more suited to Beacon Hill or to Rittenhouse Square. From the enormous front-room windows the clubmen got a spectacular view of the Hudson River and the Palisades on the opposite shore. The smell of the house was familiar, almost reassuring, compounded of good rugs and hangings and expensive British furniture polish.

Avery was treated like a piece of valuable glass. The group seemed eager to let him know that even in the midst of this great bustling vulgar university, there were a few who cared for the old gentlemanly standards and knew how to observe them. The head of the house, who wore a starched white collar, smiled pleasantly at him and said, "Did Jim tell me you'd gone to Groton, Hollister? It was Groton, wasn't it?"

"Colborn," Avery said. Colborn was to Groton what Eton was to Harrow. He was amused.

"Oh, yes, Colborn," the boy in the starched collar said. "Fine school. I went to Lawrenceville, so theoretically I'm in favor of bigger schools, but Colborn's a fine place."

At dinner they drew from Avery what they wanted to know about his family, his finances, his academic interest, his social status. He felt like a man being kissed by a woman and having his pocket picked at the same time, but he was grateful to Colborn for one thing; all the boys at the table secretly had conceded that Colborn was better than their own schools, and he realized this. It made him more than usually self-confident.

After dinner, when they sat with their coffee in the front room, he understood that he had passed the test. There would be a few more dinners, a suitable interval of sparring, but in the end he would be asked to become a member. They had made up their minds. He knew that from the point of view of honesty as well as politeness, that he should make it clear that he did not intend to join this fraternity or any other. But for some reason, he did not do this. He sat with them until one o'clock, talking about people who knew other people that they knew. When Jim Elliot took him to the door, he asked him to dinner the following week, and Avery agreed to come. He walked back to the dormitory in the bright winter starlight, a little flattered and a little impressed, pardonably relieved to have found one area at Columbia in which his background was an asset instead of a liability.

He found Dennis in a sullen mood.

"Been out?" McCoy said.

"Well, you know I haven't been here," Avery said.

Dennis looked up at him, sharply, and Avery saw that he was jealous, and resentful of the fact that he could have gone to Colborn, Groton, St. Paul's and St. Mark's and still not have been asked to dine with the young Protestant gentlemen at The Hall.

"As a matter of fact," Avery said good naturedly, "I had dinner at one of the better fraternities."

"I know," said Dennis. "The one they call St. Mac's."

"How did you know that?" Avery asked, a little irritated, feeling he had been spied on.

"Breitbart saw the committee," said Dennis. "He minds everybody's business."

"Why should Breitbart be interested in where I have dinner?" Avery asked.

"Don't be a bigger dope than you have to be, Hollister, will you?" Dennis said angrily. "Are you going to join? I'll take the room off your hands if you like. You don't have to worry about leaving me in the lurch."

"Oh, for God's sake, McCoy, lay off me, will you?" Avery said. "I just had dinner with some people. Is there a law against that?"

Dennis shook his head. "No, there's no law against it. And there's no law that says you have to live here with me, either."

"Oh, the hell with it, Dennis," Avery said. "I simply had dinner out. That's my privilege, isn't it? After all, we're not married, are we?"

"No. No, we're not," said Dennis.

He got up and went out of the room, and didn't come back that night. Avery was ashamed of himself. He knew that there had been a rule against it, and knew that he had broken it. The next day he called Elliot and broke the date for dinner.

"You're making a mistake," Elliot said, like a man selling insurance. "I think you'll find we're your kind of people."

He reminded Avery of Roger Bell, advising him not to get involved with that bog-trotter McCoy. He laughed into the phone and said, "That would be a horrible break for you, Elliot. A horrible break."

He hung up the phone and went on to class, sorry he had hurt Dennis' feelings by going to dinner at St. Mac's. If he had wanted to join a club, he would have gone to New Haven and joined his father's club. Angelo's Spaghetti House was all the club he wanted.

CHAPTER TWENTY-NINE

O F COURSE Angelo's was a club with a fluctuating member-
ship. Except for Breitbart and Klein, who were Four F, the
boys at Angelo's existed in a predraft limbo, waiting until they
were eighteen and passed into the services. Some of them went
into the navy as V12 seamen, and moved across Broadway to
Hartley Hall, becoming uniformed enlisted men, but going on
with college as before. Some didn't like the idea of confusing college with the standing of watches, and left college to disappear
into the mass of the army. It was a decision Avery didn't face, for
two years, at any rate, and he was fortunate.

The war confused him; he had been brought up to believe
that service in war was almost the prerequisite of manhood, and
a diet of Kiplingesque romance leaves its mark on the spirit. Had
he been eighteen in 1944, the chances are he would have volunteered, for part of him secretly envied the midshipmen on the
Columbia campus, and envied every soldier he passed on the
street. He knew in his heart that just by being in uniform they
were part of an adventure. He knew that this war had nothing
to do with Fontenoy, or a cavalry charge in the Crimea, or even
with the Battle of Loos, in which his father had fought, but he
could not always prevent the images of childhood from rising in
his mind, and in childhood soldiers had meant adventure, high
adventure and romance, related to the First Crusade and to the
Battle of Hastings.

One day in March, on a bright afternoon, he watched the
midshipmen parade on South Field—hundreds of them, in

straight blue ranks, the commands and the cadence ringing out clearly, and echoing back from the buildings. The music of the band got into his blood. He felt a tingling in his finger tips and his throat tightened with emotion. The rifles made an authoritative sound as the formation executed a maneuver, and the band struck up a lively march as they moved off toward their quarters on the west side of the field. Avery watched them, excited as he had been when his father had taken him to West Point once, to see the corps of cadets parade.

"You'd give your right arm to be out there with them, wouldn't you, friend?"

Avery turned. It was Dennis, smiling at him, very nearly sneering at him. He felt like a little boy, surprised while playing with some toy he has formally renounced. He wondered how long Dennis had been standing there watching him, and his face turned red with embarrassment.

"That's a sneaky damn thing to do," he said.

"Oh, hell, Avery, you'll get a chance to wear the suit," Dennis said. "Plenty of war for everybody. Just wait your turn."

Avery's adrenalin had already been brought into flood by the midshipmen's band. He turned on Dennis and said, in a fair imitation of the tone his father might have used under the same circumstances, "That's a cheap thing to say, McCoy. There are certain things you just don't seem to understand."

It was an unpleasant moment. It was Protestant, colonial, New England, facing the immigrant Irish Catholic, and the bitter prejudice of a hundred years was in the air around them, like static. McCoy's face tightened, and for a moment Avery thought he was going to hit him. Then Dennis laughed bluntly and said, "I guess you're right, Avery. There are certain things an Irish mick just can't understand."

"I'm sorry, Dennis," Avery said. "I didn't mean anything."

"I know," Dennis said pleasantly. "You have war nerves, old boy. Call it precombat fatigue. I have it too."

They walked slowly across the campus together, Avery ashamed and not quite at ease, McCoy seeming to have thrown it off. When they reached Broadway, they paused beneath the gate and looked back into the campus. It was now late afternoon and the sun was low, casting a soft golden light on the buildings, modifying their hard functional lines. The midshipmen were having their dinner. There was not a uniform in sight. On the broad stone steps of the old library, under the gilded Alma Mater, a boy and girl sat with books on their laps, their heads close, almost touching. The scene was peaceful, and in that light, both Dennis and Avery were touched by nostalgia and by an awareness of past and future, as well as the violated present.

Then Dennis said, "I know one thing. So far as I am concerned, the era of postwar disillusionment has begun." He took a long hard look at the campus, then turned away. Avery followed.

The next day Dennis was gone. He did not appear at the college for three days. When he returned, it was to pack his things. He had volunteered through his draft board, the day after his eighteenth birthday. Avery watched him stow his clothes into a new cowhide case. "What do you think you'll get into?" he said. "I mean, what branch?"

"All the good jobs are taken, friend," Dennis said. "The openings, right now, are for infantry replacements."

"Jesus, Dennis," Avery said, "why didn't you go V12? You could stay on here. The war might be over before you graduate and get your commission."

Dennis straightened up.

"Look, Avery," he said. "I told you how I feel about it. I don't give a special damn about the war, the way you do, for instance, if you'd tell yourself the truth for a change. But I'm a funny guy in some ways. I don't go to church any more, and I told you why. I don't go because I don't believe. Well, it's the same thing, in a way, with this. If I'm in college, I'm in college, and to hell with it.

I'm going to wear what I God damn please and study what I God damn please, eat what I please and come and go when I please. If I'm in the God damn war, I'm going to be in it all the way."

They had dinner together alone, in a place on Broadway, instead of going to Angelo's. After dinner, Dennis said, "I've got the old man's car. Why don't you come down to the apartment with me for a while?"

"Well, sure," said Avery. He was surprised; Dennis had never asked him to his father's apartment, and sometimes Avery thought he resented the fact that he had been there, that summer, when he had run away to New York.

They drove downtown, and Dennis turned the car over to a doorman who saluted him and called him sir. Avery followed him into the house. When they entered the apartment, he was, for the second time, struck by the painting over the mantel.

"Italian painter," Dennis said, in a cruel approximation of his father's voice. "Mood, elegance." He looked at the painting and sighed. "I bought that when I was thirteen years old," he said. "Can you imagine a thirteen-year-old kid buying a painting worth seven thousand dollars?"

Avery looked at the painting again.

"Is it really worth that much?" he asked. Some rigid Puritan realism rose in him, to protest against the idea that a few dollars worth of paint and canvas, and a few hours' effort by a man who was really enjoying himself rather than working, could possibly be worth, in American money, more than the powerful automobile that had just carried him downtown.

McCoy nodded. "I guess it's worth more than that now," he said. "There's been a kind of boom in art, you know."

They sat down opposite one another in the soft leather chairs. The bland-faced Negro maid came into the room, as if by instinct, unsummoned. "What would you like?" Dennis asked. "Beer? Glass of wine? Ginger ale?"

"Ginger ale, I guess," said Avery.

Dennis thought for a moment, then said, "I think I'll have a scotch and soda. What the hell, I'm a soldier, practically."

When the maid went out, Dennis looked at the painting again. "You know," he said, "the fairy decorator that did up this place kicked up a storm when I bought that. They can't stand having a real painting around. It drives them nuts." He looked around the room, then back at the painting. "They put together a place like this, everything perfect, everything in absolute taste, with all the humanity squeezed out of it. It's a set piece. You put a painting into it, and the painting exposes the whole damn thing. It shows them up. It's like having St. Francis walk into the Chancery Office. He would embarrass them. Probably they'd take him for a bum, and throw him out, or maybe some kind of nut, and call the wagon."

Avery didn't understand. The maid came with their drinks and Dennis took his whiskey, smelled it, then drank a little, making a face. After a while, he looked across the room at Avery. "Still think I'm a dirty Irish mick?" he asked.

"I didn't call you that," said Avery.

"No. But you meant it, for a few minutes, anyway," said Dennis.

"Oh, forget it, will you," said Avery.

"Nothing I'd like better," said Dennis. "Except that of course I am a dirty Irish mick, and Klein is a dirty Jew, and so on. You belong to the club, Holly. You ought to take advantage of it."

"Don't talk like a damn fool," Avery said.

Dennis looked at his glass. "I hate to pull out on you, Avery," he said. "I know you came down here partly because I was coming. But there isn't anything I can do."

"That's all right," Avery said. "I guess I knew you were going to do it, ever since the day I got here and you met me at the station." He hesitated, then said, "What is it, Dinny? What's wrong?"

"I don't know," Dennis said. "Everything, I guess. Or nothing."

He got himself another drink. He wasn't used to whiskey, and his speech became a little furry.

"I don't know," he said. "It's not the college. I don't give a damn about the college. The navy is welcome to it." He paused, staring at the tip of his shoe. "Remember the time I walked out of Angelo's, the night you guys were talking about religion?"

"Sure," said Avery. "You went on some kind of a tear."

"Yeah," said Dennis. "I went over to Philadelphia, to see my mother."

"Oh?" said Avery. He had never heard Dennis mention his mother. He had somehow assumed that she was dead.

"She lives over there," Dennis said. "The old man doesn't want her here in New York, but four or five times a year she breaks loose and hits Broadway, where she came from. It's always a tough job, getting her to go back. She's a drunk. She smokes reefers. I guess she does everything else, too." He paused, then said, "She ran out on the old man. It hurt him. It hurt his pride."

Avery listened, wondering how much of McCoy's mother was in Dennis and how much of his father, and how much that was simply Dennis, and had nothing to do with either of his parents.

"I sat there looking at her," Dennis said, "in a ginmill on Market Street, slopped to the ears. She fished her beads out of her bag and said, 'One thing to be thankful for, Dennis, I've got my religion.' It turned my stomach." He looked up at Avery. "I don't believe in God," he said. "I took the beads away from my mother and threw them into the gutter and then I put her into a cab. I didn't want to ever see her again, or have anything to do with her religion. I excommunicated myself, on the spot." He paused, then said, "But I guess it had been coming on for quite a while."

"How about your father?" Avery said. "Isn't he a Catholic?"

"The old man?" Dennis asked, surprised. "No. He's not a Catholic. He never was. He's nothing. I guess he was born Presbyterian, but he's nothing now. He's from Tyrone, from the

Six Counties, but I'll say this for him. He's never interfered with my religion. I got it from my mother and I lost it for myself."

The dawn showed through the tall windows that formed the east wall of the room, pink light sifting through the thin curtains, making the electric lights look yellow and tawdry, so that Dennis switched them off, and the room was bathed in the compassionate morning light, making the neutral colors of the modern furniture look more attractive. They both rose without speaking and walked to the window, watching the sun come up across the park. The city was quiet, asleep, and looked enormously potent. After a while, the sun broke through, and felt warm on their faces.

Dennis turned away. "How about some chow?" he said.

He cooked slabs of ham and fried eggs, and they ate in the kitchen.

They said good-bye at the door. Dennis looked tired and old. Avery felt the hopeless regret that overtakes one, when it is too late to say or do kind things that might have helped another human being. When he spoke, his voice was thick, and he was afraid he would cry.

"So long, Dennis," he said. "You take care of yourself."

"You bet," said Dennis. "You bet I will."

Avery took the subway back to the college. The room, with Dennis' things gone, looked as if it had been burglarized. He stared at Dennis' cleared table, then threw himself on his bed, wanting to cry. After a time he fell asleep. When he woke up it was late afternoon and he had missed his classes. He felt a pang of guilt at the wasted day. He went out into the city, which seemed dangerous with neon signs and the hurtling lights of taxis. The air was heavy with formless danger. He felt the curdling city fear, fear of the inhabited, predatory jungle. He was afraid to be alone, and hated to go back to the dormitory and upstairs to the empty room.

CHAPTER THIRTY

A FEW weeks later, one morning, he found a note in his mail-box, typed on a crisp expensive letterhead: CHADBOURNE, WALKER, PARK & BROWNE:

Dear Avery:

It's years since I've had the pleasure of seeing you, and I won't feel hurt about it if you don't remember me at all. You were ten, I think, or was it eleven, the summer Edie and I were at your father's place in Hull.

I've just had a letter from your Dad, in which he mentions the fact that you are right here in New York. Of course, I'd love to see you. I wonder if you'd lunch with me at my club? It's the Ivy, on Fifth Avenue, and next Tuesday at one would suit me fine. If that conflicts with your schedule, please call me and we'll change the date. Otherwise, I'll look for you Tuesday.

Caldecott Browne

The signature was in green ink, calligraphic and important looking. He read the note, then handed it to Angus, who stood beside him. "Read that," he said. "My father, the general, has a spy system."

Angus ran his thumb over the engraved letterhead. "Rich," he said. "Feels like high-class espionage."

Avery took the letter back, folded it and put it in his pocket. He took it as a sign of his own maturity that he was amused rather than annoyed. "Of course it's high-class," he said. "Browne is a classmate of my old man's." He smiled, imagining his father's face, had he heard himself referred to as the old man. He remembered Caldecott Browne all right: a big tanned man who liked to ride and wore a blue Yale blazer and a white terry cloth ascot. He was a man his father saw when he came to New York on business. His father must think of Browne as a kind of ally in enemy territory.

"Think you'll go?" Angus asked, as they crossed Broadway to the drug store, where they had breakfast.

"I don't know," he said. "Maybe."

"Better," Angus advised. "You can play nice for an hour or so. And you might get a decent meal for free. All those swanky clubs have got their own black-market butchers. You might even get a steak."

"I don't know," Avery said. "I don't like the idea of having the guy check up on me."

Of course, he went. For one thing, he was curious, and for another, he knew that if he didn't go that Browne would write to his father, and that might mean trouble. He was sixteen, and dependent on his father. Once, during the summer, he had thought of really striking out for himself—getting a scholarship and earning his keep by doing odd jobs, as others did. But he begrudged the time. There was no virtue in it, only work. He wanted time, and washing somebody else's dirty dishes would steal time he wanted for himself. He had no money of his own, and wouldn't have until he became twenty-one, and began to draw on the trust fund his grandfather had established for him, which, though he did not know the precise amount, could certainly not be very much. In the meantime, it was pleasant to have his own checking account, and not to worry about his fees, as some of the others worried.

Browne's club occupied a massive dark stone building on a valuable Fifth Avenue corner, with stone carving over the doorway and lofty windows high above the street. Avery sat in a leather chair in the comfortable strangers' room, across from a general in the marine corps, whose chest was covered with battle ribbons. For some time the general turned incredulous bright blue eyes on the headlines of the morning paper. Then he looked up and said, "Hello, youngster."

"Hello, sir," Avery said.

"How's life, youngster?" the general asked, his voice thin and metallic, as though transmitted through a wire. "How old are you?"

"Sixteen, sir," said Avery.

"Might miss it altogether," the general said. He had a long Yankee face, weather-bitten and shrewd.

"I hope not," Avery said, thinking it might be expected of him.

"Don't be a damn fool, youngster," the general said. "You miss it if you get the chance. War's no good for civilians. It's good for professionals. It's our busy season. But for civilians—" he made a short, rude sound—"it's no good. Two years, three years, after the war, the hero racket is done with. They'll be getting out the ticker tape for some fat little girl who's swum the Channel, or some damn fool who sat on a flagpole. No future in it. No future at all."

Avery laughed. "You don't sound much like a recruiting officer, sir," he said. There was something about the tough-faced old marine that appealed to him. He trusted him. He believed him.

"I'm not," the general said. "I've seen too many kids your age chopped to pieces in the shallow water, before they ever hit the beach. Go to college, do you?"

"Yes, sir."

"Well, stay in college. Join any kind of phoney set-up they have that will keep you in college, and out of the war." He straightened up, so the ribbons on his blouse could be seen. They were good ribbons, the best ribbons, and Avery recognized them:

Medal of Honor, Navy Cross, campaign ribbons with battle stars on them. He looked at the stars on the shoulder straps—the same insignia of rank his father wore. But this was not his father's kind of general, or his father's kind of man.

Browne arrived, a tall, tanned figure in a well-cut blue suit, wearing a starched white collar and a dark, expensive French tie that was a little too carefully knotted. He looked New York, and downtown. Avery got up and said, "Hello, sir. I guess I'm early."

"No. I'm late," Browne said, shaking hands with him. "Had to take the subway. Can't get a cab these days, and of course there's no gas."

"Sad, sad," the general said.

Browne turned and saw the general, his annoyance at interruption instantly replaced by a smile of professional geniality. "General Judson, isn't it, sir?" he asked. "I'm C. Browne. We met at Senator Shrewell's party, in Washington, but of course you won't remember me."

The general nodded and said, " 'Member you very well. You explained the Guadalcanal campaign to me. First time I ever understood it." He began to rise but Browne held up a hand.

"Please, sir, don't get up. You embarrass a poor civilian."

The general sank back into his seat. "Didn't know there were any poor civilians," he said.

Browne laughed politely and took Avery's arm. "Would you care to join us for lunch, sir?" he asked the general. "We'd be delighted, young Hollister and I."

General Judson shook his head. "I think I have a date for lunch," he said. "And if I'm mistaken, which I hope to Christ I am, I intend to go to a noisier, cheaper place than this, where I can get good and drunk and sing to the bartender in Tagalog."

Browne laughed and turned away, waving at the general, Avery followed him into the elegant dining room, where ancient waiters cruised dispassionately over a thick crimson carpet that squidged like grass beneath their feet. When they were seated,

Browne said, "Thank heaven General Judson didn't join us. You've heard of him, haven't you?"

"I think I've seen his picture," said Avery.

"MacArthur won't have him in the Pacific," Browne said. "They say he's practically a Communist. Full of mad ideas about doing away with rank, and making the officers eat with the men. Things like that." He smiled and said, "But let's forget him. He's the hell of a bore, too, by the way."

A waiter brought Browne a printed menu and a pad and pencil. Browne recommended the small steak, and Avery said that would be fine, remembering Angus' advice.

"Well, Avery," Browne said, when the ordering had been done, "what persuaded you to pass up New Haven in favor of New York? Was it the call of the fleshpots? Or are you one of those scholarly chaps, interested in some obscure subject that must be pursued on Morningside Heights under some wily Oriental?"

Avery understood that he was supposed to be amused, and smiled. "Well, sir," he said, "I'm going in for math, and Columbia seemed to be a good place for that."

"What the devil's wrong with Sheff'?" Browne asked.

"I'm not going in for engineering, sir," Avery said. "Pure mathematics." He pronounced the words with some pride, and was gratified when Browne displayed both astonishment and respect.

"You young fellows are beyond me," he said. "Mathematics, physics, chemistry, God only knows what. You seem to go out of your way to look for the hard subjects. When your Dad and I went to college, most fellows wanted a snap course that met twice a week, on the first floor of the building, and near the fraternity house."

Avery laughed.

When they finished lunch, and were having a second cup of coffee, Browne said casually, "Avery, I think I should tell you that your Dad's quite worried about you."

"Is he?" Avery asked, his pulse quickening a little. "Did he tell you so?"

"Not exactly," Browne said. "It's nothing specific." He hesitated, then went on, "It's just that he'd feel better if you were at New Haven, and he was sure you were with the right kind of people."

It was useless to try to explain to Browne that most people nowadays didn't even pick their colleges, but had them picked for them, by the army or navy. He looked at the silver coffee pitcher, then looked back at Browne. "What kind of people does he think I'm with?" he asked.

"Well, he mentioned Tip McCoy's son. Someone at Col-born apparently gave him the idea you were rooming with him."

"Hardly," Avery said. "McCoy's in a training camp, somewhere in Georgia. He's in the army."

"Oh?" said Browne. "I'm surprised he wasn't made a captain to begin with, the way his father's friend's son was."

"He's a private," Avery said flatly. "An infantry replacement."

"I'm sorry," Browne said. "I was just trying to make a joke." He smiled, then said, "Are you getting along all right? No problems?"

"Only in mathematics," Avery said.

Browne laughed. "The fact is, I don't know a damn thing about Columbia," he said. "If it were New Haven, I might be on safer ground. Of course, if you were in a fraternity it would be simpler."

Avery said nothing. He could almost smell the man-to-man talk that Browne had been delegated to make. He waited, feeling a little sorry for Browne, who was doing an awkward job for his father.

"I don't have to tell you that it's awfully easy to get into trouble," Browne said. "Especially nowadays, during the war, in a city like this one. Frankly, I think the French have the right idea. They have their prostitutes, and the girls obey the law, or bang goes their license. You know, medical exams and all that. I wish we had it here. I think in the long run a fellow's better off to go to a cathouse than to get involved with a so-called respectable girl, and maybe taken for a lot of money, or put to a great deal of inconvenience. Don't you agree?"

"I hadn't thought about it," said Avery.

After a moment's hesitation, Browne took a slip of paper from his wallet, with a name and address written on it, and said, "I don't know just how your Dad would handle this, Avery," he said, rather tentatively. "I'm just filling in for him, you might say. But if you were my own son, I'd give you this piece of paper, and tell you to use your own judgment."

Avery nodded solemnly, putting the paper into his wallet. He wondered whether Browne believed modern parents supplied their sons with the telephone numbers of reliable prostitutes in the same way they gave them the names of tailors, or whether this chore was one his father had specifically asked Browne to do. Browne seemed a little embarrassed. He looked at Avery, then smiled and said, "Thank God, I have daughters."

Avery laughed.

When they parted, on the sidewalk in front of the club, Browne said, "I don't suppose you play much squash up there, do you?"

Avery shook his head. "No, I haven't played since I left Colborn," he said, suddenly realizing that he missed the game, and sorry he had lost it.

"I'd be glad to give you a game," Browne said. "Most any evening, after five-thirty. Would you like that?"

"Very much," Avery said. It is easier to abandon belief in God than belief that virtue resides in exercise, if you have been reared as Avery was reared. The thought of the close confines of the court and the punctuation of the fast ball on the boards excited him.

Browne handed him a card. "Just give me a day's notice, Avery," he said. "I look forward to it." He hesitated, then smiled. "And of course, you must dine with us. Soon. We'll arrange it."

Avery watched him get into a cab, then put the card into his wallet beside the address of the brothel. The cab moved off toward the east and Browne waved good-bye. Avery turned into Fifth Avenue, walking uptown, past the windows of glamorous shops. The street, the city, was crowded with busy, attractive women, advance guard of creeping feminism, moving into the gap that thirteen million men had left when they departed for the war. On this bright rich street it was difficult to grasp the fact that at this moment people were bleeding and dying—people who, in ordinary times, belonged on this street. There was no sense of war. Even the men in uniform, walking in the sun with their women, did not suggest war, but holiday, festivity. Everyone was well-dressed, well-fed, well-tipped, well-heeled. The country was rich, pig rich, hog rich, rich and glutted to the point of bursting, and you could feel it in the air. Walking up the Avenue, past the dioramic windows, into the rich Continental stretch of street beside the Park, where people walked expensive dogs and aired expensive children, Avery remembered the tough-faced marine that Browne had called a Communist, and when he recalled the general's face, for an instant he thought he felt the war, out there beyond the Coast, and caught a hint of its meaning.

He did not call Browne, but ten days later Browne called him, and he made a date to play squash on the Ivy Club courts.

He enjoyed himself.

When they finished playing, he was pleasantly tired and aware of a rewarding sense of virtue. The numbness in his limbs was familiar and almost voluptuous. He had a conviction that the hour of skilled, intense exercise had actually quickened the flow of his blood, made him more alive.

He played again the following week. It corrected a deficiency in his life he had felt but not quite recognized. It didn't occur to him, though, that the reason he felt better after squash was because he was taking his father's advice, and getting some exercise, if not every day, at least once a week. And he found that he liked Browne, even though Browne was his father's agent, and liked the Ivy Club locker room, that was filled with the sound of familiar accents and talk about people and places and things he had been hearing about all his life.

CHAPTER THIRTY-ONE

T HE war in Europe faltered, then ended. On VE Day, Avery and the others went down to Times Square and watched the crowds that tried to turn the fact of peace into a personal experience. The existence of victory did not seem real; it seemed to have no general meaning. But it had personal meaning to Avery. It meant that his father would be coming home, and that his false autonomy might be called into question. The actual thought of his father's return frightened him, for himself and for his mother; it seemed to him that if his father were in the house every day that the secret behind his mother's madness would somehow be brought out of concealment, and the thought of this filled him with a dark, classic anticipation of murder, a fatal, Orestian conviction of vengeance, tragedy and death.

That night he dreamed his father was dead and he was attending the funeral, together with a crowd of implacable strangers, people in stylized uniforms whose faces meant nothing to him. He approached the stiff gray casket and looked down into the still, familiar face. He tried to utter the words that formed in his mind: *Father,* he wanted to say, *Father, I forgive you.* But the words that come from his lips in the dream were not the words in his mind. He fell to his knees before his father's body and cried: "Father! Father, forgive me!" But the dead dream face did not alter its expression. The silent lips were condemnation. There was no appeal. He remained on his knees, staring at the face, until at last masked men came and carried the coffin away, leaving him in empty prayer before the bare trestles with the flowers banked behind them. He woke up, terrified, calling out into the night: *Mother! Mother!*

The next day the dream refused to dissolve or be shaken off, but remained vividly in his mind, interrupting his consciousness with surrealistic force. He found two parts of his spirit engaged in bitter debate, one doggedly insisting that he cared not a damn whether his father lived or died, returned home or stayed away, provided he left him in peace and made no threat to his safety—the other contradicting this and reminding him that he did care very much indeed. He passed the day in morbid brooding. Toward evening it occurred to him that he was stale, physically stale. He called Browne and made a date for squash, playing so viciously that Browne stopped at the end of a game and said reproachfully, "Good Lord, Avery, there's no money up. We both know you can beat me two times out of three. What are you trying to prove."

Avery shook his head. The heat of the court, and the sweat, and the way he had forced his muscles, had relieved some of the tension. "I know," he said. "I'm sorry." He tossed the ball into the air and served, deliberately checking the speed of his game so that Browne could win.

Afterward, refreshed by a shower and considerably relaxed, he laughed at Browne's jokes and listened to Browne's high-echelon gossip about the end of the war in Asia. "Two years, they say, maybe three," Browne explained. "It's a matter of the Home Islands. The Japs will defend them to the last man."

Avery nodded. It was the war in Europe that concerned him, and the war in Europe was over.

"I understand your Dad's going to stay on in Germany," Browne said. "I suppose he's going to try to teach the Old Hun some Town Meeting democracy."

Avery's heart contracted and his head went numb with blood. They were sitting in the lounge of Browne's club and all around him people were talking, the buzz of voices crowding his nerves like a swarm of summer flies. Then he let out his breath and said, trying to sound unconcerned, "Oh? I hadn't heard."

Browne saw that he had made a gaffe. "Oh, well," he said awkwardly, "I may be mistaken. I just heard it from a fellow downtown who had talked to some people in the Pentagon, just before the Germans surrendered. It may be just talk."

"Could be," Avery said. "Could be one of those rumors."

But the man who had talked to the Pentagon people and then talked to Browne had been right. A few days later, Avery got a letter that told him his father would be in Frankfurt for at least six months, perhaps a year. *"They seem to think that a man who has had considerable business as well as military experience will be useful during the occupation,"* his father wrote. *"Of course I am glad to do my part. Beating them in the field was only half the job. Now we have to teach them to live like human beings again."*

Avery read the letter, then read it again. He knew that his father had left the desk in Grosvenor Square, to fight through France and Germany, to be wounded, heroic and decorated, not because he had been made to do it, but because he could not bear the thought of being a soldier who did not fight. And the one thing that he understood now, with stunning clarity, was that his father remained abroad at his own suggestion, or at least with his own consent—that he could come home if he wanted to, and that he did not want to. He was evading the issue at home, postponing it, hoping perhaps that it would wear out or disappear before he finally came back to Hull, and persuading himself that this failure to take responsibility was nothing more than his duty. He was corrupting his own honor, because he was afraid to face the ruin that his own honor had in part created. At first Avery felt resentment. It seemed unfair. It meant that he would have to go on trying to do his father's job when he went home on week ends and during holidays from school, that he would go on taking the rap for his father's blindness and neglect.

Then, as he thought it over, it seemed to him that his father, by clinging to the stars on his shoulders and the medal ribbons over his heart, was revealing a desperate, terrible weakness, a disinclination to face reality much greater than his own, more deep-going and more serious, and never to be overcome. It made his father seem less formidable. He felt a kind of pity for him, an oblique, partial, but quite real apprehension of his predicament.

And he understood, with a sense of depression, that his father would not come home from Europe as long as there was an excuse for remaining away from Hull and the tragedy at Hull—any excuse whatever.

A few days later, he had dinner at Browne's apartment on Park Avenue. He was given a steak cut from a steer Browne had imported from Texas on the hoof, and after dinner Browne gave him port from a heavy crystal decanter and offered him a beautifully tailored cigar.

"You were right about my father," Avery said. "He's going to be on the Occupation Staff."

Browne nodded. "I envy your Dad, you know," he said, looking around the luxurious room. "I wish I could have afforded to go. But I was in the navy in 1918, and I'm afraid one war is all my exchequer could stand." He paused, appraising his cigar, then said, "Your father must be having a perfectly wonderful time."

Avery nodded. "I suppose he is," he said. "I suppose he's enjoying himself very much."

He said this rather bitterly and Browne looked up sharply. "Oh, I don't mean he's not there to do a job," Browne said. "It's just that, well, it must be exciting."

"I Know what you mean," Avery said.

He understood that what Browne said was true. For his father the war was a variety of luxury, like fox hunting, or breeding animals for show, the kind of adventure a well-to-do man decided he wanted and could afford. His father was indulging himself with the war, and using it as an escape from home.

"You know, Avery, you should be proud of your father," Browne said, leaning forward to give himself a third glass of port. "He's a gentleman, an American gentleman, in the finest sense of the word. It's a dying breed. We get plenty of clever ambitious fellows, and plenty of the Riviera riffraff sort of thing, the New York Stork Club kind of thing, you know. But there are darned few like your Dad."

Browne was slightly mulled by the wine and taken by a mild attack of manly sentimentality. He reminisced about Avery's father when Avery's father had been at Yale, and Avery's attention wandered back to Browne's original observation that General John M. van A. Hollister of Hull was a gentleman.

It had never occurred to him to question that fact, but he had passed a good many hours speculating on the possible chemistry of gentility—his father's and his own. His father was not like Caldecott Browne. Browne placed value on the superficial attributes of class, but had long since abandoned any firm belief in the importance of things in which his father believed and would believe in to the death. His father was as simplistic about what he believed was honor and duty as one of the Barons of Runnymede. Browne had been right in his observation that men like his father were becoming rare. They were, in fact, becoming extinct. But his father was only once or twice removed from the archetypal, and superficial reproductions of him flourished in a thousand law offices, a hundred bond houses, a score of advertising agencies, and so on—men who had, at certain schools and in certain clubs, been advised that they were gentlemen, who dressed themselves like gentlemen, and thought thus of themselves, but who had no deep conviction of duty, no sense of noblesse oblige, who were, in fact, behind their accents, indistinguishable from the mass of conclusive nongentility to which they considered themselves superior. They wanted the privileges without the duties, and the deference without performance. In the old horse cavalry, he had been told, estate was expressed in order of feeding, the horses being fed first, then the men, and last of all the officers. In return for this and for bravery, the officers understood that they were entitled to the salute and what went with it. But these young men, and other men, like Caldecott Browne, were at the trough before anyone else. It would not have occurred to them to have waited until the horses and men had been looked after. Yet they wanted the salute. His father had always wanted the salute, from his wife and his children and the generality of mankind, and Avery until now had always believed that he was prepared to earn it.

"Yes, Avery," Browne said hazily, "your father is one in a million. One in a million."

"Oh, hell," Avery said, suddenly irritated with Browne, "he's probably got some schmeklige fräulein on the hook, trying to demonstrate the fact that the democratic method of fornication is superior to the National Socialist. The war's over, for God's sake. The fighting's finished."

Browne looked up reproachfully. "That's a hell of a thing to say, Avery," he said.

"Yes, isn't it?" Avery said. He got up and said good night, and left Browne baffled and offended. But when he got off the subway at Columbia he called from a booth and apologized.

"That's all right, old man," said Browne. "I understand how you feel. I know exactly how you feel."

"The hell you do," Avery said to himself, walking back to the dormitory. "The hell you do."

CHAPTER THIRTY-TWO

EARLY in June, when he finished basic training, Dennis McCoy came home on leave. He and Avery had dinner together in an expensive restaurant downtown, a big, rather vulgar restaurant where the food was good and incredibly expensive. When the bill came, Avery offered to pay his share, but Dennis wouldn't take his money. "This is on my old man," he said. "He has a charge account here."

Avery watched him sign the bill with a pencil stub the waiter brought, and add the figure 5 to the total. "What's that?" he asked.

"The tip," said Dennis.

"Five bucks!"

Dennis laughed. "If you don't come from an old and well-heeled family," he said, "it's better to leave large, vulgar tips."

They went on to a bar, instead of going to Dennis' apartment, as Avery had expected they would do. Avery had a glass of beer and Dennis had whiskey. The whiskey seemed to make him moody, and Avery felt a gap between them that came partly from Dennis' suntan uniform.

"Are you going to O.C.S.?" he asked.

Dennis shook his head. "I had a chance. Infantry O.C.S. But I wouldn't take it on a bet. The army's all right as long as you're an enlisted man. Obey their silly rules, and you can do as you please. An officer has no privacy."

It was impossible for Avery to understand how anyone could prefer being an enlisted man to being a commissioned officer.

And though it made him ashamed of himself, he knew that he would feel better if Dennis went to O.C.S.

"Will you go overseas now?" he said.

McCoy shrugged. "I guess so," he said. "I don't know. I just do what they tell me. Mouth closed, bowels open. You know." He grinned and punched Avery's shoulder, and there was a flash of the old Dennis. "Don't mind me," he said. "If I'm kind of screwy it's because I'm worried about my old man."

"What's the matter?" Avery asked.

"He's in a jam," Dennis said. "A bad jam." He paused, then said a little bitterly, "I guess he backed the wrong general."

"I'm sorry," Avery said.

"What the hell," Dennis said. "When you get out of your own league, you're bound to get hurt. He could handle things, here in New York. Down there in Washington you run into another kind of character. They operate under another kind of morality. They don't mean exactly what they say."

"How bad a jam is he in?" said Avery.

"About as bad as they come," said Dennis. "He'll go to jail, I guess."

"Jesus! You think he'll really go to *jail*?"

Dennis nodded. "Five years anyway," he said. "Maybe ten." He was trying to be dead pan, but Avery knew him; he could feel the anguish that was held just beneath the surface.

"The funny thing is," Dennis said, "the old man isn't a crook. He's a politician, but he isn't a crook. He made his money, every cent of it—with his hands at first, then in the contracting business. He was a hod carrier on the Woolworth Building when they were putting it up. Just a flannel-mouthed kid from Tyrone. And then he went in for himself, with a thousand bucks he won in a poker game. I don't think he ever had his hands on a crooked dollar in his life. But some of his friends are crooks. And he's the one who will go to jail."

"But what did he do?" Avery asked. "You can't put a man in jail for nothing."

"He introduced one man to another," Dennis said. "At least, that's what he told me when I saw him this afternoon, before he went down to Washington."

"Well, that isn't a crime, is it?"

"It is if one of the men makes airplanes that cost too much and the other man buys them for the government," Dennis said.

"Jesus, Dennis, I'm sorry," Avery said. "I'm sorry as hell."

"Yeah," Dennis said. "So am I. And I can't figure it. The old man was honest. He didn't cheat anybody, or hurt anybody. He didn't steal. He didn't tell lies. But his whole damn life was a lie. There was something left out, and I can't figure it. Maybe I'll get to it, out there in the Pacific."

A few days later, it was in the papers. There was a picture of Tip McCoy on the front page of the *Daily News,* and Avery was glad Dennis wasn't in New York to see it. He sat down and tried to write Dennis, to tell him how he felt, but he couldn't. Then he had a letter from Dennis, with a San Francisco A.P.O. number, and knew that Dennis had shipped overseas. He had another letter, from Okinawa, and gathered that Dennis had been moved up into the battle area a few days after he reached the islands. It seemed incredible to him that Dennis was already in combat, five months after he entered the army. He worried about him. Then the hideous bombs were dropped and the war ended, and he realized that Dennis was not going to be killed.

CHAPTER THIRTY-THREE

THE first Christmas after the war was the saddest in Avery's memory, sadder even than the one last year, when the war had been going badly. He went home out of a sense of duty, though he would rather have stayed in New York. There was a tree, and a package from his father, and Annie tried, but the holiday seemed grim, a kind of accusation. The day itself was gray, the sky heavy with snow that refused to fall, the air cold and very damp. The trees on the lawn looked as if they were made of cast iron.

They all went to church together, Avery and his mother and Annie, and in a pew near them sat Mrs. Choate with her little girl, the two of them looking like a kodachrome magazine cover. Avery felt a tingling in his blood as he experienced quick, stabbing recollection of the bright afternoon on the hill, when she had opened her halter and let him kiss her breasts. He detested her. He watched her singing piously, smiling down at her child, and had a burning memory of her breasts, that sagged away from one another, and the fringe of hair underneath her arms that he had seen when he leaned over her. As they filed out of church, she spoke to his mother, then smiled at him and said, "How's college, Avery? I understand you're in New York, instead of at Yale, or some proper place. Good for you."

"It's all right, thank you," he said stiffly. "Mostly navy, you know, and I'm just a civilian."

She smiled again and passed on.

"Really, Avery, you were quite rude," his mother said sharply, in the tone she would have used to a child. "I hope college isn't going to spoil your manners. You were always such a nice little boy."

"Sorry, mother," he said absently.

Seeing Mrs. Choate had disturbed him, plunging his mind into a dark channel of sex. During the last few weeks he had been besieged by sex. A trivial encounter could set him burning— the touch of a waitress' hand as she served him, being pressed against a woman in the subway, the sight of a bright silk shaft of leg as a girl climbed aboard a bus, a phrase in a book, or movie, or a brutal phrase overheard on the street. The whole area of physical desire was humiliating to him, tortuous and degrading, yet tantalizing, so that sometimes in his bed he deliberately brought sex to his mind, and lay there in the dark, half frantic and half revolted, inspired with pain, yet unwilling, or unable, to seek relief because of the biting shame that would follow. He was seventeen, and it seemed to him a sign of some fundamental deficiency that he had not yet had a woman.

The whole context boiled up in him as he followed his mother into the car. Driving home, Avery at the wheel, he was bumped against his mother and her perfume excited him. He was ashamed that his repulsive conjectures were linked to the smell of his mother's cosmetics and to the soft flesh of her thighs and shoulders that pressed against him as the car lurched. The realization filled him with self-loathing, so that when they reached the house he went upstairs and drew a scalding bath, scrubbing his body with a stiff brush until the skin was red, finding the pain of the harsh bristles punitive and desirable.

He lay in the tub as the water cooled and inspected his body, that danced in the shuddering water, disgusted with himself, attacked by imaginations of his mother, and David Fearing, and Bell's mother, and Mrs. Choate, and the sour-smelling Portuguese girl who had been on Bell's boat, all confused in his mind, a morass of flesh, naked, obscene, and in movement.

He was filled with a fear of sex that seemed to infect his body and soul. It did not help to remember the advice of the young Physical Education instructor, who had told the class: "Don't forget, fellows, everybody has a sewer in his mind. Everybody. Even the Pope in Rome. It's not the sewer you have to worry about. It's keeping the outlet open. Not letting it get bottled up inside."

He got out of the tub and dried himself with a rough towel that had his father's initials woven into it. He took a perverse satisfaction in using his father's things, his razor, socks, towels, handkerchiefs, as if in this way he were secretly displacing his father.

After he had put on his shirt and trousers, he went into his father's bedroom and opened the long closet, that had two doors. The sharp, realistic odor of camphor that sprang from the closet broke his mood and he felt less depressed. He ran his hands over the rack of suits that hung like suits in a clothing store, then took down a coat that his father had often worn when he was at home. It was made of greenish tweed ordered from a weaver in the Hebrides and smelled, as his father had explained, of the peat fires that warmed the weavers' cottages. It was a handsome coat, with great side pockets cut to hold a small bird. He slipped into it and went to the mirror. The image of his face above his father's coat was disturbing, but he did not take the coat off. It was loose across the shoulders and too long, but it occurred to him that a tailor could easily recut it. He had a new tweed coat of his own and another that was good enough for class, but he had a sudden fierce desire to own this coat, or at least to wear it. He walked away from the mirror to his father's chest and pulled out the right-hand top drawer. There was a black leather box, lined with white satin, in which his father kept his dress jewelry, a pair of gold cuff links, and a gold collar pin that he sometimes wore. Avery put the pin into his necktie, pinning the tie to his shirt with it, as his father sometimes did. All this time he felt a pleasurable tension that he could not at first understand, but that, as he stood prowling through the drawer, became centered in the odor that rose from the chest, a familiar, exciting odor: his father's smell. Recognition of the smell struck him with force, and it seemed for an instant as if his father stood there in the room with him. He felt the same compound of fear, affection, awe and glamour he had always felt as a child when he entered this room and his father was here, standing at the mirror fixing his tie, or seated on the little needlepoint stool, coaxing his feet into his polished English shoes, with the aid of a tortoise shell shoehorn that was nearly two feet long. He had a passionate longing for his father, a need for him, and the word "Daddy" came to his lips without thought.

Then he turned away from the chest and went back to the closet, intending to put the tweed coat on its hanger. Instead, he riffled through the rank of dark sleek suits, the ones his father wore when he went to his offices in Hartford, and ran his hand down the soft lapel of his father's tail coat, reading the romantic English label that was sewn to the pocket: F. Lonsdale & Son, Savile Row, London W1., and, in a space provided, his father's name, written in a curious foreign hand: Mr. John M. Hollister, Hull, Connecticut, U.S.A. October, 1937.

He felt an ache for the past and a sense of loss. He wished passionately that there had been no war, to kill his brother, remove his father, and bring his cousin into the house so that his mother had betrayed herself. He wished that he were at New Haven instead of New York and that his father were here at home, to tell him how to go about making a success of himself at Yale, as he had told Morgan, to tell him what to do about girls, as he had told Morgan, to be his friend, as he had been Morgan's friend.

He wore his father's coat at dinner. His mother looked curiously at it, but said nothing, though he understood that it had reminded her of his father, for she began to speak of him, quite lucidly at first, then losing contact with reality and placing him back in France with his regiment, in the other war. She looked across the table at Avery beseechingly, then said in a voice that resembled her normal voice, "We're all so selfish, Avery. So dreadfully selfish. We think of nothing but ourselves. It's what causes all the trouble in the world, dear, you know. All the trouble in the world is caused by self-love."

"Yes, mother."

He half listened to what she was saying and went on with his dinner. She was now involved in one of her curious, half-lighted monologues, in which her observations often had an odd, oblique ring of importance, of truth.

"You see, Avery, it's all the ego. We are all corrupted by it. When a man appears who rises above it, he becomes a saint. Pissarro. There was a saint."

She began to weep for poor Pissarro, who hadn't had a penny to buy a stamp to write to the son he loved. That winter she wept in succession for poor Pissarro, poor Cézanne, poor misguided Gauguin, poor mad van Gogh, poor depraved Lautrec, poor arthritic Renoir, at the end of life, poor Mary Cassatt, all the pauvres of the Salon des Refusées. She did not weep for poor Braque or poor Picasso or poor Juan Gris or poor Modigliani, though she would have, had they entered her mind. But they did not.

He looked across the table at her, marveling that an illness that destroyed so much inside could show so little on the surface. She was like a person murdered by some mysterious method that leaves no mark on the body or residue of poison in the blood. Her world had been smashed, and she had been smashed along with it, but she was like an empty, unused, beautiful room in some museum, still lovely, still enchanting, still graceful, but without function. He was moved by pity, an almost detached, aesthetic pity, rather than the specific pity one might be expected to feel for a stricken mother. As the waves of emotion poured over him, he realized that the sensation was not altogether unpleasant, and perceived that he was responding to his tragic mother in the way one is supposed to respond to a work of art, that what he experienced was not pity for her but a controlled emotion that was self-rewarding.

She was no longer the mother who had borne him in her body, given birth to him in pain, fed him from her breast, saved him when he was ill to death, defended him when he was weak, and then deserted him when he was almost, but not quite, strong enough to be abandoned.

She was a symbol, dispassionate as marble, of all the lovely lost dreams smashed.

She had clung to her lost causes—to art, to heaven on earth, to peace, and to faith in the good, the true and the beautiful. The broken remnants of all these were like shattered porcelain around her now, but there was too much serenity on her face. Even when she wept for the dead French artists, she wept softly and without passion, and the tears scarcely scarred her face.

It was disturbing.

It seemed to Avery that she must be like one of those huge puff-balls one sometimes finds in the woods, great things with a surface immaculate as ivory, but filled, when you break them, with festering rot and thousands of hideous parasitical grubs.

What went on inside his mother could not be guessed by looking at her face. But sometimes she gazed across the hills with a cryptic, wronged expression in her eyes, and seemed about to speak, to permit some of the festering rot to pour out in words. But when she did lose her grip, it was never to erupt. She simply receded, a layer further down, remaining in her room, in her bed, staring at the ceiling and sometimes softly singing to herself, or talking, but more often just staring, silently, for several days, until, one day, she would rise from the bed, dress herself, and appear downstairs as if nothing had happened.

This Avery learned from Annie McBain. And he learned too that Doctor Parks had called back the triptych of specialists from Hartford.

"There are certain things she doesn't want to remember," Annie explained. "She shuts them out of her mind. The tall doctor from Hartford told me that sometimes people who've seen a dreadful thing will go blind for a time. Or people who've done a dreadful thing, say, with the right hand, will go paralyzed in that hand. Or people who've heard something awful will go deaf, and so on. It's just a way the mind has of defending itself, you might say."

"Do you think it's Morgan she doesn't want to remember?" Avery asked.

Annie shook her head. "It's not Morgan. It's something else that's preying on her mind, something different." She caught his hand in a grip strong as a policeman's. "Sometimes she loses track altogether. She seemed to think, the other day, when you came, that you weren't Avery at all, but your sister, the wee one that died before you were born. She seemed to think that you, that is, not you, really, but your little sister, had been got into trouble by a soldier, and that we must all stand by the poor thing, since it wasn't her fault, but the fault of the war."

"God, Annie," he said. "She must be crazy. She must be insane."

Annie's hand tightened on his arm. "Don't say that, Avery," she said. "Don't say that."

They stood in the old familiar kitchen, that looked the same and smelled the same as it had when he was a little boy and ate his dinner there with her. This gave Annie the advantage a person has on his home grounds. The smells of the kitchen, the gleaming lights on the copper, the familiar, friendly old black stove, recalled chidhood and dependence on her, adoration of her.

"Avery," she said gently, looking straight into his eyes, "don't turn your heart against your mother. You'll regret it, when she's gone and it's too late. Mark my words, laddie, you'll regret it. You'll never forgive yourself."

She was right; he was losing his mother, his love for her, and he hated it. "What can I do?" he asked. "Annie, what can I do?"

She touched his cheek with her finger tips, then his lips.

"You can show her you love her, son," she said. "She's starved for love as a puppy. She wants love more than she wants food or sleep or the pills that fellow brings, that don't seem to work any more. She needs something to be sure of. Something she can believe in, that won't just blow away, the way everything else has blown away like smoke in the wind, her whole life, and whatever it meant."

"Annie, I can't," he said desperately. "I've tried, and I can't. It's no use."

She put her arms around him, and her old cheek was next to his. "Avery, lovey," she said softly, "what have they done to you? You were such a sweet child, such a darling, so filled with love."

"I'm not a child any more," he said. "I'm not a child any more."

She touched his cheek. "You don't need words, or education, for what's wanted in this house," she said. "You could let a dog know you loved him, or a horse, just by the tone of your voice, just by the way you move around, just by the way you breathe."

He turned and went out of the house, into the biting January night, looking off at the stars through the gap in the hills, through which he had watched the sun come up, the day after Morgan had been killed.

No doubt what Annie had said was true.

But he did not love a horse or a dog, and he no longer clearly loved his mother. It was hard enough for him to prevent the loathing and disgust he often felt from boiling over like lava. He saw his mother as destroyed and useless, to herself, to him, and to the world. That she was his mother at all was nothing more than an accident, for him, an unfortunate accident.

But this he could not explain to Annie McBain.

He could not explain it to anyone, even to himself, for when he forced his mind toward the truth, his mind suggested that he blamed his mother for failing to do something that was beyond her power. He blamed her for not being responsible, for not having turned David away, or at least in the end made his father go to New York and find David in the Ritz Hotel, and smash his face until it was bloody and unhandsome and unlike his own face, or his father's or Morgan's. He blamed her for being what she was, but that was like blaming the rain for being wet.

He had loved his mother, and now he didn't, and the lack of love for her weakened him.

He had looked up the word love, and the dictionary had informed him that love was *a strong or passionate attraction for a person of the opposite sex.* Then it had said: *sexual passion, or desire, or its gratification.* And then: *a feeling of warm personal attachment or affection, as for a friend, or between friends, parent, child, etc.*

Proximity, chemistry, habit, sex.

He shook his head.

Love was what he had seen on Annie's face a few minutes ago, when she had begged him to love his mother as she loved her, and then without any question at all, forgiven him because she understood that he could not. He stood in the cold, watching the stars, and was swept by the realization that he loved no one in all the world in the way Annie loved him and his mother, and perhaps even his father too, and that he seemed to be incapable of loving anyone in that way, totally and without question. The knowledge frightened him. He could not escape the suggestion that his lack of love was due to a lack within himself, so that he was struck again by the old suspicion that there was something unnatural in him, something left out or added, that set him apart from others.

He went into the house and sat by the fire. Why had he not, he asked himself, been able to see the fraud in the beginning?

Why had he not been able to say: "Sure. It's a phony. The whole thing is stated backward, in order to make it harder, but once you find out that dishonesty's the best policy, you should be in like Flynn."

That was what Angus would have said, or, in different words, what Dennis would have said, and it was what Roger Bell would have said. He cast his mind back to the summer before last, realizing that Roger Bell had known all along what he had discovered so painfully. Yet Roger had a third-rate mind, while his own mind was first-rate. How had Bell understood that the whole structure was a fake and not to be taken literally, that it was possible for your mother to be a damned whore and fornicate with your schoolmate's cousin, and yet for life to go on, right on in its usual pattern? How had stupid Roger Bell understood without being told, what he was in the process of learning, to the accompaniment of pain?

The next day he went back to college, a day before the holiday ended. He couldn't stand the house. Seeing Mrs. Choate in church, and then being aroused by the smell of his mother's perfume had been like turning over a stone. The day after he got back to school, he sat in Angelo's with Breitbart and Herb Klein and a thin cool-looking boy named Gowen, who had already been in the army. "Do you know a cathouse, Freddie?" he asked. "A real low-down whorehouse?" He took it for granted that if anyone at Angelo's would know, it would be Breitbart. But Breitbart shook his head.

"I know one," Gowen said. "But it's real low down. Way low."

Klein wouldn't go, but Avery and Gowen and Breitbart went, taking a cab up to Harlem. The brothel was on the first floor of a hideous brownstone tenement, and a grave-faced dignified Negro woman let them in. "Rest your coats, gentlemen," she said, leading them through a narrow hall that smelled of must and of human copulation, to a tiny parlor that contained a rubber plant, a scabrous carpet, a fringed lamp that shed a lewd light, and a horsehair sofa with a list to starboard, on which sat three painted women, wearing slack kimonos. Two of the women were white and the third was colored. They stood up and stripped, one by one, turning while the boys watched. Avery's heart pounded and his throat tightened. He could not take his eyes away from the hair on the Negro woman's body. Suddenly he felt he was going to be sick and turned blindly, stumbling in the dark through the narrow hall until he reached the door. He lurched to the curb and vomited, holding his stomach. A big self-confident Negro man approached him and stopped, "What's the matter, boy?" he said. "Had more'n your share?" He held Avery's waist in his hands while Avery finished being sick, holding him the way a parent might hold a child over the rail of a ship.

"Thanks," Avery said finally. "Thanks."

He walked east toward the lighted avenue and found a cab in front of an all-night restaurant. The sour taste of vomit was in his mouth, and the smell nearly made him sick again. He could not get the sharp focus of the brothel out of his mind. It was a caricature of his worst imaginings.

But when Breitbart came back to the dormitory, boasting about his achievement, Avery was ashamed of himself; he wished he had the stomach to go through with what had been his idea to begin with.

"God," he said. "I thought they were awful."

"Well, hell, Avery," Breitbart said, "what did you expect? A nineteen-year-old Wellesley girl?"

Afterward, Avery remembered the address Browne had given him. It would probably be a good place, with nice furniture and girls who looked like ordinary girls you would see on the street. But he knew he would never have the nerve to use it now. He took the paper out of his wallet and tore it up and threw it away.

CHAPTER THIRTY-FOUR

URING his second year at college, he found himself dining with the Brownes three or four times a month. They were a break with his routine, and the only one that presented itself. Sometimes he went to the theater with them, serving as escort to Browne's daughter Ginny, who was fifteen, and in her second year at Brearley, filled with indolent contempt for the war that had just ended, for her family, for education, for everything except herself and her collection of early jazz records. She was the kind of invulnerable girl that had always been able to put him at a disadvantage, just by ignoring him. Nevertheless, one night he called her and asked her to go to the movies with him. He was rather surprised when she said, "All right. If you feel like it."

Sitting beside her in the darkened theater, he looked away from the screen and studied her face, which was set in the professionally bored expression of a fashion photographer's model. He played with the idea of making some kind of pass at her, then remembered her father's little lecture on the subject of prostitutes and decided against it. He simply sat, watching the dull story on the screen, and made no move toward her at all. But in the taxi, on the way back to the Brownes' apartment, she put up her mouth to be kissed. He kissed her and tried to put his hand on her breasts, but she pushed him away. She had worked out a kind of table of rewards—so many kisses, so many caresses.

During that spring he went out with her half a dozen times. There was no relationship. He went out with her because he was

TRIAL BY DARKNESS

bored, and because it seemed more normal to him to have some kind of girl.

"Does Ginny ever talk to you?" Browne asked him one day. "Does she ever give you any idea of what goes on in her mind?"

"Not much," he said. "You know kids."

Browne shook his head. "They're all alike, these youngsters. They've had the world handed to them on a silver platter, but they simply aren't interested."

"It's partly the war," Avery said. "They feel left out."

"Left out!" Browne said. "She simply refuses to take any interest in anything except a piano player named Mead Lux Lewis."

Avery laughed. But it occurred to him that Ginny Browne might be a lot smarter than he gave her credit for being. The next time he was out with her, he said, "What are you going to do, Ginny, when you get out of college?"

"I'm not going to college," she said. "There isn't anything I want to learn in college."

"Well then, when you get old enough to do what you please," he said.

"I do what I please now," she said. "Except I don't have a boat of my own."

They were in a little restaurant on Madison Avenue that had a soda fountain in front. Ginny's face was reflected in the black glass table top so that he had to see it whether he looked up or down. It was a face that had cost perhaps forty thousand dollars to produce, and that would cost that much more before it and its owner were publicly bartered in St. Thomas's Church and Caldecott Browne got off the hook.

"But for the love of mike, Ginny," he said, "don't you want to *be* somebody?"

She looked blandly at him, then at the top of her ice cream soda. "Well, I am somebody already," she said.

237

"Oh, Ginny, for Christ's sake!" he said, raising his voice, so that a waitress looked at him and frowned. "Do you have to put on this cow act?"

"I'm not putting on an act," she said. "You just don't interest me, that's all. You don't know anything I want to know."

"Well, why the hell do you go out with me then?" he asked.

"Well, I don't know," she said. "You asked me."

In the taxi he went through the routine of kissing her, of squeezing her breast, once, twice, thrice, and then being pushed away, and finally moving away from her, so their bodies didn't touch.

"Ginny, do you hate me?" he said. He wondered whether she had any reaction to him at all.

"No," she said. "You've never done anything to me. Why should I hate you?"

He left her at her apartment house and took the bus back to college, frustrated and confused. It was impossible for anyone to be as indifferent to him as she pretended to be.

But of course it was perfectly possible, as he realized later, in his bed. He remembered little girls at school dances who had been impervious as leather, for whom he simply had not existed. At such moments, on the sidelines, watching the same girl brighten up when she danced with someone else, he had always been drowned in humiliation, filled with a need to shout: ME! ME! ME! THIS IS ME! and to pound his chest. It was insufferable to be ignored. It made him feel less than human.

It was a bad spring for him. He needed a girl to walk with in the warm night, to hold by the hand and kiss in the dark. But he had no girl and did not know how to go about getting one. He envied the veterans back from the war who were coming into the college, united by their common experience and by the resentment they held in common toward the world that had cheated them of youth. He felt friendless, and it seemed to him he must be being punished for something he had done or failed to do.

He searched his mind and decided in the end that if he had a friend at all, it was probably Professor Douminoff, who that year was teaching him Differential Equations. Douminoff was the one person he knew who seemed to confirm his faith in himself, that was under attack too often by his environment and the accidents of time. One day he stopped by at Douminoff's office, waiting on a bench until Douminoff had finished with the student who preceded him. When he entered the little room, Douminoff looked up, smiling pleasantly.

"Yes, Hollister? Something I can do?"

He took a chair beside the professor's desk. The room was plain as the field office of a construction superintendent, furnished with an old desk, two chairs, and a cheap wooden case filled with textbooks, the bright jacket of a modern novel standing out in the files of texts like a fashion model at a Quaker meeting.

"Well sir, I don't know," he said.

"Has it anything to do with Differential Equations?" Douminoff asked, smiling. "I'll try to answer anything you throw me on that subject. God I leave to Father Ford, and sex to the Department of Physical Education. One must draw the line somewhere, you know."

Avery smiled. As a matter of fact he would have liked to have asked about both God and sex, but what he said was, "Well, sir, what I really want to find out is whether I have any talent for mathematics, I guess."

Douminoff looked curiously at him, seeming to be making a judgment, then took a supple ivory ruler from his desk and bent it like a sword. "A talent for mathematics, eh?" he asked, slapping his palm with the ruler. "Do you like it? Do you like calculus?"

"Yes, sir," Avery said.

"You do very well," Douminoff said. "Of course, that may just mean that you're an intelligent boy and work hard." He paused and frowned. "I can't answer your question, Hollister," he said.

"It's a question you'll have to answer for yourself, in three or four years' time, when you've had a chance to splash around in the subject a bit. Then you won't have to ask me, d'you see? You'll tell me." He bent the ruler, then released it and it sprang back into shape. He smiled and put it on his desk. "What are you going in for eventually, Hollister?" he asked. "Physics? Engineering?"

Avery shook his head. "No, sir," he said. "Neither one."

"Going to teach?"

"I hadn't thought about it," Avery said.

Douminoff smiled. "You know, Hollister," he said, "mathematics as a rich man's diversion has been out of fashion for several centuries. But maybe it'll come back." He narrowed his eyes, becoming serious, and asked, "Why did you come to college, Hollister? What did you expect to find, that would be worth the fees and three years' time?"

Avery frowned, staring at the ruler on Douminoff's desk, trying to frame an intelligent answer to this question. Had he gone to Yale, the reason for his going would have been clear enough. He would have gone to have learned to be like his father, because his father had gone there and his grandfather, and because it was necessary to go there in order to become a member of his father's senior society, that Morgan had not lived long enough to belong to, and to his father's fraternity. These were the things he had been told he would do when he went to college, and of course none of them could be done here, on Morningside Heights. When he tried to answer Douminoff's question, he faltered. "Well, sir," he said, "I don't know. I want to learn what I can learn. I want to go as far as my mind will take me."

"In mathematics?" Douminoff asked.

"Yes, sir."

"And what do you expect to find, when you've gone as far as your mind will take you?" the professor prodded gently.

Avery flushed, then said bluntly, "The truth. Part of it, anyway."

Douminoff nodded soberly and bent the ruler again. "Well, Hollister, I wish you luck," he said. "It's a noble search. I hope you won't be disappointed."

Avery got up. Hardly knowing why, he put out his hand and Douminoff took it, then stood up and put a hand on his shoulder. "I should warn you, Hollister," he said. "It's catching. Contagious."

"What, sir?" asked Avery.

Douminoff laughed.

"Education," he said. "Most people, fortunately, are immune. They can pass three years, four years, in a place like this, or even seven or eight years, and come out at the other end with their bills paid and their degrees in order and nothing about them changed, absolutely nothing. It's just a cosmetic process for them, a kind of academic lip rouge. But others—well, they catch the thing in their blood, and they're hooked, for there's no cure."

The final phrase struck a chord of memory. Avery walked across the campus when he left Douminoff's office, troubled by something familiar about it. Then he remembered that the parallel phrase had been one his father had used. He had asked his father about syphilis. "Is it true, sir," he had asked, "that the best thing to do is to shoot yourself?" That had been the consensus of Sixth Form opinion at Sturgis Manor. "Well, no," his father had said. "Not exactly. But of course, there's no real cure." His father's medical ignorance was revealed to him later, but the phrase stuck in his mind. "There's no real cure."

After his conversation with Douminoff, Douminoff took him under his wing, and he began to be asked to the bull sessions that took place in Douminoff's rooms. Douminoff lived in a kind of apartment in one of the dormitory buildings, made by knocking down some walls and throwing a pair of suites together. The rooms were ancient and leathery, like the rooms of Sherlock Holmes. There were books everywhere, and phonograph records, and half a dozen handsome paintings of the early cubist period. There was a sagging sofa with a greasy cover, usually harboring a deposit of dirty laundry. There was powerful black coffee, made over an alcohol flame, and powerful conversation—supplied by Douminoff himself.

The paintings bewildered Avery. He was surprised that Douminoff was interested in anything except the pursuit of a point on a path, and the pictures themselves affronted him, for they seemed without plan or meaning, and yet disturbed him, making him physically uneasy and complicating his moral adjustment.

"It is a matter of empathy, Hollister," Douminoff told him. "You must feel, not understand. Feel with the artist. With him, mind you. Not necessarily like him. Feel into the paint. Don't try to intellectualize. Just feel."

Douminoff took him downtown and gave him lunch at the Century Club, then gave him a guided tour through the antiseptic Museum. He looked at the painting, and after a while, miraculously, he felt. It was an intoxicating experience. When he and Douminoff came out of the gallery into the cool clean evening, he felt as though he had discovered a new kind of world, that marched beside his mathematical world—the other side of the medal.

"You know," he said, "my mother is an amateur painter. One day, I called her an artist, and she said, 'Oh, Avery, I'm not an artist. I'm not an artist at all.'" He walked on beside Douminoff for a few moments remembering the way his mother had said, *An artist speaks to the world, darling. I only speak to myself, and sometimes, in a whisper, to people who love me.* Then he said, "I never understood what she meant. But I do now."

Douminoff took his arm in an old-fashioned Victorian way, and said, "Hollister, you are a nice boy, but you look for too many simplicities. You want everything tidied up. Let me give you a piece of advice. Don't get any hifalutin notions. Mathematics is a fiction. So are those paintings. Mathematics has no existence—outside of the human mind. Leave these things to philosophers. Concern yourself with the number system and with analysis. That way you will never get into trouble."

"I didn't say anything about mathematics," Avery complained. "I was talking about my mother."

"You were about to discover a relationship between art and the calculus. I am trying to save you from embarrassing yourself, in front of yourself, later on."

Avery didn't protest. The next day, when he finished his work, he went back to the Museum and looked at the paintings again. After a time, he discovered he had latent, intuitive taste—a good eye. He found himself talking painting with Freddie Breitbart, who, this fall, was the only one left of the old guard from Angelo's, Angus having gone into the army, and Herb Klein having moved to the medical school.

At college he saw Douminoff and Breitbart, and for counterpoint he saw the Brownes. Sometimes the Brownes asked him to their big cocktail parties, as an unattached and decorative male, and at one of these he encountered his father's New York whore—Ivy Calder, from Litchfield, who had fought with his father in the legislature and then had lunch with him in the candle-lighted restaurant where he had gone with his mother. He wouldn't have recognized her, but she came across the room toward him, a martini glass in her hand, her gilt hair trembling just as it had when she made her speech. "You're John Hollister's boy," she said, making it sound like an accusation. "You don't remember me. I met you with your father once, at the state capitol in Hartford."

"Yes," he said. "I remember."

He was afraid of her. She asked him about college, and expressed regret about Morgan. Then she said casually, "I'm going to Germany, next week. I expect I'll see your father there. I'll tell him how well you're looking."

"You're going to *Germany?*" he said.

"Yes," she said brightly. "I'm on a United Nations Committee." She took a sip of martini. "Just for a few weeks," she said.

She shook hands with him and moved away; he watched her, in the crowd, remembering the day in Hartford with his father, and the antagonism toward her he had felt that night, when he got home. Then Browne came over to him and put a hand on his shoulder. "Saw you talking to Ivy," he said, looking across the room at her. "She's quite a gal. Quite a gal. Has a way of getting what she wants."

Avery nodded. "I guess she has," he said. "I wouldn't know."

He wasn't surprised, a few weeks later, to see a photograph in *Life* that showed his father and some other generals explaining the occupation to Mrs. Calder, or surprised that Mrs. Calder was smiling at his father and looking at him as if she owned him. Breitbart saw the photograph, and Avery said, surprised by his own vulgarity, "That's one of the advantages of being a general, Fritz. You can import your own shack job. You don't have to depend on the local talent, the way the lower ranks do."

Breitbart was shocked, and tried not to show it. "You upper classes," he said. "You mystify me."

"We are used to concubines," Avery said, determined to be sophisticated even if it made him vomit.

It was no use. He was fanatically jealous, and his pride was hurt. It gnawed at him. He had the irrational conviction that the whole thing had been arranged, including Mrs. Calder's appointment to the U.N. Committee, for the purpose of bringing his father's mistress to his father's place of duty. He took it as a sign of his father's guilt that there was no mention in his letters of Mrs. Calder's visit.

CHAPTER THIRTY-FIVE

I N OCTOBER, Dennis McCoy came back to New York, but not to stay. They went to Angelo's for dinner, and Avery listened while Dennis told him he wasn't coming back to college, but going up to the Canadian Arctic, as a lay brother in a Catholic mission to the Copper Eskimos.

It didn't penetrate.

It made no sense.

"Where did you get an idea like that?" he asked, when Dennis had finished.

"In Rome, a month ago."

"But you weren't in Europe," Avery said. "You were in the Pacific."

"I've been out of the service for three months," Dennis said. "I was here in New York for a few days, and then I went to Rome."

"You should have called me," Avery said.

"I didn't call anybody," Dennis said. "I didn't see anyone." He leaned forward, playing with a book of paper matches, striking one and watching it burn, then blowing it out. He looked thinner and harder than when Avery had seen him last, and there was a curious intensity about him. "I heard a story in the Pacific," he said, "about an American nun. A Sister of Charity. She was dressing the gangrenous wounds of a Chinese soldier, and a war correspondent was watching her. 'Sister,' he said, 'I wouldn't do that for a million dollars.' "

Avery frowned, then raised his eyebrows. "So?"

"So she said, 'Neither would I,' " Dennis went on. He paused, then said, "The first time I heard that story, I thought it was a phony. I thought of my mother, with her beads trailing in the booze, and of every fat-faced priest I'd ever seen in a shiny Buick, with a pot gut on him that must have cost fifty thousand dollars. Maybe it is a phony, for all I know. Maybe it never happened. But I believe it. And that story stays with me. That nun is as real to me as you are, even though I've never seen her in my life." He hesitated, then said, "It was that story that sent me to Rome. I wanted to find out something, about myself, and my old man."

"Did you?" Avery asked.

Dennis nodded. He lit another match, staring at the flame. "I found out what was left out of my old man's life. And out of mine, too. And maybe out of the fat-faced priest's."

"What?"

"God."

There was no courteous comment Avery could make on this. He looked down at the table, at his empty plate, that was smeared with spaghetti sauce that looked like blood. "But for Christ's sake, Dennis," he said finally, "You don't give a damn about the Eskimos."

"About the Eskimos, no. About their souls, yes."

Avery frowned, staring at his hands until they seemed disparate objects, detached from him. "But Dinny," he said finally, feeling for his words. "Do you believe in God? I mean, really?" He had abandoned even his family's dilute God when he was eleven years old, and decided that the Resurrection was an affront to his intelligence. He shared the general Columbia view that religion was a phantasy, conceived in the fear of death.

"Yes, Avery, I believe in God," Dennis said. "I believe in Him because I can feel Him. I feel Him in my room at night, when I'm alone."

"The way you feel a burglar?" Avery said.

"No. The way a child feels his mother," Dennis said.

Avery said nothing. He poured wine for himself and Dennis, and lit a cigarette. Then he said, "Well, if you feel that way, why don't you become a priest? You could go on a diet and drive a Ford. Or even a Crosley."

Dennis didn't smile, and didn't get angry.

"I'm not fit to be a priest," he said. "At least, not now. Maybe, after I've been up there for a few years, I'll feel different about it. I don't know."

"Do you really believe it?" Avery asked. "All the way?"

Dennis nodded. "All the way," he said.

"I envy you," Avery said. "I honest to God envy you."

But it wasn't true.

After they said good-bye and Dennis had disappeared into the subway, Avery walked back across the campus, but instead of going up to his room in Hartley Hall he went through an arch to Amsterdam Avenue and turned right, walking downtown to a point where the dome of St. John the Divine rose like a great malleable shadow against the night sky. All of his feeling about religion rose in his consciousness almost palpably, as his objections to Christ's Rising had surged up in him in Bible Class.

It was preposterous.

There was no God. At least, there was certainly no God in the terms of Dennis McCoy's Church, or the terms of this other church that rose before him in the darkness. Dennis was deceiving himself, perhaps because he must deceive himself or die, but the necessity, whatever it was, didn't make the deception less. Avery sat down on a fire plug, his eyes on the cathedral that wasn't finished, and the idiocy of Dennis' venture seemed architecturally expressed. It was absurd as erecting a building according to the methods of another century. Medieval. The expanding, exploding universe was all around him, he understood, visible in the night sky, and he knew, because he had been told, that out beyond his range of vision great stars larger than the sun were rushing off into space. He knew that the sun was cooling down and that within a predictable span of years the warm earth would be cold as the moon.

"Better minds than yours have believed it," someone at Colborn had told him, when he professed inability to believe in God or in God's Son. *"Better minds than yours have believed it."*

"No!"

He spoke to the night, then stood up, his body aching from the hard iron seat. He looked at the cathedral again, this time with enmity, then went back to his room. He took down his atlas and turned to the map of the Polar Regions, searching out with his finger tip the place Dennis was going to live.

"Coppermine," he said to himself. "Coppermine."

At last he found it, a speck on the map, a speck on the shore of the Arctic Ocean.

It was incredible.

He stared at the map, the blank bare sections to the north almost suggesting the naked wastes, and thought of Dennis, who was as urban as the Library pigeons. It was incredible. Then it occurred to him that Dennis was simply looking for adventure. That way it made sense, and he persuaded himself that it was the case, whether Dennis was aware of it or not. It was a presumptuous rationalization but it was better than nothing, and he certainly could not accept the simple, monolithic truth, which was that Dennis had found his God and fallen in love with Him.

PART 2
THE JOURNEY HOME

CHAPTER THIRTY-SIX

IN THE end it was Avery's mother who brought his father home, in the spring of his third year at college, the spring of 1947. She took one of the seven straight razors with which he had taught himself to shave and opened the veins of her wrists, then got into her marble tub that she had filled with warm, perfumed water. It was simple, classic, and effective. She was dead when Avery reached the house, and the undertaker's people had carried her off in a wicker basket that creaked when they moved it.

What affected him more than the half-apprehended fact of his mother's death, was Annie McBain's grief, which was total and nearly disabling. She looked as though some actual chemical change had occurred in her body; she seemed almost literally dissolved in grief. Yet she controlled it somehow and did what was necessary, even to the point of giving him food when he reached the farm in the middle of the night, in response to her telegram.

"The poor thing," she said. "The poor sad thing."

In the morning, Avery stood on the bright green grass, looking at the borders of his mother's garden. He made a conscious effort of the will toward sorrow, an effort to feel deep, personal, unique grief and bitter awareness of loss. He did not feel it. What he experienced was formal sadness of the kind that derives from music or landscape in a certain light. He looked at the spring flowers that were just coming into bloom and tears rose, but they were less for his mother than for himself. "I must be a monster," he said. "Inhuman."

Then his eyes fell and he saw that he wore his father's gold tie pin. He took it off and went into the house, up the stairs to his father's room, where he put it back into its box. Then he crossed the hall to his mother's room. For an instant, the persistence of her perfume and a slant of light through the filmy curtains that he associated with her, gave the illusion that she was there. The smooth bed, its pillow undisturbed, was an accusation. He saw her pink wool shawl, neatly folded on the arm of her chaise, and a lump rose in his throat. He turned and went out of the room, overcome. What flashed into his mind was memory of the day she had used a blunt word that had shocked him, and then forgotten she had used it. For a few moments recollection of her was intense. He could feel her, see her, as she had emerged from the house, smiling now, to go off with the Volunteer ladies in the imitation ambulance. He went into his room and picked up a book, but could not read it. He felt that he should be doing something, taking some action, but there was nothing to do. He sat, feeling a dull ache, and a formless, vagrant apprehension.

At dinner time there was a cable from Germany, and the next day he drove to the airport to meet his father. He had not seen him for nearly three years, and was prepared for some change in appearance. He was not prepared to see him look younger and more vigorous than when he had gone abroad. His father looked hard and tough and very very soldierly. He wore a battle jacket that exploited his figure, and there were new ribbons on his chest, under the blue enameled infantry badge he had gotten for himself in Normandy.

"Well, Avery?"

"Hello, father."

They shook hands and looked at one another for several seconds. He saw the tears in his father's eyes.

"Got the car, son?"

"Yes, sir. Would you like to drive?"

"No, son. You drive. I'm beat. Just beat up."

Avery pointed the car toward home. It was just coming on dark, and he used the headlights. He had learned to drive and gotten his license during his father's absence, and he was conscious of being judged.

"Hard time to drive," his father said. "Dusk. It's the worst time."

Avery nodded.

After a while, when they were on the highway, his father stared straight ahead, at the white line on the pavement, and said, not looking at him, "How did it happen, son? Was it her heart?"

Avery turned, then looked back at the road, realizing that his father had not been told that his mother had killed herself. It was not the kind of thing you cared to put in a cablegram. For a few seconds he said nothing but drove on, keeping his eyes on the white line.

"You're going too fast," his father said. "There's a mean curve, just ahead."

"Sorry," Avery said. He touched the brake a little too hard, so that the tires squealed and the car shuddered. "She killed herself," he said bluntly. "She killed herself with one of Grandpa's razors. The one for Thursday."

He saw his father's fists tighten.

"What?" his father demanded. "What did you say?"

He touched Avery's arm roughly and the car lurched, then swayed. Avery brought it to a stop and pulled up at the side of the road. It was at this moment that realization of his mother's death, and the irrevocable quality of it, struck him. He rested his forearms on the wheel, then turned and looked at his father.

"I'm sorry, sir," he said gently. "I forgot you didn't know. She killed herself. She cut her wrists with one of Grandpa's razors."

"Good God!" his father said. "Good Jesus Christ!"

The car throbbed beneath them and the reek of raw gasoline was liquid and sickening in the warm spring air. His father hit the palm of his hand with his fist. "Poor Nancy," he said, his voice choked. "Poor Nancy."

Avery put the car in gear and started slowly. They drove the rest of the way in silence. When they reached the farm, his father stood in the front door, staring at the heavy brass knocker that had his name carved into it, afraid to enter the house he had been born in. Avery felt sorry for him, and curiously senior. He reached around him and opened the door, then put a hand on his shoulder and followed him into the hall. In the living room, his father turned, looking at him appraisingly.

"You've grown," he said. "You're taller. Heavier."

"Yes, sir," Avery said. "I'm eighteen. Nearly nineteen."

His father nodded. "Yes. Yes," he said heavily. "So you are."

Their eyes met, and Avery saw an expression on his father's face that seemed to incorporate grief, exhaustion, and a plea for mercy, or compassion. At that instant, he had a sense that things might now be all right, that the tragedy might expurgate the quarrel between them. He reached out and touched his father's sleeve.

"Ah, Avery," his father said. "It's a damned shame."

"Yes, sir," he said. "It is."

They heard a sound and turned together. Annie stood in the doorway, wearing a black dress, her composure regained, but the look of age on her face startling to Avery and more so to his father, who stood motionless for a few seconds, seeming to be shocked, then crossed the room quickly and kissed her on the cheek.

"I'm sorry, General," Annie said. "I'm sorry."

Avery turned and went out of the house, understanding that his father would want to talk with Annie alone for a little bit. When he returned he found his father in a chair in the living room, a pot of coffee and a sandwich on the table beside him, untouched. He sat down near him. "Why don't you eat something, father?" he asked. "You must be hungry. Why don't you try to eat something?"

His father shook his head.

Avery got up and poured coffee for him, then handed him the plate. He looked at the sandwich dumbly, then began to eat it, and drank some of the strong black coffee. When he had finished, he looked gratefully at Avery. "Good boy," he said. "Good lad. Thanks."

Avery looked at his father, at the gilt chevrons on the sleeve of his blouse, then at the ribbons on his chest. It occurred to him that he and his father were all that remained of what had been a family, that the family, in fact, no longer existed. He wondered what the use of it was, why people clung to life. There seemed to be no order in it, no reason.

His father looked up. "You've seen Cally Browne?" he asked.

"Yes, sir. We play squash together, sometimes."

"How are you getting on down there, Avery?"

"All right, I guess," Avery said. He hesitated, then said, "I made Phi Beta Kappa, last month. And I suppose I'll get honors in math."

"Phi Beta Kappa," his father repeated. "I don't think there's ever been one in the family. Congratulations."

"Thank you."

"I was awfully disappointed," his father said, "when you decided not to go to Yale. But I suppose you know what you're doing."

"I hope so, sir," Avery said.

"Well, I didn't interfere," his father said, almost defensively. "It's your own life."

Avery made no comment. His father frowned, seeming to be gathering his ideas, then said, "I'm afraid we don't know one another very well, Avery. It's not my fault. It's—I don't know, the war, partly, I suppose. Things haven't been right."

"No, sir," Avery said. "It's not your fault."

His father rose and stretched his arms. "I'm beat," he said. "Beat up. Good night, Avery."

"Good night, father."

"Don't stay up too late, son."

"No, sir."

After his father had gone up stairs, Avery sat for an hour, not thinking, really, but permitting himself to absorb the idea that he had regained his father's confidence, and that his father had regained his. It was almost as though his mother had rescued them both by dying, understanding somehow that the lack of faith between them would be buried by the fact of her death. She had given them a sorrow they must share, because it belonged to both of them.

Unfortunately it was not peace, but only an armistice and a short one.

The next day they buried Avery's mother in a plot beside Morgan's grave, and drove back to the house together in a black hired car, as they had done after Morgan's funeral. When they reached the house his father took Avery into his study and gave him a glass of straight whiskey, bourbon whiskey with a clean, strong smell.

"Here, Avery," he said. "This will help settle your nerves."

"Thank you."

They sat together in the familiar room. The whiskey warmed Avery's blood and made him feel more confident, dissipating part of the old fear that had risen in his throat when they entered the study, fear prompted by the known smell of the room, the known passage of light through the window, and the known silhouette of the familiar figure in its customary chair behind the desk—a tableau of authority established in childhood.

He misread his father's character.

Perhaps it was the whiskey that blunted his wits, or perhaps in his heart there was some perverse inclination to misunderstand the complex of his father's moral pattern. There was something he wanted to know, so he asked an inappropriate question. "Has anyone else in our family ever committed suicide?" he asked. "I mean, in mother's family?"

His father looked across the desk at him, then down at the glass in his hand. Avery saw his fingers tighten, and the muscles of his neck go taut. He was wearing his blouse and looked more magisterial than he had the day before. He put down the glass and took up the paper knife from his desk, turning it over, then over again, making the light glint on the blade. Behind him the French clock that Avery once had broken whirred significantly and struck. They listened to the high neurotic bell until the clock had finished striking, then his father put down the knife. When he spoke there was no anger in his voice, but admonition.

"I wouldn't use that word in connection with your mother, son," he said. "It was an accident."

"But, father—"

"It was an accident. I talked with McBain about it, and with Captain Pawling, at the police barracks. She had been sick, and she had an accident with the razor."

"That's not true," Avery said. "It's a lie."

His father played with the paper knife, making an effort to keep his temper. "Your mother was sick," he said. "Very sick."

"I know that," Avery said. "Better than you do. I've been here. *Here.*"

His voice rose, and his father said sharply, "Control yourself, Avery. Lower your voice."

"Sorry."

His father sat straight up in his chair and the light from the window struck the stars on his shoulder straps, making them flash like diamonds. The armistice of tragedy was over.

"If you are trying to insinuate that my being overseas had anything to do with your mother's illness, you are mistaken," he said slowly. "Your mother's illness goes a long way back. Back to a time before you were born. I've talked to Parks about it. I've been in touch with him. I asked him a year ago whether it would help if I came home." He hesitated, his voice going thick. "Parks thought it might do more harm than good."

"Parks is a fool," Avery said. "A God damned ignorant fool."

"Well, Avery," his father said warningly. "Joe Parks is a member of your own fraternity. He can't be both a fool and a Phi Bete, now can he?"

"Of course he can," Avery said. "What's that got to do with it?"

His father shook his head, almost sadly. "Avery, Avery," he said. "You have a genius for bringing up the right thing at the wrong time." His voice flared. "Haven't you got any consideration for my feelings? Even if you don't see the bad taste involved in tearing your mother to pieces a few hours after she's in the ground, you might consider my feelings in the matter."

"What about my feelings?" Avery said sullenly. "I'm a human being. I feel too."

"Sometimes you seem to have no feelings," his father said. "Sometimes you act as if you had ice water in your veins. God knows I've tried, but I don't understand you. I don't know what makes you tick."

"I suppose you think you understood Morgan?" Avery said.

His father thought for a moment, then nodded. "Yes. Yes, I think I did," he said.

"You did not," said Avery flatly. "You did not understand him. He never wanted to go in the war. You forced him into it."

His father's face turned white, then red, and his hands trembled. He moved quickly from behind his desk, seizing the lapels of Avery's coat with his left hand and slapping him with his right, hard, across the face.

"That's a rotten thing to say," he said. "Rotten."

Avery broke loose.

"It's true," he said. "It's true. You think you can change the truth, by putting some crap on Morgan's grave, or by talking to a state cop who knows you can get him broken. Well, you can't. You can't change it. The truth is the truth."

His father turned back toward his desk, the movement of his body almost like the closing of a door in Avery's face. Avery went out of the room, his head still ringing from the force of the blows. He went upstairs and packed his bag, then down the back stairs to the kitchen to say good-bye to Annie.

She sat at the kitchen table, having a mug of strong tea, still dressed in the rusty black she had worn at the funeral. When he entered the kitchen she looked at his bag, then said, "Are you going, Avery? There's no train for three hours."

"I know," he said.

"What's the matter, laddie?" she asked. "What's happened?"

"I'm going for good," he said. "I won't be back."

"You've quarreled with your father?"

He nodded. "That's one way of putting it," he said.

"Try to understand him, Avery," she said. "He's a proud man, and he's not really simple. He just seems simple."

"He hates me," Avery said.

Annie did not deny it. She looked up at him, then down at her cup, and said finally, "He loves you too, Avery."

"Good-bye, Annie," he said.

He bent and kissed her on the cheek, then went out the back door. He cut across the lawn to the road and walked to the highway, his feet raising little explosions of dust. When he reached the hard road he put down his bag and waited until a truck appeared, then raised his arm. The truck came slowly to a stop, air brakes hissing cautiously. "Where you headed?" the driver asked, leaning out of the cab. He was a young man in an O.D. shirt with the patch of an infantry division on the shoulder.

"New York," Avery said.

"Climb aboard," the driver said. "I'm going to Yonkers. From there you can take the car."

Avery climbed up into the cab and threw his bag into the space behind the seat. The driver coaxed the heavy truck to a start. After it was rolling, he glanced at the lapel of Avery's coat. "Been in the service yet?" he asked.

Avery shook his head.

The driver seemed disappointed. After a while, he said, "I guess you were too young for the war, huh?"

"That's right," Avery said. He was getting used to being ashamed of not having been in the war, and sometimes now the shame turned into resentment of those who had been.

"Lucky Pierre," the driver said. "Lucky Pierre."

The truck pounded along the highway, flashing past roadside stands and little towns that were crude and ugly and not at all like Hull. The smell of the truck and the heavy rhythm of the diesel engine brought back memory of the afternoon he had run away to New York and talked to Dennis McCoy's father. With a sudden, empty feeling in his chest, he realized that this expedition was not the same as the other. There would be no turning back, this time. This time he had broken. He was not a child any more, or a boy, but a man, and this flight was a man's flight. He was through with his father, and through with Hull. He had a sense of his years reaching out before him, like the guide-line on the highway, and he shuddered for a moment with fear and with excitement.

When he came out of the subway at 116th Street and passed between the university gates, he felt as if he had come home. He had made a world for himself here, however limited it might be. He had a sense of being on his home grounds that made him feel almost secure, and the familiar scene, the rigid, dependable pattern of the campus, the utilitarian confinement of his dormitory room, gave him the dramatic illusion of moving from one world to another. The interlude at Hull, from the moment he had opened Annie's wire, until this moment, when he opened the door of his room, seemed out of time and detached itself from him. What had happened at Hull seemed unreal, like the action of a play after the curtain has come down, while the fact that he had a seminar meeting in half an hour seemed intensely real and operative. He changed his clothes, glanced at his notes, and went to class, impressed by his own composure and the feeling of hardness in his mind. The break with his father seemed to have been conclusive and painless as decapitation.

CHAPTER THIRTY-SEVEN

A FEW days later he got a letter from Hull, in which his father apologized for striking him, and also informed him that he planned to return to Germany at once. *"I don't have to point out,"* his father wrote, *"that legally you are probably some kind of juvenile delinquent. However, you may do as you please. You will have your own money in two years. Meanwhile, it is my obligation to support you until you finish college, in spite of the fact that you seem to despise everything I stand for. I shall do so. You may draw on your account at Hull as before, until June. After that, you are on your own."*

It was the first time his father had ever apologized to him for anything, but of course it was too late. He tore up the letter and threw it away, then took all of his father's letters, that he had saved since his first year at Colborn, and tore them and threw them out. He was not affected by the fact that he realized that his father was partly in the right. It was simply too late.

His father's decision about the money did not perturb him. He had nearly two thousand dollars in the bank that he had saved from his allowance during his three years at Columbia, and when he was twenty-one he would have the income from the trust fund his mother's father had left him. The problem of supporting himself did not seem formidable. He had no plans, but in a few weeks' time he would be a Bachelor of Arts with a Phi Beta Kappa key and Honors in Mathematics. He understood that these were highly negotiable assets, and had he not known it, he would have learned it a few weeks later, when raiding parties from the great corporations prowled the campus in search of talent—any kind of talent at all in the fields of mathematics, physics and chemistry. A man from a famous electrical company, with a Tau Bete key and a pleasant manner, offered him a job that started at seventy-five dollars a week.

"It's a lot of money," the man said. "I don't think you'll do better." He smiled, then said rather sadly, "Do you know what I started at, in 1936? Eighteen dollars a week. And it took me almost a year to get the job. You young fellows don't know how lucky you are."

Avery said he would let him know.

He had other offers at other salaries. He was taken to dinner and on a tour of an electronics plant in Jersey. He was flattered and stimulated by these demonstrations of his economic worth. But when he thought of actually leaving the University and going to Pittsburgh or Wilmington, or Minneapolis, or Montgomery, Alabama, he was apprehensive. He had a fear of a strange room in a strange city, and a desk in an office filled with unfamiliar people who belonged to an aggressive, different world. He didn't want to leave the college. He had not found what he had come to the college to look for, and he was afraid to abandon the familiar scene, the learnt routine.

In the end it was Douminoff who made up his mind for him. A few days before graduation, he had a note from Douminoff and went to see him in his rooms.

"Well, Avery," Douminoff said, "have you hit the industrial jack pot? Three hundred a month and found?"

Avery smiled and said, "No. I'm still at liberty."

"Going to stay with us?" Douminoff asked.

"I don't know," Avery said.

"Got any money?"

"A little," Avery told him. "Not enough to see myself through.

Douminoff swung around in his chair and seemed to examine Avery for flaws. Then he said, "Hollister, I honestly don't know whether I'm doing you a favor or a disservice. Maybe the best thing for you would be a year on a farm, pitching hay. Or the army. Or going to sea as a fo'c'sle hand. I wouldn't know. It might do you good to come up against life reduced to its simpler elements. You intellectualize too much, and it's hard to intellectualize a hay fork or a chipping hammer. But maybe that's just romanticism. Anyway, it's old fashioned." He paused, then said, "I've been asked to turn up a graduate student for Karl Dormaker's project. A junior. Somebody working for a Ph.D. in mathematics." He coughed, then smiled and said, "It won't pay seventy-five a week to start, but you might like it."

Avery didn't answer. He was flattered and impressed. Karl Dormaker was one of the half-dozen internationally famous physicists in the country. He had shared the Nobel Prize with a Swiss opposite number. He had been on loan to the navy during the war, away from the campus, and his legend had grown during his absence. Avery knew that Douminoff would not recommend him merely out of friendship; it meant that Douminoff believed he had professional potentialities.

Douminoff leaned back in his chair.

"There's a great deal to be said for life in a university, Avery," he observed. "And a great deal to be said against it. I think we're less parochial here than at most other institutions, but we don't escape a certain smugness, a certain lack of contact with life on the tooth-and-claw level. On the other hand, within reasonable limits, you're a free man here. At least, you are free in your own area." He glanced at Avery, then went on. "Now, you have a certain talent for mathematics. Whether it's anything more than a talent, a real gift, I don't know. You may turn out to be nothing more, ever, than an able technician. On the other hand, you may become—anything. Two years with Dormaker should help you find out what kind of man you are."

"I'm very much flattered," Avery said. He hesitated, and Douminoff smiled. "It's nice of you to give me the chance," he said. "I—"

"Why don't you think it over?" Douminoff suggested. "Let me know in a day or two? Right?"

"Right!"

Outside, Avery stopped in front of South Field, and sat down on the concrete base that once had held an enormous marble sphere, that had cracked, somebody said, because of the rhythm of the midshipmen's marching. The flat face of the library, in the afternoon light, looked like a cardboard cut-out. He read the names carved into the stone: HOMER—HERODOTUS—SOCRATES, then faced about and read the carving on the portico of the old library, that was impressive as a great temple, planted on a high hill of steps: *King's College in the Province of New York. Founded under Royal Charter in the Reign of George II.*

It was late afternoon. The campus and the city beyond it took on a glow from the spring sky, and he felt the slow steady enormous heartbeat of the city, an inexorable, pulsing, metropolitan cadence that he seemed to hear, though actually there was no sound but that of traffic from the streets beyond the college, and of radio music from a parked car. There was an urban solemnity about the scene he found comforting and reassuring.

He was not under great illusions.

He knew that this university was not really a seat of learning, or Twentieth Century Cloister, but a great educational factory, a kind of shop that stored knowledge and offered it for sale. He had changed since the day he came here, three years ago, but the change had not been accomplished as much by the university as by events and the passage of time. If the function of education was to arm the character, to provide it with resources, as he had been told, then he had not been given education here, but only a supply of information and the use of certain skills. He did not feel educated. He felt ignorant and unsure of himself and frightened. In a few days' time his academic apprenticeship would have ended: but he knew nothing, really, he reflected, beyond the technique of mathematics and the hodgepodge of history, economics and literature served up like academic stew in the required survey courses. He knew nothing of women, nothing of men, nothing of the world of men or of the tragic sense of life that was, as Dennis had informed him, supposed to be communicated by poetry and other art. He was an ignoramus, and the only thing he possessed to his advantage was his intelligence, which now prodded him to suggest that if he stayed here at the university he might merely go on learning more and more about less and less, go on with the process of sharpening his mind by narrowing it. Yet he was afraid to leave. He understood that if he took the post Douminoff had found for him, there was every chance that he would pass the rest of his life within this red brick reservation enclosed by the city, imprisoned by it.

He looked off to the west, and at the end of the narrow street that led to the River saw a bright patch of sky and a fragment of cloud with the sun behind it, so that the edges of the cloud were gold. It occurred to him that he could walk west, and continue walking until he stopped because there was something he wanted to see or do or listen to or have done to him. There was nothing to hold him. Nothing.

But he stood where he was.

Within this quadrangular prison there was safety. Beyond the River, there was danger. "Why, I'm a coward," he said aloud, rather surprised by the words themselves as well as the fact. "I'm afraid."

"What's that?" called someone, passing.

"Nothing," Avery said. "Just talking to myself."

The next day he accepted the assistant's job on Dormaker's project. It was hard to tell whether Douminoff was pleased or disappointed.

"What will you do with your summer, Hollister?" he asked. "Karl won't be here until fall."

"I don't know," Avery said. "I hadn't thought about it." It would be his first summer off since he had started college; he had planned to go home to Hull, to loaf in the sun and ride and swim, but now he would not do that.

"Do something strenuous," Douminoff advised. "Go be a lifeguard or a lumberjack. Something that will use your muscles instead of your brains."

Avery smiled. "I was raised in a family that made a fetish of exercise, sir," he said. "I got a belly full of it when I was a boy."

"Even so," Douminoff said. "Sweat out the kinks. And come back here in September ready to work. They will keep you busy."

CHAPTER THIRTY-EIGHT

H E TOOK Douminoff's advice. He bought a pair of army shoes and a surplus army rucksack that looked expensive and Norwegian, and walked from Williamstown, Mass. to the Canadian border, through the strip of mountain wilderness, alone, cooking his own meals and sleeping in shelters along the trail. He read Thoreau by a gasoline lantern that contributed a fierce white light and burned with a dangerous hissing sound. It was a rather self-conscious conclusion to his academic career, but it did what Douminoff had suggested. It worked the kinks out of his body, and living in the open helped reduce his problems to somewhat more manageable size.

One afternoon he overtook a pair of Radcliffe girls, wearing shorts and clean white shirts, handsome as amazons and able looking. They had sleek, powerful necks and composed, intelligent faces. They were the kind of college girls who seem capable of producing exactly one and seven-eighths children, or whatever the proper fractional family appropriate to their particular year. Their skillful voices made Avery feel that he belonged to the subservient sex. They were seniors, or would be in the fall, and both were knowledgeable history majors. He camped with them for three nights, carrying water and cutting wood while they prepared the food. It was a pleasant break from the monotony of being alone, but it was irritating too. The last night they were together, he told them about the research project he was joining in the fall.

"But don't you want to take any real subjects?" one of the girls asked. "I mean, history or literature or art?"

"Don't you think mathematics is a real subject?" he asked.

"Well, it's very necessary and all that," she said. "But isn't it more or less a servant subject? Just a technique?"

They were seated on the ground before a small fire and the night had closed in. Off in the distance there were forest noises, and from time to time the disturbing sound of a fox's bark. Avery stared at the fire, trying to answer honestly. Finally he said, "I don't agree with you at all. I think mathematics is a kind of last stand of the human spirit, a kind of final gallantry. It's an island of decency, you might say, the one country where things still relate to one another and make sense, where ideas are still dependable."

He looked at the girl who had asked the question. Her face was lighted from below by the fire, and this made her look theatrical and romantic. She was impressed. She nodded and looked at him with gray solemn eyes. "I hadn't ever thought of it that way," she said.

"Neither had I," he said. "Until you asked me."

The next day they went off the trail to buy supplies and he went on north alone. He thought it was curious that a stranger had caused him to say something he had needed to say for his own sake. The more he considered the answer he had given, the more sense it seemed to make, and he was grateful to the Radcliffe girl for having asked the question.

During the first week in September, at midday, he came to the border post set into a power slash through the forest, and gazed north into Canada, spread before him flat as a map and tidy as an enormous farm. He had walked the length of the State of Vermont, up and down the granite ridge. He touched Canada with the toe of his boot, then turned down the side trail that led to the hamlet of North Troy. He drank an ice cream soda in a drug store that smelled more like a drug store than any he had ever been in, then boarded the bus that went to Newport and took the train to New York. He was in better shape than he had been since his Fifth Form year at Colborn. He looked dangerous as a lumberjack or parachute infantryman. People stared at him. In the washroom of the train he inspected himself in the mirror and smiled. He resembled a savage. It was inconceivable that the man who looked back at him from the mirror should be afraid of anything on earth.

But he was.

He was mortally afraid of the years that faced him and, now that the narcotic effect of the wilderness was gone, afraid of his singular position in the world, with his mother dead and his brother dead and his father gone back to the world where he could preserve his fictions without being challenged by bad-mannered sons. He stared through the window of the train at the familiar New England landscape and was swept by a wave of homesickness and a yearning for his mother so desperate that it choked him and made him weep.

When he came out of the subway at Columbia, someone called his name and he turned. It was Freddie Breitbart, who looked at him skeptically and said, "For God's sake, Hollister, what are you dressed for? A costume ball?"

Avery explained.

Breitbart shook his head. "Every man to his taste," he said. He wore a new flannel suit and expensive English shoes. He touched his tie and said, "Charvet, my lad. I'm just back from Paris."

"No kidding?" Avery said. "You lucky bum."

"Where are you going to live this year?" Breitbart asked.

"Dorm, I guess," Avery said. "I hadn't thought about it."

"The dorm's no good," Breitbart said. "Why don't you come in with me? I've got an apartment. The guy who was supposed to split it with me got drafted and it's too big for one."

"I don't know," Avery said. "I'm used to living by myself."

"It will do you good," Breitbart said. "Few months with me will be a liberal education for you." He opened his coat and Avery saw that he wore his Phi Beta Kappa key. "I'll give you the number. Call me in a couple of days, and I'll hold off the queue meanwhile. Okay?"

"Okay," Avery agreed. "I'll think it over."

He watched Breitbart cross the campus, looking more like a bright young man from some public relations office than a candidate for the Doctor's degree in philosophy. Avery smiled. He was surprised and rather flattered. Freddie had a good reputation and was supposed to have impressed important faculty people. He wasn't sure he wanted to live with Freddie Breitbart or anyone else, but when he looked at an available dormitory room he decided to accept Freddie's invitation. The room was small and depressing, and he suddenly felt he had outgrown his taste for regimented academic life, and was willing to risk invasion of his privacy for the chance of something more stimulating than life in the graduate school dorms.

"You're not making a mistake, keed," Breitbart told him when he phoned. "We can have the hell of a good time."

CHAPTER THIRTY-NINE

BREITBART enjoyed the task of giving Avery a liberal education. He expected to pass his life giving such an education to the better class of young Americans, and Avery made a good trial run.

There were those at Columbia who thought that Breitbart was insincere.

They were mistaken.

It was true that he was ambitious, and true that he had a flair for success. He would inevitably, in ten years' time, become a fashionable professor, appearing on television programs, writing pieces for Sunday supplements and crisp light verse for the magazines, as well as readable, intelligent, useful books that would be picked up by the book clubs. He already resembled the newer type of streamlined college professor—young, alert, informed, well-dressed, confident as a banker—pants pressed, no chalk on his cuffs. His slight tendency toward fleshiness would later add authority to his figure. He was certainly on the make, as a professor once had described him. But he was perfectly sincere. He simply recognized the fact that the university was a corporation and that a man made progress here as in any other corporation, by cultivating authority. During his four years at Columbia, he had acquired his bachelor's and master's degrees, and established himself on a first-name level with faculty people who counted. He had not made the mistake of taking undergraduate politics seriously, and had made no effort to impress his classmates, turning all of his ingenuity and power to the task of breaking into the semipermanent faculty political structure.

To achieve his position, which was not inconsequential, since it was a life-guarantee of security and status, Freddie had followed the standard procedures. He was not a radical. He had worked hard in areas where the results would be noticed, and persuaded himself to think highly of people who might be useful to him. There was nothing dishonest about him. When he paused at the conclusion of class to tell a professor the lecture had been brilliant, it was because he really believed the lecture had been brilliant. It was simply impossible for Freddie to overlook the virtues of people who might help him advance his position. It was second nature to him to select the right people to admire.

He had discovered, too, that a reputation for brilliant conversation is most easily acquired by limiting one's own observations to "Yes, sir," and "That's very true, sir." He listened, and he entered his own ideas into half a dozen black notebooks that would later supply ideas for dozens of books and articles, the profits from which, added to the salary the college would pay him and the competence his father would leave him, would enable him to live like a scholar and gentleman. He had planned his life as carefully as a young Jesuit or the heir to an enormous fortune. If he had been bitterly disappointed when the Cambridge fellowship he had wanted had gone to an athlete and war veteran, he quickly recovered from the blow. He had the best fellowship the Philosophy Department offered and he would go to Cambridge later on, if it still seemed worth while. "To tell you the truth, Avery," he said, "the real reason I'd like a Cambridge doctorate is so I can wear that floppy hat, like Henry the Eighth."

Breitbart saw himself as burdened with only one handicap. This was what he liked to call his humble birth, the fact that his origins were not Anglo-Saxon, Protestant and middle class. His people were German immigrants who lived somewhere in the wastes of Brooklyn, where they prospered. He pretended to loathe them. "Sometimes I look at them," he said, "and wonder how two lumps of Teutonic dung like that ever produced a marvel like myself. It's incredible. I must derive from some irregular, aristocratic ancestor."

Avery laughed.

"I'm not joking," Freddie said. "They're a hell of a disadvantage to me. Why don't you trade with me, Hollister? I have everything to go with your background—looks, brilliance, charm, wit."

"I might take you up," Avery said. "But I'd have to see your parents first."

"Christ forbid!"

The apartment Breitbart had found, in a year when no one could find apartments, was a floor through in a proud old brownstone house on a street that led downhill toward the river. There was a large front room that overlooked the street, and two small bedrooms in the rear, from the windows of which could be seen back yards turned into gardens. The furniture was old, but it was massive, and the chairs and sofa had been re-covered with crimson rep that made the place look warm and academic. The quarters were what Avery imagined rooms at Oxford might be like: comfortable, old fashioned, solid, gentlemanly. Breitbart's books and pictures added to the atmosphere of scholarly opulence, particularly the hundred-odd paper-backed volumes in French.

A silent bent Irish woman made their beds each morning except Sunday, and they got their own breakfast on a gas plate, taking the other meals in restaurants or the college dining halls. It was more expensive than the dormitories, but Avery thought it was worth it. For a few days he missed the monkish quality of dormitory life, and its privacy, but that passed. And, for a little while, he was suspicious of Breitbart, wondering what the catch was, and how Breitbart wanted to use him.

There was no catch, he discovered. Breitbart admired his background, and had needed someone to share the apartment. There was nothing more to it than that, and when Avery came to this conclusion he began to enjoy Freddie.

Freddie blunted the edge of his semioccupational smugness. He began to read novels again, having given them up when he came to college; he read Fitzgerald and Faulkner and Somerset Maugham, and then the great Russian novelists, in editions Breitbart owned and fed him one by one. He read *War and Peace,* and when he finished it he was not quite the same person he had been when Breitbart dropped the book into his lap. He was shaken by Tolstoi; the book illuminated his appalling ignorance and appalling insignificance. It made him feel at the same time mean as a grub underneath a stone and elevated as an angel. For the first time, under the impact of art, there was suggested to him a great controlling relationship that cuts across the whole field of human communication and links together giants who invest the same ingredient, the truth, with different forms and different spirits. In a sharp, applicable sense, the book gave freshened meaning to his own work.

CHAPTER FORTY

HIS own work, during the first months of the term, was checking the work that had been done the year before, during Karl Dormaker's absence—and involved masses of calculation, the drudgery of which was reduced by the fact that he had occasional access to a machine that did computation for him.

"The brain of the future," Dormaker told him. "Watch out for it. It will eat you up."

His first meeting with Dormaker was a shock, though he should have been more or less prepared by photographs he had seen and stories he had heard.

Dormaker was a singular individual.

He had been graduated from Amherst at fifteen and taken his Ph.D. at Harvard at nineteen. Before he was forty he had shared the Nobel Prize and everyone thought he would get another, all his own, before he finished his career. He was five feet tall, and wide as an old-fashioned football lineman. He moved with the blunt inevitability of a tank destroyer, and had an enormous head that looked as if it had been fashioned from an outsize cocoanut. The face that looked out of this head was ugly enough to be frightening, a face surrealist and grotesque. But when Dormaker spoke, the face was forgotten and an almost tangible personal charm developed in the air around him. As he went on, the ugliness receded until you were no longer aware of it, but only of the resonant, powerful voice and the presence of greatness in the room.

After giving Avery a chair, when Avery called at the beginning of term, Dormaker took from the pocket of his wrinkled coat a thin crooked black cigar of the kind Italian laborers smoke, and sat with the cigar in his hand, looking at Avery curiously, with a diffidence that seemed to suggest that he was wondering what Avery thought of him, rather than what he thought of Avery, and hoping that Avery liked him. Avery remembered something Douminoff had told him: "Most physicists are nothing but educated mechanics, Hollister. But Dormaker, although he's the best mechanic in the country, without exception, is also a first-rate mathematician, and, incidentally, one of the few people drawing breath who really believe in the validity of the human spirit."

It was that belief in humanity Avery felt, as Dormaker gazed across the desk at him, two brown eyes that were like jewels set into the cocoanut bark dancing intensely behind heavy lenses.

"What do you do for relaxation?" Dormaker asked. "Do you read? Look at pictures? Paint them? Play the piano? Pursue young women?" He smiled, lighting his cigar and blowing a cloud of rancid smoke toward the ceiling. "I always like to know how my assistants enjoy themselves. Sometimes it helps me understand the character of the work they do for me."

"Well, sir, I read and look at pictures," Avery said. "I don't play the piano."

"So?" Dormaker shook his head. "No piano? That's too bad. Every scientist should be an amateur musician. It is better, for *Life* Magazine. I myself play the flute. Einstein plays the fiddle. Douminoff plays, well, we can't say he plays, but he owns a cello. You've heard him? Good!"

Avery laughed. Douminoff's effort to produce music from the cello was a college joke.

"But you must learn to play something," Dormaker said. "Perhaps the drum?" He shook his head. "Drums are for chemists.

Not the drum. Perhaps the harp? The harp is a fine instrument. It is being stolen by women."

He reached into a drawer of his desk and took out a flute, placing it against his lips and blowing a few clear notes. In the small room, the sound was disturbing.

"And what do you read?" Dormaker asked, putting the flute away.

Avery told him what he read and mentioned Tolstoi's novel. Dormaker nodded approvingly.

"It is a good project for a young man," he said. "And even better for an old one. I am almost old enough to read it again."

Having looked it up in *Who's Who,* Avery knew that Dormaker was not quite fifty-three, almost exactly the age of his father, though Dormaker looked a great deal older.

They talked of books and painting and music and girls, of everything except the university and the science of physics, and Avery's graduate career. Avery understood that this was Dormaker's way of guessing his weight, and that all the time they were talking, Dormaker was absorbing him.

At last Dormaker seemed to have learned what he wanted to know about him. He leaned forward, spilling ash on his coat, and picked up Avery's undergraduate record, the courses and grades inscribed on a complicated form. He ran his finger down the form, nodding and grunting. Then he looked up.

"You are how old?"

"Nineteen."

"A good age to begin your graduate work," Dormaker said. "Young enough to avoid the pressure, the terrible need to do everything in three weeks, and old enough to enjoy life. I was too young, by at least one year. I've often wished that I'd taken a year off. Bummed around, or studied painting, or worked maybe as a harvest hand, the way people do in books. I was too young." He paused, looking at Avery. "But you are just the right age." He looked at the card again and nodded. "You should be a good technician," he said. "I see you have done a lot with Boris. He's a good workman, Douminoff. A good workman."

He swung around in his swivel chair so that he faced the open window, looking out over the rooftops at the campus and the city, windows of buildings glittering in the sun. "It's good to be back here," he said, raising his hands and striking the arms of his chair a pair of emphatic, simultaneous blows. "I like the military well enough. They are courteous, in their own curious way, and their intellectual stature, while limited, has been much maligned. But I'm glad to be back. I feel at home here."

He swung back and put his elbows on the edge of his desk.

"How much do you know about our project?" he asked, his voice more matter-of-fact.

"Only what Professor Douminoff told me," Avery said. "I know you're building a machine that will play a game of chess."

Dormaker laughed.

"It may do that," he said. "Among other things. Of course, it will play a dull game of chess. No mistakes. No flair. But that isn't what we are building it for. I prefer to play chess with people."

He took from his desk a thick mimeographed report, bound in tough blue paper and stamped: SECRET equals BRITISH MOST SECRET. With a blunt black pencil, he crossed out these words, adding his initials.

"So you see, the secret is out," he said. He laughed. "You know, one of the men on my signal corps project, before I went with the navy, could not do simple sums. He always kept a child's arithmetic with him, because it contained the multiplication table. The security officer made him stamp it like this one: SECRET, equals BRITISH MOST SECRET. So you see, on that project two times two equals four was just secret to us, but most secret to the subjects of George Six."

Avery laughed.

Dormaker shook his head.

"Not so ridiculous," he said. "The things in that arithmetic book are secrets to millions of schoolboys. Besides, the fellow kept his girls' phone numbers in the book, along with the multiplication table." He handed Avery the blue report that was no longer most secret. "Read it when you have time," he said, "and you'll know as much as the rest of us do." He hesitated, then smiled apologetically. "I sometimes think it's useful to state a problem in plain English," he said, "even at the risk of simplifying it into meaninglessness. Briefly, here is what we are trying to do. We know that machines can learn. What we want to find out is how much they can learn. Whether or not there is an upper limit, and if so where it is, between man's mind and the mind of what our public relations officer used to call Upper Case Him."

Avery laughed and Dormaker smiled.

"He was a great fellow," Dormaker said. "A big boy with a face like a Turk, always just keeping out of trouble. 'Doc,' he used to say to me, 'doesn't it scare you to fool around with this stuff? Maybe Upper Case Him won't like it. Maybe He's got ideas of His own.' " Dormaker chuckled, then said, "Maybe He has, at that."

Then he stood up and offered Avery his hand. It was like shaking hands with a wrestler.

"Come in tomorrow, Hollister," he said. "Dr. Bascomb will tell you what he wants you to do. I'm afraid you will be just a mathematical clerk for a while, but it will get interesting later on."

"Thank you, sir," Avery said.

Dormaker hesitated, then said, "You know, Avery, I have been three years with the military. Among the military the word 'sir' gets a good deal of use. Could you omit it, except perhaps once a day? Maybe use it just once, in the morning, the way they salute on ships?"

Avery blushed, then grinned. "Sure. Sure I can," he said.

"Good. Good." Dormaker patted his shoulder. "You're a nice boy, Avery," he said. "A nice boy. We will get along."

Outside on the flag walk in front of Pupin Hall, Avery stopped and looked down at a neat trimmed bush, feeling positive affection for it. His finger tips tingled with excitement. He felt as though he had just been assured that he was going to heaven. He looked at the thick book in his hand, then laughed and said out loud, "By God, I'm a mathematician."

He turned and collided with an old gentleman carrying a brief case, who looked at him and observed dryly, "Are you, young man? It's an illusion I once cherished myself."

"Sorry, sir," Avery said.

It was old Professor Carpenter, who taught theoretical physics and was now professor emeritus. He smiled and touched Avery's shoulder, the way Dormaker had done. "Quite all right, young man," he said. "You are quite right to believe in yourself." He peered at him, then said, "It's Hollister, isn't it? Hollister, A.?"

"Yes, sir," Avery said.

The old man nodded, his eyes showing amusement. "Good. Good luck to you."

He walked briskly away, leaving Avery alone on the walk, flattered and surprised by the fact that the professor had remembered his name, for it was two years since he had taken the old man's course.

That night he began the report Dormaker had given him, and the next morning presented himself to Dr. Bascomb, a thin, nervous energetic man a few years older than himself, six feet four in height, and already nearly bald.

"I'm as lost as you are, Hollister," he told him. "I just got out of the army. But I'll show you what you can start on."

He put Avery to work, checking what had been done before the project had been more or less suspended because of Dormaker's absence. Avery saw that it was going to be dull, as Dormaker had warned him, but he didn't care. There was a certain satisfaction to be taken even from the monotonous chore of sorting hundreds of punched cards; the conviction persisted that he was, as he had told himself and old Professor Carpenter, a mathematician, and therefore engaged in seeking out the truth, no matter how humble and routine might be his immediate assignment.

He gave the project half his time, the other half being devoted to courses that would qualify him for his master's and then for his doctor's degree. He was busier than ever before, and happier. He was inspired by awareness of function, and had enormous faith in the truth, the truth for its own sake. It never occurred to him to question the scripture presented to men for centuries: "Ye shall know the truth, and the truth shall make you free." He did not consider the possibility that the truth, in some obscene way, had made men not free at all, but enslaved to systems and techniques their own brains had discovered, and though all around him was evidence that scientific truth was neither absolute nor all-saving, but often equivocal and fatal, and though all around him were men and women eager to inform him of this, he refused either to look or listen, either to heed or observe. The idea that he might be engaged in anything less than pursuit of truth would have been intolerable. It would have torn from his existence whatever meaning it seemed to have. He was still the prisoner of the perfect shapes he had glimpsed in his room at Hull, the summer before he came to college.

And he was a prisoner of the academic life. It served him as a retreat, a putting off—a place to hide. He liked the life. Its rhythm pleased him. The fact that one lived by the half-year, rather than by the day and week, suited him, and so did the anti-quarian formality and order, and, at the level on which he oper-ated, the lack of bitter personal competition. There are men who remain thus protected by the walls of their schools for all of their lives. They are often good men, sometimes noble, sometimes great. Frequently they are more alive than their nonacademic contemporaries who consider themselves in the midst of battle. If the university was escape, so was the pursuit of large sums of money, or power, or medals, or death, and Avery saw that the schoolmen were no more evaders than other men.

Two things, however, disturbed him and prevented him from becoming truly insulated by the university. One was the fact that his life was too much monitored by a force he could not control or measure and of which he was often only half aware. This was the deep skein of buried attraction that tied him to his father. He hated this and tried to drive it from his dreams, but it was a fact and continued to haunt him. His father had been archetype too long; the press of the mold was there. In a sense every action Avery took, from selection of a necktie in the morning to the manner in which he attacked some technical problem that would have no meaning for his father, was performed under that absent eye and with that absent approval in mind. He had murdered his father in his mind, but his father would not stay dead. His father haunted him, and sometimes seemed to mock him.

The other force that bewitched Avery was the drive of unnourished sex, fighting against his Yankee reticence to exploit his body for physical pleasure, and this force, during his first graduate year, led him into adventure with a girl who had a quantity of bright gold hair and a whitewashed studio on Bleecker Street, where she lived and worked alone.

CHAPTER FORTY-ONE

HER name was Frieda von Mardo and she was four years older than Avery, according to the calendar, and several centuries older in terms of experience and approach to life.

He met her by chance.

During the fall, he and Breitbart fell into the habit of going to the brawlish, semipublic cocktail parties given by Tom and Connie Requa, people who had an apartment in Chelsea, with two enormous front rooms that could be divided with sliding doors but were thrown together for parties, making a hall the size of a small ballroom, the high ceilings reaching up, with fantastic plaster work in the center, from which depended prismed chandeliers that jingled dangerously when people danced. It was a stately, imperial house; the leavings of the perambulating rich, who had occupied this part of town for a generation or two, and then moved on.

Tom Requa had taught English to Columbia freshmen, but he had no gift for the job and the pay was bad, so he had drifted into journalism and then into advertising, which now gave him a harassed living. He was a standard good-looking man, now going a bit to seed: overneat, gray at the temples, appearing to be perpetually tired. His wife was a thin frenetic woman with long earrings and a moist painted mouth to which a cigarette seemed to have been permanently attached with glue. Neither of them much regretted the fact that Tom had quit the university, but they clung to the old associations and their parties, given on schedule once a week, were always crowded with graduate students and young instructors, and occasionally they would capture a well-known Columbia figure. There were advertising people too, and young novelists and gallery artists. It was a kind of prosperous Bohemia, a little dated and a little thin. Breitbart considered it second rate, but amusing, and it gave him a chance to display his talents. Avery found it fascinating. It seemed to him to be real life.

One evening in November they had gone to the Requas as usual, and Avery stood listening to Freddie infatuate Connie Requa with his literary flair. He marveled at Breitbart's facility and verbal change of pace. Breitbart was discussing a new novel Avery was sure he hadn't read, demolishing both book and author with a kind of courteous savagery. From time to time he glanced at Avery, to let him know he was in on the joke.

Avery was entertained, but after a while Freddie went into a routine he had heard several times before, and he turned away. He looked around the crowded room, becoming aware, after a little, of a handsome blonde girl whose hair was piled up on top of her head like a beacon, and who wore a bright blue linen dress with a reckless open throat. She turned, and he saw that in profile she was beautiful. She was surrounded by half a dozen men who seemed to be keeping her amused. She gave the impression of holding court. He watched her, fascinated by the clarity of her head, the brilliant, authentic, bone beauty. She turned and looked toward him and his two companions, attracted, he supposed, by Freddie, who was being animated and courtly, making a sophisticated appearance and giving his lines as much importance as if they had been written for him by Shaw. But Connie Requa touched his arm and said, "Avery, you're making an impression on *die schöne* Frieda. Why don't you move in? You need a girl, you know."

He looked across the room and saw that the candid gray blue eyes were trained on him rather than Freddie, and that there was invitation in them, or challenge, he wasn't sure which. He stared back and the girl smiled. He felt a tension that grew in his back-bone and a tightening of the blood vessels. Connie waved an arm that was crowded with bracelets and called, "Freida! Come here."

Frieda came toward them through the crowd. She was lovely. She looked untouchable. She had a beautiful throat, and the innocent blue color of her dress pointed up the extraordinary clarity of her skin and emphasized her golden blondeness. There was nothing in the least sexual about her until she spoke, but her voice, furred with a slight, enchanting accent, made Avery's blood rise.

"Hello, Connie," she said. *"Grüss Gott,* Herr Doktor Breitbart." She looked at Freddie tolerantly and smiled, then turned to Avery.

"This is Frieda von Mardo, Avery," Connie said. "Avery Hollister." She took Avery's hand and Frieda's and drew them together. "Be very careful, Frieda," she said. "He's a mathematician. They are dangerous people."

Frieda looked at him and said, "So that's it. I knew there was something different about him. He doesn't look like the rest of these amateur art critics, amateur literary critics, amateur economists and amateur psychologists." She stared frankly at Avery, making him blush, then nodded and said, "Of course. I should have recognized it right away. I am supposed to have an eye for these things."

Freddie laughed. "Frieda's a painter, Ave," he said. "She has just thrown away three hundred dollars a week, in perfectly good J. Walter Thompson currency, in favor of the garret and a moldy crust. And art."

Frieda smiled. Avery got the impression she was not filled with respect for Breitbart.

"Don't you ever get the desire to be a performer, Herr Doktor?" she asked pleasantly. "Of course, you come from a race of critics. You have the mind of a *Kunst* historian, and they all

hate art. That's why they try to destroy it, by reducing it to ico-
nography, paint chemistry, and biography."

Freddie flushed, then recovered and touched her cheek with
the tips of his fingers. There was a certain amount of contempt
in the gesture, as if he were touching a handsome dog, but it was
subtle.

"You know, Frieda is an excellent painter," he said. "Or at
least, she will be in twenty years' time. But she's also a semiskilled
intellectual. The city is filled with them. They have replaced the
Communists who used to enliven parties like this one. They
have read pamphlets and popular books on every subject about
which pamphlets and popular books have been written. They can
speak the official expertise, and provided they aren't permitted to
discuss a subject for more than fifteen minutes, they seem to be
well-educated people. Consequently, they can see no sense at all
in a man who devotes twenty years to really informing himself
on a subject."

He smiled and moved away. Frieda laughed. After a moment
Connie said, "I've got to see that there's food and stuff. Excuse me
will you, you two pets?"

Frieda and Avery stepped behind a chair in a corner of the
room, defended by it from the crowd. On the wall behind them
was a modern head, a flat painting of a shrewd, corrupt, aristocratic woman, so painted that the line of the skull was indicated
beneath the hair. Avery glanced at it, frowning, then saw the signature: von Mardo. "Why it's yours," he said.

"An old one," she said. "Last year's."

He looked at the painting, then at the girl beside him, who
was an inch or two shorter than he and whose face was turned
up to him. It was impossible to reconcile the painting with the
artist. The painting aroused awareness of evil; it was touched by a
strain of evil, that must have been known to the painter too. The
face was corrupt and unashamed, the face of a woman incapable

of feeling guilt. But the girl who had painted it was beautiful, and her face expressed integrity and the absence of evil.

She touched his arm. "Never mind the picture," she said. "I don't paint that way any more." She smiled at him, then said, "So you're a scientist, a mathematician?"

The low, slurring accent went through him.

"Well not exactly," he said. "I'm going to be."

"Good! I like mathematicians. My father was one, you know."

He turned quickly, his mind ticking over, then said with a note of excitement in his voice, "Your father was Friedrich von Mardo? From Vienna?"

She nodded. "Yes. He was my father."

He felt a sense of compassion. He knew the story of Friedrich von Mardo. He had heard it from Douminoff, and read a clipping Douminoff had saved. Von Mardo had been Austria's greatest mathematician, a famous teacher and the author of a standard book on the number system. The Germans had killed him, but not for a long time after they arrested him, and not before they had first attempted to suborn his mind. Memory of the newspaper clipping and of Douminoff's recollections of von Mardo passed through Avery's mind. He looked at Frieda, a little awed. She smiled at him, and he felt a powerful attraction, an absolutely commanding need to know her, to touch her.

"Look, would you like to get out of here?" he asked. "Will you come and have dinner with me, somewhere?"

"I'd like very much to get out of here," she said. "And to have dinner with you. Unfortunately, I've promised some people."

His heart sank.

"But I would like very much to have dinner with you tomorrow night, if you're free."

"Of course," he said. He would have made himself free if it had meant committing murder.

She wrote an address on a bit of paper torn from an envelope, and gave it to him. "Come about seven," she said.

Then she leaned forward quickly and kissed his cheek. She went back through the crowd to the group she had been with when Connie called her. Avery stood where he was, watching her, over the heads of the others.

CHAPTER FORTY-TWO

HER studio was on Bleecker Street, in the Village, reached by ascending a narrow staircase that creaked under Avery's weight and smelled of foreign cookery. Frieda's place was on the top floor—one large room with a skylight fitted on the north end. The impression was one of monastic severity. One would not have been surprised to see a well-bred crucifix on the wall. The walls were rough plastered and whitewashed and there was a bare floor of wide boards, painted black. During the day the skylight softened and diffused the sun, so that everything was bathed in a flattering, motionless light. At one end of the room stood an easel and table. Against a wall was a box spring and mattress, raised to comfortable sitting height by two sections of four-by-four lumber. At one end of this couch was a table and lamp, with a clean porcelain ash tray that looked like laboratory equipment, and nearby was a straight bentwood chair of the kind once used in restaurants, enameled black, and looking like an expensive piece of modern furniture. On a packing box in one corner was an electric plate, a tin of coffee, and a pair of cups and saucers made of imitation white Limoges. The simplicity was self-conscious, but it was effective. Avery was impressed. What affected him at once was the smell, that was exactly like the smell of his mother's studio at home—the smell of oil and turps and canvas, plus the smell of a woman. He looked around the room, perhaps a little too critically. Frieda smiled and said, "Are you looking for the john? It's down the hall. Come, I'll show you."

She guided him to the malodorous communal toilet. There was simply a closet with a toilet bowl—no tub, no washstand, no window. There was a hook inside the door, and on the wall someone had pasted an advertisement for a prophylactic. It was depressing. He waited for a moment, then flushed the bowl though he hadn't used it, and went back to the studio.

Frieda had put on her hat. She was wearing a gray tailored suit with a white shirt open at the neck, and looked impeccable. He wondered how she managed without a bathtub. She guessed what he was thinking and laughed.

"The convenience is a little primitive, I'm afraid," she said. "But one manages. Do you know where I bathe?"

"Where?"

"At the St. George pool, in Brooklyn. It's marvelous."

She took his arm and they went downstairs and out into the vivid street, the curbs crowded on either side with pushcarts piled high with food, fires burning here and there in corrugated iron cans, the air filled with Latin voices raised in argument and supplication. At the corner, a man was selling chestnuts that roasted over a charcoal brazier and smelled delicious.

"Italians," Frieda said. "I love Italians. Don't you?"

"I don't know," said Avery. "I don't think I've ever known one."

She squeezed his arm. "You haven't been touched by the breath of life," she said. "They are a great people. First the French, then the Italians. But in some ways the Italians are better."

They passed through a series of crowded streets, narrow and dirty and filled with life, making a number of arbitrary turnings that bewildered him, until they reached the restaurant Frieda had suggested, when he told her he didn't know the Village. It was in a cellar on Thompson Street. In the rear of the room was a pool table, around which a trio of dangerous-looking youths in sharp clothes stood watching a fourth youth take aim with his cue and fire. There was sawdust on the floor and wine on the tables. It was

Avery's first experience of the carefree Life of Art, and he wanted to appear knowledgeable, so he agreed when Frieda suggested that they begin their meal with the mussels, though he had never eaten a mussel in his life and had to be shown how to spear the things out of their shells. But the wine put him at ease, and the food was so good he forgot to be embarrassed.

"Have you known Connie very long?" asked Frieda. "Connie Requa?"

"Not long. She's a friend of Breitbart's really. He knew them last year."

"She's fearfully impressed with you," said Frieda. "She tells me you come from what she described as a terribly good family."

"Oh, no. Not me," Avery said.

"Oh yes," Frieda said. "She told me all about your family, and said you'd gone to some frightfully posh school in Boston or somewhere, and that your ancestors had distinguished themselves by slaughtering thousands of Red Indians."

Avery laughed. "She doesn't know anything about me," he said.

"She went to the public library and looked it up," said Frieda. "Apparently there is a special room devoted to the records of distinguished American families."

"I thought she was supposed to be left-wingish and above all that," Avery said.

"Well, of course she is," Frieda said. "She's very advanced, but she also reads *Harpers Bazaar* and things like that. She has a great interest in the high well born."

"She must be a fool," Avery said.

"Certainly. But I like her," Frieda said. "She's good hearted, and perfectly honest and she has a rather pathetic life."

The meal progressed through a pasta course to the inevitable veal cutlet, this time cooked with a bland cheese.

Avery was enjoying himself, but he was on guard. He had never met anyone remotely like Frieda before, and so had nothing to go on, no area of experience to which he could refer, and be had the kind of mind that doesn't make much progress until it has recognized or established certain postulates. The only beautiful woman he had known until now had been his mother, and it did not seem to him that his mother had been in the least like Frieda von Mardo.

Frieda carried the ball for him. She knew something about his work, because of her father, and he found himself telling her about old Douminoff and Dormaker.

"What is it you're making?" she asked. "Something that will explode and blow us all up?"

"I am a mathematician," he said. "I deal with equations, and equations do not explode. Only bombs explode."

"Bombs are made only to explode," she said, rephrasing his statement. "And they are made by scientists just like you." She looked at him and sighed. "It is incredible that a boy who looks like a tennis champion should be dealing with these sinister profound things."

He laughed.

"Bombs are made by mechanics," he said. "I'm not a mechanic. I deal with the truth, pure and simple."

"You don't really believe it?" she asked, looking at him suddenly in a new way, as if she had just noticed something different about him. "Not really?"

"Of course I believe it," he said, seriously. "Scientists are concerned with the truth, after all."

"You mean they are concerned with certain facts that can be given the appearance of truth, and that maybe will work, when you build something. Not with the truth. They don't like the truth, as a general thing. It interferes with their facts."

Avery shook his head. "I suppose you think there's truth in art?" he said.

"I don't know about that," she answered thoughtfully. "I haven't decided. But about science, that is another matter. My father was one of those people who like to play with systems. It is a Central European vice, like hunting animals with the English. He thought the National Socialists were an enormous joke, the funniest thing Europe had ever seen. And he continued to think they were a joke, until one day they murdered him and then hung his body in a public toilet and announced that his mind had failed and that he had killed himself."

"What did they want him to do?" Avery asked.

"Nothing, really," she said. "Merely to go on with his work and stop laughing at them."

She talked about Vienna and her childhood, and how the Germans had entered the city and how they had come for her father in the night, carried him off, then brought him back, carried him off again and brought him back, and finally carried him off and killed him. She repeated these things in a flat tone, without much emotion, almost as though she were reading a case history or a bill of indictment in a war crimes case.

When she had finished, Avery touched her hand and said, "I'm sorry."

"So am I," she said. "I loved my father, even though he was a fool in some ways."

"What happened to you?" he asked.

"Oh, the usual thing," she said, making a fatalistic gesture with her hands that was intensely European. "We were in a camp for a while, my mother and I. Then we were released. We sold what we had and got to Lisbon, then to Central America, and finally I got here to New York. My mother died in Guatemala. She was only forty-seven."

They sat for a little while without saying anything, then Frieda said, "Let's have a brandy, shall we?" and Avery ordered it.

He was shocked by what he had heard, and struck by humiliating awareness of his own insularity and ignorance. She had taken the lid off hell for a moment and given him a peep inside, and it made him ashamed of his own protected existence. He knew, because people in classrooms had informed him of the fact, that the German government had been operated by one Adolf Hitler, and he knew that the Nazi Party program had included extermination of the Jews and others. He had seen photographs and a movie short of the murder camp at Belsen. He had even heard Hitler on the radio, and heard the sea of terror behind him: *Heilsiegheilsiegheilsiegheil*. But he knew these things no more personally than he knew the facts that surrounded the American Civil War. Buchenwald had as little to do with him as Cold Harbor. He realized, sitting across the table from Frieda, who had been in a concentration camp, that he had been living outside the world. The flat way in which she had described her father's murder gave him, all at once, a glimpse of the paranoid actual world, and he was swept by a wave of guilt at his own lack of participation. He shuddered, as if struck by a chill, then drank the brandy at a gulp, burning his throat.

"Why do people do such things?" he asked.

"I don't know," she said. "And I have stopped wondering."

"People should wonder," he said.

She shook her head. "I don't agree. I don't think the past has anything to teach us. Or the future. We live a little bit at a time, a second, a fraction of a second, at a time. And if there is anything for us to learn it must be learnt from that moment, and not from history or tradition or some pattern of finite eternity that can be worked out on graph paper. There is no continuity, my friend. We live in a random world."

"No," said Avery. "You don't believe that."

"But I do," she said. "Take my father. He was at one instant walking down a city street in a university town, having been turned out of the Gestapo cells—forty years of learning balanced in his brain, a perambulating encyclopedia. A few seconds later, when the Storm Troopers had finished with him, he was dead flesh, soaking in a pool of piss."

"But the books are still there," Avery said. "Your father's books, for instance. We use them here, at Columbia. The books hold things, even though people die."

"The books can be burnt," she said. "Or, given a little time, turned into lies."

"Then what do you think is permanent?" he asked.

"This moment," she said, touching his hand. "Or this one," touching his cheek.

"You're wrong," he said. "I don't know why, but you're wrong. Dead wrong."

"I am right," she said. "But you are young and I am old. And it is time for us to go."

They went to a dim cellar night club and listened to a handsome tawny girl sing ballads, and to a black man with hands like spades, who pounded the bass end of the piano and made the low ceiling tremble, and then went to a cafeteria that looked like a public bathhouse and was violent with the clatter of crockery and trays and the contention of political voices. They ate scrambled eggs and drank coffee from heavy mugs. Someone slightly drunk tried to persuade them that the Fourth International glowed like a beacon or a burning star and was the final hope of the world.

When they came out of the cafeteria they walked slowly through the streets of the Village, that were quiet now in the late night, aware of the thousands upon thousands of people sleeping in the crammed soiled tenements that crowded the narrow sidewalks. The city seemed romantic and promising. It was warm for the time of year, like a night in early fall. She took his hand, and they walked that way, not speaking. When they reached her place, he stood facing her, her flickering color close to him, picked up by the street light. He wanted to tell her that he felt more alive than he had ever felt before in his life, and that it was because he had been with her. But he said nothing. She produced her keys and handed them to him, then said quietly, "Well, Avery, have you decided to sleep with me or not?"

His mouth went dry and his heart began to pound. He took the keys and his hand trembled as he fitted the large one into the lock. Then he swung the door open and stepped back, permitting her to enter the dark hall. For an instant he was overwhelmed by panic and the urge to flee. Then he stepped into the hall and followed her, his eyes on the flashing white movement of her legs as she mounted the stairway quickly. When he entered the studio and was struck by the smell he had recognized earlier, he had a sudden anticipation of ecstasy.

"Do you want the light?" she asked.

"No," he said. "I don't want it," surprised by the thickness of his voice.

She moved toward him in the darkness. As she touched him, a shaft of moonlight came through the glass roof, and he saw her face turned up to his. He kissed her slowly, then kissed her again. She drew away and he stood in the center of the room, trembling, aware of fear and of destiny. In the pale heatless light, he watched her take off her coat and shirt, so that the top of her body showed white, then watched her drop her skirt to the floor and step out of it. She was naked in the wet moonlight, and lovely. He was paralyzed and tried to cry out, but the cry remained in his throat, seeming to strangle him. Then it burst forth and the sound of the sob from his own lips startled him.

"Darling, what is it?" she asked. "What's wrong?"

"Nothing," he said, choked. "Nothing."

She came to him and he felt her fingers loosening his tie, then undoing the buttons of his shirt. She threw back the cover of the studio couch and the sheets showed white as a snow bank. She got into the bed and held her arms out to him. He sank beside her and buried his face in her breasts, then raised his head and kissed her.

"*Herz, mein Herz,*" she said softly, stroking his cheek.

His body trembled and he was afraid. He felt her hands on his back, then on his chest, and she whispered, close to his ear, so that he felt her warm breath: "*Herz. Mein Herz.*"

She was kind to him.

She was gentle as a mother.

"Avery, sweet ... you mustn't be frightened. You mustn't."

He lay beside her on the narrow bed, exhausted and filled with a sense of peace. Then he raised his head, propping himself on one elbow, and looked down into her face. She looked calm and maternal; he thought she was beautiful.

"I love you," he said.

He bent and kissed her on the mouth.

"You are an idiot," she said, laughing gently. Her arm rose in the faint light and surrounded his neck, pulling him down. His body was drawn close to hers. He seemed to submerge. This time he had a sense of conquest. He was exultant. As he made love to her, his body tense and filled with power, his heart seemed to counsel him, to repeat: *I am a man, for Christ's sake. I am a man.*

"*Herz. Mein Herz.*"

He kissed her throat and her breasts. He felt excruciating happiness.

He walked back to the college in the hour before dawn, his limbs numb, his mouth bruised, enchanted with himself.

He was in love.

It was a miracle.

He was in love, and he was a man.

He was just as much a man as Morgan, just as much a man as his father.

By the time he reached the college, dawn had broken. He had no desire to sleep, so he took a shower and changed his clothes, then made a pot of coffee, sitting in an easy chair in the front room, permitting himself to emerge slowly and pleasurably from the narcotic effect of love, still filled with astonishment by what had happened to him, not quite believing that the moonlit ecstasy had been real or that Frieda had been real. He sat this way, his mind roaming euphorically, until Freddie appeared, clad in a limp pair of shorts, yawning and rubbing his eyes. His tight marcel had been disturbed in sleep and this gave him a raffish, whorish look.

"What time did you get in?" he asked. "I didn't hear you."

"I don't know," said Avery. "Five. Five-thirty, I guess." He rose and poured coffee for his roommate, who sat down and stretched himself, still half asleep, obscenely pink. Freddie drank some of the coffee then looked up and said, "Well, did you?"

"Don't be an ass," Avery said.

Freddie nodded serenely.

"You have been to bed with the beautiful nihilist," he said. "You betray yourself." He wrinkled his nose. "Also, if you don't mind my saying so, you give off an odor of animal lust that I find offensive at this hour in the morning. You smell of rut."

Avery's ego overcame his sense of honor.

"She's not a virgin," he said.

"No!" Breitbart exclaimed. "You don't mean it?"

Avery flushed. "Oh, well, I mean it's not as if—"

"Oh Hollister for God's sake! What did they do to you at that bloody school?"

Breitbart finished his coffee, then padded barefoot into the bathroom. In a moment Avery heard the drumming of the shower, then Freddie's mock scream as he turned on the cold water. He smiled, then frowned. Of course Frieda had not been a virgin. The fact that she had slept with other men was inescapable. It was he who had been the virgin. He experienced a moment of panic, and a flash of crude jealousy. Then he remembered the conversation with her at dinner, when she had talked about her father, and her white arms reaching up to him, and her voice murmuring in his ear: *Herz, mein Herz,* and he was ashamed of himself. She was beautiful. Beautiful. And he was madly in love with her. The idea suited him and supplied his requirements. He had begun to suspect that he would never experience the kind of careening grand passion enjoyed by young men in books. But here it was, sudden as a storm, violent as an explosion. He sank back into his chair, comfortable as a cat, almost purring with self-approval.

CHAPTER FORTY-THREE

THE fall passed and the damp city winter began, the streets
clotted with dirty snow.

For Avery, that winter was Frieda von Mardo.

He could not get her out of his mind. Had she given him the
chance, he would have abandoned his work and devoted his days
and nights to her. He made an unconditional surrender, and it
was difficult for him to understand that she had not surrendered
too.

He took too much for granted.

Mentally, after the first night, he had taken possession of
her, made her his exclusive property. It was not possible. She was
nobody's property, and she had a work schedule and social context undisturbed by the fact that she had taken him to bed. It
would not be accurate to say that he was the victim of unrequited
love. She was kind to him, and liked him. But he was not the
central fact of her life, as she was of his during that winter.

They moved in different areas of experience and this caused
complication. He made an effort to penetrate her half-Bohemian
world in the Village, but it didn't work out. He went to dinner
with her and to espresso joints, along with the crowd of young
painters she knew—all of them veterans of the war, studying art
or just painting under the G.I. Bill of Rights, self-consciously
poor young men, even the ones who had money of their own,
dressed in dungarees smeared with paint and combat boots of
reversed leather, rough and heavy as laborers' shoes, making a
group of them walking together sound like a military patrol.

They were Murger's young men, jet-propelled, the hunger taken out of the poverty by modern institutional methods ... *vie de Bohème* with the fees paid and the garret inspected by the Board of Health. They regarded Avery as an outsider, because he had not been in the war, because he wore a collar and tie, but mostly because he was not a painter, and therefore of doubtful existence. He was jealous of their fraternity and of their proprietary attitude toward Frieda. He complained about it. "That fellow Lennert," he said. "You'd think he owned you."

"Don't be jealous, darling," she said. "Nobody owns me. I don't even own myself."

"I am jealous," he said. "I hate the idea of anyone putting his hands on you, the way he does, as if you were just a, just a—"

"Well?" she said brightly. "Am I not?"

"Oh, Frieda!"

She laughed. "Avery, darling," she said gently, "you mustn't act as though I'd been kept for you in a little box marked A. Hollister, Do Not Open Until Christmas."

"Don't talk that way," he said.

She caught his hand. "You must take me as I am, darling," she said. "Otherwise you will be miserable. And I don't want to make you miserable, believe me."

He had a need for her that was absolute as his body's demand for air and water, but he was lucky to see her twice a week, and sometimes other people joined them. He was jealous, and that winter he came to understand the murderous content of jealousy. Sometimes she didn't permit him to come upstairs with her when he brought her home, but sent him away after saying good-bye at the doorway in the street. He became obsessed with the idea that someone waited for her in the studio, someone she preferred to him. One night when she said, "Run along, *liebe'*, I'm fearfully sleepy," he had only pretended to go away, waiting at the corner until she was in the house, then going through a dank alley that led to the back yard, standing under a pitiful tree, staring at her lighted window. He was ashamed of himself and humiliated but he could not resist the impulse to spy on her.

He saw nothing but a bright oblong of light. After a little that disappeared and he was alone in the yard, under the bare, pathetic tree, confronted by the flat brick wall of the house, that betrayed no hint of life. From a tenement behind and high above him came the sound of a man berating his wife, then the strident wail of an awakened child. Someone threw a bottle from a window and it smashed in the concrete court behind him, making him move quickly, in fear. He shivered, then pulled his coat collar around his neck and hurried out of the garden, denouncing himself and feeling like a fool.

What confused him most about Frieda was her inconsistency. Sometimes, tonight for instance, she treated him casually as a stranger, seemed almost bored with him. But sometimes she made him feel that he was the only person in the world about whom she cared a damn. When she wanted to, she could make him feel that he was the most desirable, the most handsome, the most intelligent, the most witty, the most charming individual on the face of the earth. Sometimes she fed his ego the way a mother feeds her child. She made him feel self-confident and worldly. Then they would go back to her studio, where they would make passionate love, the achromatic light through the glass roof throwing a pattern across the bed, like shadow pictures. They would be thrilled by one another and by the sense of mystery that derived from the secretive, pleasantly dangerous quality of the skylit room, and the sense of concealment in the center of the great moving city that was all around them like a populated sea. She was kind. She had no inclination to sexual cruelty. She led him out of his awkwardness and for a time almost dispelled the cloud of guilt that he associated with his body.

On these occasions, when they were attuned, he was happy, and he departed from her filled with a heightened sense of self.

He was in love. He felt it. He could feel it in his blood and taste it on his tongue.

And in a certain, limited sense, he was loved in return, but not as the center of the universe.

It was not enough for him.

He wanted to be loved alone, like the sun.

And he lacked decent sophistication, having no understanding of the formal requirements imposed by the kind of relationship he had entered. He assumed rights that had not been granted.

"For God's sake, Avery," Breitbart said to him one night, "why don't you grow up? You're one of the luckiest characters in the world. You've got a good-looking girl to sleep with, who isn't a tramp, and who likes you, and who doesn't cost you more than the price of a meal or tickets to a show once in a while. Why don't you take it as it comes? Do you have to own her too? Do you have to carry the key to her chastity belt around in your pocket?"

"I know. I know," he agreed.

He reasoned with himself. Frieda had told him not to be a fool. She had warned him against exactly what he had fallen victim to. "You must take me as I am, darling," she had said. "Or you will be miserable."

It did no good.

She was in the air around him, wherever he went, like a heavy inescapable perfume. A phrase, a color, a flash of silk, were enough to turn his mind to her. Once in the crowd on a street he saw a blonde head in the distance that looked like hers. He hurried recklessly after it, bumping into people. When he overtook the girl she turned and he saw her face, heavy with some liquid make-up that made her skin look like pink felt. She smiled at him encouragingly and his stomach turned. She was hideous. It was part of a scheme to humiliate him.

He turned back the way he had come, walking slowly with his head down. He crossed a street against the light and a heavy truck nearly hit him, swerving, and grazing his coat, so that the buttons made a noise like pebbles in a bucket. The driver leaned down from his cab and yelled: "Whyncha look where yer goin', ya mockie bum?"

Avery drew back, his mouth filled with salt. When the truck moved on he crossed the street, then paused at a drugstore that had a thermometer with a narrow mirror bolted to the wall outside. He rubbed away the film of dust and examined his reflection in the glass. Why had the driver called him a mockie? He had a sudden idiot idea that he might have grown to look Jewish as a result of his sojourn in New York. But the face that stared back at him was his own Hollister face, that someone had said was *'pure nordic, Avery, pure nordic.'*

It would not have surprised him much to see a Cruikshank rendering of Fagin replying to him from the mirror. He was a tangle of confusion, and desperately in need of a hint of who or what he was. His self-hypothesis had been destroyed by his affair with Frieda, for in it he dealt with uncertainties, with things that changed like the sea in the sun, and he had no equipment for uncertainties. Heretofore what he could not be sure of, he had avoided; but he could not avoid Frieda.

During fits of depression that winter he brooded a good deal over his childhood and youth. Sometimes he bitterly regretted not having gone to Yale, making gentlemen's grades as his father had and playing on the football team—conforming, as he had been expected to conform, and in the end being rewarded with a place in his father's office and the deed to his father's farm, and a good marriage to a girl from Hull or Avon or Farmington, and the privilege of waiting in a well-appointed limbo for his father to expire. Perhaps, he sometimes reasoned, if he had done what his father wanted his father might have left the army when the war came to an end, and his mother might still be alive.

CHAPTER FORTY-FOUR

O NE evening he was seated in a restaurant with Frieda and a young naval officer approached them, rather unsteadily, having gotten down carefully from a stool at the bar. He stopped at their table and bowed. "Aren't you Einstein Hollister?" he asked.

Avery looked up, struck by the familiar nickname that he hadn't heard for years. It was Roger Bell, tanned and accoutered and slightly drunk. Avery rose and shook hands, then presented Roger to Frieda.

"Mind if I join you?" Roger asked. "I've been sitting at the bar by myself for an hour and it's grim. I guess I've been stood up."

There was no way to refuse short of deliberate insult, and one of the things that prevented him from employing insult was the fact that Roger wore a uniform. "Sure. Why not?" he said, drawing up a chair for Bell.

Roger sat down and put his hands on the table, so that Avery could observe that he wore a Naval Academy ring. "I hope you don't mind," he said to Frieda, his voice framed in a Colborn accent that made Avery realize he had almost lost his own.

"Not at all," Frieda said. "We are honored to have the navy with us."

Roger smiled at her easily, then called the waiter and ordered whiskey. "What are you drinking?" he asked Frieda.

"We are not drinking," she said, glancing at her plate. "We are eating. But don't let us interfere with you."

Roger laughed, then touched Avery's arm. "What are you doing with yourself, old man? In your Dad's business, getting rich?"

"I'm up at Columbia," Avery said. "In the graduate school."

"No kidding," Roger said. "Doing what?"

"Math."

Roger whistled, then laughed. "Good old Einstein," he said. "I wish you'd been at the trade school with me. I just managed to squeeze by math. Darned near broke out."

He prattled on about the Naval Academy. Avery was uncomfortable, and afraid he would turn up some oddment of schoolboy gossip that would embarrass him in front of Frieda.

Of course, Roger did.

"One thing I'll say about young Hollister," he said to Frieda. "He's sure improved as far as women are concerned. When we were in school he was so scared of girls you couldn't get him to a dance except by force. One time he—"

"You were schoolmates?" Frieda interrupted.

"Roommates," Roger said.

"Oh? Then you must be good friends."

"You bet we are," said Bell, clapping Avery on the shoulder. "You bet we are. We're buddies, old Einstein and I, even if he did walk out on me. Buddies." There was a dangerous undercurrent in his voice that came from the whiskey. Avery got up and excused himself, not certain that he could keep his temper if he stayed. He made his way between the tables to the men's room in the back of the restaurant. It was claustrophobic—an ammoniac cubicle with no window, fitted with a blower that produced a perpetually rising sound and might have been used as an instrument of torture. He bent over the scabby basin and sloshed his face with cold water, patting himself dry with a coarse brown paper towel. He was afraid of Roger as Roger, and afraid of him as the advertised hero. When he came out of the men's room he saw that Roger had moved his chair and now sat close to Frieda.

He heard Frieda laugh. When he got back to the table he sat sullenly until Roger finally said, "I've got to be going now, fella, but I wish you'd give me your phone number. I'd like to see you."

"Aren't you on a ship?" Avery asked. "I was under the impression that the navy went to sea."

"Well, so it does, old boy," Bell said easily. "I just happen to have a job in the Navy Yard."

"I'm afraid I don't remember the number," Avery said. "I never call the place myself. You can get it from Information."

"Avery!" Frieda said. She looked up at Roger. "I know his number," she said. She repeated it, and Roger wrote it down in a little book.

"Thanks," he said. "Thanks a lot."

Avery watched him move away, then watched him get his brass-bound coat from the hat-check girl. He was a j.g. already and Avery wondered vaguely how long he had been an ensign.

"Why were you so rude?" asked Frieda. "He seems a perfectly nice boy. Did he steal your girl or something, when you were in school together?"

"Of course not," Avery said. "I just happen to dislike him, that's all. For one thing, he's stupid."

Frieda shrugged. "Of course he's very stupid. He is magnificently stupid. But he seems harmless. And he has very nice manners."

"Did he try to make a date with you?"

"As a matter of fact he did not," she said. "While you were out fixing your hair he told me what an important man you were at school. He gave you quite a build-up, and he was absolutely correct."

"Naturally," he said. Now that Bell was gone, it seemed silly to have been mad at him simply because he was in the navy. "He was the great politician at school."

"Of course."

"He is a perfectly typical Colborn boy," Avery said. "He is the ideal product. The one they made the mold from."

Frieda smiled. "Is that what you are running away from?" she asked. "Are you afraid that if you don't run you will turn out to be like your friend, a pleasant nonentity?"

"Perhaps."

"Don't be afraid," she said. "You are different. You were different when you were born. There is another ingredient." She touched his hand and the warmth of her fingers excited him. "These things aren't decided by schools, darling, believe me."

"Say it again," he said, catching her hand.

"Say what again?" she asked, smiling.

"Darling," he said. "Say it again."

"Of course," she said. "As often as you like. Darling *Liebschen. Lieb' Herz.*"

They went home to her place and made love. It was exquisite, unmarred, perfect. Afterward they sat in the dark and drank coffee that she made on the electric plate. The room was warm; he had an awareness of peace, a sense of security. "Frieda," he said. "Frieda, will you marry me?"

She turned her head sharply. "Oh, darling, what would be the point?"

"I love you," he said.

"Today you love me, in a way," she said. "Maybe even tomorrow. Maybe next week. And I love you too, in a way. But next year, another year. That will be another matter."

"I love you," he said stubbornly, like a boy clinging to a lie. "I will always love you."

"I hope so," she said gently. "At least I hope you will always remember me with love. But you will not always want to marry me." She hesitated, then said, "I am your first woman, Avery. You must not let it confuse you. It passes."

He didn't answer.

She had been naked, but now she put on her robe and walked to the window, her body outlined against the light. She looked down into the garden, then up at the face of the tenement, across the yawning back yards. She turned and faced *him*.

"I would betray you in six months," she said quietly. "You know what I am."

His heart pounded. What he had known and hated to admit that he knew, now had been stated as brutal fact.

"You sleep with the others," he said. "With Dagget and Lennert and Bourne. With the whole damn city, for all I know."

"You have no right to question me, Avery," she said, her head coming up angrily. "No right."

"I have."

"No," she said. "No right. I owe you nothing. No one has the right to question me. I was once questioned for fourteen hours, and not about my chastity either. I will never be questioned again. I am what I am, and I owe nothing to anyone."

He stood up. "You are a bitch," he said. "A perfect bitch."

"So?" She looked at him very candidly, then said, "In any case, I think you overlook something. You are nineteen. You need your father's permission in order to marry anyone, and I don't think that he would like to have you marry me."

It was too much.

He dressed himself quickly, furious, then stormed out of the studio, going down the steep stairs three steps at a time. It was snowing and the pavement was covered with a light white flocking, treacherously slippery. His feet left the ground, and he felt his body rise in the air as if he had been lassoed, then he hit the concrete sidewalk with a jolt, scraping his chin, half stunned by the force of his fall. A man helped him to his feet: "You all right, mister?"

He brushed the snow from his clothes and said, "Yes, thank you."

"You're bleedin'," the man said. "Here." He offered a hand-kerchief, and Avery dabbed at his face.

"Thank you," he said. "Thanks a lot."

"You bet," the man said. "Watch your step, now."

He got into a cab and rode uptown to Morningside Heights, careless of the extravagance. The hard fall had done him a service. It had cleared his head, and the sharp rational pain in his chin brought him down to earth. By the time he reached the apartment he had persuaded himself that Frieda von Mardo was nothing but a tramp, just anybody's girl, like the Farmington girl his brother had taken out on the grass at Sturgis Manor—just anybody's girl at all, that anyone at all could take to bed who bought her a meal and a bottle of wine. She was a tramp, a roll in the hay, just someone you slept with, the way men used to sleep with chorus girls. She was disposable as kleenex; use once and throw away.

Nevertheless, for a long time that night, before he went to sleep, he saw her face and her white teeth and the long shaft of her body in movement, as she had moved in the darkness, coming toward the makeshift bed where he lay waiting for her. He woke up in the middle of the night, calling her name: *Frieda! Frieda!*

CHAPTER FORTY-FIVE

FOR a month, he did not see her.

It was a month of torture.

He would sometimes sit for an hour, staring at the telephone, congratulating himself on his own toughness in being able not to phone her and tell her that he was sorry. He had an insatiable curiosity about her movements and found it difficult not to spy on her like a private detective.

He missed her, as a physical fact, and missed his life with her. He was surprised to discover how much of his time must have been devoted to her, when he measured it against the long dull passages of loneliness with which he was now confronted. What in God's name had he done with his time before he met Frieda? he asked himself.

He went to the Requas with Freddie, half hoping Frieda would be there, attended by somebody else, so that he could organize his speculative jealousy around an actual face and voice. She wasn't there, and he was embarrassed when Connie said brightly, "Where's your girl, Avery? Where's Frieda?"

He made an effort to divert himself with a compact dark girl who had plump red lips and a Bennington manner and who wrote advertising for a store. It was no good. She was a pretty girl, with soft compliant brown eyes, and she had chosen him, he sensed it. But all he saw was a slight and nondisfiguring growth of hair on her upper lip. It disgusted him. He turned away, excusing himself, and stood in a corner all alone with a warm drink in his hand, daring anyone to approach him. From time to time the dark girl, now captured by a bald-headed man who looked prosperous and eager, glanced beseechingly at him, as if she wondered what she had said to drive him away.

Finally he went off by himself, leaving Freddie with a party of people who were working up to an alcoholic meal and a pub crawl on Third Avenue to which they invited him. He had dinner by himself in a cafeteria on Sixth Avenue, then walked up lower Fifth. At this hour, the street was deserted, the office buildings closed and silent as if the city had been evacuated, mournful Victorian façades rising sadly on either side of the long silent street, that had no conceivable beginning or end, but reached off north and south, toward the vanishing points. On the empty street, his endemic loneliness was heightened and dramatized. He felt homeless and nameless, without positive identity. It occurred to him that no one would care if he lifted a manhole cover in the street and simply vanished from the face of the earth. This mood of alienation was sharpened by the sight of an old derelict asleep in the doorway of an office building. He stopped and looked down at the man. There was blood on his chin and his face was gray. Standing above him, Avery was aware of the desperate alcoholic breathing. Then he touched the man's face with his toe, and the man groaned and stirred in his sleep, but did not awaken. Avery looked down into the face that had been made almost subhuman by alcohol. One night, he understood, the man would die in such a doorway and be carried off to the island in the East River where the city buries such individuals in great common graves, unless someone appeared at the morgue to claim the horrible body—a tired woman in shabby black or a silent embarrassed son.

He was intoxicated by depression and self-pity, and so romanticized his predicament that it seemed to him that no one, not even this hopeless gray creature, anesthetized and immune to normal pain, could be less loved or more forlorn than he. As he stood staring at the sleeping drunk, a young policeman came toward him with slow hieratic step, swinging his club in a gentle, ominous arc. He looked at Avery, then at the drunk, and stopped, the club dangling at his side.

"I thought he might be sick or something," Avery said defensively. "He's bloody."

The policeman shook his head. "They fall down," he said, "but they don't get hurt much. It's hard to kill these fellows." He prodded the man with his club and said dispassionately, "Come on, get up. Wake up now."

The man stirred and groaned.

"On your feet now, or I'll have to take you in."

Slowly the drunk came awake, staring up at the policeman, then at Avery, with bewildered pleading eyes There was a cut on his forehead and the dried blood had mixed with the grime of the street. The policeman caught his arm and swung him to his feet. For a moment he swayed, staring at the policeman, who poked him gently with his club. "On your way now," the policeman said. "Get along downtown where you belong and don't be freezing on this beat."

The man lurched obediently off, heading south. At the street intersection he paused and turned to look back. He staggered, then steadied himself and walked on, head down, hands thrust into the pockets of his soggy coat.

"Where will he go?" Avery asked. "It will be cold later on."

"Bowery," the policeman said. "They have their own place, just like anybody else." He did a juggler's trick with his club, so that it spun in the air for an instant, then continued on his beat, the confident sound of his footsteps echoed by the deserted street, given back by the silent walls. Avery watched him, marveling at the way he had done his job, with neither anger nor love, clinically, without reprimand or kind word. It seemed inhuman. It would almost have been less disturbing had he kicked the man or beaten him with his club, made any concession whatsoever to his personality, not treated him like an object, rather than a living, breathing animal.

Avery walked on uptown, depressed, wishing he had gone with Freddie and the people at the Requas. He envied Freddie's ability to manage women on a sensible level. Freddie seemed able to take what was offered, or what he could get through his own skirmishing, at its face value. Freddie would never be a damn fool, the way he was being about Frieda. Freddie would simply go out and get himself another girl.

That month, Freddie was engaged in pursuit of a girl named Noreen Culpeper, who had once walked on in a Broadway play but who now had a job as receptionist in an agent's office in Radio City. She came from a red clay village outside Atlanta and had studied dramatics at the state university, so that she spoke in honey-chile southern, overlaid with the affectations imposed on her drawl by a voice coach. The product was disconcerting. It was rather like hearing Latin uttered with a Swedish accent.

Noreen was a tall, ample girl, voluptuous as a cat; when she walked across the room the air around her was charged like the air around a tiger in his cage. She was a protégée of Connie Requa's and Connie was in a quandary about her, torn between desire to sponsor an actress, and the complicating fact that Noreen aroused Tom Requa's weary lust, that Connie had considered banked forever. Had Noreen given him any encouragement, Tom would have risked his marriage and status for the privilege of sleeping with her. Fortunately for Connie's peace of soul, she found Tom unappealing, though as far as Avery could gather, this made Tom unique among males under sixty.

Noreen had sex.

She combined blatant challenging sex with masterful stupidity. She was, as Freddie observed, "built." She had animal authority. And she was sentimental. One evening someone played Connie's recording of "The White Cliffs of Dover," and

Noreen broke down, weeping ardently on Freddie's immaculate gray flannel shoulder.

"I'm just a sucker for paytritism of *enny* kind," she explained. "I just can't he'ep myself, honey."

Freddie nodded gravely, patting her cheek and winking at Avery. When she retired to repair her face, Avery said, "God, Breitbart, how can you stand her? She's a moron."

Freddie laughed. "Her stupidity is her greatest asset," he said. "One day her lack of intelligence will be recognized, and rewarded with a gross of mink coats and a long shiny automobile."

Avery laughed. "She's like something out of a comic book," he said. "I admit she's stacked, but ... "

"You've been so corrupted by education that you don't recognize true innocence when you see it," Freddie said. "I like Noreen, and she's the best damn piece of tail in New York."

Noreen came across the room, her true innocence refurbished. "I'm sorry I was such a *darn fool*," she said. "I al-ways cry. My mummy says I'm nothing but a rivvah. Al-ways have been."

The cloying, affected voice made Avery wince. Noreen looked blandly at him and said, "You know, Freyad, your friend just doesn't like me. An' it's such a shame, 'cause I think he's just sweet. He's just the kind of man I admiah. Sort of *clean* an' *fine* an' in*tell*igent."

"Of course I like you," Avery said. "If you weren't Freddie's girl I'd make a play for you myself."

"Oh, I'm nobody's girl," she said innocently. " 'Ceptin' Mummy's. That is not yet, anyhow.'

Breitbart took her arm. "You come along with me, sweetie chile," he said. "Hollister's a bad man. A BAD MAN."

"How can you stand her?" Avery asked, when Freddie came home that night with lipstick on his collar and the look of achievement on his face. "I mean, I can see sleeping with her, but how can you stand it to listen to her?"

Breitbart sat down and looked at him pityingly. "Have you ever been drunk?" he asked. "I mean arm-waving, falling-down drunk?"

Avery shook his head. He had been given to understand that there were two occasions on which gentlemen might get themselves uncontrollably drunk. These were home leave from the front, during war, and the eve of a Yale victory over Harvard in a major sport. On other occasions gentlemen drank but didn't get drunk. Muckers got drunk and Dartmouth men.

"It might do you good," Freddie suggested. "Go out and get pie-eyed. Get into a fight in a ginmill. Wind up in a black whorehouse in Harlem. Steal a policeman's horse. Get yourself thrown into the can."

"What good would that do?" Avery asked, grinning.

"I'm not kidding," Breitbart said. "It might scrape the enamel off that phoney county-family snobbery of yours and give you the chance to act like a real human being, instead of feeling as if you'd committed a crime just because you've been to bed with a girl." He paused, stripping off his soiled shirt, then went on. "I like you, Avery. You're a good type," he said. "But you're a Cotton Mather at heart. Just a God damn Puritan. A real blue-stocking Puritan."

"My people are Episcopalians," Avery objected. "And I'm a full-fledged member of the anti-god society. You know that."

"Sure sure," Breitbart said. "All the same, you're a Puritan. There are guys whose families haven't been inside a church for generations who still carry Plymouth Rock around on their shoulders. You have a nose for the pit. You just haven't found out that it's possible to enjoy yourself and still be serious."

"I enjoy myself," said Avery stubbornly. "But I can't see any sense in getting half drunk and making love to a moron who talks like a blackface comedian. If that's life, give me death."

"Ahhhh." Freddie laughed. "Get drunk and find a cop to fight."

"I have better things to do," Avery said, a little more smugly than he intended.

Freddie's eyes narrowed and he looked candidly at Avery. "Look, my little son of the revolution," he said. "You don't by any chance regard yourself as my intellectual superior, do you? I once passed a night in the cells, for throwing a can of milk bottles through a plate-glass window, or at least for being along with the damned fool who did. And I have been passing out drunk and I've been to a nigger whorehouse. But I've also got a Phi Beta key and a degree that's just as good as yours."

"Oh hell," Avery said. "I didn't mean to be snotty. I just can't see getting drunk, that's all."

"Don't try to turn your deficiencies into virtues, my friend," Breitbart said pleasantly. "You'll just prolong the confusion."

Later, Avery brooded over this interchange. Freddie was at least partly right, he admitted to himself. He did consider it somehow inappropriate, and therefore somewhat immoral, for a graduate student in a university to be diverted by the frivolous, and to carry on an affair with a girl who belonged on Seventh Avenue working as an underwear model. And Freddie's personal challenge had teeth in it. Noreen or no Noreen, Freddie was a first-class intelligence, and had the born scholar's instinct for systematic work. Avery was a craftsman himself, and Freddie's talent was something he respected. And he understood that this was the real Breitbart; the rest was just on the surface.

Nevertheless, he could not persuade himself that it was quite suitable for Freddie to finish a paper on Bhakti, then go to dinner and a trashy movie with Noreen Culpeper, and afterward to fornicate with her in the hallway of her apartment house, as he said he had once done on an evening when Noreen's roommate had a cold and could not be persuaded to leave the one-room flat.

Nor did he appreciate Freddie's flair for the one-night stand. He wanted his experience with women to be invested with at least the formal appearance of stability and order; he wanted the illusion of committed love.

"You are a flaming repressed neurotic," Freddie told him. "You'd give some psychiatrist a run for his money."

"I don't think you'll find many neurotics among mathematicians," Avery said smoothly. "They're more apt to turn up in your field. Or in literature."

"Crap!" said Freddie. "There are no special qualifications. If the slide rule boys seem to be more stable it's just a matter of appearance. And fashion. They're in the saddle. Not so very long ago the mad scientist was all the thing. A guy had to be a little cracked to go in for science. You know: longhaired, wild-eyed, apt to be secretly constructing a machine that would blow up the world. Now they've made the bloody machine, and they go around looking and acting like bankers."

Avery laughed. He knew that scientists had no special claim to emotional stability. But he liked to think that the stiffness of the work, its abrasive discipline, somehow improved the character. He looked up at Freddie, who was putting on one of his gorgeous Charvet ties. "Going sharecropping?" he asked.

Freddie nodded. "Why don't you come along?" he said. "You can take Noreen's roommate."

"No thanks," Avery said. Noreen's roommate was like Noreen, without the physical equipment.

"You're a dope," Freddie said. He turned, looking at Avery seriously. "Why don't you call up Frieda?" he said. "Tell her you're sorry you called her a bitch. She'll take you back. On parole, anyway."

Avery shook his head. "No," he said. "I won't do that."

"You're a jerk," Freddie said. "A jerk's jerk."

Avery went into his bedroom and shut the door. Freddie was right. He was a jerk. He was a jerk's jerk.

CHAPTER FORTY-SIX

ONE afternoon a few days later when he came back to the apartment he got the sense of an intruder in the room, an intuitive, animal sense that frightened him.

It was Frieda.

She sat in Freddie's favorite chair, her legs crossed, a book on her lap, looking as though she had moved in and made herself at home. It was early spring and she wore a light tweed coat and a white beret. She was lovely. He stopped in the doorway, looking at her, then said, "What are you doing here?"

She raised her head and smiled, closing the book. "Waiting for you," she said. "Your old woman let me in. I'm afraid she thought I was a call girl."

Avery put down his brief case, then turned, fumbling in his pockets for his cigarettes. "What do you want?" he said.

"I've got Connie Requa's car downstairs," she said. "It's such a beautiful day. I thought you might like to drive out to the country and have dinner somewhere."

She was as natural as if he had seen her yesterday or the day before. It took him off guard. "Well, sure," he said. "That would be swell."

She got up and pulled the beret down a little, then moved toward him. He was aware of her smell.

"Shall we go?" she said, handing him a ring of keys. "You can drive if you like." She took his arm and they went downstairs.

He was exhilarated by the sensation of power he got from handling the heavy car. It was months since he had been at the wheel and this was a good car that responded well and gave the driver confidence because of its weight and powerful engine. It was a fine April day and the top was down, heightening the sensation of speed and reckless luxury.

"Why didn't you phone me?" Frieda asked, when they were on the parkway, going north.

"Why didn't you?" he said.

"You were the one who went away mad."

"I went to Connie's a few times," he said. "I thought I'd see you there."

"I've been busy getting ready for a show," she said. "I haven't been going out much."

"Oh?" he said. "Congratulations." She had never shown him any of her work, and he had sometimes wondered what it was like.

"Wait until after the show," she said. "I'll send you a card."

They drove on for a little, then he pulled over to the side of the road and stopped the car, turning toward her. The engine purred, making his hand vibrate.

"Oh, Frieda!" he said.

She put up her face and he kissed her roughly, almost brutally, a kind of implied rape in the way he pulled her toward him. It was a frank sexual kiss. There was no sentiment in it, only hunger.

"Did you miss me?" she asked, when he let her go.

He looked straight ahead through the polished windshield at the immaculate parkway. Far off a man was trimming the grass with a tractor and in the distance he and the machine looked like a child's mechanical toy. "Of course," he said. "Of course I did."

"I missed you," she said. "You're a sweet boy."

"I'm not a boy," he said. "I'm a man."

"Of course," she said. "I'm sorry."

He pressed the gas and made the motor roar, then swung out onto the highway. He got the car up to sixty, then seventy, then eighty, holding it skillfully on the road, then eased the pressure with his foot and let the speed fall back. "Where shall we go?" he asked.

"It's your part of the country," she said. "Any place you like."

He remembered a place Morgan had told him he used to go with his girls, an inn outside New Haven, on the way to Savin Rock. He found it and they had dinner there, under a tree, and stayed the night. The bell-boy was too familiar, and eager to let Avery know that he too was a man of the world. The room had an old-fashioned double bed with brass knobs on the posts, high off the floor. The mattress was lumpy and smelled of mold. There was an illicit atmosphere that was gross enough to be amusing. They lay on the huge sagging bed, smoking, the sheet thrown back, their bodies parallel and naked, looking up at the accusative, water-stained ceiling.

"Do you think I'm a whore, Avery?" she asked. "A real tramp?"

"Of course not," he said. "It's just a rotten hotel, that's all."

"It's a sinful hotel," she said. "It was conceived in sin. The architect was a procurer and the first owner was vice overlord of the colonies."

Avery laughed. "The first owner was probably a straitlaced ship's captain who made his pile in the China trade."

"Don't you feel sinful?" she asked, teasing him.

He turned toward her and his body touched her. Their faces were close together. He took the cigarette from her hand and put it out. "I do," he said. "Sinful as hell. Just sinful as hell."

During the rest of that spring he saw her more or less regularly, but it was not the same as it had been during the fall, when he had been in love with her. He tried to exploit his good fortune, to use what was offered of Frieda and forget the rest. He went out with her and the others in the Village, and tried to be sensible about everything. He tried his damnedest not to mind when Bill Lennert put his hand on Frieda's breast and said,

"Frieda, you are one lovely Kraut trollop, one lovely delectable Kraut trollop," though he wanted to punch Lennert in the face. He went with her once when she bought clothes in a bargain basement on Fourteenth Street. He got drunk with her one night and they made love in the park, under the stars. One week end when Freddie was away, she stayed at the apartment uptown. They didn't go out at all, but lounged around for two days, not bothering to get dressed, eating delicatessen food they ordered by phone from a place on the corner, drinking a considerable quantity of dry white wine. It was exactly the kind of week end he had read about in neo-Hemingway novels; it combined tenderness and nostalgia with hearty sex that had smell to it. It was bright and brave and brittle. He found himself talking like Jake Barnes, and referred to Frieda as a lovely piece. "I say Frieda," he said, imitating the English Character, "you are a lovely piece."

He was rather pleased with himself.

He was taking things as they came, the way bull fighters and soldiers did. For several weeks, that spring, he thought of himself as the hell of a fellow.

It should have been, as Breitbart pointed out, the ideal situation. Everything was under control.

But it turned sour.

One morning, in Frieda's studio, just after the dawn light broke through the clouded glass of the roof, he looked down at her while she slept and was swept by a wave of disgust. He stared at her breasts, that sagged down, and saw them as glandular and revolting. He had the urge to get up and go home, before she awakened. Then she woke up and smiled at him, drawing his head down and kissing him good morning. Her mouth tasted sour with sleep. He pulled away and she looked at him, surprised.

"Darling, what's the matter?"

He lay on his back, staring at the ceiling.

"Nothing," he said. "Nothing's the matter."

She got out of bed and crossed the room in the pale morning light, and though he had always been excited by the movement of her body, it now appeared gross, almost ugly. She was nothing but an object, a seminal sewer. He was sick to death of sex, as a child sickens suddenly of the sweet dessert he has for months demanded. It was over and done with. The enchantment was gone. It was as though someone had rung down the curtain.

She brought him coffee, and took the chair at the foot of the bed, holding her cup and saucer on her lap. She looked at him, understanding what had happened, then said cheerfully, "Well, Avery, are you still sorry I wouldn't marry you?"

He didn't answer.

"What would you have done?" she said. "I told you these things pass."

He looked up at her and said, "Have you ever loved anyone, Frieda? Really loved anyone?"

She put her coffee cup on the floor and linked her hands together, looking at them. "Yes, I loved my father," she said. "And I loved myself, when I was small and really quite lovable. I would stand in front of the mirror by the hour, doing my hair in different ways, just loving myself to death." She paused, lighting a cigarette. A spark dropped on her leg and she uttered a cry of pain. "But I don't love myself any more," she said.

Avery sat up, looking at her, wondering what had happened. There had been no process, no preparation. Yesterday he had wanted her and today he didn't. The unreliability of his temperament troubled him. She smiled at him. "Don't blame yourself, Avery," she said. "You have simply had enough, that's all. The thing to do is to turn down your glass and say 'No thank you' politely." She blew him a kiss, hamming the gesture. "No regrets?" she said.

"No regrets."

He was embarrassed and ashamed of himself. He got up and dressed quickly. When he was ready to go, she rose and came toward him; they stood close together, their faces almost touching.

"Good-bye, Avery," she said gently, becoming maternal and considerate of him. "Don't think badly of me, will you?"

"No."

"Promise?"

"Of course," he said.

It was a promise he intended to keep, but he couldn't. He had run through his course with her, and he did think badly of her. She was a classic bad woman. She had all the qualifications. She was beautiful, she was foreign, she was an artist, she was indifferent to censure, she was reckless.

He thought badly of her, disapproved of her, but he missed her. As she had once reminded him, she was his first woman.

Breitbart told him he was a fool. "If I had a set-up like that," he said, "I certainly wouldn't walk out on it."

"Why don't you make a pitch?" Avery said good naturedly.

"No chance," Freddie said. "I'm not the type. She likes a clean-lined youth, like yourself."

CHAPTER FORTY-SEVEN

H E DID not see her again, but in May he got a card from a gallery inviting him to a first showing of the work of three young artists, one of them Frieda von Mardo, whose photograph on the back of the announcement looked quite unlike Frieda herself. He went out of curiosity. The gallery was a new one in an old building on Madison Avenue north of 57th Street, on the fourth floor, and reached by a perilous tiny elevator with an open cage. The proprietor was a bald refugee, German or Austrian, who wore shabby expensive clothes and spoke beautifully accented English. There were nearly forty canvases and the effect of the bright clean gallery when he entered it from the dingy hall was one of overwhelming, assaulting color. It took him a few minutes to get his visual bearings.

Frieda was showing a dozen pictures; he looked at them first with interest, then with considerable respect. They were not what he had expected. He had expected cleverness and wit and a good deal of surface facility ... not real painting.

What he saw was real.

She was, he supposed, fundamentally an expressionist painter and sometimes her forms dissolved into purely emotional experiments with paint. But in her best work he saw that she was striving to bring to the tempting and often artistically suicidal method, a kind of solidity that recalled Cézanne, an inevitability of form and color, so that the painting became implicit as well as impressionist.

He was moved; he had no way of knowing it, but the effect on him of Frieda's paintings and his own honest formation of opinion, entitled him to take a more sanguine view of his fundamental character than the one he generally held.

As he looked at the pictures, particularly at a pair of related still lifes in which she had very nearly got exactly what she was after, he was struck by a contradiction in her temperament that had not suggested itself to him before. This was not ephemeral painting. It was not decoration, intended to be authentic only for the few moments it was actually in the beholder's presence—the kind of painting that is produced by certain accidentalists, in which are exhibited perplexing and sometimes irritatingly nostalgic or atavistic patterns that seem to have meaning, but that is essentially art without purpose, whose meaning, really, is rejection of purpose, so that the paintings become in the end a fashionable spoof that laughs at art.

Frieda's work was modern, often elliptical and daring, but it was never without purpose. It was in a tradition and made a bid for permanence.

"Why do you paint?" he once asked her.

And she had told him, "Because it is necessary to do something, and painting is the most pleasurable way of passing the time I have encountered, aside from having you make love to me." She had laughed and added, "Also, because there are kind individuals who encourage me from time to time with sums of money too small to be useful to them, but quite useful to me."

He realized, looking at the paintings, that she had not told the truth.

She was an artist, who painted because she had to, as others must breathe or drink or acquire money or secure brutal, murderous power, because they must do these things in order to live. He saw that he had been the victim of a hoax. A woman who painted in this way did not live merely for the brief springing instant. Frieda's nihilism, that she made a cliché, was phony as Breitbart's clubmanesque manner, a mask for the privacy of seriousness. Fundamentally, she must be solid as the rock spine of

Manhattan Island, and she must have extraordinary awareness of personal dignity, a high sense of her own worth. What he felt, as he looked at one of the larger paintings, an arrangement of objects on a table in the light of the morning sun, was a sense of poetic integrity, at bottom thorny and intransigent as Luther's mood at Wittenberg. He was experiencing with emphatic directness a part of Frieda's being that was beyond painting, secret as a river underground.

He understood with a pang of regret that he had not touched Frieda at all. He had known nothing but her body and her taught conversational facility, her intelligence. What he felt, here in the paint, was her soul.

He had cheated himself.

He had missed the heart of the matter.

And he understood now what Frieda had meant when she told him he did not love her, and was not in love with her.

He had not been, for he had not known her.

He turned from the painting reluctantly, aware all at once of the crowd of people pressing against him, and moved into the other part of the L-shaped gallery. Where the L bent was a table that held a cut glass bowl filled with poisonous-looking cerise punch, in which a jagged chunk of ice was moodily melting. The space near the table had been taken over by a collaboration of young men in mass-produced ultrafashionable clothes, who might have been aspirant juvenile actors or clerks in the drapery department of a Fifth Avenue shop. They looked at Avery admiringly and one of them smiled.

Avery turned away, moving vaguely from one to another of the paintings by the other artists, then found himself again looking at the still life that had impressed him earlier—the painting of bread on a sunlit table. He felt an affinity for the painting, strong as affinity for a human being, and was taken with the desire to own it, though he had never owned a painting or particularly wanted to own one.

The beebling of the young men came between him and the painting and he went out.

The next day he returned. The gallery was empty and the proprietor sat in his little office sorting bills. The silence, after the twittering noises that had filled the place the day before, was valuable as light, and it was possible to stand back and look at the paintings as he pleased. He had come to find out whether the still life he had admired yesterday would have the same effect today. The effect was greater. It was like encountering a familiar face in an alien room, and gave the same lift to the heart. He felt an odd, triumphant thrill of recognition, related in kind to the rich controlled thrill he sometimes felt when he had concluded an intricate mathematical journey, an intense, personal Q.E.D. He took enormous satisfaction in self-confirmation of his own judgment. He wrote the gallery man a check for two hundred and fifty dollars and watched him paste a red star in one corner of the frame.

"You are getting a fine painting, Mr. Hollister," the man said in his taught English. "It is a real statement." He paused, inspecting the painting. "She is not always absolutely successful, yet. But she is real. You have the honor to be her first buyer."

"Oh," said Avery. He looked at the painting. "I like it," he said.

"Of course," the man said. "It speaks to your condition. One felt that from the way you looked at it."

They stood for a moment in silence, the roomful of paintings around them. Then the man said, "Since this is the artist's first sale, we should drink a toast. Will you join me?"

"Certainly," Avery said.

The man produced brandy and glasses, pouring ceremoniously. They stood before the painting that now belonged to Avery and raised their glasses.

"Fräulein von Mardo!"

"Fräulein von Mardo!"

The brandy burned Avery's throat and he coughed, spoiling a little of the effect. Nevertheless, he felt invigorated and aware of a rare sense of autonomy. He felt reckless and daring as he left the gallery and turned into the street of rich discreet glittering shops, and was pleased with himself. But to leave it at that would be unfair. He had not bought Frieda's painting merely in order to impress himself, but because it did, as the man had observed, speak to his condition.

In two weeks the show closed and the painting was delivered by a sad-faced Negro messenger who helped him strip away the wrappings, then accepted a dollar and carried off the paper and rope for him. He had not mentioned his purchase to Freddie and now that it was in the room he was a little apprehensive. Breitbart had attitudes toward art and inclined toward intolerance of what didn't appeal to him. Fortunately, he liked this picture. He looked at it for a long time, squinting and turning his head, then moved back a little and continued looking, saying at last, "That's a good painting, Avery. A damn good painting. You've got a good eye."

"I suppose I should have asked you," Avery said. "A painting's a kind of personal thing."

"I like it," Freddie said. "Did she give it to you, or is it just a loan."

"I haven't seen her," Avery said. "I bought it."

"Oh?"

Freddie understood Avery; he didn't ask any questions.

A few days after the picture was delivered, Avery got a note from Frieda:

If you have nothing better to do, drop by for a drink on Thursday. Bring your Teutonic paramour, if you like.
There will be others.

F.

The note was written in india ink and the page had a neat professional quality that gave it the character of a formal invitation. He handed it to Breitbart, who read it and said, "Are you going?"

"I don't know," Avery said. "I wonder why she asked me. Maybe she thinks the artist's patron has a kind of *droit de connoisseur.*"

"Maybe she just wants to be civilized," Freddie said. "You know, friend. *Politesse.*"

Avery didn't go. Breitbart went and reported a conglomerate talky party, with nothing to drink but cheap red wine and nothing to eat but pizza pies Frieda had tried to heat on the electric plate, so that the cheese had run and burnt, making the place smell awful.

"Did she ask about me?"

Freddie shook his head. "I hardly talked to her, keed. She has a new guy, a painter-chap, complete with beard and flannel shirt. He wears the beard, someone told me, because without it he looks like an ad for toothpaste or breakfast food. An all-American boy type, like you, under the hair."

"She's a good painter," Avery said. "But she's a tramp."

"In-con-tes-tab-ly," Freddie said. "Didn't they warn you about wicked women like Freida at that ersatz Eton you attended?"

"No, that wasn't in the course," Avery said coolly.

He was surprised that he felt curiosity rather than jealousy about the man with the beard and the flannel shirt.

"I don't love her at all," he said to himself, and really believed it to be true.

The painting continued to give him pleasure. After a time it took on the character of a basic possession, something meaningful and important, toward which he had a personal relation, and that had very little to do with the woman who had painted it.

CHAPTER FORTY-EIGHT

WHEN his work slackened off he found himself going to the Requas' Friday night brawls again, sometimes with Freddie and sometimes alone. People had stopped asking him about Frieda, having been briefed by Connie Requa and given a description of the man with the beard. He became used to the Requas' parties, used to the faces, and to the rather anticlimactic quality of the evenings, which always began in an atmosphere of tension that seemed to promise excitement and petered out at the end, with people getting tired or bored with one another, or simply drunk and incompetent.

Tommy Requa, during the last year, had taken to getting more and more drunk, whether because of the savage competitive demands of his job or disenchantment with the pattern of his life, no one seemed to know. The turning point of the Requas' parties usually occurred after Tommy had passed out or gone to a saloon to drink by himself, and Connie had fed herself enough gin to flirt with one or another of the young men alcoholically encamped in her apartment. It hadn't occurred to Avery that she did anything more than flirt until one evening when the party had reduced itself to six rather groggy people, in addition to Connie and him. Tom had departed after a bitter, public little row, and as Connie had informed them all, was drinking himself pig-drunk at some place on the water front for which he had recently formed an attachment. Avery sat with Connie on a couch with broken springs, a little mulled by drink, and bored. He got up, intending to go, but Connie seized his hand.

"Come and help me get some ice, will you Avery lamb?" she said.

She towed him into the kitchen. There were dishes in the sink and a smeary towel hung from a distorted wire rack. She drew his hand around her waist and then raised it to her breast. He had never thought of making love to Connie Requa, and his reaction was one of shock. She was half drunk and the incident was grotesque. There were small children's clothes on the dryer that hung from the ceiling, and there was a vague, persistent odor of cookery, together with the smell of her powder, and the rank, chemical odor of gin and stale lemon juice. Her mouth was slack as a warm wet rag. She leaned back over the kitchen sink, her skirt pulled up in a wad around her waist, and held him to her, her sharp painted fingernails, under his shirt, biting into his back.

It was brutal and frightening. When he left the Requas' half an hour later, he was trembling. What disturbed him most was a conclusive awareness of animal entrapment. He did not care much for Connie Requa. She did not appeal to him as a woman or as a person. It had never occurred to him to make any move toward her at all. But he knew that he could not, after she had kissed him with her tongue, have failed to go on to the end. It was an awful demonstration of the crude fact, of the short distance beneath the surface that the beast lives. That spasmodic uncomfortable fornication in the dirty kitchen had been ruthless as the mating of dogs in the street. He was disgusted with himself and felt physically contaminated. Yet he did not regret the experience; he felt that it had taught him something, though he wasn't quite sure what. Breitbart was amused when he told him about it.

"Never get caught with Connie after 10 P.M.," Freddie advised. "You're sure to be raped."

"Why does she do it?" Avery asked.

"Christ, who knows?" Freddie said. "When you look at Tom you can hardly blame her."

"Well why doesn't she leave him then? Clear out?"

"Well hell, she loves him," Breitbart said. "They've been married for years. They were kids together in Paris."

He avoided the Requas' for two weeks, persuading himself it was fastidiousness but knowing it was really fear. When he finally went back, Connie whispered to him: "You bad boy Avery Hollister. Raping your hostess in the kitchen! Is that the kind of thing they taught you at Colborn?" She wagged a finger at him and moved off, her preposterous earrings dangling. He smiled at her simple-minded ability to convince herself that he had taken advantage of her. As he watched her moving about the room, her hips undulant and suggestive, he found himself wondering what it would be like to make love to her in a bed, unscrutinized by roaches and infants' underwear. He was not curious enough, however, to make an effort to find out.

CHAPTER FORTY-NINE

THAT spring he was getting to know Dormaker.

Occasionally Dormaker took the staff of the project to lunch in the Faculty Club dining room, located on a high floor that overlooked the city. He sat at the head of a long table—paterfamilias—and entertained the young men with tales of his days at Göttingen, where he swore he had fought a duel with swords, and with stories about the military. They didn't talk shop very much, though it was shop that drew them together. They were all men who had been attracted early on by the lure of ideas for the sake of themselves, and even Lewiston, the engineer who was to do the actual construction of the machine, sometimes was betrayed into revealing his fascination with the essence of the thing—the complicated web of relationships built up out of nothing but pure idea, the system actually without a subject, the imaginative heart of mathematics, that he ordinarily professed to regard as highbrow and useless.

Avery, being junior to the others in both age and academic status, did more listening than talking, though he fell into a pleasant working relationship with Bascomb, his immediate superior, and sometimes had dinner with him and Lewiston and one or two of the others. He liked them, but the imperative force at work on him was Karl Dormaker.

During the year that had passed he had developed intense respect for Dormaker, and affection, but Dormaker sometimes perplexed him and often made him feel inadequate or improperly gifted. He had embarked on his graduate work still fired by

a romantic notion. It had seemed to him that the ideal mathematician would be suprahuman, less a man than an intellectual instrument—a kind of Western European yogi, with body
and emotional system so controlled that he could become, for
extended periods of time, almost pure idea. Such a conception
applied to Dormaker was ridiculous, yet Dormaker was without
question one of the stalwarts of modern science. He was about as
detached and disembodied as a ball game. He was as human as
an Indiana farmer, brimming with life, and in intimate, sharply
aware contact with the details of daily living.

"You are an idiot," he replied to Avery's half serious suggestion that a longish term in prison might be a useful thing for a
scientist. "One wants to be in the midst of life. I had one of my
best ideas when I was pushing a baby carriage. I had another one,
years ago, you understand, when I was young, watching a very
pretty girl in Berlin, sitting in front of a mirror brushing her hair.
It was long hair you see, and the shape of the curve into which it
fell gave me my solution."

He looked at Avery, his eyes twinkling, and Avery never
found out whether or not he was being fooled. Dormaker's
humor and love for exaggerated skepticism bewildered him, and
he was sometimes puzzled by Dormaker's apparently casual attitude toward the work of the project. When he had been given
the assistantship, he had expected to be driven. After all, this
was a serious business, not a matter of courses and grades. If
Dormaker finally built his machine that might, among other
things, play a dull game of chess, he might change the world, or
at least the appearance of the world. It seemed to Avery that such
work should be approached in the way a washed and sanctified
priest approaches the altar of God, that all of them should be self-
impressed with the high significance of their mission.

Dormaker did not in the least suggest a laved and sanctified priest. He was as unconcerned as a man playing a game of
croquet.

"You are working in an area," he once told Avery, "not following a white line down the center of a scientific highway. Think
of it as a section of forest with dense undergrowth, populated by
wild animals and dangerous reptilian manifestations. We have
this section. Down the hall they have another. At Cambridge
another. In Moscow another. *Und so weiter.*" He smiled and said,
"You could not run a hundred yard dash through the forest, could
you? No. You must beat about carefully and take your time. Also,
you must watch out for the beasts. They are in every tree."

Avery had laughed. But when he thought about it afterward,
Dormaker's meaning had become more clear and he found that
the forest was a useful concept applied to the kind of research they
were doing. For a long time now he had thought of mathematics
as a structure that was above reality. He began to see that it was
all mixed up with reality, that the real and ideal were inseparable
as the fibers of the human brain itself. He found himself trying to
draw together the ideas of reality he had acquired and the formal
structure to which he had been introduced during the last four
years. As he brooded over this attempt at synthesis, he became
dissatisfied with himself, for he realized that he seldom felt reality, and that when he did feel it his impulse was not to embrace it,
to possess it, but to flee. He was subject to a good deal of ethical
tension, and sensed the need of some moral catalyst that seemed
to have been left out of the formula that had produced his Yankee
mind.

"What is it we lack," he asked Dormaker. "I mean what do
Americans lack? What's been left out?"

"The sense of tragedy," Dormaker told him. "We lack the
conviction of tragedy the Greeks had, and that some Europeans
have. We forget, or maybe never really understand, that the environment is hostile and that every time we take a step forward
we risk the unholy wrath of the gods and are dead certain to be
punished for our defiance. We like to think of the environment
as a kind of private Coney Island established for our enjoyment.

You pays your money and you takes your choice. But it isn't so, my young friend. The world is a very dangerous place and there is no security, except that rather negative security of walking humbly before thy God."

"There doesn't seem to be much sense in it," Avery said. "You have lost before you even start."

"That's right, Avery," Dormaker said. "It's a fixed wheel. But it's the only game in town, as the man said."

"That's true," Avery said. "It is the only game in town."

Toward the end of the college year, Mrs. Dormaker asked him to dinner. He presented himself at seven o'clock, nervous as a schoolboy calling on the teacher.

The apartment was large and old fashioned, built to the scale of the last century. There were eight or nine rooms, leading off a long narrow hall that had a number of turnings and was covered with dense carpet, so that one had the sensation of approaching in secret, without sound. The air was heavy with the peculiar and nostalgic smell of well-kept old houses—wood and age and food and furniture polish and heavy fabrics. There was a feeling of space and height unusual in New York apartments, and the atmosphere was not quite American. There was a hint of the Central European, emphasized by a cabinet of china in the hall and the quantities of substantial, shabby furniture. It was the kind of flat one could imagine Freud's inhabiting, or some gigantic Teutonic poetic dramatist. There was an aroma of prestige, beyond the bought position of wealth or the inherited position of birth.

As he entered the twin front rooms that had a bank of windows facing the river, Mrs. Dormaker rose from a chair and came toward him. "Mr. Hollister?" She offered her hand. "I'm Erna Dormaker."

Her voice was tinted with a German accent and reminded him of Frieda's. He bowed. She was fifty, with a blunt figure and a handsome head covered with fine paper-white hair, drawn tight and finished in a bun. She looked like the Dowager Queen of Holland, and had a quality of warmth that put him at ease. They sat down together in a pair of chairs near the windows, looking out across the park and river to the cliffs on the Jersey shore. The sun, going down behind the cliffs, came through the windows and flooded the room with a poignant evening light.

"So you are one of Karl's young men," she said, looking at him. "One of his aspirant young men."

He smiled. "I suppose I'm aspirant," he said.

"All of Karl's young men aspire," she said. "It is the first requirement." She paused, then said, "What do you think of my husband?"

Avery was taken off guard. "Well, it's a privilege to work with a great man," he said awkwardly. "I, uh—"

She laughed. "I suppose Karl is a great man, for it was once printed so in the paper, and one has no choice but to believe what others have gone to the trouble to print." She smiled, teasing him. "Of course, I agree with the papers," she said. "It is just that for thirty years I have had the privilege of watching the great man shave."

Avery laughed. There was a sound at the door and the great man came into the room, bearing a tray that held three glasses of pale astringent sherry.

"I suppose you would like a martini," he said, handing his wife, then Avery a glass, "but you won't get it. They are a barbarism, cocktails. A barbarism. When I think of the amount of gin I consumed, in defense of my country, during the war, I shudder."

The sherry was good. Avery followed the lead of the others and drank it slowly. He was not offered another glass. When they had finished they filed down the narrow hall to the somber impressive dining room that was lighted by candelabra, and the colored maid who had answered the door served them a meal Mrs. Dormaker had cooked—bits of veal in sour cream and little potatoes with fresh dill on them, and after that a sweet rich cake and powerful coffee in fragile, feminine Meissen cups. The esprit was Austrian and gemütlich. There was elegance about the meal and the simple way it was served, elegance, together with homeliness, a combination Avery wasn't used to. After the plates were taken away the maid brought in a bowl of fruit and a pot of fresh coffee. They didn't leave the dining table, but sat around it with their chairs pushed back a little. Only the table was lighted; the rest of the room was in shadow and the high ceiling rose mysteriously. Avery felt very much at ease. He was glad that he was the only guest, for another person would have detracted from the sense of family he felt.

"Well Avery," Dormaker said, lighting one of his awful cigars, "in a little while you will be a Master of Arts. Have you made up your mind about being a scientist yet?"

"Sir?" Avery asked.

"Have you decided to go on with us, or are you going to leave us? I have the impression that you were using this year as a kind of test, trying us out, so to speak, in the same way we were trying you."

"Well in a way I guess that's so," Avery said. He hesitated, staring at the sentimental pattern of the china cup. "Do you think I'll make a scientist?" he said.

Dormaker carefully tipped the ash from his cigar onto his saucer, then glanced at his wife and made a mock gesture of fear, and drew a small ash tray toward him. "I think that in time you may become a very valuable human being," he said. "Whether in the field of mathematics, or science at all, I do not know and certainly wouldn't try to guess. You have intelligence and a certain talent for exploration. And you're a good workman." He spread his hands as if to beg the question. "There's no doubt that you can take a respectable Ph.D. and become a useful member of somebody's faculty." He paused, looking candidly at Avery. "But I don't suppose that would suit you, would it? You have more serious ambitions."

"I wouldn't put it as extravagantly as that," Avery said. "I would like to do more than just teach, yes. But I don't want to get ambitions that are too big for my abilities."

Dormaker leaned forward and the candlelight fell full on his face, emphasizing its ugliness and the pattern of struggle engraved upon it. "All ideas that are worth anything are too big for the abilities of the men who encounter them, Hollister," he said. "Do you think Leibniz exhausted the idea of the calculus? Or Newton? Do you think Cantor had the last word on the *Mengenlehre,* Theory of Classes? Or Einstein on Relativity?"

Avery opened his mouth to protest but Dormaker smiled and waved his hand. "I know, I know. You don't want me to get the idea that you are presumptuous. You want me to understand that your ambitions are in good taste, and that you don't regard yourself as a heaven-tapped genius. Very well. I will understand that. But don't forget that Newton and Leibniz and Cantor, Galileo Galilei—they were men too, just as you are. They were not gods or angels, but men. There is no point in having ambition at all, unless you point high. Very high. Then even if you miss, you get somewhere. Point low and you never get off the ground."

Mrs. Dormaker made a clucking sound. "Karl, you will frighten this nice young man with your speeches." She smiled at Avery. "He is always this way with young men. He asks them to dinner, then lectures them like a sour old bishop reprimanding a young priest."

"Erna, Erna," Dormaker laughed. "Do not indulge in connubial treason." He turned to Avery. "As for being a priest—the young scientist today wants to be priest, soldier, politician, businessman, diplomat, as well as scientist, if he hopes to stay alive. Scientists are not very much trusted. They are regarded as dealing with suspect forces. Do you know who is the prototype of the scientist, young man?"

Avery shook his head.

"Prometheus," Dormaker said. "The hero damned. The bound god. Chained on the Caucasus with the vultures gnawing at his liver. Bring them fire and they will warm themselves and cook their meat with it. But they won't thank you. They'll be afraid. Afraid the god you stole it from will be down on them with an ax in his hand, looking for their heads. The scientist nowadays has to be the scapegoat as well as the hero."

"Karlchen, you exaggerate," his wife protested. "Your experience with the military has made you suspicious." She laughed merrily and looked at the handsome table, then around the room. "You are not chained on the Caucasus are you? You have everything you want. Just because a stupid general spoke stupidly to you, you pervert the lesson of your experience. Is that scientific? It's childish."

Dormaker waved his cigar. "I was speaking in symbolic terms," he said. "Besides, it was an admiral, not a general. You confuse these things."

"What did the admiral say?" asked Avery.

Dormaker laughed. "Oh, he was one of those fellows who yearn for the days of wooden ships and iron men. He wanted to know how he could be expected to fight the war with a lot of kike scientists waving slide rules in his face."

"You mean he said that to you?" Avery asked.

Dormaker laughed. "I was the only kike scientist handy," he said.

"But you're not a Jew!" Avery said.

Dormaker smiled. "To a certain mentality, Avery, all scientists are Jewish Communists. If you go on in the field you will discover that this is true." He paused, frowning. "Of course it is not really so funny, this business with the admiral. We permitted a group of self-willed ignoramuses to erode the soil of the country to a very dangerous level. We mustn't let the sons of the same men erode the brains of the country too. We need a conservation program for ideas." He lifted the silver coffeepot and poured coffee for himself and Avery. "If we don't stand up and walk like men, realize our full potential, we are not long for this world. Hail and Farewell."

"We once had an old colored cook," Mrs. Dormaker said, "who used to say: 'This world an' de nex' one, an' den comes de fiahworks.' Now we have the fireworks, in this world."

"It's not that," Dormaker said. "I think we're more apt to yawn ourselves to death than to blow ourselves up. It's the inertia of the human spirit that's dangerous. Worse than a million bombs. Maybe worse than being blown up." He looked at Avery and asked, as if just struck by an idea, "Tell me, young Hollister, why did you go in for mathematics instead of engineering or medicine or physics, as is the fashion among the young men nowadays? What made you pick pure theory?"

Avery stared at his hands, spreading them on the tablecloth, then raised his eyes and looked at the face of a clock on the wall behind Dormaker. "I wanted to find out whether anything was true," he said slowly. "Or dependable." He paused, looking back at his hands. "Or whether the whole thing was a fake, an enormous lie."

Dormaker nodded.

"I thought so," he said. He frowned for a moment, then went on. "Has it ever occurred to you, Avery, how significant the accident of time is, so far as the individual is concerned?"

"I don't understand," Avery said.

"I mean to say, had you been born in New England, in the same house, two hundred years ago, you might have attempted to become a Protestant saint. Or if you'd been born say a hundred years ago, you might have been a naturalist, a biologist, instead of a mathematician. Or if you'd been born forty years ago the times might have made you see things in closer perspective, in terms of disinherited people instead of disinherited stars. You might have been an economist or an historian—one of the bright young men your Alma Mater sent to Washington in the early Thirties, filled with a mission and the determination to make America over."

Avery shook his head. "I don't think so," he said.

"Perhaps not," Dormaker conceded. "I was just speculating. It doesn't really matter, for you weren't born forty years ago, or a hundred. You were born in this generation. And you haven't answered my question."

"What?" said Avery. "Which one?"

"About whether or not you've decided to go on," Dormaker said. "It is not altogether a personal question. It is partly business."

Avery thought for a moment then said, "Yes I'd like to go on, if you will have me. And want me."

"We want you very much," Dormaker said. "And we need you. We are lucky to get you." He paused. "But there is one thing I would like to tell you, Avery," he went on. "For your own sake."

"Sir?"

"Please," said Dormaker. "No sir."

"Sorry."

"What I wanted to say, Avery, is this. And it comes from an old man. Science is a part of life, not a substitute for it. People who use science or art or anything else as an escape from life rarely become more than hacks. It is only in religion that withdrawal from life sustains the passion and science is not religion." He glanced at his wife, then back at Avery. "Do you mind if I say something frank?" he asked.

Avery shook his head. "No. Fire away," he said.

"I think you are inclined to be afraid of life."

"Karl!" Mrs. Dormaker said. "Why should a handsome boy like this be afraid of anything? He should have the world at his feet."

"Perhaps," said Dormaker. He smiled at her. "According to your theory of the coincidence of courage and physical beauty I should have passed my life in terror, crouching in a cave." He slapped his chest and raised his arm above his head, imitating a gorilla. The effect was realistic enough to be disturbing. "But I am not in terror. I feel brave as a lion."

His wife laughed then rose from the table and they followed her into the front room, where they listened to phonograph records: Beethoven, then some strange French songs that Avery had never heard, curiously atonal, mysterious and unsettling to the spirit as cave drawings. When it was time to go, Avery said good night to Mrs. Dormaker, and Dormaker walked to the door with him.

"What will you do with your summer, Avery?" he asked. "Are you going to Connecticut? That's your native heath, isn't it?"

"Are we closing the shop?" Avery asked. "Aren't we going to work this summer?"

Dormaker smiled and touched his shoulder. "My boy," he said, "I am fifty-three, and in my bones I sometimes feel almost ninety. I have not had a vacation since the year before the war. I am going to Paris with my wife, and we shall pretend to be young again."

Avery's disappointment showed on his face; Dormaker laughed.

"There is nothing to be discovered that won't keep until September, Avery," he said.

Avery grinned and said, "I guess not."

They shook hands.

"Have some fun," Dormaker said. "I will see you in the fall."

"Right," said Avery. "Thank you. Thank you very much."

He walked slowly back to his apartment. He had been disturbed by some of the things Dormaker had said and excited by others. What had impressed him most was the familial aura that surrounded Dormaker, the sense of family, even though his children were grown now and gone away. There had been the suggestion of the pram in the hall, of bourgeois well-being. He could not help contrasting this with the almost ascetic way in which

Douminoff lived, alone and unmarried, in dormitory rooms, detached almost completely from the surge of life beyond the university gates. That way of life, the monkish way, had seemed to him appropriate, the proper setting in which to conduct a search for impeccable truth. Yet Douminoff, as Dormaker had gently hinted, was nothing more than a reliable hack, while Dormaker himself was a lion, a man who was filled with daring, as far from fear as anyone Avery had ever encountered.

He saw what Dormaker was trying to tell him: that there was no place to hide. He didn't like to accept this. It made him feel naked and alone and gave him an image of the world that resembled a windblown steppe.

CHAPTER FIFTY

A FEW days later he was given counsel from another source. Ivy Calder telephoned him and asked him to come and see her.

"I'm just back from Europe," she said. "I came in a bomber. It was marvelous."

It was the voice of the enemy; it made him bristle.

"I'm very busy," he said. "It's almost the end of the term."

"But you can take time out for a drink. Please do. I want to see you."

"Very well."

She had a suite at the St. Regis with a sitting room that was elegant as a room in a private house, with deep comfortable velvet chairs and a pale French rug. She offered him whiskey and gave him sherry when he told her he didn't care for whiskey. She wore a belted black dress with a skirt that swirled when she moved and fragile shoes with astonishing heels.

She was charming. She looked like a beautiful Congresswoman out of a Hollywood light comedy. She did not really fit his conception of a New York whore at all, but that didn't prevent him from being suspicious of her and opposed to her. He wondered why she had gone to the trouble to have him down here.

"I've seen your father," she told him, after she had given him the wine and the best chair. "He looks marvelous. He's done a grand job, you know. You should be proud of him."

He nodded politely.

She told him about his father's contribution to the re-estab-lishment of Germany, about his father's political realism, that was so useful to General Clay, about his father's art with the former Nazis. She sounded like a campaign orator, and he said, "You know I don't vote yet. I'm just twenty."

She laughed and said, "I suppose I sound silly. But I thought you would want to hear about it."

"Naturally."

"You know, Avery," she said, changing the tone of her voice, "I was terribly sorry to hear about your mother's death. I never knew her, of course, but I had met her. She was a lovely person, and very beautiful."

"She killed herself you know," said Avery. "It wasn't the way the paper said."

It backfired on him. "I know," she said. "Your father told me. It must have been dreadful for you both."

"It was unpleasant," he said. His heart pounded. He had been denounced and slapped across the face for asking a ques-tion about a fact his father had pretended wasn't a fact, yet had told this woman as a matter of course. It seemed disloyal, to him and to his mother.

There were a few moments of silence, then Mrs. Calder said, "You may think it presumptuous of me, Avery, but I'd like to say something personal to you."

"Yes?"

"Your father's coming home soon. In a month, at the most. Perhaps he's written to you?"

He shook his head.

"He said you'd quarreled," Mrs. Calder said. "He's unhappy about it. He wants to see you."

"He knows where I am," Avery said.

"He wants you to come home," she said. "Where you belong."

Avery looked at her, wondering how much of this was her own idea and how much was his father's suggestion. "Did he send you to see me?" he asked.

"No. It was my idea. He said it wouldn't do any good." She smiled. "He said you were a stubborn Yankee, stubborn as he is." She paused. "He's a proud man, Avery," she said. "But he loves you and he misses you."

"What does he want from me?" Avery said.

"He wants your friendship," she said. "Your approval. You're almost a grown man, Avery. Doesn't it occur to you that your father is a human being too?"

Avery stood up, his resentment out of control.

"The only thing he could do that would get my approval would be to die," he said, the words coming from somewhere deep inside him. "I hate him. He's a selfish bastard."

He turned and went out of the room, furious, feeling that he had been invaded. On the bus going back to college he calmed down a little. It occurred to him that his father's woman had mis-read his father's character even more grossly than he had done. His father didn't want his approval, or at least, would never have asked for it. His father took the blanket approval of the whole damned world for granted.

CHAPTER FIFTY-ONE

A FEW days later, he became a Master of Arts in Mathematics. He was conscious of no sense of achievement. He might as well have been graduated from a barber college or institute of shorthand and typing.

He passed out of the roped arena and took off his cap and gown. In a drug store on Broadway he drank a coke and unrolled the degree the smiling general had handed to him. It was his fourth diploma. If he followed his present plan he would have at least one, perhaps two more. The degree informed him that Avery Hollister now enjoyed the rights and privileges of a Master of Arts, but it did not tell him what the rights are, or how he took advantage of the privileges. He sat at the marble counter with his hand in the wet, struck by a sense of disillusionment, and by the suggestive urge to abandon his pattern that had touched him a year ago: the urge to leave whatever he owned where it was, to strike off in the clothes he wore, with the few dollars in his pocket, toward the West, in search of what or to escape what he did not quite know. He felt the need to take some action that would be independent, unorthodox, identifying... action that would be for him a statement of autonomy. But he did not get up. He simply sat at the counter, contemplating his Coca Cola.

He felt a sudden wave of disenchantment with science. It seemed to him, after the year of work, correct but sterile as the world of the painter Mondrian—a region of bare walls and empty rooms, informed with a blighting ethical neutrality that he respected but that failed to satisfy him. It was not the world a man could live in. It was without scent, sound or color, merely the hurrying of material, endlessly and meaninglessly, unless one took the beauty of the patterns to have meaning in themselves. He had turned to science in search of meaning, and the answer science seemed to give was that the universe had no meaning with which science was concerned.

"Just graduate?" the soda clerk asked, looking at the fake parchment degree.

Avery nodded.

"I guess the hot breath of the draft board will be blowing down your neck, eh?"

"I'm deferred," Avery said. "I'm a math major. In the graduate school."

"Gee chum you sure are lucky. I was in the service four years, and it looks like I'll be tapped again, just because I was dumb enough to take a commission in the reserve." He shook his head. "I still go back to Mannheim, nights, sometimes."

"It doesn't seem fair," Avery said. "To make a guy go twice."

"You wouldn't like to trade, would you fellow?" the soda clerk asked good naturedly.

"No thanks," Avery said. "I'd rather stay here and learn to add and take away."

But when he was in the hot street he frowned and thought about it. Among the people he knew, it was taken for granted that you were lucky if you could avoid being drafted into the pointless peacetime army. But for a moment, he was uncomfortable. The mood of disillusionment persisted. He had a feeling that his life was passing him by while he stood still: the war, love, any real education, any real growth. Maybe that boy behind the soda fountain had learned more about himself during five minutes in the box barrage over Mannheim than he had learned about himself in four years on Morningside Heights.

He shook himself, wiping the sweat from his forehead. It was just the end of the year, he told himself. He was stale. He was fed up.

When he got back to the apartment he found Breitbart busily packing two large new bags. There were chauvinistic French Line stickers pasted to the fresh cowhide. Freddie was off to Europe again, this time to the south of France. Avery felt a pang of envy. He knew that Freddie would see all the paintings, improve his French, do a stint of professional reading, present the letters to famous people given to him by faculty members, and at the same time manage to enjoy himself recklessly as a soldier on leave. Breitbart had an acceptance of life and a greed for experience Avery felt were denied him. It did not do a bit of good to remember Freddie's occasional vulgarity, or to be amused by his sartorial concern. The fact that Freddie looked like a men's clothing advertisement didn't wipe out the fact that Freddie had a much better time than he.

"Why don't you come with me?" Freddie asked. "Everyone should see France before he's twenty-one. It's educational too."

"No thanks," Avery said.

"Dormaker's gone. You've got nothing to do."

There was actually no reason why he should not go to France, except that it seemed preposterous. "I thought I'd get started on my thesis," he said. "You know, get some reading done."

"You'd be much better off with me," said Freddie. "I'll show you the sins of Paris." He picked up a batch of ties and began to hang them on a wire traveling rack, singing a song in French that wistfully asked why blonde women weren't blonde all over: "*Si tous les femmes blondes, ont les poilus noir....*"

Avery laughed. He was tempted to go and might have, except for the suggestion of his conscience that it would not be quite moral to go abroad for his own amusement. And he had an idea that it might be unhealthy to try to run away in place from what could not be escaped in time.

Freddie lit a Turkish cigarette, blowing the cloud of rich erotic smoke across the room at him. "Well, are you coming?" he asked.

Avery shook his head.

"I think you're screwy," Freddie said. "Why don't you go home and sit in the stocks all summer? Then you can really feel like a martyr."

Avery saw him off, and met his parents for the first time. They stood stolidly behind Freddie, like the peasant servants of some minor Bavarian count, the father dressed in a suit made of cloth that looked like dark gray cardboard, wearing a vest in spite of the heat and a heavy gold chain with a charm; the mother topheavy as a tank, with hair in plaits and a bun in the back, a standard issue hausfrau, almost smelling of cinnamon and yeast. They embarrassed Avery by bowing politely, as if he were some meinherr and they were a pair of tenants.

"You will be al-zo a professor?" Freddie's mother asked.

"I guess so," Avery said. "I haven't decided."

"It is best," she said firmly. "For a professor, everyone has respect."

"Ma, don't forget to mail my shirts will you?" Breitbart inter-rupted. "I wish you'd sent them out when I asked you to, so I could have taken them with me."

"As soon as they come, *liebe*," she promised. "I don't forget."

Freddie surveyed the passengers coming up the gangway. "I'll bet there are five hundred high school teachers of French on board, and not one of them could order a decent meal in the language."

"Don't be intolerant, Fritz," said Avery. "They have to live."

"You call him Fritz?" Mrs. Breitbart said, surprised. "At home he will not have it. Only Frederick."

The ship's whistle gave a warning blast, the sound shuddering back from the pier, and a small sailor in a pom-pom hat called out with a French accent: *All ashore that's going ashore.*

Avery smiled, watching Freddie move toward his mother and put his arms around her. "*Wiedersehen,* Mama," he said softly, kissing her cheek, then kissing his father, old-country style. They gazed at their son, in his fine clothes, on this fine ship, and adored him. Avery watched them and watched Freddie, for some reason relieved to discover that Freddie's pretended contempt for his parents was just part of Freddie's act.

He stood on the dock with Freddie's parents, watching the liner being coaxed out into the stream. Mr. Breitbart stared at the ship, that was bright with a thousand flags, and shook his head. "When I came to this country I had nothing," he said. "Not a thing but my two hands, and my wife here. We came in the steerage, like animals. The first-class passengers came to look at us, just like animals in a zoo. And now my son goes back to Europe, first class, in that ship."

"You should be proud," Avery said.

"We are proud of him," said Freddie's father. "He didn't have it so easy always."

They made their way back through the pier, that smelled like a kind of maritime barn. The Breitbarts insisted on driving Avery back to the college in their big new car, but when he asked if they would like to see the apartment they declined. He got the impression they felt it would be an intrusion on Freddie as much as on him. He got out of the car and shook hands with them, feeling humble. For some time after they had driven off he stood on the sidewalk, looking in the direction in which the car had gone. He understood that these people were glad to have traded a lot of their lives for the boy they had left on the fine ship, and were certain the achievement was worth what it cost. There was Freddie, the Herr Professor, whose very rudeness, or affectation of rudeness, was proof that he had entrenched himself higher than they on the social scale. It was enough for them; they were proud.

The apartment was stifling and depressing. Freddie's empty closet and stripped bed were accusative. Avery sat down in the front room, oppressed by the heat, and felt a wave of loneliness and a quick flash of regret that he wasn't on the ship with Freddie. He wondered what in the name of God to do with himself during the summer. It occurred to him that he might have gone to Hull, at least to see Annie, if Mrs. Calder hadn't tried to talk him into it. Well, he would not go now. He would stay here in New York for the whole bloody blistering summer and he didn't give a damn how miserable he was.

CHAPTER FIFTY-TWO

THE Museum of Modern Art was open all summer and air conditioned. As the heat turned into an adversary to be outwitted, Avery found himself drawn to the sleek cool building, looking at paintings he knew well by now and sometimes going to a movie in the swank secretive basement theater. In the Museum, one afternoon in July, he bumped into Frieda von Mardo, looking cool and desirable and lovely, in a bleached blue dress that had white petals sewn to the skirt, the same color blue as the dress she had worn the first time he saw her at the Requas'. The young man with her had no beard, but he wore a tee-shirt and dungarees properly decorated with paint.

"What are you doing in the city in July?" Frieda asked, shaking hands with Avery.

"Nothing," he said. "Just loafing." He looked at the young painter and the man glared at him. A strong current of animal antagonism passed between them, a ruffling of feathers. There was a moment of tension.

"Oh sorry," Frieda said. "Avery Hollister, Bill Cameron."

They shook hands. Cameron gazed off, in the impatient attitude of a man waiting for his wife in a shop.

"We are just going to have a drink," said Frieda. "Will you come along?"

Avery hesitated, then said, "Well, no I don't think so. But thanks."

Cameron looked relieved.

"Well then," Frieda said. "It's nice to see you." She looked straight at him and he thought he saw a message in her eyes. He wanted her. He was sorry he had ever let her go.

"Good-bye," he said.

Cameron nodded and took her arm. When they reached the stairway, Avery heard him say, "Who's the Groton type, Frieda? Someone out of your rich past?" "Shhhh!" said Frieda. "Don't be childish." Then he saw her make a face at Cameron and laugh. She turned and waved at him, smiling. He waved back woodenly, wishing he had gone along and cut Cameron out. He stood in front of a Swiss poster that seemed to advertise venereal disease, matching the three languages, until he was sure Frieda was out of the building. Then he climbed the stairs and passed through the clammy cold of the lobby into the street. When he opened the heavy glass door the heat struck him like a blow. It was sickening. He walked slowly west, sweat running down his face, so that before he had walked a block his collar was soaked and clung to his neck like a tight wet rag, choking him. It was intolerable. He got on a bus and went home, taking a shower then lying naked on his bed, too hot to read or even to think.

The next day, during the morning, he found himself remembering the way Frieda had looked at him in the Museum. Maybe she would go out with him just for a one-night stand, the way she went out with other men. He picked up the phone and dialed her number, not at all surprised that he remembered it. He was a little at a loss when she answered after the first ring with a bright: "Miss von Mardo speaking!" that sounded almost business-like.

"It's Avery," he said. "I wondered if you'd like to have dinner with me. Tonight."

"Well I'd love to, Avery," she said. "But I'm going to Woodstock in an hour. I'm all packed."

"Oh."

"I'm sorry," she said. "Some other time?"

"Oh. Sure," he said. "Sure."

He hung up, feeling like an ass, irrationally jealous of Bill Cameron and of everyone Frieda had ever slept with. He was even jealous of himself. It was senseless, but he could not help himself. He was like a child who smashes a toy in a fit of rage, then blames the mother who gave it to him for having permitted him to break it.

After a while the jealousy passed, but the flash of remembered sex did not. His dormant physical desire flared up, fed by his idleness and the heat. He haunted Riverside Park in the evenings, aware of the al fresco love that could almost be smelled in the superheated night, tortured by the sight of men and women stretched indolently on the grass, tormented by the doll-like Porto Rican girls who scuffled and cursed with their Porto Rican boys, and then went off into the bushes with them amid peals of tantalizing tropical laughter.

One evening he telephoned Connie Requa, whom he had not seen for months, and she asked him to come downtown. She gave him a sweet sticky cocktail and they talked dispiritedly, sitting in the shabby airless living room, that he had never seen except when it was filled with people and that now looked pitifully dreary. He had called her with some idea that the kitchen adventure might be repeated, but she was sober and tired and beaten by the heat. When he put an arm around her waist she made some excuse to get up and move across the room. He followed her and caught her arm, pulling her toward him. He kissed her, but she pushed him away. "Avery, don't," she said. "The kids are still awake and Tom will be home in a few minutes."

He let her go and sat down. She picked up the cocktail shaker and said, " 'Nother daiquiri?"

He shook his head, regretting having traveled all the way downtown for nothing. After a while Tom arrived, wearing a wilted cotton suit, looking tired and vanquished. "God, I'd just as soon work all night," he said. "At least the office is air cooled."

He didn't seem surprised to find Avery there. Avery got the impression he was used to finding almost anyone in the house. "I'm going to have a collins," he said, looking at the shaker and making a face. "Will you join me, Avery? We'll leave this alcohol soup to Connie."

"I'd like one," Avery said.

The tart cold drink was refreshing and cut the cloying taste of Connie's cocktail. Avery shook his glass, making the ice cubes tinkle, then touched his forehead with the cold tumbler.

"Teaching summer school?" asked Tom.

"No. Just loafing," Avery answered.

"Why didn't you go to France with old Breitbart? We had a card from him. He seems to be having a terrific time."

"I know," said Avery. "I wish I'd gone."

Connie turned, putting a hand on Tom's arm. "Wasn't Paris wonderful, Tommy?" she said. "Wasn't it fun?"

"You're not kidding," Requa said, shaking his head, then looking at the ice in his glass and the squeezed half lime. "You're not just kidding."

"How long were you there?" asked Avery.

"Five years," said Tom. "My glorious youth. Just long enough to spend up what my old man left me and to find out I wasn't a novelist, but just a guy with a flair for words that was good enough to impress an English instructor who had already found out the same thing about himself." He smiled and drained the melted ice from his glass. "But it was fun," he said.

"It was wonderful!" said Connie.

They began to talk about Paris, before the war, and of people they'd known and places they'd lived, both of them stimulated by recollection, so that they forgot Avery and simply talked to one another. Avery saw suddenly that Freddie had been perfectly right when he told him that the Requas were in love. Of course they were in love, with one another and with themselves and with the youth they had passed together. The ugliness in the kitchen and Tom's Third Avenue rebellions had nothing whatever to do with it.

After a while Tom looked up and said, "Are we boring you with these tarnished reminiscences?"

"Not at all," Avery said. "Everybody likes to hear about Paris."

The conversation, the repetition of familiar place names, had made him remember his mother and the way she had loved to talk about Paris. For a moment he had a vision of the map she used to get out for him and spread on the studio floor. Connie began to hum a song called "Two Loves Have I" and it made him sad. He got up to go.

"Have one for the road," said Tom.

"All right."

"Help you sleep," Tom said. "Or stay awake, whichever you're doing."

Avery smiled. It was the first time he had seen Tom Requa sober and stripped of his party manner. He seemed quite old and rather pathetic, but likable. It was impossible to imagine that he had ever thought of himself as strong enough to be an artist, a serious writer. Yet he had done so, and memory of the risk involved remained the central fact of his life.

"Come again," he told Avery, shaking hands at the door. "Always welcome."

A week later there was a note from Connie asking him to a party. He didn't go, though he was bored and had nothing to do. He was afraid Connie might be drunk and revert to the mood that had taken her the night she had led him into the kitchen. The chance that this might happen troubled his conscience. Tom no longer seemed to him anonymous and ridiculous, but was a pathetic human being with spoilt aspirations, who loved his unhappy adulterous wife and was fond of his ill-mannered children, who loathed his job yet clung to it because it enabled him to live in something approaching comfort and to pretend to enjoy himself on Fridays, when his apartment was turned into something that resembled a jazz age *boîte* and an existentialist cellar. He was one of those people who never reach any degree of excellence whatever, whose lives are failures as soon as they begin, the hopeless, timeserving kind of man with his future behind him, a long way behind him. He wondered what Tom would be like if he had inherited a competence, and thus been able to put off the need to make any kind of challenge whatever. It was possible, when Tom was young, for a man with even a tiny income to follow the sun. Had Requa's father left him three thousand a year for life, Tom might have been quite a different man, for economic security offers a disguise to failure that even fools the man himself. At any rate, he felt pity for Tom, even compassion, and for his wife too. He did not want to risk being guilty of adding pain. So he stayed away.

CHAPTER FIFTY-THREE

AVERY himself, until this year, had given almost no thought to his own economic future. He was not extravagant and his stipend, together with what he had in the bank, supplied his needs. He knew there was a trust fund in Providence and that after he became twenty-one he would have some kind of income, but he had no idea of how much it would be, whether twenty dollars a week or sixty. He was disinclined to think about it, for he realized that even knowing the amount would in a way make a change in his status. And he didn't know how to find out even the name of the bank except by writing and asking his father, which he could not bring himself to do. He had wondered about it and realized that he should make some kind of move, but he had put it off.

It was taken care of for him, as other things had been.

During the last week in August he answered the phone in his apartment and heard Caldecott Browne's voice. "Avery? This is C. Browne. I'd like to see you."

"I don't know," Avery said. "I'm a little busy." He had not seen Browne since his mother's death and did not want to see him now.

"This is a matter of business, old man," Browne said. "I think you'd better come down to the office."

"Very well," Avery said. He made a note of the address and the time and hung up the phone.

The next day he presented himself at Browne's offices on Pine Street, which were dark and rather British looking, and decorated with oil portraits of former partners, looking slick and fake, as if the paintings had been done in a batch from a stack of photographs. Avery shook hands with Browne and sat in a deep green leather chair.

"Long time no see," said Browne pleasantly, smiling at him.

"Well sir, I've been busy."

"Don't apologize," Browne said. "Why should you bother with an old fogey like me?" He glanced at his watch, then said, "I won't take much of your time, Avery. It's good of you to come down." He pressed a buzzer that summoned a girl in a black linen dress; she looked cool and self-possessed as a nurse. "Linda, get me the Hollister file will you please?" said Browne. The girl went out and came back in a moment with a tan manila folder that had Avery's name lettered on it. Avery wondered what went on; it occurred to him that his father might be disinheriting him in some intensely formal way. Browne glanced at the contents of the folder, then said, "Your Dad thought you should have the dope on your trust fund. The one your grandfather set up for you and your brother."

"Oh?"

"He seems to feel," Browne explained carefully, "that since the money comes from your mother's side of the family, that it should be handled formally. That's why he's asked me to take care of it. He, uh, when I talked with him over the phone, he said he'd only just gotten back from abroad and hadn't seen you yet. But he wanted this cleared up."

"I understand," Avery said. He was annoyed by Browne's elaborate diplomacy and said bluntly, "We're not on the best of terms."

Browne nodded; he looked out the window, then back at Avery, and said, "Have you any idea what provision your grandfather made?"

"Not exactly," Avery said. "I know there's a trust fund, that's all. I'm not even sure I know exactly what a trust fund is."

Browne smiled. "I think you'd better be prepared for a shock," he said. "Oh a pleasant shock. Very pleasant." He glanced at the papers, then went on. "Your grandfather set up this trust a long time ago, and when he did it he probably thought it was a modest affair. It was a hundred thousand dollars, as a matter of fact, the income to be divided between you and your brother."

This conveyed nothing to Avery.

"Since your brother is deceased," Browne explained, "the whole thing goes to you."

Avery stiffened. "I don't want Morgan's share," he said.

"I don't think there's much choice," said Browne. "The whole thing goes to the surviving brother." He paused. "The important thing is though, that the hundred thousand isn't a hundred thousand any more. They are conservative in Providence, but they're not fools either. It's closer to half a million."

Browne sat back, giving Avery a chance to digest what he had said. Avery was stunned. He felt his hands tremble and his mouth went dry. It was a reaction similar to fear.

"Do you mean to tell me I'm going to inherit a half a million dollars?" he demanded. "That's ridiculous!"

"You don't inherit the half million, Avery," Browne explained. "And you're darned lucky you don't. You inherit the income from it. Something in the neighborhood of thirty thousand a year, before taxes."

"But I don't want it," Avery said.

Browne laughed. "You won't find it hard to give away," he said.

"I don't mean that," Avery said. "It's just that—well, I knew there was a trust. My mother mentioned it, sometimes. I thought it might be twenty or thirty dollars a week."

"Well it's a good deal more than that," said Browne. "You will be rich, Avery. At least according to my standards."

Avery stared through the burnished window of Browne's office, which was high above the street and had a view of the harbor and the flat island beyond it.

"Well who's been getting the income all along?" he asked, wondering whether or not it had been going to his father.

"It's been accreting," Browne said. "It reverts to the fund. That, plus the war and the fact that your grandfather knew what he was doing, accounts for the size of the fund now."

"What happens to the money when I die?" Avery asked. "Do my children get it?"

Browne shook his head. "No. Unless the Russians get it first it goes to Brown University, when you are no longer able to make use of it."

"Fantastic!" Avery said, staring at the Statue of Liberty and the red brick barracks on Ellis Island.

Browne agreed. "Did you know your grandfather, Avery?" he asked. "He must have been a remarkable man."

Avery shook his head. "I didn't know him," he said. "But I was with him when he was killed. He and my grandmother."

"Oh?"

He explained.

"Those old fellows had guts," Browne said. "Call 'em whatever names you please—economic royalists or robber barons—they were the making of this country. We'd be better off if we had a few like them around today."

"I can't say I agree with you," Avery said, looking down at the beautiful harbor, trying to absorb what he had been told and to take some meaning from it.

"Point of view," Browne said. He swung around in his chair, facing Avery. "Does this change your plans?" he asked. "I mean to say, I don't suppose you can keep a string of polo ponies on thirty thousand, after the bite the government takes, but you can do a lot of things. A lot of things. I envy you."

"I don't think it will change my plans," Avery said, making up his mind as he answered. "I think I'll go right ahead with my Ph.D., just the way I had intended to."

"Oh?" Browne looked up. "Won't the army be knocking you off? Or have you got some useful defect like a punctured eardrum?"

"I'm a science major," Avery said. "On a project. The university wants me deferred."

"I see," said Browne. He hesitated, then asked, "How do you feel about it?"

"I feel damned good about it," Avery said, more sharply than he intended. "I gave up reading Kipling a long time ago. I have no desire to rot away a couple of years in some barracks. If I'm drafted I'll do my best to be an efficient soldier but if the government thinks what I'm doing is more important than carrying a gun I don't see why I should argue with them."

"Well of course neither do I," Browne said easily. "I just wondered whether you felt you might be missing something."

"I don't think so," Avery said. "My father was in two wars. That should take care of the duty side, as far as the family is concerned. And I have no desire to be shoved around by some half-witted sergeant just to show that I'm one of the boys." He paused, then said, "Especially when there's no war on."

"I agree with you," Browne said. "I just wondered how you felt about not going along with the crowd."

"What crowd?"

"Well, fellows your own age. Classmates. Friends."

"We don't go in very much for class spirit at Columbia," Avery said. "And most of the fellows in my class weren't at Columbia by choice. They were there because the navy sent them there to study engineering or pre-med. And I don't have any friends, except for a guy who's a Catholic missionary up in the Canadian Arctic. He's already been in the army."

"How about the chaps who were at school with you?" Browne asked. "Surely they're your friends."

"I haven't seen a soul from Colborn since I left the place," said Avery. "Except for my old roommate, Bell. He's a regular officer in the navy."

Browne shook his head. "Can't understand why you didn't go to New Haven," he said. "I should think—"

Avery cut him off. "Is there anything I have to do?" he asked. "Do I have to sign anything?"

Browne shook his head. "Not a thing," he said. "Just cash the checks when they start coming, about a year from now."

He led Avery down the corridor and waited until the elevator came, then shook hands with him. "Like to see you, Avery," he said. "Call me, will you?"

"I'll do that," Avery said, knowing he wouldn't. He was half amused and half disgusted by Browne's special deference to him, now that he was by Browne's standards a rich young client.

He walked through Pine Street to Broadway and went downtown to the Battery, the end of New York, as far as one could go. It was a pleasant August day, a beautiful day to get rich on, he reflected, staring out across the harbor at the occupied islands and the Statue and the little ferry that headed toward him like a small dog running toward his master.

He watched the harbor for half an hour, refreshed by the smell of salt and the cool breath of air that rose from the water. Then he found the subway and rode uptown to Morningside Heights. He understood that it was ungracious of him not to feel elated, but he didn't. He felt disturbed and a little imposed on, the way a child sometimes feels when he is offered unnecessary help. The money his grandfather had left him was a fortune, what most men struggle all their lives to acquire, cheat for, kill for, debase themselves for and so on. It gave him the right, that he hadn't earned, to make independent decisions of scope. Yet he didn't really want it.

It was ironic.

"You young gentlemen," the headmaster of Colborn had informed them, "you young gentlemen are the most fortunate group of individuals in America. A world has been prepared for you. Live up to it, gentlemen. Live up to it."

He smiled, remembering Dr. Collamore's fervor. Then he smiled at himself. He felt sorry for himself—the poor little rich boy—and it was absurd. He washed his face and went out to dinner, eating alone, at Angelo's.

A few days later, his father wrote:

Browne tells me he has talked with you about your money. I hope you understand how fortunate you are. I wonder whether you would find the time to come home for a few days before college starts? I plan some changes in my own life that concern you, and I should like very much to see you.

For a little while Avery considered going home to see his father. Then he remembered Mrs. Calder, and what he had told her, and decided against it, partly through fear and partly because what he had told her had been true in a way, just as the lie he had told his father about David Fearing had been true in a way. He sat down and wrote his father a short correct note that explained that he was too busy with his work to take time out to visit Hull and that congratulated his father on the splendid job his father had done in Berlin. When he read over what he had written he was surprised by its tone; it seemed almost to have been written by someone else. It had all the emotional content of a military letter written in soldierly third person.

He mailed it anyway.

His father did not write again.

CHAPTER FIFTY-FOUR

WHEN the students began to drift back for the fall term he was relieved. He felt an eagerness to be back at work. The disenchantment he had felt at the beginning of summer, the staleness, had passed. Dormaker, tanned and younger looking, returned a few days before the term began, and Avery told him about his talk with Browne.

Dormaker nodded, listening carefully, then stared at the edge of his desk for several minutes before he made any comment. Then he looked up and said, "So you will be rich, young Hollister, eh? Rich mathematicians are out of fashion."

"I know," Avery grinned. "So Douminoff once told me."

"What will you do?" asked Dormaker.

"Nothing," Avery said. "I mean, I will go on just as before."

"Why?" Dormaker asked. "You could do almost anything you please. Travel. Take up sin. Or art. You could keep women, or expensive animals."

"I know, so Browne told me," Avery said. "But I think I'll just go ahead with my doctorate."

"Why?" Dormaker persisted.

"Because I started it," Avery said.

"Really?" Dormaker said. "Do you think it's just a matter of character? Or is it because you are afraid of what you might find if you made a change? Because you feel you're safe here and might not be out there, somewhere else?" He made a gesture with his hand that was intended, Avery gathered, to indicate the world.

"Partly, I guess," Avery said. "I wish I knew."

"Look, Avery," Dormaker said. "Don't try to get from us what we haven't got to give. Mathematics is a language. Maybe in time it will answer some questions, but it is only a language, a fiction. What a man says in mathematics, in your terms, he has to find elsewhere. Otherwise he just repeats what has been said over and over again, by rote, like a kid in school in the old days, learning to spell CAT. C-A-T Cat. I see the C-A-T. The C-A-T sees me."

"Mathematics is more than a language," Avery said. "It is a system."

"Are you interested in baseball?" Dormaker asked.

"Not at all."

"Well pretend you are for a minute," Dormaker said. "You know in baseball a pitcher can pitch for himself or for the team. He can pitch with the game as a whole in mind, or he can pitch a really selfish game, throwing to each individual batter. You know it is possible to pitch a no-hit game and still lose?"

"I don't understand," Avery said.

"You refuse to understand," Dormaker said. "I am only trying to tell you again what I have told you before. Technique for its own sake is worthless. And probably immoral."

"But it's necessary, isn't it?" Avery asked.

"Sure it is," Dormaker agreed. "So is your nose. But your nose doesn't make the smell or decide what's pleasant and unpleasant. The nose is only a reporter." He looked at Avery speculatively, then said, "Have a good year with us. Before you become rich and different."

"I won't be rich," Avery said. "Only well off. And I'm different already."

Dormaker laughed and stood up. Avery smiled. It was good to be back in this office again, and good to see Dormaker's face. It put him in touch with the only world he even partly understood. He shook hands with Dormaker and went out into the corridor. The Federal guards were gone this year, though a wooden fence and sentry's wicket were there to remind you of them, and there were still certain floors in Pupin Hall on which you needed a pass to get into the laboratories. Waiting for the elevator, he looked down the long, familiar corridor. He had the feeling that it was going to be a good year. "A damned good year," he said to himself. "A damned good year." He had the feeling that the summer had been shaken off. When he came out onto the campus there was a light breeze from the west, presaging fall, though the day was hot.

It wasn't until he bought an evening paper and noticed the date that he realized that it was his twentieth birthday. Nobody had remembered it, not even Annie, who had always sent him something. He felt a little warning chill and wondered if she might be ill, then shrugged it off. She must have simply forgotten the date just as he had forgotten it himself. It would be unthinkable for his father not to let him know if anything had happened to Annie.

The next day, the first day of his twenty-first year of life, he went back to work even though the term had not actually started. His summer of loafing was over. He hadn't been working more than an hour before he realized, with a sudden warmth in his heart, how much he had missed his job. He was happy. It wasn't until someone called to him in a friendly voice: "Shut up Hollister, will you?" that he realized he was whistling.

That fall the Dormaker project was given more space and Avery was moved from the bull pen into a small office of his own, with a window that looked south toward the dome of the old library. He had a new desk that glistened with varnish, a swivel chair with a rubber pad, and a bookcase with glass doors in which he installed his professional library. He liked the sense of isolation. One day he brought Frieda's painting from the apartment and hung it where it got the light. Having the painting in the office gave him a feeling of absolute proprietorship, a conviction of autonomous place he had sought in the dormitories but never found.

CHAPTER FIFTY-FIVE

BREITBART came back from France to begin the last year of work for his doctorate, three days after classes started. He had seen Gide and Matisse and talked with a glamorous lady philosopher about the Ethics of Ambiguity. He had lively tales of evenings passed in crowded cellars on the left bank of the Seine, where people studied gobbets of spit in search of the meaninglessness of life.

"Of course," he explained, "they're either American girls from Sarah Lawrence or Frenchmen who have found out it's the easiest way to get drinks for free. The people who really created the movement all look like members of the bourse and are never seen in such places."

He brought Avery half a dozen French ties that Avery was too self-conscious to wear, and a bottle of French toilet water that made him feel like a whore when he rubbed it on his face after shaving.

"Just what you need," Freddie insisted. "You should look gayer and smell more voluptuous." He inspected the tie Avery was wearing and said, "What's the point of a dreary rag like that, for instance? Protective coloration? Or is it by chance a school tie?"

Avery glanced down and reddened. "As a matter of fact it is," he admitted. "Someone gave me half a dozen and I couldn't see any sense in throwing them away." He turned the tie over and saw that it had Morgan's name tape sewn to it.

Freddie assumed the expression of a parent whose child has told an expiatory lie. "Now Hollister you can be frank with me," he said. "You wear it for the purpose for which it is intended—to let the initiated few know that you went to the proper school."

"You can get a damn good education at Colborn," Avery said irrelevantly.

Freddie laughed. "Also the right to wear a tie, just as if you'd gone to Eton."

There had always been a thin line of touchiness between them about Colborn. Freddie was jealous of the school's prestige and amused by its preposterous affectations, so that he was confused in his attitude toward it and made no effort to conceal this confusion. One of the things Avery envied about him was his ability to keep his contradictions on speaking terms. It was a gift Avery admired and associated with maturity. He could not, for example, comfortably admit to himself that he was proud of the cabalistic tie and at the same time frankly ashamed of the Colborn pretense, that he didn't like being a Colborn boy but would have hated not being one. "Don't be an ass," he said to Freddie. "You know you'd give your left ballock to have gone to Colborn."

"Maybe not that," Breitbart said. "But I would have liked it. I'm a snob. And I would have had sense enough to have exploited the advantages, unlike you and your friend McCoy."

"I'd be glad to give you a Colborn tie," Avery said, smiling.

Freddie shook his head. "Doesn't suit my coloring," he said. "Besides, I wouldn't be surprised if some old Collie has had a law passed making it a misdemeanor to falsely wear the Colborn colors."

The next day Avery wore one of the French ties Freddie had brought him from Paris, and though the bright colors made him feel conspicuous, he continued to wear it and wore the others; he did not use the erotic cologne. He went through his things and found he had five school ties in various stages of wear. He wadded them up and threw them away. Of course Freddie had been right. He had really worn the damned things in the hope that the few people in the know would recognize the haberdashery and therefore the man.

He got used to the French ties and settled down to his work, which, this year, was on a more creative level than it had been the year before. Sometimes he was aware of vague idealistic excitement in his work, that did not interfere with his ability to get on with the job but was auxiliary to it—a sense of personal validity elusive and impossible to isolate as the subtle effects of light, but real and warming to the spirit. He felt like a scientist, a working scientist as well as a student, and this gave meaning to his life.

For the good of his professional soul, he attended the mathematical colloquium held every other week and one evening early in the term he sat next to Sarah Greenway. The meetings were predominantly male and he noticed her. She was a solemn-looking girl with ingenuous gray eyes and a pretty mouth. Her face was placid. She had very clear, luminous skin and light brown hair that was beautifully brushed. She looked like a Yardley advertisement, and smelt the way a Yardley advertisement is supposed to smell—of lavender soap and cleanliness. Avery was conscious of her lavender smell and vexingly foreign appearance and stared at her until she blushed and turned her head. She was certainly not American. He guessed she was German or perhaps Dutch. When she got up later to ask a question, raising her hand rather timidly, he was surprised by her British voice. It made his heart pound. It was reminiscent of David Fearing's voice, but unlike it too—a sturdy voice for a girl. The accent belonged to another social class; the pitch was different and there was a broadness to the speech that he guessed was northern. Nevertheless, the similarity was strong enough to be disconcerting and gave him a sense of David that was not welcome. He felt a vague antagonism toward the English girl, irrational but real and combined with it he felt a strong sense of curiosity and attraction.

As the crowd passed out of the auditorium when the lecture was over he brushed against her and apologized. She told him it was quite all right. She had a shy attractive smile. She gave the impression of modesty and of good manners that verged on the genteel.

"You're English aren't you?" he asked.

"I'm afraid so," she said. "Do you mind very much?"

"No, of course not," he said awkwardly. "I just noticed your accent that's all."

"Most people do," she said. "But I'm to be here for a year and when I go home I shall probably speak exactly like an American."

They were outside in the September night. He fell into step beside her. She was tall and walked more confidently than most American girls, as if she were used to walking. She wore a suit that was too heavy for the time of year, cut in such a way that it could be worn through all vicissitudes of fashion, since the idea of fashion would never be associated with it. It was a suffragette's suit, but somehow it looked attractive. It was right.

"Are you working in math?" he asked.

She shook her head. "Chemistry actually," she said. "But I go to all the lectures I have time for just to, oh well, just for something to do."

"Chemistry," he said.

"Yes. You know, bad smells, smashed bottles, washing up, all that sort of thing."

He told her his name and she said that it sounded like an English name. "My name's Greenway," she said. "I'm afraid my first name's Sarah. Do you think it's awful?"

"I think it's nice," he said. "I like an old-fashioned name."

"I don't mind it now," she said. "I didn't like it when I was at school. All the girls were named for American film stars."

"Oh it's a nice name," he said. "Sarah. It's a very nice name."

They reached the library. He felt like a fool and could not think of anything to say that didn't sound asinine, though he wanted to establish himself with her. They stood on the steps for a few seconds and she seemed to be waiting for him to speak.

He felt tongue-tied, helpless, the way he had felt at dancing class when he had been paired off with some impermeable little girl. She smiled at him and said, "Well good night," and turned quickly, walking away, her stride not masculine at all but somehow faintly military. He stood watching her, tempted to follow, but not knowing what he would say when he overtook her. He went on home, dissatisfied with himself. It was her voice, he decided. It made him uncomfortable. It reminded him of David, and that night he dreamt about her and in the dream she seemed to resemble David, though actually there wasn't the slightest similarity between them.

He met her again a week later, crossing the campus early in the evening while it was still light. He saw her ahead of him, recognizing her hair and the blunt, take-it-or-leave-it silhouette the cut of her permanent suit presented. He quickened his steps and caught up with her. "Hello," he said. "No lecture tonight?"

"Not tonight," she said. "I'm just coming from the lab."

He walked along with her for a bit, caught again by his feeling of schoolboyish inadequacy. Out of his childhood he heard the voice of the dancing mistress at Sturgis Manor: "Don't simply dahnce about like a stick, Master Hollister. Engage in conversation. A few wöhhds often put a gühl at ease and give her confidence in her pahtner."

"It's, uh, a beautiful night," he said, looking around him at the night.

"It is lovely," she agreed. "I came in August you know, and I thought the heat was going to last forever."

They walked along for a bit.

"Would you like to have dinner with me?" he said. "I mean if you don't have a date or something."

When the words were out he felt reprieved.

"Well, I don't know, really," she said.

"You have to eat somewhere," he said.

"Well yes, then, I would," she said.

He took her to Angelo's and when the young men stared he looked at her and realized that she was a very pretty girl. She had a glow. When the food came he watched her eat it European fashion, holding her fork in the left hand. It reminded him of David, then for a moment, of Frieda.

"Do you live in the dormitory?" he asked. "In Johnson Hall?"

"No. I'm here on a curious kind of fellowship that includes the use of a flat. There were to have been two of us, but the other girl chucked it at the last minute and got married, so I have the place to myself. It belongs to a woman named Mrs. Dorrance, whose son was in the RAF. She's offered this bursary or whatever you call it to a graduate student, veteran, female British, one each."

"Were you in the war?" he asked incredulously.

"Well not really of course," she said. "I mean to say, I wasn't abroad or anything like that. I was in the WAAF. The Air Force. Just toward the end, you know. For two years."

"Oh?"

"Were you in the army?" she asked.

"No, I was not in the war," he said bluntly. He detested her for having been in the war. She could not be much older than he, and it gave her intolerable advantage over him. It was bad enough for her to be English, but to have worn a uniform as well was too much. There was a long uncomfortable silence, then she said, "You're doing maths, aren't you?"

He nodded. He felt as if he were made of wood. She was perfectly agreeable and he had no desire to be rude to her, really, simply because she was English and had been in the Air Force. But he was rude and the meal was a failure. When the bill came she opened her purse and said, "What's my share, please?"

"I'll pay for it," he said.

"Oh, please don't!"

Avery handed the waiter some money. "I'm not in the habit of asking a girl to dinner and then letting her pay the bill," he said priggishly.

"We often do in England," she said.

"Well this is not England," he said. "This is America."

"Oh, I'm so sorry," she said. "Was it wrong of me to offer?"

He was suddenly ashamed of his rudeness. "No. Of course not," he said. "I'd like to pay, that's all."

She seemed relieved. "I am strange, you know," she said. "I don't know all the customs, and it's quite different from the University of Manchester."

He took her home. Her apartment was in a quiet street south of the university. The building was modern and had a Tudor lobby and a self-service elevator, over the automatic door of which hung a tasseled spurious halberd. They said good night in the lobby. She thanked him for dinner, rather shyly, and didn't suggest that he come up.

"I'll see you," he said.

"Oh, yes. Yes of course."

He watched the brass door slide to, making the tassels on the halberd tremble, then went out and walked back to his own place, wondering why he had behaved like a schoolboy on his first date. He was twenty years old, and he had practically lived with a woman, you might say, he reminded himself. He should know how to operate. He should know how to make a play for a girl without getting all balled up. Finally he said, "To hell with it." It was just because she was English and strange, he told himself. He really wasn't attracted to her. He didn't feel any of the passion he had felt toward Frieda, the thin desperate need to know her, the promise of ecstasy and misery together. If she had been an American girl he wouldn't have bothered about her at all. It was just her accent, her damned English way of making him feel inferior and gauche.

Freddie was out when he reached the apartment. He took up a book and began to read, but he could not clear his mind of

Sarah Greenway. There was something about her that challenged him, something familiar. She came between his attention and the pages of the book, so that he abandoned it. "Oh not really," he said, imitating her speech. "I mean to say I wasn't abroad or anything like that." He had seen Waves and Wacs during the war, square shouldered and contemptuous, drinking alone in bars like men, cruising the city in pairs or threes, reckless and independent as men. It was difficult to visualize Sarah in that kind of intensified life.

When Freddie came in, he asked, trying to be casual, "Fritzie, are you afraid of the English? Do they make you feel as if you were always about to do the wrong thing?"

"Natch," said Breitbart. "Everybody's afraid of the English except the French and certain highly developed Italians, who have better tailors." Freddie took off his coat and sat where a strong light fell on his expensive striped shirt. He looked like an advertising executive at a conference. "What brings up the English?" he asked.

"I don't know," Avery said. "I was just thinking. They make me feel inferior. Guilty. Almost like an ungrateful child. Actually, I suppose I feel as though I had somehow deliberately decided not to be English and that I should be ashamed of it. And sometimes they make me feel like a guy who has been passed over by a club his father and grandfather belonged to and that people expected him to join."

"Well of all the God damned Anglophilia," Freddie said. "What do they do up there at Colborn? Import genuine English blood in plasma and inject it into your veins?" He shook his head. "I didn't know you were going Kipling on me," he said.

Avery smiled. "Then you're not really afraid of the English?" he said. "How come? You're not French and you're not an Italian with an expensive tailor."

"Well, I'm not afraid of them the way you mean," Freddie said. "I certainly don't feel like a kid whose pledge pin has been lifted when some Limey high-hats me or takes my hotel reservation. I'm afraid of them, sure, the way everyone's afraid of the boss. The bastards have been boss for so damned long it's hard to remember that they aren't any more and that the place has been taken over for taxes."

Avery laughed. Breitbart looked at him appraisingly. "Sometimes you make me feel I'm lucky to have had my humble origin in a Brooklyn speakeasy, Hollister," he said. "With me things are simple. It's just a matter of exploiting the talent God gave me, and making the kind of life for myself a man of my sterling character deserves. You rich are so complicated. You should keep a psychiatrist on staff, along with the cook and the butler and the nursery governess."

"We never had a butler," said Avery. "Or a nursery governess. And I'm not rich. At least not very." He had an impulse to tell Freddie about the money his grandfather had left him, and the urge was not totally divorced from the idea that it would make Freddie jealous. "As a matter of fact," he said, "I won't be rich until next year."

"What happens next year?" Freddie asked. "Do you poison your old man, or what?"

Avery explained.

Breitbart looked at him and whistled. "A half a million bucks! The ideal man. Handsome, charming, brilliant, gallant, scholarly, *hochwohlgeboren,* and now rich. Think of the use I could make of that dough. There is no justice. Why was my grandfather a woodcutter in the Schwartzwald? Why wasn't he patrician and wealthy?" He overplayed his clowning just a trifle and the resentment showed through.

"What would you do, Fritz, if someone left you a potful of money?" Avery asked. "Buy a harem? Open a tailor shop?"

"I don't know," Breitbart answered seriously. "I honestly don't know." He stared at Avery as if suddenly observing something he had always overlooked. "Why it would louse me up!" he exclaimed, as if pleased by this conclusion. "It would louse me up completely."

"Why?" asked Avery, agreeing with Freddie but not understanding the reason behind his agreement.

"I wouldn't be anything," Breitbart said.

"Why should it be any harder to create an imitation meaning for life just because someone left you some money?" Avery asked.

"I don't know," Freddie admitted. "But I think it would be. For one thing, if you haven't got any money the process of acquiring it serves as a kind of substitute for meaning in itself. And once you begin to acquire money on your own it becomes a technique, and a way of life too." He frowned. "But to start out with your pockets full. That's another matter altogether."

"I don't see your line of reasoning," Avery argued. "I should think it would just eliminate one more blind alley."

Freddie thought for a moment, then nodded. "It's a point," he said. "I saw people in France last summer who were so poor that for them the whole meaning of human existence, the entire human search, was most of the time reduced to the size of a cheap loaf of bread. The rats of Paris were once sold as food, for thirty dollars a pair. Or maybe you should say a brace. People fought with one another for the privilege of buying them. Of course things aren't as bad as that now, but in certain places they are bad enough so that people make jokes about *rôti de rat.*"

Avery had a vivid image of a pair of rats, skinned and dressed, hanging like pheasants in a luxury market. He was swept by nausea.

"Horrible," he said.

"Yes, it is horrible," Freddie said. "You want to stop and strip yourself, give them your money, your clothes, your valuables, everything you have. They make you ashamed to be human, and they make you feel responsible."

Avery nodded. He was ashamed to tell Freddie that he had used the word horrible not out of pity for the poor of Paris, but in disgust at the thought of men cooking rats and eating them. Breitbart's compassion for the people embarrassed him and made him conscious of a vacancy in his own spirit. It was a vacancy with which he was familiar. Again and again, he understood intellectually how he should feel in a given situation, when he should feel pity or love or compassion; too often he felt nothing at all, or an emotion quite different from the appropriate one.

His mind turned back to the English girl, who had been through bombing and strafing, perhaps seen airmen dying or dead in the planes that landed after operations, somewhere on the dark Lincolnshire countryside.

"I met a girl," he said. "An English girl."

"Oh?" said Freddie. "You need a girl. You're fresh out. Is she a candidate?"

Avery shook his head. "I don't think so," he said. He thought for a moment, then said, "No. No she isn't." He got up, pretending to yawn. "I'm beat," he said. "I'm going to turn in."

"Stick around," Freddie said. "I'll make some coffee."

"No thanks."

He went to bed, but didn't fall asleep for hours. He was thinking of Sarah Greenway. She wasn't a candidate for Frieda's place. Not at all. But she was a candidate for something.

When he met her again a few days later he took her to tea in a place called the Lion's Den and afterward, on the street, she asked him to dinner at her apartment, then shook hands with him, British fashion, briskly, almost perfunctorily. He walked away, buoyed up by an unusual feeling of confidence. Nothing of importance had been said and no passage of meaning had occurred between them that could be isolated, yet he was aware of a positive shift in his attitude toward her from one of awkwardness to one in which he sensed the advantage. He felt much as he had one day at school, when he had got up and realized that for no specific reason he was no longer afraid of a certain master who until then had terrified him. "All men are afraid of waiters,"

David Fearing had once informed him. "It's just that they show it differently. Some cringe and are positively obsequious. Others bellow and bully the poor chaps. Others pretend an enormous indifference and attempt to behave as if the waiter were no more human than the serving cart he pushes. You might say that the British Public School is intended among other things to teach a boy the technique of regarding a waiter as an item of furniture."

Colborn was an ersatz British public school, but it had not passed this technique on to Avery. He was awed by waiters and servants generally, and mortally afraid of uniformed police and enlisted personnel of the services. He was capable of being timid before almost any kind of person at all, and so used to the fact by now that he was able partly to conceal it. He had been awed by Sarah Greenway because she was British and had been in the WAAF. The fact that the fear had passed so quickly reassured him. "She's just a girl after all," he said to himself. "She's just an ordinary girl."

CHAPTER FIFTY-SIX

THE apartment Mrs. Dorrance had loaned Sarah consisted of a single large room with an alcove let into one wall big enough to hold a studio couch. There was a compact modern kitchen, like the galley on a dining car, decorated with French pots of burnished copper marshaled along one wall according to size. These were for show, Sarah informed him. The actual cookery was done in a set of lethal-looking stainless steel. "I was told particularly not to use the copper pots," she said. "They've been treated with something or other so that they won't tarnish." She smiled. "It was all in the letter. I've never actually seen Mrs. Dorrance, you know. She lives in a place called Columbus, and apparently she kept this flat to use when she came to New York for her clothes. But it is nice, isn't it?"

"Very," Avery agreed, looking around.

The main room was decorated in the bare modern style. The walls were dark gray, except for the one away from the light, which was lemon yellow. There was an arrangement of pale wood furniture of expensive, Scandinavian-looking design. There were three excellent contemporary paintings and half a dozen lithographs, the whole lot worth, Avery guessed, about six or seven thousand dollars. He was surprised that this negotiable art had been loaned with the apartment. When he had been given a chair, a drink and a light for his cigarette, he said, "You have quite a collection of modern painting. Or at least Mrs. Dorrance has."

Sarah laughed. "Aren't they frightful smears?" she said. "I suppose they were done by friends or relatives and she doesn't dare burn them or throw them out."

For a moment he thought she was trying to make a feeble joke. Then he saw that she was serious. "Do you mean to tell me you don't know what they are?" he asked.

She looked at him, perplexed, and said, "I'm afraid not."

"Well aside from the fact that the paintings are fairly good examples of the work of three of the greatest artists alive today, they have an absolute value of five or six thousand dollars. Even if you don't like painting you can't be unimpressed by that much money."

Sarah looked at him blankly. "These paintings?" she said, walking quickly from one to the other, giving each a nervous glance. "Surely you're joking. Six thousand dollars. Why that's nearly three thousand pounds."

Avery nodded. He was amused by her ignorance. It seemed inappropriate to her accent. Among the people he knew at Columbia modern painting was a kind of fad. Almost anyone, even people in the School of Business, could pick off museum prints of Picasso, Braque, Rouault and so on. It was expected of them, just as they were expected to know the names of band leaders and certain advanced writers.

"You're not really serious?" he said, suspicious of her. "You know they're valuable pictures, don't you?"

She shook her head and made a helpless face. "I'm afraid I know nothing about art, at least this kind, you know." She paused, searching her memory. "Mrs. Dorrance did say something about the pictures in her letter, and now that I recall it she made quite a point of them. But I'm afraid I'd forgotten all about it by the time I arrived in America."

Avery laughed. "You'd better not let any drunken sailors poke holes in them," he said. "The owner wouldn't like it."

She gave him a forthright British meal of mutton chops and steamed potatoes and refused when he offered to help with the dishes.

"That's one thing our girls thought awfully odd about your GI's," she said. "They were forever trying to do the pots and pans. It simply wouldn't occur to an Englishman and I must say I'm just as well pleased. It makes me uncomfortable to have a man in the kitchen. It doesn't seem suitable."

"Oh quite," he agreed. "Frightfully bad form. Shocking."

She laughed and told him not to make fun of the stranger within the gates. When she finished the dishes she brought out a pot of coffee and they talked. She deferred to him. He talked of food and art and discovered that he could dominate the conversation without much effort. They dropped automatically into hierarchical position, with Sarah falling into step two paces to the rear.

He could not help comparing this role of knowledgeable male to the one he had played opposite Frieda, in which he had been the innocent juvenile, the fresh-faced boy awed by life and passionate for experience. He realized with some self-amusement that he preferred this role. It was less demanding. He wondered idly, watching Sarah, whether if he married he had not better pick out a neutral wife. With Frieda he had been the novice—in art, sex, society, life itself. The position was a humiliating one and had stirred rebellion in him. This girl, perhaps because of temperament, perhaps because she came from a society in which deference to the male was taken for granted, awarded him precedence, took it for an axiom that he was domestically superior simply because he was a man. He sensed something familiar in the subtly expressed convention but it did not occur to him that he was approximating the household role his father had played at Hull.

He stayed until nearly midnight and when he rose to go he realized that for several hours he had been almost entirely at ease. There was something about Sarah that dissipated tension and made him feel sure of himself. It was a feeling that seldom overtook him and he liked it. There was nothing abrasive about Sarah, nothing thorny, and it didn't seem important that this was because there was nothing positive about her at all.

During the next few weeks he fell into the habit of having dinner with her two or three nights a week, sometimes at Angelo's, sometimes at her place, very occasionally downtown in some foreign restaurant or other. What began to grow up between them was not intimacy, or even real familiarity or friendship, but a kind of useful interim relationship of the variety common in schools and military units. Sarah provided something he needed—companionship on a simple level—and he accepted it.

He took a good deal of pleasure in showing her New York. Playing guide gave him a sense of belonging to the city that he had never quite achieved before. He thought of himself as a New Yorker, but his alliance with the city had not been altogether authentic. Even after five years he was still sometimes more like a proper young New Englander on holiday than a committed New Yorker with roots in the life of the city. His father had always approached New York as an Englishman might approach his tailor—with knowledgeability and respect, but never for a moment forgetting the essential master-servant basis of the relationship. His father's attitude toward New York was something like the conventional Englishman's attitude toward Paris, too; he regarded the city with profound suspicion and assumed an undercurrent of naughtiness and duplicity, taking it more or less for granted that outside of the Yale Club, Brooks Brothers and the Prince George Hotel, people would automatically attempt to cheat him or lead him astray. He saw the city as organized around a colossal bunco game. In New York, he had once warned Avery, one must always be careful to count his change.

Avery had absorbed this attitude when he was a boy and never succeeded completely in ridding himself of it, so that New

York had remained in a sense foreign and dangerous to him, less his city, really, than Boston, which he had seen only once, or London, which he had yet to visit. Serving as guide to Sarah Greenway helped obscure this lack of ease with New York. He found himself proud of the city's power and of the kinetic sense of life that captured people and held them here.

Sarah was not at all like the traditional English visitor, who is supposed to bring the prejudice of Trollope in his kit-bag along with his loofah. She had an instinct to please and a horror of offending. She found fault with nothing. She admired what she was told to admire, exclaimed over what she was told was spectacular, and did not comment when New York would have fared badly in comparison with London. Sometimes her good manners made her seem insufferably self-possessed or blandly unresponsive, according to Avery's mood.

One afternoon he took her to the observation tower on top of the Empire State Building, where he had never been. It was a clear fall day and they saw all of New York as it appears in colored aerial photographs, an extravagant presentation that is not altogether credible. Sarah looked with her own eyes, then through the glasses bolted to the rampart, and turned to him with an enigmatic smile. He looked off toward the Jersey flats, then south at the harbor. "Well what do you think of it?" he asked. "Do you think it's impressive?"

"Oh yes of course it is that," she said eagerly. She paused, then said, "It's extraordinary, really. Quite unreal."

"Don't you think it's vulgar?" he asked.

"Vulgar?"

"Don't you think it's typical American vulgarity?" he insisted. "Size for the sake of size, meaningless vulgarity?"

"Oh no," she protested. "It's lovely really. It's quite beautiful."

"For God's sake, Sarah, it's awful," he said. "It's obscene."

An expression of bewilderment crossed her face, then one of hurt. He took her arm and led her to the elevators. They rode to the street in silence. In the crowded elevator, Sarah's face was close to his, and he saw her confusion. He could not account for what he had done. She had been prepared to admire or to remain silent, and he had bewildered and hurt her for no reason he could discover except the pleasure of inflicting pain.

On the bus going back to Morningside Heights they sat on the upper deck. He glanced at Sarah, who was staring at the flat wall of buildings, and saw two enormous tears that stood for an instant on her lashes, then, as the bus staggered and stopped, tumbled from her eyes and rolled slowly down her cheeks.

"I'm sorry," he said. "I didn't mean to make you cry."

He gave her a flat clean handkerchief and she wiped the tears away. "You didn't make me cry," she said. "It's just that I'm homesick. It's not your fault."

"I don't really think the city looked vulgar," he said. "I don't know why I said it. I thought it was beautiful." He took her hand and held it; he felt the vibration of the bus through her hand, which was very cool to the touch. She turned her head and smiled at him and he felt a glow of warmth and a feeling of relief. He kissed her cheek, without thinking, and blushed when a woman with an armful of bundles looked across the aisle at them and smiled understandingly.

When they got back to her apartment she gave him tea and buttered toast and offered him jam her people had sent that was better than any jam he had tasted. He sat in the best of the Finnish chairs, watching her pour him a second cup of tea. "Why are you so nice to me?" he asked. "I'm not nearly as nice to you."

She handed him his cup. "Oh I'm fond of you," she said. "You are the nicest American I've met. Besides, I rather like being nice to people, and I've no one else to be nice to, after all."

He laughed and drank his tea, remembering Freddie Breitbart's having asked him, "What's with you and the Limey girl? Do you just have crumpets with her, or what?" He looked across the room at her. She looked as pretty as a girl on a calendar, but he had absolutely no impulse to make love to her. Sometimes it occurred to him that for form's sake he should make some kind of token advance, just to get the rebuff on record, but he didn't. The idea of sleeping with her, after having slept with Frieda, was anticlimactic.

"I'm fond of you too," he said. "You're a nice girl."

It was the right word. Fondness was what he felt toward her, almost the kind of fondness one might feel for a favorite setter or a favorite suit of clothes. She became associated in his mind with comfort, with an atmosphere of ease. There was something durable about her that gave him satisfaction; and she had a maternal instinct that he satisfied. She enjoyed cooking his dinner and serving it to him, enjoyed waiting on him and giving him his figurative pipe and slippers. For a long time it didn't occur to him that she never really talked about anything at all, even herself. What he found out about her he got in the form of answers to his own questions; she never volunteered a word.

CHAPTER FIFTY-SEVEN

S HE was a Lancashire girl, the daughter of a factory manager who had once been a factory foreman. She had grown up in a black town that rose early to the factory whistle and that was crowded with workingmen's pubs and loud with the authority of workingmen's boots. She had gone to a day school for girls in a neighboring town, and thus been moved a notch above the class to which her parents belonged by birth. She had joined the Air Force at eighteen and served on a bomber station in Lincolnshire. She didn't talk about the war, but she once showed Avery some photographs that had been made at Scampton, of herself with other WAAFs, of herself alone, and of herself with a young man with an observer's wing sewn to his tunic, over the striped medal ribbon. He had a bushy RAF mustache and a pipe, and one of his arms was around Sarah's waist.

"Who's that?" Avery asked.

"That's Tommy Bryce," she said. "He was a navigator during the war." She looked at the photograph then turned it over and read the date on the back. "Nineteen forty-four," she said. "Of course he looks older here than he is. It was made the week they went to Cologne four nights running."

"Nice-looking guy," Avery said.

"Yes, isn't he?" she said. "Actually we're more or less engaged. But I don't know that it will ever come to anything."

"Well you're either engaged or you aren't," he said.

"Well you see, when he got out of the RAF he went home to Leeds, to work in his father's place, and I wasn't demobbed until six months later, and then I went straight on to the University of Manchester, so it seemed rather senseless to marry. Then I got this chance to come to America and everyone said I mustn't miss it, if only for the food." She paused, then said, "He writes me, every fortnight. And I write him once a week."

"It doesn't sound like a grand passion," Avery said.

"Well it isn't, really," she said. "It's just that I am fond of Tommy. Quite fond of him. And my Dad likes him. They get on well."

He wondered whether she had gone to bed with F/O Bryce and for a moment was tempted to ask, but he didn't. He simply said, "I suppose he's quite faithful to you, back in Leeds?"

"Oh I'm sure of it," she said. "He's a nice boy, you see. His people are very nice."

Their hands touched, handling the photographs, and Avery caught hers and held it for a moment, then bent his head and kissed her mouth. Her lips were cool. Her body was immobile as a cotton mattress. It was like kissing an aunt. He let her go, then said, "Is that the way you kiss Mr. Bryce?"

"I don't know," she said. "We didn't do much kissing actually. You see I was in Squadron Records and he was aircrew, and an officer. That made it awkward, seeing one another."

She baffled him. She wasn't stupid, but trying to enliven her was like trying to strike a light from a wet match. He decided that this quality in her was what was meant by the term British phlegm.

"Why did you go in for chemistry?" he asked her one evening. "Why not astronomy or botany or library service?"

"No reason really," she said. "Except that I'm rather good with my hands and like working in a lab. And I do have a goodish memory for facts. It seemed as sensible a choice as any."

"But aren't you really interested in it? I mean *really* interested, as a scientist?"

"I should think so, yes," she said. "I do like it."

"You might just as well be talking about cookery," he said.

"It is rather like cookery," she said, smiling. "Especially the washing up."

Avery, that year, was concerned with the old family quarrel between the basic scientist and the engineer, with the question of learning for its own sake as opposed to learning for practical use. But there was no point in trying out his arguments on Sarah. Sarah didn't think of herself as either a basic scientist or an engineer, but simply as a young woman working in a laboratory. She was learning something she had been told was useful, to the Crown, to herself, and to society. It did not seem wrong to her that she was learning it by rote. She once showed Avery her notebooks and he discovered that she took down the lectures in shorthand, retaining every word that was uttered in class, transcribing them later and apparently committing them to memory. He was horrified.

"It's so mechanical," he said. "You're supposed to follow the thought, not just the words."

"Perhaps you're right," she said agreeably. "But I can never understand quite what's meant, during the lecture. If I take it all down and study it afterward I manage better."

"I hope you aren't deluding yourself by thinking you're doing independent work," he said stuffily.

"Oh, I hadn't thought about that," she said, smiling at him.

It occurred to him that she might be poking fun at him, behind her bland gray eyes. He looked at her suspiciously, and saw nothing but utter innocence.

There was nothing else there.

She was absolutely innocent and absolutely honest, as honest as triple-distilled water.

She was literal. She wept quietly during the appropriate sequences of the sadder Hollywood films and was always frankly relieved when the story turned out right in the end. She read nothing outside the field of her work, and had never seen a play until Avery took her to one on Broadway. She would have been content to have dined on steamed potatoes, steamed cabbage, steamed sprouts and steamed beef for the fifteen thousand evening meals she would eat before she died. She did not arouse his passion. There were no sparks between them, physical or intellectual. There was nothing between them that he could isolate. But she fed his ego. She made him feel masculine and urbane and extraordinarily intelligent. She was soothing as old Annie McBain. He got used to her and without quite understanding the process became enormously dependent on her. He did not have enough understanding of the chemistry of human beings to realize that she was drifting deeply and hopelessly into love with him.

CHAPTER FIFTY-EIGHT

BUT Breitbart saw it.

One evening Avery and Sarah had dinner with Freddie and then went back to the men's apartment, where they drank coffee and an acrid plum brandy that Freddie had brought back from France and that tasted like benzine mixed with potato spirits. It brought tears to Sarah's eyes and made Avery cough, but it did loosen everyone up.

Breitbart approved of Sarah and seemed eager to make Avery understand that he approved. He put his sarcasm aside, and went out of his way to be diplomatic. He talked about England just enough to please Sarah and not enough to irritate Avery, who sometimes felt inferior because he had not been to Europe. He was playing a character part and he enjoyed it—the role of the faithful university friend, at the service of his friend's inamorata. He was attentive to Sarah without being in the least on the make, and she liked him. She thought he was sincere.

When he came back to the apartment after taking her home, Avery had an impulse to thank Freddie, or to do something for him in repayment for his effort. But he could think of nothing to say or do that would not seem sentimental or false. They had another glass of the fierce French brandy and Freddie said, "That's a nice girl, Hollister. Lots of character."

"She's all right," Avery said. "She's no ball of fire, but she's all right."

"Are you going to marry her?" Freddie asked.

"Good Lord no!" Avery said. "She's just somebody I know, that's all."

"She's in love with you," Breitbart said. "Take my word for it. She's in your pocket."

"Are you crazy?" Avery said. "Anyway, she's engaged to a guy in England. A fellow she knew in the R.A.F."

"You mean he gave her a pair of his birdie wings and said 'Pip pip old gel, we must toddle up to the altar one of these days'? She may be engaged, old boy, or married for all I know, but she's in love with young Mr. Hollister. You've been chosen, friend. She's your girl. Take it from Poppa. I know women."

"I've never even made a pass at her," Avery said. "I don't even care about her that way."

"Then you're a damn fool," said Freddie. "She's a dam good-looking girl and all she wants is a little warming up. Get the cold English fog out of her blood and she'd give you a run for your money."

"I haven't the faintest interest in her," Avery said stiffly. "Warm or cold."

"Have it your own way," Freddie said. He got up and corked the brandy bottle. "By the way, there's a letter for you. From Canada. It's in your room."

"Thanks," Avery said. "You're a nice guy, Fritz," he said, after a moment, looking up at Freddie. "You put on a good show." He grinned. "But you're wrong about Sarah. I like her, but that's all there is to it."

"Who do you think you're kidding?" said Freddie. "Yourself, maybe. But not old F. the Great. You will be fumbling with her woolen underwear, just you wait and see."

Avery laughed and went into his bedroom. The letter from Canada was on his dresser, propped up against the mirror, a bedraggled-looking blue envelope. It was from Dennis McCoy and had been written six weeks earlier and posted at Copper-mine in the Canadian Northwest Territory. It told Avery that

Dennis was coming back to the United States, to enter a semi-
nary where he would be prepared for the priesthood. He planned
to be in New York for a few days at Christmas time and wanted
to see Avery.

Avery read the letter standing up, his elbows resting on his
dresser top. When he finished reading, he looked up and was
confronted by his own reflection. The letter had a queer effect on
him. He felt numb. And he felt a sickening wave of depression.
He had the conviction that once Dennis had taken his vows he
would be finally and irrevocably lost, lost as if he were dead on
the coral where he had just missed death.

He sat down on his bed, the letter in his hand, remembering Dennis the day he had seen him after Dennis got back from
Rome. Then Dennis had said to him, "I'm not fit to be a priest.
Not fit." He wondered how much Dennis had changed up there
in the Arctic. He wondered what it was that had made Dennis
change his mind.

Then a question rose in his own mind that he recognized as
improper but could not suppress. He wondered whether Dennis
truly believed that when he became a priest and officiated at mass
that he would actually receive into his body the Body and Blood
of Jesus Christ. The probability that he did believe this with all
his heart and mind and soul, caused a shudder of fear and mystery to pass through Avery, and then a wave of revulsion.

It was obscene.

It was incredible that Dennis McCoy could literally believe
what Avery knew he must believe in order to have found himself
worthy of becoming a candidate for the priesthood.

Avery went to bed confused. In a sense he envied Dennis his
faith. At least Dennis believed in something. But he recoiled in
horror, with Protestant horror and the distaste of the scientific
rationalist, from the costumed expression of that faith. And he
could not get out of his mind the contemptible suspicion that
Dennis had not traveled in a straight line, but must somewhere

have skipped a step, ignored some contradiction and left it unresolved, like a golfer who secretly moves his ball from a sand trap to the fairway and plays the rest of the round, pretending to himself that it is actual achievement. It seemed to him that Dennis professed to believe in magic and that his religion, however beautiful and time-endowed, was in the end a mass of repulsive superstition, unworthy of a first-rate mind or an honest one. It was simply impossible for him to understand that Dennis McCoy really believed, for example, in Transubstantiation or in the Assumption of the Virgin. He took it for granted that the Virgin for one thing had not been a virgin, and that her bones had long since rotted into the dust of some arid Middle Eastern hillside. He realized that he was suggesting to himself, in brutal terms, that Dennis' renewal of faith was phony, or else that Dennis was nervously unbalanced.

Yet he understood the illogic and unfairness of his suspicion; this was an area of human experience he knew nothing about and had no means of investigating. Dennis once had said to him: "If a mathematically ignorant professor of literature looked at the equation $E=mc^2$ and boldly announced that the equation was nonsense and the Theory of Relativity a hoax, you'd put him down as a pompous ass, wouldn't you? So would anyone else. Yet if the same man, equally ignorant of religion and religious experience, announced that God was a hoax and the Church a fraud, you'd nod your head in agreement and think he was a perfectly normal modern intellectual and not a pompous ass at all."

He had seen the point of Dennis' argument then, or at least he had not been able to break the argument down. But the prejudice remained, deep in his heart. His grandmother, his father's mother, had drawn back her skirts when she passed a nun, and that blood was in him and so was the blood of Cromwell's men, whose broadswords had lopped the heads from a thousand miniature saints in the chapel at Ely Cathedral. Rome was a harlot, vulgar, jeweled and false. There was something sickening to him in the thought of Dennis, prostrate before a bishop, being invested with holy orders.

"Better minds than yours have believed it," came old Mr. Cobble's voice. "Better minds than yours have believed it, Hollister, to their great advantage, one might add, in this world as well as the next."

In the morning Breitbart asked, "How's with our friend St. Francis of the North? Has he got his belly full of God yet?"

"I don't think so," Avery said. "He's coming down here at Christmas time. You can ask him yourself."

He did not tell Breitbart about Dennis' decision. He was somewhat ashamed of Dennis, as well as afraid of what Freddie might say. He wrote to Dennis and said he would expect him during the holiday, but said nothing about Dennis' plans; he didn't know the correct form of congratulation used in such a situation.

CHAPTER FIFTY-NINE

THE sources of cruelty are often concealed and what appears to be deliberate brutality may be only the end result of a process confused and shot through with obliquity and contradiction.

It is probable that Avery's father made several attempts to write a proper letter, but each time failed. In the end what Avery got was one of several hundred engraved announcements of the coming marriage of John Morgan van Ameringe Hollister to Mrs. Ivy Prewitt Calder, addressed in the anonymous professional hand of Mrs. Calder's secretary.

His first reaction was one of unbelief similar to the unbelief aroused by announcement in dispassionate type of the death of a friend only recently seen and touched or another friend's sudden acquisition of eminence or notoriety. The thing described with the authority of journalism must not refer to the person you know, but to someone else with the same name. It is simply incredible that so-and-so has been made president of a college or died or been sent to jail or decorated with the Medal of Honor. The photograph on the newsprint page, however accurate the likeness, cannot really be of the person you had dinner with on Thursday, or fought with twenty years ago when you were boys, or made love to in another year in an episode the intensity of which is now oddly unbelievable and faintly shameful.

Avery literally could not believe what he read on the card that Tiffany & Co. had printed. It made no difference that attempts had been made to prepare him for the event, and even to secure his approval of it and possible collaboration. He did not at first find it possible to believe the intelligence offered him in a form compact and economical as one of his own equations. What his mind understood, his heart rejected.

But after a little he realized that the card meant exactly what it said, in spite of the elegant format and costly paper. It meant that his father was getting married to the New York whore. His mouth went dry and his heart pounded dangerously, clogging the passage of blood to his brain. He experienced a wave of vertigo and put a hand on the wall to steady himself.

She had no right. She had simply no right.

The fact that she seemed to have no home of her own, so that the wedding was going to take place in Hull, in his mind placed her more firmly in the role of invader. He felt murderous personal jealousy. It was not until some time later that he remembered his dead mother and realized that this woman, his father's woman, who looked like a photograph in a magazine, was going to take his mother's place, assume his mother's prerogatives, possess his mother's belongings: her bedroom, her very bed, her gardens, her studio, her name, her husband.

It was intolerable.

His father had no right to marry. He was already married, to a corpse. His father wanted two of everything—two wars, two wives.

He went into his room and threw himself onto his bed, giving way to his emotions, sobbing like a poisoned child, wishing himself dead or unborn. His maturity abandoned him; it was like a wall breaking and giving way before the waters of a flood, or a house going down in bomb blast. He had contained himself with dams that he had built with his mind, but the dams broke. He felt agony, and the formulated, untrue conviction that his father had thrown him out so that he could take his woman in, and even though he knew this wasn't the truth, he could not rid himself of the will to believe it. He lay on his bed for a long time, aware of a sense of incarceration. Finally he got up and took the wedding announcement out of his pocket. He read it again, then burnt it, holding the flaming cardboard over an ash tray, exorcising the devil in the print. He washed himself and went about his business, but he could not get away from the fact. It came back to him throung the day, without warning, like asthmatic attack.

During the next few days he made an effort to take an adult, sensible attitude but he failed. He did not seem to have the equipment needed to control his jealousy and resentment and his insistent persuasion of betrayal. He reacted like an adolescent, and was ashamed of his own thoughts, yet he could not control them. He felt a desperate, irrational need to know whether the marriage merely regularized a relationship that had existed in one form or another ever since the afternoon he and his mother had encountered his father and Mrs. Calder in the awful restaurant with the orange candles, or whether Mrs. Calder came to his father as a figurative virgin. In terms of ordinary common sense he had no doubt that his father was simply entering the notarized phase of a long affair. But in those areas of human consciousness not governed by common sense, he experienced torturing uncertainty, and the wedding took on powerful, brutal, sexual significance. He was disgusted with himself but he could not banish imaginations of his father's approaching wedding night, conjurings so realistic they were a form of torture and the source of obscene confusion. He had dealt for twenty years with the beast in his flesh that had been born when he was placed on his mother's breast, yet it was still his half-time master, beyond control of his intellect. He had been celibate for months, having seen no woman but Sarah, and perhaps the accumulated pressure was partly to blame for the violence of his thoughts. Whatever the reason, the terrible scenes that rose in his mind prevented him from seeking relief.

What troubled him most was his immaturity. He was behaving like a child and he knew it, but he could not help himself no matter how angrily he debated with his emotions. *"Your father is a man. It's been two years. He has a right to marry,"* his mind seemed to say to him. But the answer was a paroxysmal No! and the answer was stronger than the argument.

He told himself again and again that it was none of his affair, that it no longer mattered to him what his father did or failed to do. There was nothing at Hull he wanted, not a stick of furniture, not a single rose bloom, not a picture or book or blade of grass. He had not seen the farm for more than two years and had adjusted himself to the idea that he would never see it again.

He did not want the farm. He did not want to get back on line, behind his father in the place he had relinquished. He wanted neither honey nor sting, neither cuff nor caress. He didn't want his father's living body or his mother's ghost.

Yet the idea that the house he had been born in would now be inhabited by his father's woman made him sick with jealousy. He didn't want the farm or his father, but he didn't want anyone else to have them. It was the old problem again. He wanted always what he could not have: to be loved and to be loved alone, insisting that his place be saved whether he intended to use it or not.

He had read somewhere that mathematicians were the most intelligent of all scientists and it seemed to him that they should therefore be the best balanced individuals. Gross doubts rose in his mind concerning his own professional fitness.

Dormaker reassured him.

"Avery, we have healthy artists and unhealthy ones," he said, "and we have healthy scientists and diseased ones. Look at——." He mentioned the name of a physicist sent to prison for treason, who had made in the courtroom an elaborate Freudian confession of guilt.

"But if a man devotes himself to truth shouldn't it make him a better person?"

"No," said Dormaker. "Only a better chemist or physicist or mathematician."

"It seems to me—" Avery began, but he broke off and decided not to utter the thought that had occurred to him, which was that if science did not make men moral then science was nothing but a game or a branch of mechanics. If it didn't improve a man's moral fiber to know that a certain star was three billion light-years from the earth, or that a body in motion tended to remain in motion, then the first fact was meaningless and the second no more profound in nature than the knowledge required to take apart the carburetor of a cheap engine. He had thought for some time now that he was better than his father and more moral, because his calling was more honorable. Dormaker's viewpoint didn't suit him; it invalidated his own.

But he didn't say this. He said, "Well I don't have any secrets the Russians would care about buying from me, so maybe I'd better not worry about it."

He went back to his work but his brain was sluggish. The pale blue grid of the graph paper blurred before his eyes and he could not concentrate. He took a freshly sharpened pencil from the pot on his desk and snapped off the thin point, making a sharp destructive sound. The bit of graphite rolled across the desk and fell to the floor. He took the pencil in both hands and snapped it like a stick of kindling, taking pleasure for some reason in the destruction of the harmless tool. Tomorrow at about this time he knew that his father would be getting married in the church in Hull where he had gone with his mother when he was a boy, and where his mother had gone to pray out her madness and confusion on the day of the Normandy invasion. He had an obsessive desire to see the wedding, combined with fear of the meeting with his father that must occur if he did attend.

He brooded about it all morning and that afternoon, instead of going to his classes, he packed a small bag and took the train to Hartford, going straight from the station to a hotel, where he got a room and locked the door behind him. He had no plans. He didn't know whether or not he would go out to Hull tomorrow or sit here in this room until his father was married again. He had acted on impulse that arose from inability to sit in New York, where he belonged, and do the work that had been placed before him.

It was early evening and from the window he had a view of the city, the sun on the gold dome of the Capitol, where his father had taken him when he was a boy and where he had first seen Ivy Calder, the Lady Democrat from Litchfield County. He remembered the day, the excitement in the lobby that smelled of whiskey and cigars, the pride in his father when his father spoke, and the little edge of fear when Mrs. Calder had stuck her tongue out at him.

In that light, the city looked intensely groomed. He was so used to New York, seen always through a veil of haze, that the clarity of the Hartford landscape, the sharp outline of the buildings, seemed remarkable and gave the city a foreign aspect that was exciting and romantic. There was a sense both of familiarity and of strangeness. He sat at the window, smoking, and watched the lights come on as darkness fell. It was warm for November and the window was open, so that he heard the street noises. He had a heady sense of anonymity, of secrecy. He felt like the hero of a thriller who has at the beginning of the book arrived incognito in a strange Balkan town, where adventure and danger await him.

He also had the feeling of playing truant. At this hour he would normally be at a seminar meeting in Havemeyer Hall, and since he never cut classes they must assume that he was ill. He had said nothing to Sarah or Freddie, and it occurred to him that Sarah might be worried about him.

When it was completely dark he felt a languorous, vague unease, as though he were suspended in time. The sound of water running in the next room gave him a start. He wanted suddenly to be out of the dark imprisoning room. He went downstairs to the lobby, where he bought a Hartford paper and sat in a deep leather chair, glancing at the headlines, amused by the English appearance of the paper, which looked the same as it had looked when he had seen it at his father's place on the breakfast table at Hull. It was a paper made up in such a way that it would not have been embarrassed at being warmed before the fire in preparation for the master's hands. When he finished the paper he folded it and put it on the table beside his chair, instead of simply throwing it away as he would have done with a New York paper.

He sat in the chair, staring through the lobby windows at the landscaped hill on which the Capitol stood. He had not eaten since noon and it was now nearly nine, but he did not feel hungry or feel anything else, except a vague unsafety and awareness that his destiny for the time being was not in his own hands. He felt rather like a hospital patient who has been entered and made comfortable the evening before an operation, knowing it is too soon to be frightened but not trusting the environment.

He went into the bar and sat on a stool, ordering whiskey. He wasn't used to drinking alone and felt conspicuous, but it seemed the proper thing to do. The hotel was old but the bar was new, with pine-paneled walls and amber light bulbs shaped like candles. It looked like a colored photograph of the rumpus room in a modern house. He drank his whiskey and ordered another. He had almost finished his third, and his lips were numb, when somebody called his name and he turned.

"Aren't you General Hollister's boy, from Hull?"

It was Mr. Sweeney, who owned the Hull Supply Company and had been in the legislature with his father. He was sixty now and wore polished, clinical-looking rimless glasses. Avery admitted his identity and shook hands with him.

"Up for the wedding, I suppose?" Mr. Sweeney said.

Avery nodded. "Yes, I'm up for the wedding," he said.

They had a drink and Mr. Sweeney told about his son Sam, who was in the army now and married to the prettiest darn girl in Hartford. Avery looked at the photographs of Sam and Sam's wife and Sam's baby son that Mr. Sweeney took out of his wallet, and admired all of them. It seemed strange to him that Sam Sweeney who was exactly his own age, should already be the father of a son, while he had scarcely started his life.

Mr. Sweeney put the pictures away and touched Avery's arm. "Don't see your Dad as much as I used to," he said confidentially. "But if you ask me it's a durn good thing he's gettin' married, even if the lady is a Democrat. It's not good for a man to be all by himself, and your Dad's no exception, general or no general."

Avery nodded; he felt the whiskey, it made Mr. Sweeney's face look evil and made his eyes behind the vicious lenses look inexorable. His voice went on, thin, Yankee and inescapable.

"Don't think he's been the same since old Mrs. McBain died," he said. "It got to him somehow. Guess she'd been with your folks so long it was just like having a member of the family pass away."

Through the blur of the whiskey Avery felt a stab of pain. He put down his glass very carefully and said, "What did you just say?" There was a suggestion of threat in his voice that made Mr. Sweeney look at him strangely.

"I said your Dad hasn't been looking just right since Annie McBain died," he repeated.

Avery felt a blunt sense of shock, then was struck by a wave of nausea. He put his hands on the bar to steady himself.

"Say, you knew she was dead didn't you?" Mr. Sweeney asked, "You haven't been having some kind of row with your Dad, have you?"

"When did Annie die?" said Avery bluntly. "Exactly when?"

Mr. Sweeney was embarrassed. He took out his handkerchief and polished his glasses, then ran a hand over his hair. "Well let's see now," he said. "Couple of months ago, I reckon. Just keeled over one day in the kitchen. Heart just stopped beating, the doc said. All over in a minute." He paused, looking cagily at Avery. "There was an item about it in the paper. But I s'pose being in New York City you wouldn't see the Hartford papers."

"No," said Avery. "No I don't." He finished the whiskey in his glass and ordered another for himself and for Mr. Sweeney. Mr. Sweeney reminisced, while Avery sat with a hand on the bar, trying to steady himself.

"Fine woman, Mrs. McBain," Mr. Sweeney said. "She'd have made some fellow a fine wife. Wonder she never got married. Didn't want to leave you folks, I guess."

"Look, I don't feel well," Avery said abruptly, prompted to smash his fist into Mr. Sweeney's enunciating face. "I wonder if you will excuse me?"

"Well, sure," Mr. Sweeney said. "Sure." He was disappointed; he had hoped to find out what kind of row Avery had had with his father.

Avery got down from the stool and made his way to the elevator, unsteady on his feet, feeling a combination of shock, grief and raw whiskey. He fell to the bed in his room and as his head whirled sickeningly he realized that he was quite drunk. He began to cry softly and after a while subsided into a sodden alcoholic sleep.

When he woke up the morning sun was streaming through the window. He felt sick at his stomach and uncertain of his whereabouts. He had slept through the night in his clothes, so that he felt wretchedly dirty. He was besieged by the formless guilt sometimes encouraged by liquor, a vague sense of duty forgotten, unspecific but troubling as a fly in the room. He got up and walked to the window, staring at the State House dome, and remembered that he was in Hartford and had come for his father's wedding. Then he recalled the dark bar and Mr. Sweeney's face, filled with confidence. The fact of Annie's death hit him like a blow in the stomach. He sat down heavily on the bed. He was stunned, and could not suppress his outrage at having heard the news from an outsider. He could not understand it. It did not fit the correct pattern his father usually followed. After all, Annie had really been his mother's servant. He felt that the insult had been deliberate and that his father intended to convey meaning with it, to let him know that he was not missed at Hull or wanted, that it was good riddance to him.

He shaved and bathed and put on the clean shirt he had brought from New York. It was nearly eleven and his head throbbed. Through the window came the noise of the city, a low murmur of people and traffic with a vicious counterpoint of automobile horns; somewhere far off there was the mournful sound of a steam whistle. In the strange room in what was now a strange city, he had the feeling of being illegal, of being hunted.

He ate his breakfast in the empty dining room, then went out into the city. It was a bright fall day, warm enough so that people carried their coats on their arms. The familiar streets and familiar neat policemen that somehow suggested British policemen, brought back a rush of memory of afternoons passed with his mother, shopping or being taken to the doctor's or to the photographer's studio to have his semiannual portrait made. The nostalgia was overpowering. He was filled with yearning for his childhood and his mother.

He wandered up and down Main Street, then turned and went downhill then up again to the State Capitol. A trooper stood in the driveway managing traffic and he realized that it was the same trooper who had saluted his father the night they had left the legislature. He was in his father's territory. If he loitered in front of the Capitol the trooper would not salute him, but order him to move on. As he stood staring at the gilt dome he understood that at least part of his rebellion had been fake. His refusal to go to his father's college and there be taught how to emulate his father had not been altogether based on his rejection of his father's world and the things his father stood for, but on fear as well—the secret deadly knowledge in his heart that the task was too great, that he could never have equaled or surpassed his father on his father's home grounds. Morgan might have, but he never. The knowledge that he had rejected a challenge had of course been with him all along, but he had suppressed it.

He speculated as he had done before on what kind of man he would be today had he gone to Yale and then to the army and, when he had finished with the army, into his father's business in Hartford. His appearance would not be much different. He had never abandoned the rules of dress passed to him by his father. He still wore the plain suits and plain shirts that went over the head, the stodgy, correct things one wore until it was time to go to England and begin having his clothes made there. He would have looked the same. But he would not have felt the same inside or seemed the same to other people.

An impressively long black car came up the drive and the trooper snapped to attention. It was the Governor. He got out of the car and hurried into the Capitol, carrying a brief case. Avery saw the license plate: 1, and caught a glimpse of the Governor's face, a long friendly equine face, often photographed and familiar. The trooper glanced at Avery and frowned and Avery moved off, going down through the park again and up the hill to Main Street.

He wanted very much to go to Hull and if possible to see something of the wedding. But he was afraid someone on the Hull bus would recognize him and he did not want to be recognized. He was engaged in espionage. He found a taxi and persuaded the driver to take him around the village of Hull, to the dirt road that led to the farm. He got out of the cab and paid the man, then approached the house on foot, secretly as a thief, not certain of what he planned to do, but drawn by an attraction morbid as that which draws people to a public execution. When he saw the house and the front door with the brass plate on it he curdled. He knew that he could not face his father or his father's new wife. But he could not turn back either and return to the city, to New York, to his own territory.

Something made him stay.

There was a place he knew from which he would be able to watch the front door of the house—a little room in the horse barn that was closed off from the hay loft and used as a storage place for oddments of disused harness and gear. He left the road before he reached the house and cut through the underbrush to the barn. There was no one in sight; he felt pleased with his maneuver. He slipped into the barn and climbed the ladder to the loft, entering the little room and closing the door behind him. He was overwhelmed by the strong, erotic smell of hay and animals that filled the barn, a smell that had always in his mind been closely related to Hull and to childhood.

From the window he could see the house and part of the terrace where his mother and David Fearing had danced together during the storm. He could see the broad sweep of lawn that ended in the perennial borders his mother had loved and then neglected. As his pulse slowed down he was struck by the irrational quality of his behavior and for a moment questioned his sanity. He was nearly twenty-one. He had been invited to the wedding and it was his privilege to attend or stay away. There was no reason for him to hide. But he could not bring himself to descend the ladder, brush off his clothes, and present himself properly at the front door. The fear might not be rational but it was real. He could not go down to the house and he could not turn away and depart without making his presence known. He was held there at the barn window, conspiring with himself, by the hypnotic power of the unresolved conflict with his father that created within him conflict with himself: perpetual guerilla warfare between intelligence and emotion, body and soul.

He saw his father come out of the house, dressed in a dark suit and carrying a pair of gloves and a coat over his arm. He pressed his forehead against the windowpane, watching his father stand for a moment in the doorway like an officer reviewing troops, then go into the garage. A few seconds later he saw a big new car that he didn't recognize being backed out of the garage, then swung in an arc and turned toward town. He had a sense of identification with his father that was uncanny, so that having watched him cross the drive was like having watched himself on film. The stride, the turn of the head, the contour of the body, were all his own and the tense physical resemblance, that had never seemed so strong before, seemed to contest his own identity.

He had been on his knees at the window, but now he sank back to the floor, pulling a horse's collar toward him and using it as a pillow. By now his father must be at the church. In a few minutes the wedding would have taken place. He settled down on the floor, intending to wait until the wedding party came back to the house, and fell into revery, half asleep, half awake, unconscious of the passage of time. He fell into real sleep for a little while and woke up with a start, going to the window. The sun had moved and the house was in shadow. It occurred to him that they were not coming back to the house at all, and the absurdity of his adventure struck him all at once. He burst into laughter that was on the verge of hysteria. What a fool! he said to himself. What a God damned bloody fool. He stared through the window at the silent house and realized that of course they weren't coming back.

He climbed down from the hay loft and stood for a moment looking at the house, undecided, then crossed the lawn quickly and went around the house to the kitchen door. He knocked and the door was opened by a young woman wearing a light blue uniform and a very clean white apron.

"Yes?"

"Excuse me," Avery said. "I used to know an old woman that worked for the Hollisters here. Mrs. McBain. Annie McBain." He hesitated. "Someone told me she was dead. Someone in Hartford."

"She is that," the woman said, her speech touched with a brogue. "She died a couple of months ago."

"How did it happen?" he asked.

The woman looked at him curiously. "Did you know her well?" she asked. "Were you related to her now?"

"In a way," Avery said.

The woman swung the door open. "Well, it was a strange thing," she said. "She was sittin' right there at that table, peelin' some apples, an' she looked up an' said to me, 'You know Rose, the fall always makes me think of Mrs. Hollister. She'd put those gardens to bed the way you'd tuck in a child.' Then she made a kind of funny noise and went all rigid like. Before I could get around the table she fell right into the apples." The woman paused, looking at the empty chair, then said, "It was a queer thing to see. She was a strict old devil you know, but good as they come. Good as they come."

Avery felt a kind of chill pass through his veins. His throat tightened and the tears rose. He attempted to speak but his mouth was stiff and the words wouldn't come.

"That was the first Mrs. Hollister she meant, you know," the cook said. "The general just got married again, this afternoon, an' now he's off to France with his brand-new wife."

Avery nodded. He looked at the woman, then through the door at the familiar kitchen, catching a glimpse of the old black stove. "Thanks," he said thickly. "Thanks for telling me."

He walked back to the highway in the dusk and caught the bus into Hartford. He went to the hotel and packed his bag, then took a cab to the station. It had turned colder and he felt chilled in his light coat that had seemed too warm when he left the city yesterday. As he climbed aboard the train and took a seat near the window, he had the illusion of being released from nightmare. The interlude in the hayloft and the Irish woman's reconstruction of the scene of Annie's death took on the character of events that had happened in sleep. His imagination returned to his father and the fact of his father's marriage, which now was total fact and irrevocable. He felt a dull eroding jealousy. It did not seem fair.

He was almost twenty-one.

If anyone was getting married, he should be the one. His father was old. He had gray hair on his head and his body. The idea of his getting into bed with Mrs. Calder in the New York hotel where they now must be waiting for the Paris boat, was intolerable, disgusting. He had a vivid imagination of them unclothed and abandoned to passion in the hotel his father always used. When he got down from the train he went to a phone booth and called the hotel. He was told that Mr. and Mrs. Hollister had registered but did not wish to be disturbed. He hung up the phone, imagining that the room clerk had had a giggle in his voice. He sat on the little hard bench, his shins pressed again the sharp edge of his bag. He was filled with poisonous physical jealousy of his father and his father's wife, a consuming, lewd envy, and then he had a sharp memory of the night he had surprised his brother and the Farmington girl on the grass at Sturgis Manor, memory of the girl's marble thigh and stricken face and of his brother's nonchalance afterward: *"We weren't playing marbles, kid. We sure weren't playing parchesi."*

His forehead rested against the mouthpiece of the phone and he thought for a moment he was going to be sick. Then there was a knocking on the glass door and he raised his head. Outside was a heavy woman with gray marceled hair and a face thick with powder. He swung the door open and the woman said, "Young man this is a telephone booth, not a place to sleep."

"I'm sorry," he mumbled. "I felt sick."

She looked at him indignantly then entered the booth and slammed the door. She gave off sparks of matriarchal authority. He turned and walked away, toward the subway, then changed his mind and went through the station to the cab rank on Vanderbilt Avenue. He gave the driver Sarah's address and sat back watching the street lights as the cab rolled up Fifth Avenue. They passed a jeweler's clock set on a stanchion at the curb. He leaned forward in the cab. "Driver, is that the right time?" he asked. "Ten minutes to four?"

"That's right, bud," the driver said. "The ginmills are closed." He slowed the cab, turning his head. "Unless you feel like going way uptown. I know a joint in Harlem stays open all night. They oney close an hour a day to sweep the place out."

"No thanks," Avery said, sitting back again and folding his arms across his chest. It was late, too late to go to Sarah's apartment, too late to go anywhere but home and he leaned forward to tell the driver to take him to his own place. But he changed his mind. He didn't feel like going to his own place and he did feel like going to Sarah's. To hell with what time it was. To hell with her too, and with his father and his father's God damn whore of a wife.

As the cab turned west and climbed the hill, he was filled with intense predatory excitement. He felt as though a bomb were ticking away inside him and had an urge toward physical violence—almost the desire to murder, to smash someone to death with his fists just for the sake of inflicting pain, for the sake of the pure animal response. When the cab pulled up in front of Sarah's house he had a moment of hesitation at the sight of the tall faceless building with all the windows dark. He brushed this aside and paid off the cab, then went into the atrocious lobby. There was an arrangement of bells on a brass plate with a circular grill into which one spoke and an earphone that hung from a hook. He rang until Sarah answered, then said bluntly into the mouthpiece, "It's me. Avery. Let me in."

"Why Avery, what on earth—"

Her voice was metallic over the wire, and heavy with sleep.

"Let me in!" he said.

"Just a minute," she said.

She pressed the button that released the lock and he hurried up the stairs, ignoring the automatic elevator that always responded slowly. She was waiting at the door, wearing a pale blue flannel robe, her hair down and tied back with a ribbon. "Are you all right?" she said. "I've been worried."

"I'm all right," he said. "I'm fine."

He followed her into the apartment and put down his bag. Then he took off his coat and loosened his tie and sat on the sofa, staring at her. He was used to seeing her with her hair done up and her body armored in some kind of tweed. With her hair down and in bare feet she looked smaller than usual and more vulnerable.

"Avery, you look worn out," she said, embarrassed by the way he stared. "Shall I make you some coffee?"

"No. Come here and sit down," he said.

She crossed the room and sat down beside him. He kissed her brutally, without affection, hard, so that his teeth bit into her lip. He pushed back her robe and kissed her neck and breasts, then forced her down and opened the robe.

"Avery darling, please be good to me. Please," she said. "I've never let a man handle me like this before you know. Please be kind, darling. Please."

He only half believed what she said. But it was true and for some reason the fact that she was a virgin seemed retributive and providential, as did her tears and cry of pain. He wanted to hurt her and he did. It was the classic masculine assertion: the defloration. He felt triumph, raw brutal triumph so crudely physical it frightened him.

The light was off and he heard her crying softly in the darkness. In the dim light that came from the courtyard her body looked ghostly. He leaned back on the sofa and his breath slackened. He felt numb and confused by the power that had swept through him. He listened to the sound of her weeping and experienced no regret, only a sense of victory.

After a little she stopped crying and sat up, then rose and put on her robe. She bent and kissed his forehead. Then she picked up his trousers, that he had kicked to the floor, shaking them into their creases, then folding them neatly and putting them on a chair. "It's all right, Avery," she said quietly. "I do love you so. It's all right."

She went into the bathroom and he heard the water running. He got up and put on his pants, then sat in a chair. She
came out of the bathroom with the tears washed away and made
a pot of coffee. They sat and drank it in the dark room, that was
now obliquely illuminated by the light from the kitchen, so that
he could see her face in profile. She looked peaceful and quite
happy. He remembered the way she had cried before and could
not understand it.

"It's almost morning," she said. "Would you like to see the
sun come up?"

"That would be nice," he said. "If you like."

He wondered whether she sensed his need to get out of the
room, or whether the suggestion was accident.

"We can go to the roof," she said. "It's lovely from there. I
often go. You can see a bit of either river."

The roof was covered with tar and light gravel that
crunched under their feet. A faint smell of oil smoke came
from the chimney pots, mixing with the smell of the morning.
They stood near the water tower, facing east. Far off through
a gap in the buildings was the glimpse of East River she had
promised. Beyond that, over the Bronx, was the pink evanes-
cent morning.

"Isn't it beautiful?" Sarah asked. She looked up. "And the sky.
There's so much of it from here."

Avery nodded. He was on the edge of exhaustion. He felt an
ache in his bones and a wooden dullness in his nerves, as if he
had been ill for days with devastating fever that had drawn the
energy from his body like an electric current from a battery. But
his mind was in turmoil and he felt no desire for sleep but only
for the kind of respite one associates with a warm bath. Things
were in contest in his mind, Annie and his father and Sarah
Greenway. He looked at Sarah, whose innocence was emphasized
by the pale morning light. He felt as though he had committed
rape, and that somehow the act of violence had in some measure

reasserted the manhood that had deserted him in Hull when he hid in the barn.

They watched the sun rise, standing close together, saying nothing. When it had risen and the city horizon showed clear against the light, Sarah said, "Do you love me, Avery? Truly?"

"Of course," he said. "Naturally."

He uttered the words mechanically, as if he had scarcely heard the question. Then he turned and looked at her. She had put on a skirt and a rough wool sweater and tied a silk square over her head so that it formed a kind of coif and made her look innocent and wholesome. He bent his head and kissed her on the mouth.

"Do you really love me?" she asked again. "It's all right if you don't. I mean, you musn't feel you have to, just because of what happened."

He stared off toward the east. He didn't know whether he loved her or not, but he did know that he needed her, and he felt, without quite understanding it, a desperate need for the forms of love.

"Yes," he said. "I love you. I must."

She put her arm through his. "I'm glad," she said. "I do love you, Avery. I expect I have, right from the beginning, when you bumped into me at that silly meeting."

"Why?" he asked.

"Well, I don't quite know," she said. "I like the way you look, of course. And the way you walk and do things. But it's not that. It's—I simply love you, that's all. I feel right with you."

They went downstairs and made love again. This time there was no rape in it, only pleasure and, for Avery, a kind of conformation of identity.

CHAPTER SIXTY

O NE night a few days later he fell asleep in the bed beside her. When he woke up it was daylight, and he smelled fresh coffee. Sarah sat on a chair beside the bed, watching him. "You looked so peaceful last night," she said. "I hadn't the heart to wake you up."

She brought him his breakfast in bed. It is a great thing for the ego and he enjoyed it. After that he often stayed overnight at her place, and he drifted into the kind of arrangement many men believe they would prefer if it were socially more acceptable: a combination of bachelorhood with domesticity. He was getting something for nothing and should have been aware of the danger in this, but he wasn't. He simply took what was offered. He was loved and the love warmed him, and he was made to feel like a little king, for he was always given precedence. It was not an exciting relationship, sexually or in any other way. Sometimes it was almost dull. But it was soothing; it was comfortable. It was a form of modified marriage, and nothing at all like the kind of affair Breitbart tried to make of it.

Breitbart amused himself by referring to Sarah as Avery's paramour, making the word sound wicked and swanky. He had a weakness for shopworn literary situations and sometimes liked to pretend that he and Avery were Regency bucks, living in digs on Jermyn Street and amusingly going to the Jews each year to borrow against their expectations. Of course he was a little jealous, and this made his buffoonery palatable.

"Will you be at the digs tonight, old boy?" he would ask, "or are you passing the hours of darkness with your paramour?" He would stand in the bathroom doorway, clad in his extravagant dressing gown, doing a clever burlesque of a movie actor being British.

Most of the time Avery would fall into his act. "Actually," he would reply, "I thought I would pop in on the old gel tonight, you know."

"Oh bad show!" Breitbart would say. "I'd rather looked forward to your companionship tonight old boy. Bottle of sack and all that, what?"

"So sorry, old man. Tomorrow perhaps?"

By any logical system of accounting, Avery knew that he should have been perfectly satisfied with his situation, or at least content with it. He was in fact far from content. There was something missing from his life and he was aware of the lack but he did not know what had been lost or what had never been put into him. It did not occur to him to try to love Sarah, and it would have done no good to have suggested this to him. He had lost the will and liberty to love anyone when he had tried to stop loving his father. It was a matter of sequence and to a member of Avery's profession sequence has quasi-magical significance. He had undertaken to follow the path of a moving point and had presumed that he would move sequentially as a point would move through empty space. It is not an applicable idea. It is only valid when one creates the world in which the point is to be made to move, and he had not created his own world. He had only spoiled the world that had been created for him. "In Euclid's world," they had told him, "where there are absolutely plane surfaces and where parallel lines never meet, every proposition that Euclid proved is true. Euclid only becomes unreliable when you put him into someone else's world—Einstein's, for instance, or the tiny world of Planck."

"But where is the true world," he would have asked, had he not been ashamed of betraying his naiveté.

"In the Mind of God," would have been the answer. "Or perhaps nowhere."

That fall he was investigating, among other things, the contradiction between the anthill world of Planck and the careening universe of Einstein—microcosm and macrocosm, infinite smallness, infinite largeness, autonomous systems that seemed to ignore each other, thus bedeviling a Yankee mind that searched for order and yearned for perfection and unity. The irresolution was a barrier in thought. He brooded over it, though the others working in the seminar, two in mathematics, four in physics, seemed to shrug off the disharmony. The indifference of the physicists Avery accepted. They were a people used to taking approximations as good enough. But to a pure mathematician the contradiction, it seemed to him, should be conspicuous and unsafe as a building on the verge of collapse.

Dormaker made fun of him.

"You have a disease," Dormaker said. "A slight case of philosophy. It's not a dangerous ailment in itself but one must watch out for complications."

"Such as?"

"Such as an attraction to the mystique of the false absolute," Dormaker said. "And a tendency to make religious observations in esoteric scientific idiom. That is a bad one. Always fatal. Not a chance of recovery."

On another occasion, more seriously, Dormaker told him, "Look, Hollister, you are forever looking for absolutes. Absolutism is the enemy of science. The enemy of true speculation. We aim to describe, describe, describe, not to establish a redoubt."

"How can you describe a thing unless you take a point of view?" Avery asked.

"The point of view is auxiliary. You are like a man on a raft going downstream with the current. From here one thing, from there another."

Dormaker waved his Italian cigar and smiled at Avery.

Avery scarcely realized how lucky he was in his superior. There were men in the Physics Department and in the Department of Mathematics who would not have been tolerant, but would have told him gruffly to get on with the job and to leave cosmology to other people, nonscientists with plenty of time and no political responsibilities. Dormaker listened to almost anything Avery had to say and never reprimanded him except with gentle chiding.

"Protestant priest, Hollister," he said. "You were born in the wrong time."

Avery laughed, but he didn't think the observation was funny. He envied Dormaker's power, he envied Freddie's intellectualism, he even envied Sarah Greenway's inclination to busy herself with her washing up and to leave the heavy thinking to him.

CHAPTER SIXTY-ONE

WHEN the fall passed and December began, he found himself impatient for Dennis McCoy to arrive. He felt that seeing Dennis might somehow clarify his own life, even though he couldn't stomach Dennis' religion. He thought just talking to Dennis would improve his outlook, for he trusted Dennis in a way that he didn't trust anyone else. He was disappointed. In mid-December he got a letter from Dennis, saying that Dennis had been delayed and must remain in Edmonton for several weeks before coming on to New York. Avery got the impression that the delay had something to do with Dennis' being approved as a postulant, though the letter gave no details.

He was depressed. It meant that he would be alone at Christmas time, for Sarah was going to England. Mrs. Dorrance was the kind of woman who liked to produce stunning surprises and she sent Sarah a round-trip ticket on the transatlantic plane.

Sarah didn't want to go. "I'd much rather be here with you," she said. "I'd looked forward to our being alone. But I suppose I must."

He agreed that she must and took her to the airport, a day before the holiday began. When he got back to his apartment Breitbart said, "Your girl gone, old chap?"

Avery nodded.

"Well you won't get your breakfast in bed from me," Freddie said. "In fact since I'm the senior member, I think you should bring me mine."

Avery laughed. "As a matter of fact I'm glad she's gone," he said. "I'll be glad to have a little time to myself."

"You mean marriage is a chore?" asked Freddie. "All that copulation and care?"

"It's not that," Avery said. "It's just that a steady diet of even temper gets to be a bore sometimes. She's so God damned well *mannered*. She never gets mad."

Freddie laughed. "You are hard to please, my friend," he said. He hesitated, then asked rather shyly, "Would you like to come out to Brooklyn for dinner on Christmas? It'll be dull but you'll get some good food."

"I'd like it," Avery said. "Thanks for asking me."

He was relieved. The thought of being alone on Christmas had morbidly depressed him, partly because he had looked forward to seeing Dennis but mostly because being with Sarah so much of the time had made him unused to being alone and he had lost part of the technique being alone demands.

It was a family party in Brooklyn, with various polite German relatives and friends and an enormous meal constructed around a fat goose. There was a huge elaborately decorated tree and the table was set with a quantity of heavy Continental silver. Breitbart's people went out of their way to make Avery feel at home and fed him quantities of food. He felt his embarrassment slip away. He looked down the table at Freddie's mother and smiled, saying, *"Danke, danke, gnädige Frau."* She blushed and smiled back at him. After dinner someone sat down at the upright piano and they all sang tender German hymns and sipped pale sweet wine that was served in small fragile glasses. He sang with the others, ... *Stille Nacht, Heilige Nacht* ... and was warmed by food, wine and sentiment. They tried to persuade him to stay the night but he declined, afraid the memory would be spoilt in the morning. He rode all the way back to New York in a taxi, gratified by the reckless extravagance and giving the driver too big a tip. He had been more touched by human kindness than he had been in a long time, and the fact that Freddie's parents had treated him like a member of the British aristocracy did not irritate him but added to their old-country charm.

The tenderness of Christmas passed and the rest of the holiday was dreary. Freddie stayed with his people, and Avery was alone. He went out into the city on New Year's Eve, not wanting to really but unable to bear being alone or to bear the din of a fierce undergraduate party being held across the street.

The city was gross. It inspired a kind of prowling fear, the feeling of being in a sacked city, on the streets of which conquering troops disport themselves with the dangerous enthusiasm of victory. The faces of the crowds in Times Square seemed cast by the honkytonk light into expressionist attitudes of cruelty and vice, so that the celebrating hordes seemed to be an enormous collaboration of rapists and murderers and not just shipping clerks and their girls or people from states on the prairie attempting to enjoy themselves in harmless spurious orgy. There was a warning of violence in the air, wanton violence for its own sake. Avery felt like a doomed Jew under the German terror, abroad without his yellow badge, terrified that someone would recognize him and point a finger, bringing the brutes with the truncheons.

When he left the university area he had drifted without much thought toward the center of the city. Now he found himself trapped, jammed between a sailor and a girl wearing the sailor's hat, and two youths who were wearing vivid identical overcoats. The sailor's voice, thick with drink, bellowed into his ear: "We won't go back to Subic any more. No we won't go back to Subic any more...." Then there was a loosening of the crowd, like the sudden irrational shifting of sand, and he was free. He made his way to the curb, looking for a path out of the mob. A voice hailed him.

"Hey Hollister! Hollister!"

It was Beasley Smith, from Colborn, wearing a marine officer's uniform, buoyantly drunk and with two friends wearing the same uniform.

"Holly, Holly, Holly, old boy," he said. "You come with us."

He took Avery's arm and they stumbled across Times Square to the Astor bar. Smith and his friends wore pilot's wings, and ribbons that Avery didn't recognize. He had not known Smith well at Colborn, having been two forms below him, but Smith behaved as if he had been his firmest Colborn friend, pounding him on the back and saying, "Avery Hollister, you guys. Friend of mine. One of the best. One of the incontestably very best."

The two marines with Smith conceded that Avery was one of the incontestably very best and shook hands with him. The bar was a madhouse. A cacophonous pick-up band was playing somewhere out of sight, beyond the mirrored shadows, and half a dozen groups of people sang loudly and without reference to this official music. Behind the long oval bar immaculate bartenders worked efficiently and without excitement. They had a drink, then another, then Smith looked malevolently at the crowd and said, "Let's get out of this rat race."

They drifted uptown, stopping at numerous bars, wandering without destination through the celebrating city. Avery felt like a hostage. He didn't particularly want to pub-crawl with them, but Smith had adopted him and would not hear of his leaving. "Early yet," Smith insisted, an arm around his shoulder. "Early yet, Hollister. Plenty of time. Plenty."

They tacked east and reached Third Avenue, stopping at a tough Irish bar where a party of army enlisted men regarded the officers with hurt unfriendly eyes. Toward three in the morning they found themselves in a dance hall on 125th Street. Avery danced with a tall brass blonde who felt as though she had been constructed over a sculptor's steel armature and who smelt defiantly of raw gin and spearmint gum, then with a plump, short girl whose flesh felt like foam rubber and who smelled faintly of sweat and cosmetics. During a pause between dances, he leaned against a pillar near the booth where they sold tickets, vaguely ill from too much to drink and oppressed by the heat and smell of the place. One of Smith's comrades-in-arms approached him confidentially and said in a whisper, "Beasie's got something lined up, kid. For all of us. Soon as the joint closes up we gonna meet 'em."

Avery looked at him blankly.

"Pigs," the boy said, grinning. "Tramps. Quail. Wimmin, guy, wimmin."

A girl approached, reaching for tickets in Avery's hand.

"Dance, honey?"

He was out on the floor again, staggering through the dance. The band seemed to be all horn and drum.

"By God I'm drunk," he said to the girl.

She was chewing gum and she shifted it to the side of her mouth like a farmer shifting a cud of tobacco.

"Honey, you're tellin' me," she said.

When the place closed, they rode out to the East Bronx, eight of them illegally crowded into one cab. Three of the girls lived together in a crowded, fetid apartment, and the instant the door was closed behind them the radio was turned on, giving out dance music, loud. Someone opened a window on the court and yelled: "Turn that Gawd damn thing down, you bitch." The girl cursed and turned down the volume a little. Beasley Smith, his blouse unbuttoned, was doing a dance in the middle of the room.

Avery asked for the bathroom and one of the girls, a heavy brunette whose skin was coated with pancake make-up so that it looked like starched pink blotting paper, took him by the hand and led him down the hall to a toilet that reeked of dampness and strong lye soap and was hung with underwear and silk stockings. She switched on the light and he waited for her to go but she made no move. "Go ahead honey," she said. "Don't mind me. I seen a guy take a leak before."

He turned his back and tried to make as little noise as possible. When he had finished, the girl hoisted her skirts and sat down. He watched, overcome through the blur of liquor by a kind of hideous amusement. When he came back into the front room one of the girls had pulled off her dress and was doing a kind of ersatz harem dance. She was naked and the various elastic accouterments just removed had left lascivious ridges on her flesh. Beasley and his friends sat in a row on the couch, clapping their hands in determined rhythm. Avery began to clap too. Then the lights were turned off and he was on the floor in the darkness, entangled with the girl who had led him to the bathroom. He felt sick and not quite competent.

"Whatsamatter, honey?" the girl whispered hoarsely into his ear. "You queer or something? Or just plastered?"

She kissed him on the mouth and he tasted her lipstick and gum, peppermint mixed with cocoa butter. Then she got up and he watched her in the half light as she pulled her dress over her head. "No use rooning a good dress, is there honey?" She came down beside him and he lost himself, running his hands over her body, feeling her hot tongue in his mouth. *I'm like an animal*, he thought. *Like a bull in the ring or a dog in the street.*

It was what he wanted; it was degrading and the degradation seemed to be something he had been looking for and not found.

At dawn the four of them stood in the cold morning air on a barren street intersection. It was snowing and there were no cabs. There were car tracks in the street that looked as though no car had traveled on them for years. It was forlorn, a residential desert. They gave up hope of finding a cab and walked to the subway, stamping up and down the platform, all of them sheepish and somewhat chastened, all hungover.

"God what pigs!" Smith said. "What dogs!"

"You can say that again," agreed one of the others.

"By the way," Smith said, "you gentlemen owe me ten bucks apiece. I paid off."

"You mean they were whores? I thought it was a party for the sake of the flag. Semper Fidelis and all that."

"They're not exactly whores," Smith explained. "They just take money that's all. I thought it would be nicer if you all paid now instead of last night, but you can't make a book account of it. Come on, fork over."

Avery gave him ten dollars and his friends reluctantly did the same. One of them looked knowingly at Smith and said, "You sure you're not getting a cut on this, Bease? I wouldn't put it past you."

"Well natch," Smith said. "You know me, Pimp's Mate, first class. It's my regular work, when I'm not employed by Uncle Sam as an intrepid birdman."

Finally the train came and they rode into Grand Central, finding an all night Child's, where they washed their faces and ate pancakes and drank coffee. Avery now had a frantic need to get away from Smith and his friends and from the cyclonic, incredible night. He looked at his watch and said, "I think I'd better shove along."

"What's the rush?" Smith asked. "Nowhere to go on New Year's. Stick with us. We're going to get shaved and then do a little gentlemanly drinking and have a rich lunch somewhere."

"Sure, Hollister," said one of the others. "What can you lose?"

The three young men in their snobbish black-buttoned uniforms made Avery uncomfortable now that everyone was sober. He was not a member of the club and didn't care to pretend that he was. He took a dollar from his wallet and put it on the table. "I don't think so," he said. "I'm beat. I haven't had any navy training."

Smith laughed. "I guess you think we're low types," he said. "But we were pretty well on the way when we ran into you last night. We do nice things too. We give to the poor and we dance with debutantes all up and down the coast. You just caught us in one of our cruddy moods."

"Oh sure," Avery said. "I was plastered myself."

He shook hands all around and went uptown to his apartment. He felt dirty and ashamed of his body. He took a long scalding shower, scrubbing himself with a stiff nail brush so that the skin on his body was red and sore to the touch. He felt contaminated and no amount of toothpaste seemed to obliterate the aftertaste of the girl's mouth, that had been greasy with cheap lipstick.

A few months ago, when he had imagined himself progressing through scenes of utter depravity and degradation, there had been only the visual synoptic effect of the dream or half dream, without the imagination of smell or taste ... gutter expeditions that were recorded on silent film. The reality was horrible now that he was sober, and memory of the sour apartment with its brothel stench filled him with disgust.

Yet the others, Smith and the others, who were nice young men from nice schools and nice universities, who were officers and gentlemen commissioned by the President, had not seemed vitally disgusted. They had taken the development of the night as a matter of course, one phase, the next phase to be the gentlemanly drinking in the Ritz bar and the rich lunch in some good restaurant in the Fifties off Park Avenue.

He envied Smith and the other marines. He felt a yearning to be part of something, a member of something—anything—the Cottage Club, the Marine Corps, the Department of Sanitation—anything at all that would give him automatic status and a special suit to wear or charm to hang from his watch chain or secret grip or whatever.

He passed the day in a mood of depression. Toward evening, bored and unable to tolerate the apartment any longer, he dressed himself and went to his office, using his pass and key. A neat stack of graph paper was on his desk. He took the top sheet and began to work. Soon he was lost in his computation; the unease he had felt all day was pressed down into a dark part of his mind. He worked steadily for nearly seven hours, unaware of fatigue or the passage of time, occasionally looking up from his desk to Frieda's painting on the wall, drawing a kind of reassurance from it that served him as fuel. In spite of the fact that he had not slept he was in superb working form. As his mind sharpened to the task he got the effect of exhilaration one derives from doing a thing expertly and without apparent effort.

When the sheets were done he was surprised. He leafed through them, only then realizing that as he had gone through the data he had shortened the method, almost as in a trance or dream, seemingly without thought. He had made no mathematical discovery, but it was a creative application of skill, a professional achievement.

He was pleased with himself.

He got up from the desk, his muscles aching, and went to the window, looking down at the exhausted city. He felt a sense of glorious detachment, of isolation. "By God," he said aloud, speaking to the ignorant illuminated world twenty stories below him, "by God if I'm nothing else I'm a mathematician."

He carried the finished work sheets into Dormaker's private office and placed them on Dormaker's desk with a heavy weight on top of them. The sight of the great batch of work, neat as a bound volume, gave him considerable satisfaction.

It was not until he had left the building and was halfway home that fatigue overtook him, and ravenous hunger. He bought two turkey sandwiches at an all-night delicatessen and carried them to the apartment, where he made coffee and sat in the living room, enjoying the secret meal. He was filled with awareness of his powers and of rightness in himself that was comforting as milk. He finished his meal then went to bed. Just before he closed his eyes he had the feeling that he had rescued himself from something sinister and dangerous, he knew not what, unless it was the trap of his own flesh.

When he woke up he was refreshed. The night passed with Smith and his friends was submerged, though it flared back for an instant when he put his laundry into the hamper and noticed a smear of lipstick on the collar of his dirty shirt. He dropped the shirt into the hamper then let the tin lid fall, making a conclusive, clanging noise.

That night he went back to his office and for several hours checked the work he had done the night before, in order to satisfy himself that the short cut he had devised was really adequate to the problem.

It was, and the fact reassured him.

CHAPTER SIXTY-TWO

A FEW days later, Sarah returned. She brought him a good English tie and a bottle of whiskey that she said came straight from Scotland.

"I didn't get anything for you," he said, ashamed of himself for having forgotten. "I've been working through the holiday."

"That's all right," she said cheerfully, "After all, I'm the one who's been away."

She finished unpacking her bags and they went to Angelo's for dinner, then came back to her apartment. She had seemed a little strange at dinner, but he had put it down to the abrupt airborne transition from one world to another, the scene shifting that was too swift for human adjustment. But now, sitting in the familiar room, she seemed distressed. When he tried to make love to her, she began to cry.

"What is it?" he said. "What's wrong?"

They were seated on the day bed. She turned away from him, looking at the wall, then said, "I don't like to tell you, really. But I'm afraid I must. The fact is, I think I'm going to have a baby."

He felt as though someone had stabbed him in the chest. The possibility had not even occurred to him. He had taken it for granted that Sarah, in some mysterious feminine fashion, would automatically have known how to take suitable precautions. Then he remembered, with a feeling of hopeless regret, the night he had come here to her, when he had returned from Hull, wanting to smash someone, to murder someone, to rape someone.

"Are you sure?" he said finally.

"I think so," she said, turning to face him. "Of course it may be a false alarm."

"Have you talked to anyone?" he said.

"Well no, Avery," she said. "I've no one to talk to, except you."

He nodded.

She touched his arm. "I am sorry," she said. "You see I hadn't any experience, really. I didn't know what to do."

"It's all right," he said dully, "it will be all right."

He felt like a man who has been told he has a brain tumor that will kill him. The idea of a child, of himself as the father of a child, was intolerable. He didn't want to be anyone's father. It was grotesque. He had not even considered the fact that the seeds of fatherhood were in him; it implied a confidence in his own power that he had never entertained and that he now rejected.

They went to bed together, holding one another like a pair of children lost in the woods. They were both afraid. They had the conviction of having somehow blundered into crime.

"What shall we do?" he asked, his voice sounding thin and inadequate in the dark room.

"Perhaps it will be all right," she said. "They say you can't be sure right off. Perhaps it will be all right."

Of course it was not all right. A week passed and another, and she admitted that there could not be any doubt. They were in Angelo's and he was painfully aware of other people, as if her condition might already be betrayed by her appearance, at least to other women. Beyond his personal desperation, he had a sense of outrage at his ignorance, his pathetic lack of practical information.

"It's my fault," she said. "I should have known what to do. It's my fault."

"No,' he said. "It's not your fault." He looked down at his plate; it was one of Angelo's vitreous plates that he had been eating from for years and that had *U.S. Shipping Board* baked into the clay under the glaze. He suddenly hated it. "It isn't anyone's fault," he said.

"Do you mind so very much?" she asked. "It needn't make too much difference, really. You can go right on with your degree. But I suppose we should get married, just for form's sake."

He nodded. "I suppose," he said.

She took it for granted that he loved her and that they would be married. He didn't have the courage to tell her the truth: that he wasn't prepared to be married to anyone. He didn't love her. He had never loved her. He had only let himself be loved, and now he had been caught by it, as a fly is caught by one of those carnivorous tropical flowers. It seemed fantastic to him that what had developed with so little excitement, so little passion, could now have been turned into a trap. He couldn't get married to anyone; he had hardly begun to breathe. It seemed unfair.

"Sarah," he said, looking across the table at her, "Sarah I—"

"Yes, darling?"

"Nothing," he said. "I was just thinking."

He must tell her the truth. He must. But he didn't know where to begin. He couldn't simply say to her: *I don't love you. I never did. I only said I loved you because you asked me to say it and because it was easier to say it.* He couldn't have said it even if he hadn't given her the child. But the idea of being married to her, of living with her in an apartment, of seeing her every day of his life, appalled him. It was like facing a sentence to prison. It meant that he would give up his freedom before he ever set eyes on it.

He turned to Breitbart for advice, because he had no one else.

"What can I do?" he asked Freddie. "She expects me to marry her. She takes it for granted."

"You could do a damn sight worse," Freddie said. "You've got that dough coming next year. There's no reason why you shouldn't marry her. After all, you knocked her up."

"Don't put it that way," Avery said.

"How do you want it put?" said Freddie. "After all, you would play house."

"I don't want to marry her," Avery said. "I don't want to marry anyone."

"I know," Freddie said. "But you should have picked another kind of girl. I told you Sarah was in love with you, a long time ago. Why didn't you tell her the truth? Why didn't you tell her it was just a shack job as far as you were concerned? You could have slept with her anyway, if you wanted to. Why did you tell her you loved her?"

This was a question Avery had been asking himself for several days, without finding an answer. "I don't know," he said. "I honest to Christ don't know."

Freddie laughed. "You know you're not a kid any more," he said. "You're a college graduate, a grown man, damn near it. Nobody's going to bail you out."

"I thought you were a friend of mine," Avery said.

"I am a friend of yours," said Breitbart. "But that doesn't mean I have to approve of everything you do."

"You could help me," Avery said. "Instead of sitting there and pointing out what a bastard I am. I'm willing to do what's right. It's just that I can't marry her, that's all."

"What do you think is right?" asked Freddie.

"I don't know," Avery said. He drew in his breath then let it out, and finally phrased what had been gathering in his mind. "She doesn't have to have the baby," he said. "She can get rid of it."

Freddie smiled; Avery realized, looking at him, that he had come to the wrong quarter for help. Breitbart was amused by his predicament. It gratified Breitbart's jealousy.

"If you mean that I'm supposed to consult my little black book and turn up the name of a disbarred surgeon for you, I'm sorry," Breitbart said. "I simply haven't had occasion to require that kind of medical work." He paused, looking skeptically at

Avery. "Besides," he said, "what makes you think Sarah will go for it anyway? Have you asked her?"

Avery shook his head. "No," he said. "But she'll do what I want."

"You may be in for a surprise," said Freddie. "She's from Lancashire, don't forget. They're a tough breed, those people from the Black Country. They have character. Of course it's not the kind of character they breed at Colborn, but it's character just the same."

Freddie was baiting him and Avery flared up. He used a gutter word. He had counted on Freddie's support and he was outraged by his amusement. Freddie laughed softly. It was not a friendly laugh at all.

"The Brooklyn kid and the Colborn boy, they're sisters under the skin," he said. He leaned forward and touched Avery's cheek. "Hollister, you amuse me," he said. "All that expensive breeding, yet you lead such an untidy life." He smiled, pursing his mouth. "Being of humble origin, I am satisfied with a lower grade of milk-white body, and thus avoid these complications."

It was the contemptuous touch on the cheek more than the words Freddie used that made Avery lose his temper. The crust was broken and the mutual distrust, class-based and ignoble, was there like a wound with the bandage removed. Avery felt the blood pound in his forehead and his lips trembled. He wanted to hurt Breitbart, and the phrase he used tumbled out of the depths of his mind, a phrase he had once heard his father use.

"Please try to remember," he said, "that you are not in the steerage now."

Breitbart's body stiffened. It was almost as though an electric current had been passed through him, immobilizing him for an instant. Then he said, his voice steady, "I'm not quite an immigrant, Avery, having been born in Bensonhurst. But I understand what you mean all right and I appreciate the fine scientific detachment with which you phrase your point of view."

Avery put his head in his hands, waiting for his heart to stop pounding. After a long time he looked up. "I apologize," he said. "I'm sorry."

Breitbart nodded.

"So am I," he said. He turned away and went into his bedroom, coming out a moment later wearing his overcoat and hat. He looked at Avery in the way one might look at a broken plate on the floor, then said, "But don't think it hasn't been fun. I've enjoyed the opportunity of mixing with the upper classes."

He went out, closing the door quietly behind him. Avery sat in the chair, ashamed of himself and resentful of Freddie because Freddie had kept his temper. It was the end between them, he understood. The relationship had been destroyed the moment its essential lack of stability had been brought to the surface by Avery's crudeness, of which he was now ashamed but did not honestly regret. His mind turned to the source of the phrase he had used in his anger against Freddie, and he saw his father standing in the barn, dressed in immaculate white breeches and black beautiful English boots, raising his head and saying dispassionately to the groom who had offended him, "Please try to remember, Higgins, that you are not in the steerage now."

The thought of his father carried his mind straight to his father's friend Browne. Browne would know what to do; Browne had tried to warn him once against getting involved with a nice girl. He got up and went to the phone, asking the girl to give him an appointment just as soon as Browne was free.

CHAPTER SIXTY-THREE

B ROWNE listened sympathetically, then began to advise Avery of the legal problems involved.

"There's the chance of a paternity suit," he explained. "And she might make it stick. But there's no way she can make you marry her. Absolutely none." He paused. "You'll probably have to contribute to the support of the child," he said. "Not much, but something."

"It's not that," Avery said. "It's—I don't want her to have the child," he said.

Browne nodded.

Avery leaned forward in his chair. "Can you tell me where to go?" he said. At that moment he felt as though the name and address of a doctor would compactly solve his problems: all of them, including the lifting of blame for having taken love without giving anything in return.

Browne looked at him candidly and said, "I can't, because I'm a lawyer and it is generally healthier for lawyers to avoid breaking the law." He thought for a moment, drumming on the top of his desk, then looked up. "But if you happen to be in the Strangers' Room of the Ivy Club in, say, two hours' time, there might be a gentleman there who could advise you."

Avery glanced at the silent electric clock that stood on Browne's desk. It was twenty minutes past two. "I'll be there at four-thirty," he said, getting up to go. "Thank you."

"Not at all," Browne said. "These things happen in the best of families." He laughed reminiscently. "I remember getting a little wop girl big when I was at New Haven with your father. I didn't know quite what to do and I called my Dad on the phone. He asked me what the girl's name was and I said, 'Mary Manicotti, sir.'" Browne laughed again. "He was so darned mad he just hung up. But there was a check in the next mail." He chuckled. "Mary Manicotti, sir," he repeated.

Avery felt contempt for Browne and for himself and for the relationship between them. Under all the gloss of his impressive front, Browne was cheerfully doing the job of a common pimp. It was disgusting. Nevertheless, at half-past four he was in the Strangers' Room at the Ivy Club and at twenty minutes to five came out of the club with the name and address he wanted, together with the preposterous amount of the fee.

He visited the clinic, a kind of small private hospital in a nice street off Madison Avenue, and handed over some money in cash as he had been advised to do. The whole thing seemed absurdly simple. A nurse wearing the pin and cap of a perfectly respectable hospital assured him that there was no risk. "He's a genius at this sort of thing, Dr. Ullman. Absolutely a genius." She smiled. "It's really a simple operation you know, if it's properly done," she said.

It would have been simple except for the fact that he had underestimated Sarah, as Breitbart had suggested.

"You can't be serious, Avery," she said, when he told her about the arrangements he had made. "I couldn't do that."

"There isn't any risk," he said stubbornly. "No more than having the child would be."

"I don't mean that," she said, looking at him challengingly. "Do you think I'm afraid?"

"Well then what's wrong?" he asked. "It's the only thing to do. It's all arranged. What's wrong?"

"Just that I simply couldn't do it," she said. She looked at him, her face incredulous. "Why it's like murder," she said.

"I didn't know you were religious," he said.

"Well I'm not, really," she said. "At least not formally, you know, as far as taking Communion goes and things like that."

"Then what do you mean by calling it murder," he said resentfully. "You can't murder something that doesn't exist."

"But it does exist," she said calmly. "And it's part of you and me. It's alive." There was an unfamiliar note of firmness in her voice, of insistence. He looked at her curiously. Her chin was set in a firm line and she looked across the room at him in a way she never had before, her face showing independence and a very definite point of view. She was the embattled Briton, and she looked entirely out of place in the self-conscious, sham apartment.

"I don't understand you," he said.

But he did. It was what Breitbart had warned him he would find under the even temper—the Black Country stubbornness. She was stronger than he, and he knew it. He turned away and went to the window, looking down into the courtyard at a file of corrugated garbage cans.

He was miserable.

Since childhood he had often been obsessed with the idea that other people, for their own purposes, wanted to trap him, to get their hooks into him. He had been on the alert ever since the afternoon his father drove him out of the study at Hull and refused him the right to defend his mother by telling a lie that was really the truth, and he had been on guard at ease since long before that, perhaps since the day of his birth. Now he was face to face with what had been only an imagination. He was trapped. Here was a living human being who wanted his soul, his body, his life, who wanted to possess him in the name of love.

She could not have him.

He belonged to himself.

It was not fair.

The trap had been camouflaged with comfort and baited with food for the ego, but it was a trap nonetheless and made of steel, with steel jaws and a spring that would snap and ensnare him forever. He could almost see the steel teeth of a fox trap concealed in the earth and the imagination made the salt taste flood his mouth.

He was cornered and in terror, and panic should have supplied him with a species of courage, but it did not. It was Sarah who supplied it.

"You don't love me, do you Avery?" she said quietly.

He felt his throat tighten and the voice he produced was not familiar to him. "I didn't say that," he said. "I—"

"You don't have to say it, Avery," she said.

He remained at the window, staring down at the garbage cans, watching a cat that prowled through the concrete alley. It was coming on night. The courtyard was illuminated by a thin sad light. It looked like a place of execution. He turned around and saw that she was crying bitterly, simply sitting with her head erect while the tears streamed from her eyes. Her body shuddered as though she were being struck rhythmically with a lash. It was terrible. He felt the indictment. Had she shrieked at him, raged, struck him, accused him, it would have been less denunciatory than this silent weeping. He wished she would leave off weeping in this silent shuddering way and say something to which he might reply, touch off a quarrel that would let the blood. He felt that in some way a quarrel might give him the chance to discover some words that would justify him; he felt no justification now but only necessity, the urge to self-preservation.

"Please," he said. "Please, Sarah."

She did not seem to hear him. After a time he became worried and went into the kitchen, getting down the bottle of whiskey she had brought to him from Scotland. It had an intense, clinical smell, like iodine. He poured a good-sized drink into a water tumbler and carried it in to her.

"Drink this," he said. "It will do you good."

She shook her head.

"Drink it," he said bluntly. "Drink it."

"Very well."

She drank off the whiskey and shuddered, coughing. "Please bring me some water, Avery," she said, her voice almost under control. "I'm not used to whiskey this way."

He got the water for her. After a time she stopped crying and her shoulders slumped a little. She had the appearance of a person who could be dissolved to dust by a breath of air. He sat down across the room from her.

"I'm sorry, Sarah," he said.

"There's no need to be sorry," she said. "I suppose I've known you didn't love me, really, ever since I came back from England. I just wouldn't permit myself to admit it. I'd tell myself you'd gone all strange over your work, that it wasn't me, but something outside that would pass. Or that the idea of the baby was something that you wanted getting used to. But I should have known. I did know."

He got the impression that she had surrendered. "You can see now why it's better not to have the child, can't you?" he said.

"I'm going to have the child," she said. "It has nothing to do with you any longer."

"But you can't!" he said. "You can't do that."

"It has nothing to do with you," she said. "It's my affair."

"What will you do?" he asked.

She raised her head. "I shall go home to my own people," she said.

"But your fellowship," he said. "Your degree. You'll lose everything."

"It doesn't matter," she said.

"It's insane!" he protested. "You can't just throw everything out the window."

She looked at him then laughed rather bitterly. "Can I not?" she said.

"I'm sorry. I didn't mean to be amusing," he said.

CHARLES GORHAM

"You're not amusing, Avery," she said. "You are sad. You are the saddest American I know. That's one of the reasons I love you."

There was nothing more to be said. He felt almost cheated by the lack of drama. The fact that he had not been accused left him without a defense and with a flat, helpless awareness of guilt.

"It's not my fault that I don't love you," he said. "I don't see how you can blame me for it."

"No, Avery, it's not your fault," she said.

He crossed the room and stood beside her, not knowing how to put into words what he wanted to say. The flat Picasso above her head had lost its color in the evening light and looked monochromatic, the meaning gone out of it.

"If you need any money or anything," he said, looking at the painting, "of course I'd be glad to give it to you."

"Thank you, Avery," she said. "As a matter of fact I should like to borrow enough for my fare home. I'd intended to ask Mrs. Dorrance but it would be awkward."

"I'll give you a check," he said. He took out his pen and checkbook. "Will five hundred dollars be enough?"

"Oh, quite," she said.

"You don't have to send it back," he said.

"Thank you, Avery. I'll send you the money as soon as I can. Of course it's just a loan."

He did not argue the point. The act of writing the check and handing it to her was conclusive and made him feel better. At least he had done something. He stood waiting for her to make a move, but she simply sat and stared at the wall, the pale blue check in her hand.

"Well good-bye," he said lamely. "I—"

"Good-bye, Avery," she said.

She didn't look up. He hesitated for an instant, feeling a rush of pain, then turned and went out, leaving her alone in the dark apartment.

CHAPTER SIXTY-FOUR

T HE next few weeks were desolate.

At the beginning of the new semester he moved into a single room in the Graduate Students' dormitory, for it was impossible to repair the breach with Breitbart and as Breitbart pointed out, the apartment was his and had been his before Avery moved into it. "Sorry to put you out," he had said, "but I'm afraid I have a priority."

Avery found he had lost the technique of living in a small institutional room. He missed the apartment and its privacy. He detested using the communal shower rooms. He found the room so confining that he was sometimes driven out into the unfriendly weather to walk the slushy streets for an hour or into a dark anonymous theater to see a film that bored him, simply to rid himself of the sense of imprisonment and retrogression. One night he half emerged from sleep in the narrow dormitory room and imagined himself back at Colborn, in a cubicle, and the impression was so strong that he got up and switched on the light to assure himself that he had not been somehow moved backward in time.

He and Breitbart had parted in civilized fashion, promising each other that they would occasionally dine together at Angelo's, but of course they didn't. Breitbart was preparing to defend his thesis and adhered to a rigid schedule. Avery avoided Angelo's because he knew he would be asked embarrassing questions about his pretty English girl that Angelo thought was *"Bella! Bella!"* He ate most of his meals in the John Jay Dining Room or the drug store on Broadway.

It was bleak. He was intolerably lonely and yearned for companionship, but he lacked the will to reach out for friendship or even acquaintanceship and actually rejected overtures made by people in his classes. He simply hadn't the energy to select new people or to make a campaign for them.

He relied on his work and used it as a narcotic against his loneliness. He began to take monkish satisfaction in conducting tests of his own endurance, and pressed himself, often working in his office until midnight or later, until he was drugged by fatigue.

One night quite late Dormaker came back to his office for something he wanted or had forgotten and saw Avery's light. He knocked and entered Avery's room. He was wearing a full-dress suit and looked like the concertmaster of a provincial German orchestra, his simian ugliness exaggerated by the starched white and smooth black satin. He looked at Avery, a cigar shaped like a cigarette between his lips instead of the crooked Italian one, probably regarding it as a concession to the elegance of his attire.

"Hollister, you are a fool," he said. "You will never find what you are looking for in that conglomeration. You would be better off in a church, at midnight mass somewhere."

Avery looked up, startled. Dormaker winked solemnly, tipped his silk hat, then turned and went away, leaving the door open. Avery heard his heavy footsteps going down the corridor, then heard the whirr of the motor as the elevator rose in the silent building, then the crash of the doors as the professor departed for wherever his finery was taking him.

He smiled and shook his head, turning back to his work. He took a sharp pencil from his pot and tested the point on the ball of his thumb, the sharp punctative pain reassuring to his numbed body. He drew the paper toward him, but he could not concentrate. He stared at the papers as though they were an enemy. Of course Dormaker was right, he thought, staring at the neat piles of paper on his desk. He hadn't the faintest hope of finding anything but labor in what Dormaker had called his conglomeration. What he was doing was mechanical and meaningless as jogging around a quarter-mile track. He would find nothing in all this that he didn't already know. What he really sought wasn't there, and in any case he wouldn't have found it since he didn't know what it was. "It's like searching in a dark cellar for a black cat that isn't there," Breitbart had once said, quoting someone or other at Harvard. "But it's gallant, friend. Gallant."

What black imaginary cat Avery sought he didn't know. He did not think that it was God, as Dormaker had suggested, or even traces of God's art. He didn't believe that he was concerned with God's existence or lack of it. What concerned him was his own existence. He wanted evidence of his own freedom or else evidence of his serfdom. He had an awareness that he lived in shadow, and a sense of being passed by and of regret for the years that were falling away from him like dead leaves from a tree. It was a feeling inappropriate to youth that has no understanding of death and it caused a chill to pass through him.

He put his papers together and stowed them in a drawer, then walked back to the dormitory, his heels making a challenging sound echoed back by the silent campus. He had a sense of error that plagued him. He felt like a laboratory rat in a maze, systematically bewildered so that some psychologist could watch him and tabulate his confusion. He went to bed thinking of Sarah, filled with need for her to be in the bed with him close to his body or at least there in the dark room, breathing, making some sound that would let him know he was not alone. It was not simply that he needed a woman to sleep with, though he needed that. He needed the mother in Sarah, the dependability in her.

The next morning, in the curious way in which these things sometimes seem to have been presaged, there was a letter from her, or rather an envelope from her, for there was no letter but only a draft for the five hundred dollars he had loaned her. For a moment he was tempted to destroy it and enjoy whatever symbolism might be thus expressed, but in the end his Yankee respect for capital intervened. He folded the draft and put it in his wallet and later in the day found time to deposit it in his bank.

CHAPTER SIXTY-FIVE

ARCH passed and the bright forsythia burst into bloom along the campus walks. Early in April Avery got a note from Dennis McCoy that told him Dennis expected to arrive in New York a few days later and would Avery reserve a room for him at the King's Crown Hotel.

Avery reserved a double room and went down to meet the train. When he saw Dennis step onto the platform he understood why Dennis had not been in New York at Christmas time. Dennis had lost an arm, his left, and the pinned-up black sleeve looked so conclusive that tears rose in Avery's eyes. He was shocked and for a moment repelled by Dennis's appearance. Dennis had the look of death one associates with a charity ward. He had lost perhaps thirty pounds and his face displayed the marks of pain. He looked unbelievably older and moved slowly, as though he had not completely recovered. He was dressed in a clerical suit with a plain white shirt and black tie and wore a black anarchist's hat. When he saw Avery he grinned and waved his good arm. It was the same old McCoy, the same old mick grin. It made Avery feel better.

"Hi, kid," Dennis said. "You look good. Good."

"Hello, Dinny," Avery said. "I'm glad to see you."

In the cab going uptown Avery glanced at Dennis's clothes and said, "Are you ordained already? I thought—"

"I shall never be ordained," said Dennis.

"You mean your arm?"

Dennis nodded.

"But it happened on duty. It's not fair."

"Let's talk about something else, shall we?" Dennis said. "How is college? How is the higher mathematics? Still a little ahead of its pursuers, or have you all caught up with Aleph Null or whatever it was you were talking about?"

Avery told him about Dormaker and Dennis said that was swell. Then he stared through the window of the cab and said, "I used to wonder sometimes whether I'd ever see New York again."

"Why didn't you tell me you were hurt?" Avery asked.

"What was there to tell?" Dennis said. "It was a question of living or dying and the decision wasn't mine."

There was a simplicity about Dennis that was unfamiliar and that would require some getting used to; he seemed composed almost to the point of being fatalistic.

"I got a double room," said Avery. "I thought we might bunk together while you're here."

"Swell," said Dennis. "If you don't mind living with a cripple."

"Don't be a darned fool," said Avery.

They looked at one another and grinned; the old sense of fraternity between them seemed to move back into place like a set of gears meshing.

They had dinner at Angelo's, where the waiters made a fuss over Dennis and called him "father." Dennis told Avery how he had been hurt.

"It was almost comical," he said. "There was an Eskimo named Igorok who found out that one woman wasn't enough for him and decided to take over another guy's wife, one of our people, a Catholic Eskimo. He came into the mission after her with his gun in his hand. He was the most anti-Catholic Eskimo I've ever seen. He was even more anti-Catholic than one of the Anglican missionaries. And he was a good hand with a rifle."

"What happened?" Avery asked.

Dennis laughed. "He got my arm, but he didn't get the guy's wife," he said. He looked down at his good hand. "They're a rough people, Avery. A rough people."

He told Avery about the country and the people, about the night that was six months long and the short miraculous summer, about the cruel distances, the relentless weather, the hard bitter way of life that had made the Eskimos arrogant and strong.

"The end of the world," Avery said.

"Almost," said Dennis. "Our mission, the one furthest north, was about thirty miles from the magnetic pole."

"It must be awful."

"I like it," Dennis said.

He picked up the wicker bound carafe of wine and looked at the bright Italianate label, then filled Avery's glass and his own. The restaurant was crowded and buzzed with life. It smelled wonderfully of food and wine and there was a suggestion of the Mediterranean, of the warm, benevolent South, that Avery could not help placing in contrast with the country Dennis had described.

"What is there to like about it?" he asked. "It doesn't sound like a place that was meant for men to live in."

"I don't know," Dennis said. "There's something about the country that gets you. The distances for one thing. And the sky. It's the most beautiful sky in the world. You feel free." He drank a little of the wine that had come from a contradictory part of the world. "And I like the people," he said reflectively. "With all their faults, I like them. They are men. We could take a lesson from them."

"Are you going back there?" Avery asked.

"I'd like to," Dennis said. "But a guy with only one arm wouldn't be much use. It's no country for cripples."

Avery realized suddenly, from something in Dennis' tone, the catastrophic character of what had happened to Dennis. The whole plan of his life had been destroyed, for he had fought his way through his own doubt and set his mind on becoming a priest. He was as tragic as a barren wife who had planned her life around the idea of being a mother.

"What will you do then?" he asked.

Dennis shrugged. "First off I'm going to make a retreat with the Trappists, down in Kentucky. Then I don't know. Maybe I'll go back to school. Maybe not."

"Here?" Avery asked.

Dennis shook his head. "I don't think this place has anything more to offer me. If I go back to college it will be to Holy Cross." He looked at Avery, then down at the table. "My old man's dead you know," he said. "He died in prison."

"I didn't know," Avery said. "I'm sorry."

"Yeah," said Dennis. "I was sorry too. I wish I had seen him before he died. I might have helped him. I don't know." Avery had a memory of Dennis' father, the lonely man who had lived by himself in that monstrously dispassionate apartment. He would never forget him, though he had talked with him only once. Tip McCoy had touched his faith, as he had touched the faith of a thousand men and impelled them to believe him.

"Your father could have been a great man," he said. "He just got a rotten break."

Dennis shook his head. "They called him the fall guy," he said. "He was, but he was the fall guy for himself. He started wrong. He started out with the wrong idea. He thought that being an honest man meant just always keeping your word. And he was wrong."

"What does it mean?" Avery asked.

Dennis smiled. "I don't think you'd agree with me on that point," he said. "And I didn't come down here to proselytize you. Don't try to sell me any formulas and I'll leave you in your heathen peace."

Avery laughed. "Okay, Dinny," he agreed. "It's a truce."

They kept the truce, but during the next few days Avery began to get some idea of what had happened to Dennis and of how much Dennis had changed. In the Arctic, during the interminable winter darkness when he had traveled across country through a blizzard behind a team of dogs, or sat in some ice-house at the side of a dying Eskimo, watching the man's inscrutable face by the light of a seal oil lamp, Dennis had become not merely formally religious, but religious to the bone. The idea that he might become a priest had become the central, informing fact of his life. It was a vocation, a Divine call, and to be a missionary priest had seemed to him the way in which he was intended to serve God. Denial of the priesthood had seemed to him at first quixotic beyond comprehension, a monstrous joke played on him by God. He had wanted to die when they brought him out of the Barren Land in the mission plane, filled with morphine and whiskey against the pain of his shattered arm. When he came out of the anesthetic in the hospital at Edmonton and learned that his arm was gone, he had turned his face to the wall like an Eskimo, resigned to death that would deliver him from the sense of loss he felt he could not bear.

But time and the kindness of the sisters had drawn him away from despair. The beginnings of hope had returned. He had faith that during his retreat with the Cistercians he would perceive the meaning and understand the purpose of what he regarded as the Will of God.

"It must have a meaning," he told Avery. "Though of course I may never understand it."

Avery tried to imagine a comparable tragedy in his own life, but he could not do it. It occurred to him that he didn't possess anything worth the effort of stealing, as Dennis' prospective priesthood had been stolen from him.

"How are the guys?" Dennis asked. "Cotton and Breitbart and Klein and the others?"

"Cotton's still in the army," said Avery. "He's in Germany, or was. I got a letter from him a few months ago. Herb's up in the Med School. Breitbart's around but I don't see him." He hesitated. "You know I lived with him, last year," he said.

"Yeah," Dennis said. "One year was enough, I guess?"

"That's about it," said Avery, modifying the truth a little. "We sort of used one another up."

Dennis laughed. He was stretched out on one of the single beds in the hotel room. His mutilated arm was out of sight, and his face was relaxed. He looked almost the way he had when he and Avery had roomed together in the Divinity School dorm nearly five years ago. It carried Avery back and softened some of the things that had happened during the years between.

He was starved for companionship and could not get enough of it. He had arranged to be almost free of work, and he and Dennis enjoyed themselves. They went to the theater and to galleries and ate meals in good restaurants, once going to Chinatown to have dinner in a cellar that looked like a Hollywood reconstruction of an opium den and where they served food that was unbelievably subtle and almost unbelievably expensive.

Dennis had the wonderful experience of rediscovering his native city. He was like a tourist from Texas, becoming enthusiastic over the mid-town lights, the subway, the crowds, the sheer vibrant sense of life. But when Avery said, laughing at him, "Do you mean you'd trade this for the Arctic?" Dennis had said, "In a minute, kid. In a minute."

They were on the upper deck of a Fifth Avenue bus. The street below them was crowded with swarming fashionable women and banked with fashionable elegant shops. The day was clear and there was a sense of cosmopolitan luxury and of pace.

"This is wonderful," Dennis said, looking down at the street. "It's exciting and beautiful. But it has no real meaning for me, any more. I'm a stranger here. A tourist. An observer. In the North I used to feel that I was finally where I belonged, doing what I'd been born to do. I never felt that here. I never will." He paused, brooding for a moment while the bus growled impatiently, waiting for the traffic light to change. "It's a good feeling," he went on, "the feeling that you have a function, a meaning."

"Must be," Avery said. "I wouldn't know."

They got off the bus and walked east, passing four young naval officers, cropped and scrubbed and nicely tailored.

"I suppose you've heard about Bell?" asked Dennis, glancing at the officers. "Your old roomie?"

"What about him?" Avery said. "Is he dead?"

"No. But he's a fully authenticated hero," Dennis said. "He was on a ship that blew up and he saved all the sailors. They gave him the Navy Cross. It was in the paper. I saw it in Edmonton."

Avery nodded. It was inevitable that Bell would get some kind of medal, war or no war. He was surprised at the fact that he didn't care very much.

They went into Brooks Brothers to buy Dennis some ordinary clothes. The clerk looked at him suspiciously when he asked for a gray suit.

"He probably thinks I'm absconding with the parish treasury," Dennis said. He picked up the black coat he had just taken off. "I thought my clothes problem was settled for life when I got this," he said. "Now I feel like a phony in it."

"It doesn't seem fair," Avery said, putting into words what he had thought ever since Dennis arrived.

"Don't you think God has a right to expect physical perfection in his servants?" Dennis said, smiling. "A deformed priest would be ... "

"You're not deformed," Avery said. "You lost an arm in an accident. It happens to lots of people."

"Of course," Dennis said. "How do you like this tweed?" He backed into the coat the salesman held then stood off so that Avery could judge the fit. The empty sleeve, unpinned, hung loose from the shoulder like a dead man's arm.

"It's a little dark," Avery said. "Why don't you go all the way and get something colorful? This for instance." He took a bright plaid jacket from the pile and held it up.

Dennis shook his head. "I'm not going to run a race track," he said, "even if I am a washed-out priest."

There was a little tension. Avery understood that Dennis was turning off his comment about what seemed to him unfairness. He decided not to mention it again. After a while Dennis made up his mind to take three suits. "I think I still have an account here," he told the clerk. "If not I'll give you a check."

"You can use mine," Avery said.

"Thanks," said Dennis. "I think mine will be okay. The old man left me some dough. Not a lot, but enough."

Avery was disappointed. Financial help was the one kind that he seemed to have to give.

CHAPTER SIXTY-SIX

DENNIS stayed for ten days. It was not until the night before he left for Kentucky that Avery managed to tell him about Sarah Greenway. He didn't like to tell the story. It put him in a bad light and he was afraid that Dennis might exhibit a Savonarola streak and denounce him to the pits of hell. But he had a feeling that it would be dishonest not to tell Dennis. He told the story in detail, from the beginning to the scene in her apartment when he had left her alone in the dark. Dennis listened, not interrupting. He was wearing one of his new suits, and didn't look like a priest at all, which made it easier for Avery to talk.

"She sent back the five hundred bucks," Avery said. "Just the money. No letter, no nothing. Just a draft for the money."

Dennis shook his head. Avery waited, half expecting some kind of storm to break, but Dennis didn't say anything. Finally Avery said, "What do you think about it, Dinny?"

Dennis looked up at him. "I suppose you expect me to go into some kind of act," he said. "Maybe carry on like a priest out of James Joyce or James Farrell. I"m going to disappoint you. For one thing I'm not a priest and for another I'm not in the denouncing business." He paused, striking a match and watching the flame burn down to the end. "But I feel sorry for you. You've got a conscience and it's not going to be a healthy thing to carry around for the rest of your life."

"Look, Dennis," Avery said, defending himself in spite of the fact that Dennis hadn't accused him of anything. "She went back to England. It was her own idea."

"I think you forget one thing," Dennis said. "There's a human life involved. A human being that will be born and live and breathe and grow and have a soul. You're not just dealing with a social complication out of a novel or a play. And you're not dealing with an equation. You are dealing with a human life that you are responsible for."

"To God you mean?" Avery said. "I don't accept that. I don't believe in God."

"No." Dennis shook his head. "To yourself. You are responsible to yourself." He thought for a moment, then said, "You do believe in yourself, don't you?"

"I don't know," Avery said. "I don't think so."

"It takes a certain kind of guy to be a sonofabitch successfully," Dennis said. "And you aren't it. You haven't got the tail to swing it."

"I know," Avery said.

The next day Dennis was gone, to the monastery in Kentucky. He might as well have returned to the Arctic or to the South Pacific. There was no way to communicate with him. He had dropped out of life again.

Avery went back to his work. This year he would complete the course requirements for his Ph.D., leaving his thesis to be written and the two examinations to pass. When he had done these things he would have his scholar's operating license and be certified as an independent thinker. It seemed absurd. It was nothing but the certification of time passed in certain rooms and of certain books that had been read and partly understood. At the end of May when he was finished he had no sense of achievement or conclusion. It was a dead end.

He did not know what to do with his time.

The month of May had been clear, with scarcely any rain. As June approached, relentless distillate heat descended on the city before people expected it, so that they sweltered more resentfully than usual.

Avery's room was paid up and he stayed on in the dormitory even though he had nothing to do. One day, crossing the campus, he met Angus Cotton, whom he had not seen for three years. Cotton was wearing a white linen suit and had lost his old Bolshevik look. He was delighted to see Avery. "Jesus, at least there's somebody left," he said. "I was beginning to feel like Rip Van Winkle."

They found an air-cooled place and drank some beer together. Cotton told him that he had been in Europe for a year after he got out of the army, at the University of Paris. "I'm coming back here in the fall," he said. "I don't know how I'll like it."

"What are you doing for the summer?" Avery asked, wondering what he was going to do with his own.

"I'm staying down at my brother-in-law's farm on Long Island," Angus said. "It's the closest thing to a home I've got any more. How about you?"

"I don't know," Avery said.

"Why don't you come down to the Island with me?" Angus said, half seriously. "Do you good to push a tractor around for a couple of months instead of a pencil. Bad pay but good food."

"Are you serious?" Avery asked.

"Well sure," Cotton said. "Why not? Hands are hard to get and we could use one."

Avery was tempted for a moment; he had nothing to do and it would be a change of scene. Then he realized that it would mean living in a house with people he didn't know. He wasn't prepared to make the effort. "I don't know," he said. "I may go off somewhere and work on my God damn thesis."

Angus wrote a telephone number on a paper napkin and gave it to him. "Well call me up if you change your mind," he said. He had made the suggestion as a joke, but now it seemed to appeal to him. "You might like it," he said. "And we could have a swell time together."

Avery nodded. He had always liked Cotton, but there had been a kind of chalk line between them that both had observed and that originated in Cotton's hostility to Avery's background. The war and time seemed to have obliterated this; they had both grown up a little. There was warmth between them, tentative and based more on the accidental fact that they had both been members of the Four F Club at Angelo's than on anything positive, but real nonetheless.

"Could be," Avery said. "Look, would you like to have dinner with me? We could go downtown somewhere." He suddenly didn't want to let Cotton go.

But Cotton said, "I'd like to, but they expect me down on the Island for dinner." He looked at his watch. "As a matter of fact, I'll just about make it."

Avery wasn't expected anywhere for dinner. When Cotton had gone he went back to his room, but it was insufferably hot so he went to a movie without bothering to find out the title of the film being shown. It was an English picture and the actors' voices brought Sarah into his mind.

Ever since he had talked with Dennis his imagination had been turning back to her. He was aware of the child growing in her body as one is aware of a clock ticking away the minutes. He knew that she was home with her people and safe, as she would have said, as houses, but he could not get over apprehension about her and had a recurrent dream in which he saw her alone on a wide empty plain, gross with child so that she staggered, wandering across the stylized desert, seeming to be trying to call his name. It was a horrible dream and filled him with guilt. The memory of it invaded his thoughts during the day and he had no peace. He was miserable. He was prosecuting himself.

He went often to Riverside Park to sit in the sun and watch the river. One afternoon a nursemaid pushing a baby carriage stopped for a moment in front of the bench on which he sat. He stared at the sleeping infant, pink and angelic as a baby on a magazine cover, but alive, inarguably alive. He was struck by sudden meaning of what Dennis had said to him. "It's a human being, that will live and breathe." The actuality of his own child, inside Sarah's body, came to him with force. He was oddly moved and felt tears in his eyes. He had a rush of excitement and the desire to put things right.

He got up and walked back to the university slowly through the sluggish, palpable heat. He decided abruptly that he would go to England as soon as Caldecott Browne could make the arrangements for him. He went to a phone booth and called Browne without considering the matter further.

CHAPTER SIXTY-SEVEN

SARAH'S town was in the heart of Lancashire, several hours from London by train. Avery arrived early in the evening just as the mill shifts were changing, in the midst of an endless northern drizzle. The town smelled heavily of dampness and beer, of wet wool and of brassy Virginia tobacco smoke. He got a room at the Railway Hotel and a meal of sawdust sausages. In the morning, which was clear, he telephoned Sarah. She did not seem startled by the sound of his voice or surprised that he was in England and this put him off a little.

"I want to see you," he said.

"If you like," she said without expression, and told him how to get from his hotel to her father's house.

He walked, asking directions occasionally, conscious of the fact that he was conspicuous in his American clothes. He was appalled by the dreariness of the town. The only note of beauty was the deep rose color of the brick that formed most of the houses. A pall of soot hung in the air and clung to the walls and pavements. The whole landscape looked like a workhouse scene out of Dickens. It was as though every nonutilitarian note had been rigidly ordered removed by a committee for the preservation of drabness. It was impossible to believe that all of this had once been pleasant countryside; that all this ugly monotony was a deliberate creation of man. The faces he saw were blankly tired. Only occasionally did he see a girl or a young man who did not look shabby and resigned. The country seemed worn out. The endless rows of red brick houses stirred a dim memory in him of the abandoned mills at Amoskeag he had seen when he was a boy.

He passed through workingmen's streets and entered a brighter section of the town, where the houses stood on terraces above the level of the street and were defended by iron railings and neat well-tended gardens. It was not as grim as the area he had just traversed but it was relentlessly dull. It expressed a determined mediocrity that he reasoned must be intentional and sought by the people who inhabited these houses. It occurred to him that perhaps they found safety in the mediocrity, safety in being like one another in their houses, their diet, their dress and their speech.

At last he came to Sarah's house, indistinguishable from the houses to its left and to its right except by the fact that painted on the gate were the words: Wandsea Villa, H. D. Greenway. It was the place and he was astonished at how accurately he had imagined it months ago. The front door was half stained glass and there was a brass bell-knob with a card beneath it. He pulled and heard a tinkle inside the house, like a shop bell's tinkle in an English movie. Sarah came to the door herself. She was dressed in a loose blue smock that flattered her coloring. She looked aggressively pregnant. She led him through a crowded hall to a tiny sitting room that was filled with late-Victorian furniture. There was a paper fan in the fireplace and tea things had been set out. The room was neat and gave the impression of being tended methodically with an old-fashioned feather duster. He was asked to sit on a mohair sofa with springs that reminded him of the seat of a buggy they once had had at Hull. Sarah sat across from him. Her body was monolithic, sculptural, classic in outline. Her face looked fresh and extremely pretty.

"You don't seem very glad to see me," he said.

She handed him a cup of tea and a cake and said quietly, "Why have you come, Avery? What do you want?"

"I want to marry you," he said, his heart pounding.

"Oh?"

For several seconds there was total silence in the room. Sarah poured tea for herself and there was the clinking sound of the china. "That's very kind of you, Avery," she said. "But I'm afraid it's impossible. I'm going to be married next week, so you see you're a bit late."

Avery was stunned; there is no other word for it.

"You see I was engaged to Tommy long before I met you," she said. "It's not really so startling."

"But what about us?" he asked. "Doesn't he care anything about—"

"Of course he cares," she said, an impatient note in her voice. "He's a man. Of course he cares. He cares very much." She paused. "But you see, Avery," she went on, "he loves me."

"But you love me," Avery said accusingly. "You said you did, in New York."

"We're not in New York now though, Avery," she said. "We're i' Lancashire, luv', where the folk are blunt and straight." She took on a music hall north country accent.

"I'm only trying to do what's right," he said, confused and resentful that he had been put in the wrong.

"It's nothing to do with you, Avery," she said. "Nothing to do with you at all."

"Then you don't love me," he said, making it a kind of challenge.

"I feel sorry for you," she said. "You're afraid of yourself. You're afraid of your own heart." She paused, frowning, then said, "Do you know what your friend Breitbart said about you once?" she asked.

He shook his head.

"He said you were in a deep freeze." She smiled. "I didn't understand what he meant. We don't have deep freezes here, you see. But he explained. I didn't agree with him then, but I do now."

He was silent. She leaned forward in her chair, staring at him curiously. She seemed to be aware of the dignity of her swollen body. When she spoke again her voice was kinder.

"When I was in New York alone," she said, "I thought my heart would break. I hoped to die. But when I got home and people were kind to me, I knew that my heart wasn't going to break." She broke off, thinking for a moment, then said, "Do you know what my Dad said, when I told him the whole story?"

Avery looked up.

"He said, 'Well, lass, we wouldn't want our girl married to a chap that wasn't fond of her, no matter what.' "

Avery stared at the paper fan; it was made of newsprint and he wondered how the intricate folds were contrived. "So you won't marry me?" he said dully.

"It's not a matter of won't," Sarah said cheerfully. "It's a matter of can't. I've already promised someone else."

Avery looked at Sarah then back at the fan. This was a turn he had not been prepared to face. During the time that had passed between his decision to come to England and the present moment, he had prepared himself for recrimination and tears, for praise and joy, even for physical violence on the part of Sarah's father. He had not taken up with himself the prospect of a summary refusal. It was humiliating and it offended his sense of order. He had retraced his steps so that he might correct what he had discovered was in error, in the same way he might have gone back over a long tedious piece of computation until he came to the place where the mistake had been made. It had seemed straightforward enough ... just a matter of putting things right, correcting the error then going on. He simply could not understand that the whole problem had been changed at the moment he walked out of Sarah's apartment and left her alone in the dark.

He got up.

"Will you let me know when the baby is born?" he asked. "I'd like to know."

"If you like," she said.

"I don't live with Breitbart any more," he said. "You can write to me at the university and they'll forward it, wherever I am."

"Are you sure you want to know, Avery?" she asked, her voice rather kindly.

"Yes. I want to know," he said.

"All right," she said. "I promise that I will let you know, whatever happens."

She took him to the door. He bent quickly and kissed her cheek, then felt a lump rise in his throat and was afraid that he would cry. He turned and hurried down the concrete steps through the little garden in front of the house. When he looked back the door was closed and the dull sun winked on the polished brass bell-pull.

He walked back to the Railway Hotel, a kind of desperation in his heart that was unclear. He felt that he had been a fool and been made a fool of, and that he had come on a fool's errand. He had a sense of despair and deprivation at the thought that he would never see the child and that it would grow up bearing someone else's name. The rejection had been absolute; there had been no chance to appeal. As he walked he recalled Breitbart's observation: "Don't underestimate Sarah. She's from Lancashire and they have character."

It was incredible to him that he was not required; he had thought of himself, ever since Sarah left New York, as the central element, the controlling one. He could not get it through his head that she did not want him or his money or his name or even, at this point, his love. It was more degrading for him to face the fact that he did not matter than it had been for him to admit to himself that he had behaved like a scoundrel and betrayed a human being. He felt morbid jealousy of the man who was going to marry Sarah, that he had never seen. He had an awareness of defeat. It was unreasonable. He had not got what he had not wanted and been given quitclaim. It should have settled the problem, but it didn't.

Breitbart had told Sarah that he was in a deep freeze. He turned the phrase over in his mind, worrying out the figure of speech, and in the end admitted to himself that Breitbart had been right. He was in a deep freeze all right, and he could feel the ice in his veins. He wanted thawing out. But he wasn't quite sure of how to begin the thawing process and there were no directions on the package.

He returned to London on the train and sat at the window of a West End hotel, looking down into the street. Across the Channel was Europe; he could pass the summer there. But the idea of Europe by himself was forbidding. He wanted to get away from England and away from Europe. There was no seat on the plane and no cabin on the fast boat. The best he could get was passage on a ten-day intermediate ship sailing from Liverpool in the morning. He took it. When he landed in New York he called Angus Cotton from the pay booth in a water-front saloon across the street from the pier.

"Sure I was serious," Angus said. "Come along. We'll put you to work though, fellow. This is no gentleman's farm. We're in the bean business."

"Suits me," Avery said. "You've hired yourself a boy."

CHAPTER SIXTY-EIGHT

HE CAUGHT the Long Island train with a few minutes to spare and bought a magazine from the candy butcher who passed through the car. But when the train emerged from the tunnel and cut eastward he abandoned the predigested news and stared at the depressing landscape ... thousands of acres of defiant mediocrity that reminded him of Lancashire. But after a bit the country began to look challenging and exciting. From time to time he had a glimpse of the sea over low sand dunes. It was not like any country he knew and the strangeness, together with the sense of the sea, gave him a feeling of cyclical awareness; he had an odd sense of being directed by a force outside himself—God, Fate, whatever—and of not being totally responsible for his decisions. He had the conviction that he was deliberately stepping out of the past like a moth undergoing mutation, less through choice than something inevitable in his nature. He had made no real decision but he had a compelling and warning anticipation of conclusion, of a turning point.

When he got down from the train he was struck by the hot dense air, overpowering after the air-conditioned coach. He felt lost. Then he saw Angus down the platform, dressed in dungarees, looking efficient and part of the landscape.

"Jesus, Avery," Angus said, "you've lost weight. You look as though you'd just come from combat."

"Limey food I guess," Avery said. "I've just come from England."

"No kidding?" Angus said. "How long were you there?"

"Three days," Avery said.

"Are you nuts?"

"I didn't like it," Avery said. "I'll tell you about it later."

Angus led the way through the station and they climbed aboard a battered pick-up truck. They drove through the hot little town and turned onto a black-top road that skirted the shore line. The landscape was flat, flatter than any Avery had ever seen. It was sandy country, with scrub pine growing along the verge of the road. There were dozens of inlets from the sea, thick with tough grass and marsh mallow. He could smell the ocean. It was exciting. He had a sense of strangeness that was keener than what he had felt in England, on foreign soil. Then the broad shallow bay came into view. Far out he saw a cluster of sails, reaching to starboard.

"That's the kids," Angus told him. "They race all the time. Bob's kid Brenda's probably out there with them. She'll come back tonight too beat up to do the dishes." He slowed the car and squinted against the sun, peering at the sails. "She's a great kid though. They're crazy about her."

They passed a field planted in beans; the plants looked withered and the earth was dry. "Need some rain," Angus said. "It's awful dry."

"Can't you irrigate?" Avery asked. "I saw some pipe back there a ways."

"We could if we had the pipe," Angus said. "Bob bought himself a pump last year and that left him fresh out of money. I guess we'll have to depend on God Almighty this year. I told you this was no gentleman's farm."

They came to a dark place where the dirt road that approached the farm passed between double rows of handsome maples. It was like a French *grande allée*. "House is just ahead," said Angus. "And here's Bob now." He stopped and touched the horn. Bob Cutler straightened up and walked to the truck. He was a big man with sandy hair bleached by the sun and skin that was an even tone of red. This redness was emphasized by the washed blue of his work shirt. He was unmistakably a farmer but there was a suggestion of the sea about him too. He looked simple, able and intelligent. He gave Avery a square hard hand and said, "Glad to meet you. Heard about you."

"Glad to meet you," Avery said. He felt an instinctive conviction of trust, the recognition of total honesty.

"You go on up to the house," said Bob. "I'll be along in a minute, soon's I get this coffee mill to running." He turned back to the engine he had been working on and Angus shifted gears. They drove through the alley of trees and pulled up in front of the house. The house was white, with a lot of lawn, and as they stood for a few moments in the blazing sun, Avery had the sensation of coming back to a place he had known before, though actually he had never seen this house or been on the south shore of Long Island before.

"Come on," said Angus. "I'll show you where you're going to sleep and you can change your clothes. You must be beat."

"Yeah," said Avery. "I guess I am."

He took a bath and changed into cotton clothes, then sat in a chair near the window of his room, from which he had a clear view of the bay and the open sea that was beyond the sandbar of Westhampton Beach. He felt relaxed. Then he recalled Angus' observation about his appearance and went to the mirror over the bureau. He saw nothing but the face he had been looking at all his life in its various stages of development: a standard New England face set on a narrow nordic skull, the face of a documented Yale boy or Princeton boy or Williams boy. He could not see on his face any evidence of the spiritual bankruptcy that had brought him to this Long Island farm in search of a breathing spell instead of to his own home in Hull, or to the university that he had tried to turn into a substitute home.

He went back to the chair beside the window and stood with a knee on the chair arm, gazing at the open sea. A long tow of seagoing barges moved east along the coast. Out of the haze came a squadron of torpedo bombers, pitch black against the sky, making a simulated attack on the barges, coming in low then gaining height quickly, one after the other, resuming formation ... playing war with the precision of a corps de ballet. He could imagine the men in the planes: people like Beasley Smith and the two marines with whom he had cruised the town on New Year's Eve. There was a contradiction in it, just as there was contradiction in Smith and his friends. There was beauty in the precision of the closely teamed formation, and terror in the racks under the planes that could just as well have been loaded with real torpedoes with the warheads ready.

"There is a funny thing about human thinking," Dormaker once had told him. "Opposites become blended with opposites and the contradictions disappear."

He felt the contradiction in himself, the contradiction of love and hate, the contradiction of fear and courage, unreconciled and at war inside him, giving the power to the cooling system that ran in his private deep freeze.

There was a knock at the door. "Avery? How about some chow? Five minutes, huh?"

"Okay," he called.

Molly Cutler put him at ease. She was a good deal older than Angus and Avery remembered that there were a sister and brother between them. She wore a pink wash dress and looked capable. She shook Avery's hand and told him where to sit, then took her own place at the foot of the table, facing Bob. They had a big meal of beef and potatoes and lima beans that Avery thought were wonderful but that everyone else belittled because they hadn't just been picked.

When they were halfway through the meal Brenda Cutler, aged fifteen, bounced into the room. She was a teen-age caricature, snub-nosed, freckled, pert-mouthed, with a mop of dull gold hair and a plump, budding figure that she handled a little self-consciously. She had an effervescent voice that filled the room and so much energy that it seemed to spill over. She went around the table quickly, kissing everyone including Avery, to whom she said, "I don't know you but I'll kiss you anyway." Then she sat down, her navy white hat on the back of her head, and began to eat what her mother gave her with the single-minded efficiency of a bailing machine. It was impossible not to respond to so much life; Avery watched her and grinned and she looked up for a moment and grinned back.

"Hi!"

"Hi," he said.

He felt at home.

At the end of the week he had settled into the routine of the farm. He got up with Bob and Angus, just before the first light broke across the bay, and passed the day in the fields. Angus taught him to drive the tractor and he learned to handle the dusting gun. He also learned to glance at the sky from time to time during the day, in the hope that by some dispensation a cloud might have appeared in it while he wasn't looking. There was a drought this year, on Long Island, and up and down the Eastern seaboard. Things in the fields were burning up. The earth was dry as powder and dust rose in clouds as they moved between the rows of plants.

"I think Bob's had it," Angus said one day when he and Avery were at work. He bent and touched one of the plants. "It'll take a miracle to pull these poor bastards through now."

"A real good soaker ought to do it," Avery said mechanically, repeating the words he had been hearing several times a day ever since he arrived at the farm. "A real good all-day rain."

"Sure it would," Angus agreed. "But I don't see any sign of it, do you?"

Avery looked up at the sun and felt personal hatred for it. It seemed enormous and diseased, perilously close to the earth. "No," he agreed. "I don't."

Late in the day thin clouds appeared in the sky, meaning-less filmy streaks like chiffon, drawn toward the retiring sun. The next day dawned pale and clear with no sign of rain. They heard a radio broadcast that announced water rationing in New York. Beyond the city, to the north, the reservoirs were dry and there were photographs in the papers that showed the mud bottoms dried in polygons like the arctic tundra.

As he watched the drought, it seemed to Avery that it was somehow more merciless than other natural afflictions—fire, storm, flood. There was nothing to fight. It was inexorable. Nature inflicted nothing man could combat with his hands or his brain. She merely withheld. There was no appeal. The few farmers on Long Island who owned irrigation gear tapped the water that was a few feet below the surface and soaked their fields. Bob had no gear and he simply watched the drought burn away his farm.

He was like a man being consumed by cancer, but he sur-vived; and his survival was a lesson to Avery for it involved the question of human freedom and freedom was something that interested Avery, in the abstract as well as the concrete. As the days passed and he came to absorb Bob's character by working with him in the fields, in the same way a man absorbs the char-acter of a quiet landscape, he felt profound respect for Bob and a kind of love. There was a sense of substance about Cutler that was rare as quality in painting and that gave Avery the hint of a new point of view about human character. In some ways Bob was simple to the point of banality, but he touched the great banality that art must have in order to detach itself from method or time or mere effect. It was not simply that Bob reflected certain old-fashioned virtues—honesty, courtesy, respect for work and so on, but the fact that Avery felt in Bob an ingredient of goodness, of human integrity, of faith in his own manhood. Bob was intui-tively moral, and it was upon a search for morality that Avery had embarked years ago in his room at Hull when he had on his own grasped a fragment of the Cartesian system, and for this reason he felt a kinship with Bob that was fundamental and did not have to be put into words. They were looking for the same thing, he and Bob. They were looking for unity and cosmic support.

But Bob had the advantage over him. Bob was in love with his wife and his wife and child loved him, so that the biting edge of loneliness was blunted for him and the struggle was warmed with human meaning.

This love was a fact that informed the household and made living in it almost a healing process, as far as Avery was concerned. As he observed the passage of love between man and wife, he began to understand some of the lack in his father's marriage, and saw that the necessary mutuality had been missing. He saw that in crisis his parents had not been drawn together at all, but instead had withdrawn to previously prepared positions and become not allies but well-bred antagonists. His father's marriage to his mother had had more in it of the duel than of love, and he understood that at Hull he and Morgan had lived in the atmosphere of covert war, and that his father and mother, since long before his memory began, must have lost the ability to communicate with one another in more than formal terms. One evening in a kind of revelation, he saw why it was that his father had been prompted to abandon his mother when her defenses broke and the world swept over her like a wave. The situation had demanded resources his father did not possess, and for lack of which he could not be blamed. It was not his father's fault that his father had not loved his mother in a way that might have salvaged and sustained her. It was not a thing that could be summoned by the will. He had blamed his father for deserting his duty, but he saw now that in a sense his father had been deserted too.

He was struck by a wave of pity for his father. It was the beginning of understanding and he realized this. He fought back the sympathy in the way one attempts to suppress inappropriate sentiment, for he did not want to make moral concessions to the enemy. Nevertheless, once his speculations had suggested that it was not his father's fault that his father had not loved his mother, the idea remained with him. He saw that love could not be commanded but either was or was not. It could be developed and guarded, like talent, and it might deepen with time and the play of events, but it could not be willed into existence and certainly was not automatically supplied to the relationships in which it was formally supposed to reside.

This discovery was of importance to Avery. It helped him to understand his father's defection and it lessened his guilt about Sarah, for he saw that he had told the truth and not merely phrased a convenience when he had insisted it was not his fault that he had not loved her but had only let himself be loved.

CHAPTER SIXTY-NINE

THROUGH July and early August, Avery was given over to a considerable amount of stylized brooding. This mood was intensified by the closeness of the sea. The context of sea and sky and impeccable endless reach of sand induced detached awareness of doom and this was punctuated by the oppressive philosophical overtures of the surf. The scene was stagy, almost overdone, but at root it contained austere inexorable beauty, at the same time modern and ancient, timeless, atavistic. There were stretches of beach as lonely as the moon. The dunes and planted beach grass and washed immaculate beach gave the impression of an unexplored area, somehow not related to this planet, suggesting the fantastic world of a poet concerned with the formalization of loneliness.

Angus loved the beach and the sea. "I get a sense of peace from it that I don't get anywhere else," he told Avery. "It's a matter of temperament, I guess. You have part of it."

"I know what you mean," Avery said. "You can get outside of yourself in a way, and look yourself over."

Angus nodded. They were stretched out on the beach at a place they liked, half a mile or so from the bridge that led to the farm. It was a deserted reach of shore line, beyond the colonies of bright umbrellas and modern bleached redwood houses, and the beach changed direction slightly, so that nothing could be seen in either direction but sand and sea and the clumps of tough-bladed grass planted in military rank and file. The sky was like blue chalk, cloudless and prophylactic. There was a still dry heat, and the sound of the surf that tantalized the sand in a rhythm regular as a metronome.

"You know I came down here after I got back from Europe," Angus said. "I was a mess. I was a mess when I got out of the army. That's why I stayed overseas and went to the Sorbonne. I was afraid to come home. I hated the war, or the peace rather. It was supposed to be peace when I got to Germany. I had to make an effort to be a soldier and I brutalized myself to a point where I began to doubt my own humanity." He paused for a moment, raising himself on one elbow and looking off at the sea horizon. "Do you know that I shot a German prisoner between the eyes just because he kept muttering '*Cigaretten, bitte. Cigaretten, bitte, Herr Leutnant*'? The sound of his voice with a whine in it just seemed to drive me nuts. I shot him in the head with my forty-five and I said, 'There you Kraut bastard, you won't need any God damned cigarette now.' He was a young guy, about our age. One of my people looked at him, on the ground with his head blown off, and said, 'Jeez, Lieutenant, you didn't ought to done that. It's against the Geneva Convention to shoot 'em.' "

"What did they do?" Avery said. "The army I mean?"

"Nothing," Angus said. "They were S.S. prisoners. They had been at Malmedy. The army didn't do anything, but it did something to me. When I came down here last spring I was shot. I didn't have the energy to go on living. I felt like a guy who'd been in jail for something he didn't do."

Avery nodded. "How do you feel now?" he said. "Do you think you can go back to college in the fall and study history again?"

"I think so," Angus said. "I hope so." He hesitated then said, "How about you? You must be almost finished. Are you satisfied?"

"I don't know," Avery said. "Academically, I suppose I am. What I can do on my own I don't know. So far I'm a good mechanic. To go further, to be an originator, you have to make a leap of the mind, and I don't know yet how far my mind will leap.

But I'm going to find out." He paused, looking off at the sea. "You see, I tried to get something out of mathematics that isn't there. I went knocking at the wrong door."

"Looking for what?" Angus asked.

"I don't know," Avery said, looking up at the sky. "God, I guess. Somebody who would prosecute my old man for murdering my mother. Justice maybe. Or the Devil. I don't know. The funny thing is, you really couldn't get him for the first degree. I guess involuntary manslaughter is about the toughest you could make it." He smiled. "Vehicular homicide, maybe. But I guess she let some of the air out of the tires, so maybe you couldn't even get him for that. You could just put him down as a lousy driver and let it go."

"I saw your father in Germany," Angus said. "He looked like a damn good driver."

"On his own road, in his own car, there isn't any better," Avery said. "But put him in a car with a right-hand drive and he's licked."

"Why don't you put it in plain English?" Angus said. "I'm not sure I get your point."

"I guess not," Avery said. "But in plain English it wouldn't make any kind of sense at all."

"What are you going to do when you get your degree?" Angus said. "Teach? Or research?"

"I don't know," Avery said. "That's one of the things I came down here to find out."

They got up and went into the ocean for a moment, feeling the salt bite of the water. Then they walked slowly down the beach and crossed the bridge over the inlet, heading toward the farm. Neither of them had noticed the darkening of the sky, but suddenly from far off came a low rumble of thunder.

"Jesus! Jesus Christ!" Angus yelled. "Rain for the love of mike. Rain."

They began to run toward the house. By the time they reached the yard the rain had started, big drops that made emphatic splashes and pockmarks on the dusty road that were the size of half-dollars. Bob stood in the shelter of the porch watching the storm and they joined him. There were rain marks on his blue shirt and his hair was wet. The air near the house was split by a vivid flash of lightning and the rain began to pour down. Bob nodded at the gullies the water made in the dry earth. "Won't be enough," he said. "Most of it'll run off." He smiled. "You might say it'll just prolong the agony."

"It's rain isn't it?" Angus said. "What do you want, an egg in your beer?"

Avery looked at the rain. "My mother was a great gardener," he said. "She always used to say, 'Water well, Avery, or not at all. It's terribly frustrating to grass to be sprinkled. It's like giving a starving man a cracker.'"

Bob nodded. "She knew what she was talking about," he said. "Your mother living, is she?"

"No." Avery shook his head. "No. She's dead."

It was the first time since his mother's death that he had spoken of her naturally, and the first time she had come into his mind the way she had been before she broke up, unaccompanied by an image of the awful bloody bath water. He felt a wave of tenderness for his mother.

Abruptly the rain stopped, conclusively as though someone had turned a switch. The dead silence after the hysteric storm was uncomfortable and no one spoke. Then Brenda, wearing tight corduroy shorts and a soaked cotton shirt, streaked across the lawn from the garage where she had taken shelter, her bare feet splashing in the still puddles. She looked at Bob and kissed him quickly. "Rain's no good is it, Daddy?" she said.

He shook his head. "Just enough to get the darned beans mad," he said, grinning at her.

"Hi, youngster," Avery said. "Why don't you change your clothes and maybe we can get an hour's algebra done before dinner, eh?"

Brenda made a face and said, "Okay, teach', okay."

Avery changed into slacks and a shirt and went to the living room where Brenda waited, her algebra text opened to the lesson she had been asked to prepare. She had failed the subject last year and was making it up in summer school. For a month Avery had been coaching her and she was sufficiently flattered by his attention to make the effort she had declined to make during the term. She would listen to him with absolute attention, her innocent gray eyes almost comically serious, her plump mouth set, the navy white hat shoved back so that a strand of corn-colored hair fell across her freckled cheek. She had a crush on Avery of course, as she had on all grown men.

Usually she was cheerful, for she had an outgoing nature and lots of energy, but this afternoon, after the abortive storm, she was unusually serious. When the lesson was over Avery sat back in his chair and lit a cigarette. "What's the matter, kid?" he asked. "Are you worried about this?" He touched the textbook. "You'll pass it all right, even if I have to get dressed up in a skirt and take the darned test for you."

She shook her head. "No it isn't that," she said. "I was just thinking about Daddy." She looked directly at him and he saw two large tears form and roll down her cheeks. He took out his handkerchief and dabbed at them. "Thanks," she said. She frowned. "You know I love Daddy better than anyone in the world," she said. "But I wouldn't marry a farmer for anything. Not for anything."

She was usually about as solemn as a jukebox; her seriousness touched him. "Don't worry about your Dad," he said. "It'll take more than a drought to lick him."

He looked at her, suddenly realizing that she was about the age he had been when Morgan was killed. He could not help wondering if he had been as filled with complex innocence—a combination of awareness of subtlety with demand for the simple truth. He remembered his terrible confusion in the face of the freedom just beyond childhood that imposed a necessity for moral choice, and the way in which he had turned from it to look for another safe prison. In Brenda he saw something of himself as he had been, and he recognized the monstrous test of endurance that confronts the adolescent who is titillated everywhere by art, commerce and adult behavior, yet forbidden more than symbolic experiment on pain of social exclusion.

"The thing about Daddy is," she said, "he's stubborn. He won't do what other people do. He could go in with the freezer company and not have to worry so about money. Or he could plant potatoes. Then the government would pay him."

"Would you rather he did that?" Avery asked. "You know he wouldn't like it."

She shook her head. "No, I want him to be the way he is." She hesitated for a moment, then said desperately, "But I hate to see him suffer so."

"I know," Avery said. "But he's a free man. He wouldn't be the same if he signed up with the freezer company or tried to latch on to the spud money."

Brenda got up and tucked her books under her arm. She looked like a Coca Cola ad. She smiled and kissed Avery on the cheek, then said, "Sure, I know. I just get blue sometimes." She looked through the window at the sky. "I just wish to God it would *rain*, that's all," she said. "I just wish to God it would pour."

CHAPTER SEVENTY

O N SATURDAY evenings they went to the beach and had
their supper on the sand, cooking hamburgers and hot
dogs over a driftwood fire, drinking cold beer from the cans.
Sometimes they sat around the fire until midnight, talking and
watching the starlight on the sea. The beach and the sea and the
food cooked in the open were a part of the pattern of their common life and they made Avery feel part of it, just as they made
him feel part of the farm. To compare the sense of security he felt
with them he had to go far back in time, into childhood and the
long safe days in his mother's studio, days from which detail had
evaporated and which were now remembered as a climate of love,
an atmosphere of permanence once felt, now gone.

The particular setting and group of people might not have
worked the same change in another individual; often the cata-
lytic situation seems the result of chance. Chance or not, it suited
Avery. It was what he needed at this turn of life. He was beginning
to thaw out. He did not know whether he had changed because
something had been added or whether he had simply aroused a
latent part of his character, the part that had been frozen. But he
knew that he was changing. He could feel it in his heart and in
the muscles of his body. He felt sometimes as though he were like
a man emerging from a great sleep, during which the heartbeat
and the passage of blood through the body have been chemically
slowed to the limiting point at which life will be sustained.

Early one morning when they were dusting before the sun
had a chance to burn the dew from the plants, he thought of

Freddie Breitbart and imagined the astonishment with which Freddie would regard him could he see him now, stripped to the waist, burnt brown by the sun, his hair whitened by the dusting powder. The imagined expression of Freddie's face made him laugh. Angus looked at him and said, "What are you feeling so good about at this time in the morning?"

"I don't know," Avery said. "I just feel good."

"That's more than these beans do," Angus grunted. "They feel awful." He paused, wiping the sweat and dust from his face with a bright red bandanna. "Bob'll have to turn 'em under next week sure as hell. They're goners."

Avery looked down at the stunted plants and was struck by a sense of tragedy at the thought of what these helpless fields represented in terms of labor and money and investment of human spirit. He had a sudden vivid perception of the divine indifference of nature. "The environment is hostile," Dormaker had told him. "To live you must defy the gods and take some primary risks." He had accepted Dormaker's words as obvious to the point of banality, once he had managed to accept them at all. But as he stood under the cruel sun in the midst of Bob's desiccated fields he saw that he had not grasped Dormaker's meaning at all, or understood that Dormaker was trying to tell him that danger was man's proper companion, that danger and risk belonged to freedom, safety and the long-term hedge to self-oppression and the slave spirit. Now that he felt Dormaker's meaning, in terms of the round malevolent sun and the rain from heaven that had gone on strike, the idea seemed majestic and terrifying. He saw that we are all at war with the gods, that the simplest protective act, the mere drawing on of a coat against the cold, is a skirmish in the struggle the final engagement of which is for every man lost at birth when he began to die. He remembered a phrase that had been burnt into his mind when he first read it in Joyce's novel: *Reproduction is the beginning of death.*

He felt a mild controlled depression during the rest of the morning. If death was the goal, he asked himself, then what was the sense of living at all? Logically then his brother and his poor mother in her crimson bath were really victors rather than vanquished and had conquered life rather than been destroyed by it.

He was depressed because he realized that his line of thought spun out would lead eventually to the idea of God, and the idea of a God whose thought could be diluted in sufficient proportion to contain the affairs of men was an absurdity to him. If there was a God at all he must be transfinite beyond conception. The tragic fact of death in life he took as self-evidence that man, beast, and the planet itself were alone in the struggle, which meant that the end of life had no meaning distinguishable from death, and that, to Avery, was definitively without meaning. Mathematics was no help here. Science, and especially mathematics, was only a fictional tenant of the mind of the race and only proved that finite man could think beyond his life span. What presented itself to him that summer was a question of pure belief, like the belief of a child in his mother or man in the beauty of the sky; all the casuistry proceeded from belief, belief, belief, belief, and thus at the outset the argument was reduced to the status of sophisticated play, like Dormaker's three-dimensional chess. Maybe you had to be born with God in your pocket, he thought, like old Annie McBain, or feel Him in your room at night, the way Dennis said he felt Him.

Avery thought these things over, contemplating the blue chalk sky and the hideous sun that seemed to squat close to the earth and be part of the landscape.

In the meantime Bob's crop burnt to death.

There was no rain and the following week the neat rows were turned under. Bob was going to plant again as soon as there was enough rain to wet the soil, too late to be sure his crop would mature, gambling with nature on a late frost. It was as if there had been a human death, the day they plowed the condemned plants under. "Mercy killing," Bob said, sitting on the iron seat of the tractor. "What they call euthanasia."

It was the only joke he managed all that day. They came into dinner that night exhausted and depressed, unwilling to talk about the central fact and unable to talk about anything else. Bob ate his food quickly and left the table before the others were finished. They heard him outside on the porch, his heels making a heavy sound on the board floor, then heard the sound of a chain being dragged. Everyone paused, aware of the desperate man outside in the gathering darkness. Then his wife said almost irritably, "Well we might as well eat our dinner, for heaven's sake!"

Avery looked up quickly, startled by the tone of Molly's voice. She was thin, too thin, and the strain of the summer showed. There were tears in her eyes and her lips quivered but the tears didn't fall. After a moment she smiled at him and said, "We've been in lots worse fixes than this and we're still here. Let's not turn the meal into a wake."

"Take it easy, sis," said Angus. "Everybody's tired."

"I know," she said. "It's him I worry about. He'll take that tractor apart and put it together again all night long, just for something to do."

While they were eating dessert Brenda's current boy friend joined them. He was an angular, acned youth named Barringer whose father owned a neighboring farm. He detested Avery, having convinced himself that Avery was a city slicker from New York who regarded the hicks with contempt. He attacked his plate of berries and ice cream after he had glared at Avery and did not raise his eyes from the dish until he had finished. Then he pushed the dish away from him and said, "Hear you folks lost your crop. Bet you wish you'd planted spuds now, the way my dad did. Don't matter if they are like marbles. Gov'ment pays up just the same." He laughed, a kind of comedy-farmer, well I s'wan laugh, and said, "Don't see what's wrong with spuds anyhow."

Brenda got up, rattling the crockery. She was on the verge of tears. "You can just go home and eat your old potatoes," she said. "That's all you're fit to raise anyway."

The boy looked up, shocked by her anger. "I didn't mean nothin'," he said.

"Go on!" Brenda cried. "Go on home."

The boy's doltish face turned red. "Thought you wanted to go to the show," he said. "Good picture."

"Well I don't," she said. "I've got better things to do."

There was a moment's pause, then young Barringer rose clumsily and stood for a few seconds, looking at Brenda then at the others. He turned and went out, slamming the screen door. Brenda sat down, staring at what was left of her dessert. The ice cream had melted and she stirred the cerise-colored soup with her spoon, then hesitantly ate a berry.

"That wasn't necessary you know," her mother said. "He's entitled to his opinion."

"Well let him be entitled to it somewhere else," Brenda said defiantly. "I don't like him anyway."

"Well don't come complaining to me when you've got nothing to do," Molly said.

"Oh mother, don't rub it in!"

Avery glanced at Angus then said, "Your dumb uncle and I were thinking of going to the movies ourselves. Want to come along?"

"Would you take me? No kidding?"

"You bet," said Avery. "We'll even pay your way."

"Gee, you're swell!" she said. She came around the table and kissed him, then kissed Angus.

They went to the drive-in movie and saw two Wild West pictures and ate a lot of pop-corn that had plenty of butter and salt on it. The big screen, under the sky, was apparitional and strange. Afterward they had ice cream sodas at a place near the theater and drove back to the farm through the night, the three of them on the front seat of the pick-up truck. The headlights cut the ground fog into evocative sculptural shapes and they sang popular songs together to ward off the ghosts in the fog. When Brenda got out of the truck she stood for a moment with the moonlight on her face.

"Gee, thanks!" she said.

She looked radiantly young and totally happy. She turned and ran into the house and Avery laughed.

"That was a good idea," Angus said, "taking the kid to the movies. She's a nice kid and it's not so easy for her, all the time."

"I guess not," Avery said. "She's a lucky kid though. Darned lucky."

They walked away from the pick-up toward the house. There were lights on in the kitchen and as they approached the door they heard Bob and Molly quarreling bitterly, an undercurrent of desperation in their voices. Angus shook his head. "Farming's tough on people," he said. "Especially if they love one another." He banged on the door and yelled, "Is this a private fight or can anybody get in on it?"

Bob opened the door and grinned sheepishly. "Free-for-all," he said. "Come on in and have some coffee."

They sat around the kitchen table and drank coffee and for the time being the quarrel was put aside. But Avery saw the distraction that came up on Mollie's face like an image emerging on a photographic plate, and the dogged, almost grim expression of Bob's face when he was off guard. They were people being pressed by forces outside their control, almost beyond their understanding: a money system that took no accounting of the proportion of rainfall to sun, and the developing season that was ignorant of bank loans and mortgage payments.

A few days later Avery drove into town with Bob, taking a plow that wanted fixing to the welding shop. They stood on the street in front of the shop with half an hour to wait. The air was moist; it clogged the lungs like damp warm cotton. The asphalt sidewalk under their feet cooked audibly in the sun.

"Like living in an oyster stew," said Bob. He thought for a moment, then said, "I don't know about you, Avery, but I'd like to get myself outside a good cold beer right now."

They went to a dark small-town saloon that had a gumwood bar and a smeary encampment of bottles and glasses in front of a mirror that had a price list written on it with soap. It was meaner than bars in city slums because there was no noise or color or hint of violent ruin, but only dreary resignation. Half a dozen sunburnt men in work clothes nodded and said " 'Lo, Bob," when Bob and Avery entered. Then they turned back to their beer and gave attention to a radio voice filled with southern plausibility, describing a ball game in New York.

The beer was metallic and fearfully cold, so that the first taste of it was like touching a cold sled runner with the tongue. Bob drained his glass and wiped his mouth with the back of his hand. He looked at the empty glass with an expression of mock astonishment, and said, "I could have sworn that glass was full of beer. Wonder where it went?"

Avery drank his beer and Bob went to the bar for more. The radio went on and overhead a fan with indolent paddle blades stirred the warm beery air.

"How much chance do you think you've got of beating the frost?" Avery asked, when they were halfway through their second round. "If you get a chance to plant again?"

"Not much," said Bob. "Not much."

"What will happen if you don't make a crop?"

"Darned if I know," Bob said. "I guess I'll worry about that in the fall."

Avery hesitated then said, "Bob, I've got some money my grandfather left me. Quite a lot. I'd be glad to loan you whatever you need." He did not look at Bob as he spoke, but stared at a beer ring on the table. There were a few moments' silence, concluded by a roar from the radio as someone got a two base hit and scored a runner.

Then Bob said, "That's darn nice of you, Avery. I appreciate it." He grinned. "Of course you'd be in competition with the government, subsidizing a farmer. Uncle Sam might not like it." He glanced at the clock above the bar and said, "Let's see if that plow's ready, shall we?"

They walked out into the sun, exchanging the smell of dampness and beer for hot asphalt and exhaust fumes. Avery understood that his offer had been refused, but he was not sorry he had made it. He was sorry that he had nothing to offer but the money that he had not really wanted and of which he was vaguely ashamed. Like most of his generation, he had not been touched by the politics of the left that beguiled young men in the Thirties. He belonged to a generation that was nearly neutral in politics, deliberately almost unaware of the sinister political fact to which they might expect to be offered as sacrifice. Nevertheless, he felt that his inheritance challenged him with want of justification. In this he followed his generation, which looked for meaning where its predecessor had looked for method.

Under the double row of maples at the entrance to the farm, Bob pulled up for a moment. The engine throbbed beneath them, making the windshield vibrate.

"I never got around to thanking you for helping Brenda with her schoolwork," Bob said. "I sure do appreciate it. Mean a lot to her mother, if she gets through. Mean a lot to Brenda too."

"She'll pass all right," Avery said. "All she needed was a little encouragement." He was embarrassed at being thanked for something he had done for its own sake, without expectation of praise. Bob understood this and said no more. He drove on through the arch of trees and parked the truck. Brenda ran out to meet them.

"There's some mail for you, Avery," she said excitedly. "One of them's a letter from England. I put them in your room."

He got down from the truck slowly, not wanting to go upstairs and read the letters, sorry he had asked the university post office to forward his mail. He crossed the lawn reluctantly, aware of the pressure of the heat. In his room a little stack of mail lay on the table beside his bed. He picked it up, running through the letters. The message from Sarah was short and told him simply that she thought he had a right to know that the baby had been born dead, or at least almost dead, having lived less than two hours. It had been a boy and she had named it after her father. He read her Lancashire accent into the words on the air-mail paper and felt himself go to jelly. He sat on the edge of the bed and read the letter again. Then he recovered himself. He did not know whether he was relieved or terribly saddened. There seemed to be an element of fate involved in the death of the child, as though something had intervened to prevent the expression of his guilt from living and perhaps surviving him.

He sat with the letter in his hand for a long time before he opened the rest of his mail. There was a letter from the university with a form about his draft deferment, some advertising matter, and a letter from Dennis McCoy that he didn't like to open. Our Lady of Gethsemane, the return address read. The place of Christ's Agony. The words sent a little current of fear up and down Avery's spine. He read the letter and found out what he had probably known already—that Dennis was going to stay with the Trappists as a lay brother, forbidden the priesthood, forbidden the sacrament of ordination for which his heart yearned, but living out his life within the sound of the sanctus bell, in silence and in retreat from the world.

Avery lay down on his bed and stared at the ceiling, thinking of Dennis and of Sarah and of his own dead child. He was aware of a flat colorless nostalgia of the kind prisoners must feel. He fell asleep for a time, then drifted out of sleep into an area of waking dream, hypnotic and physically pleasant. He became aware of a familiar hissing sound at the window and leapt from the bed.

It was raining, a slow steady drizzle that caressed the earth. He watched it and felt an almost grim sensation of triumph, then a surge of clear unselfish gratitude to God or whatever Benevolence had at last intervened.

Downstairs, he found them on the porch watching this rain as they had watched the thunderstorm. But Bob had an arm around Mollie's waist and the anguish was gone from his face.

"Plant tomorrow?" Avery said.

Bob nodded. "You bet we will," he said.

There was more rain, then three days of sun. The new plants came along quickly and there was a great amount of work. Avery fought the heavy tractor, taking pleasure in the response of his summer hardened muscles, a simple elemental joy in hard work. A week passed and they watched the sky lower and darken for a full day before the rain came down as before, in timeless gentle fashion.

The drought was broken.

That Saturday they had a party on the beach that turned into a celebration. As the night closed in they drew close to the fire and sang songs that everyone knew. Angus pounded Avery on the back. "You wouldn't think a man could be so God damned happy just because it rained, would you?" he said. "Just because the God damn rain came down."

Bob grinned, his face lighted by the dying fire. "Let's not be Gawd damnin' the rain now, Angus," he said. "Let's treat that rain with quite a lot of respect."

Avery sat on the sand, watching Bob's face, and he was aware of a sense of peace in himself and of maturity. He didn't quite know the source of the change, but he felt it. Nothing had happened, but everything had happened; he felt as though he had been put through a kind of trial by darkness designed to establish his character. He was not out of the darkness yet, but he could see the light off in the distance, like the light at the end of a tunnel.

"Rain comes from heaven," he said to Angus. "It's entitled to special deference."

The fire burned down to coals and they sat for a while in the darkness. Then a chill wind came in from the sea and they got up, walking back along the beach, their feet heavy in the sand.

CHAPTER SEVENTY-ONE

A T THE end of August, Brenda took her algebra examination and passed. When she showed him the summer school certificate Avery had a feeling of accomplishment that he had never experienced before.

"You see I told you it was easy," he said.

"It isn't easy," she said. "It's hard. It's just that I can understand it the way you explain it."

He bowed gravely and said, "Thank you."

"Gee, thank you!"

There was a whistle on the porch. She kissed him on the cheek and ran out of the room. The pimply Barringer who liked potatoes had been replaced by Donald, who had both a clear skin and a Star class boat that he sailed in the junior races. Avery heard them greet one another.

"Hi, Stoop!"

"Hi, Brain!"

He smiled, feeling a sense of extraordinary well-being. The summer seemed over, and he felt the restlessness that comes with the turn of a season, the feeling of loss and of need for change. During August he had thought a great deal about his return to the university. He had tried to put it out of his mind, for it had not been appealing. It had been like contemplating a return to prison. He did not realize how far his thinking actually had gone until a few days later, when Bob said, "What'll you do this fall, Avery? Go back to Columbia with Angus or get a job somewhere?"

"Neither one I guess," said Avery, staring off at the fields that now were densely green with fresh plants. "I'll be twenty-one in a couple of weeks. I suppose the draft will get me."

"Can't you get out of it, being in college?"

"I guess I could," he said. "But I think I'd rather get it over with at the right time. I've got plenty of time. A lot of time. A whole damn lifetime."

Bob nodded. "Probably a good idea," he said. "Think you'll like the army?"

"I don't know," said Avery. "As well as anyone else, I guess." He hesitated then said, "I think I'll go home first, if you don't need me here any more."

"You go ahead," said Bob. "It's a good idea. Been a long time, I guess, since you've been home?"

Avery nodded. "Yes. A long time," he said. "A hell of a long time."

Now that he had announced his plans he understood that he had been forming them all summer long. He had really started his journey home when he had gone to England. The summer had been a delay en route. He faced the idea of going home with confidence and a certain detachment. He wrote to his father, telling him that he planned to enter the army and would like if possible to come home for a few days and enlist through the draft board in Hull, since that seemed to him more appropriate. He had his answer in three days. Bob drove him into town to make the dawn train for New York. He felt odd in his city clothes and was sorry to leave a place that he had learned to love. But he was confident. He had the feeling that the thaw had set in.

At the station, before they got down from the truck, Bob said, "Been good to have you, Avery. Thanks."

"I think I got more than I gave," Avery said.

They shook hands. It was not necessary to say anything more. Avery got aboard the train and waved through the window. Bob stood on the platform, his faded blue work clothes a beautiful color in the pale light. He waved back, then the train gave a long lonely whistle and moved slowly out of the station. Avery took a book out of his bag and began to read, not looking at the flat countryside. He did not look up until the train had passed into Queens and the busy suburban streets.

He took a taxi across the city to Grand Central Station and bought a ticket for Hartford, then on a chance went to a booth and phoned Dormaker at his apartment. Dormaker was there. He listened to what Avery had to say, then said, "I see."

Avery waited for him to make some further observation, praise or blame. The phone hummed in his ear. Finally he said, "Do you think I'm right?"

"Do you?" Dormaker asked.

Avery thought for a moment, staring through the window of the booth at the crowds moving through the station. A troop of boys from a summer camp, sunburnt and dressed in shorts and dark green jerseys, was herded into line by a young man wearing a pale blue Columbia sweat shirt. He looked young: younger than Avery could imagine that he himself had ever been.

"Yes," he said finally into the phone. "Yes I do."

"Then you probably are," Dormaker said. "I hope you come back to us when you're finished with the military." There was a pause, then Dormaker said in a lower tone, "We like you Avery. And we can use you. Your work is here."

"Thank you, sir," Avery said. "Good-bye."

"Good-bye Avery. And good luck to you."

Avery hung up and came out of the booth. He had half expected Dormaker to protest his decision and Dormaker's neutral attitude left him a little flat. Then he smiled, walking across the station with his bag. This time he had made up his own mind.

A conductor in a porous blue-serge suit stood at the brass railed gate. "Hartford train!" he called. "Bridgeport, New Haven, Hartford Express!"

Avery showed his ticket and walked down the ramp into the steamy underground level and got a seat at the window of a glassy air-conditioned coach, settling himself for the long ride home.

CHAPTER SEVENTY-TWO

H E HAD not seen his father for more than two years and the fact that struck him first was that he was as tall as his father or perhaps half an inch taller. It was disconcerting.

"You look well, father," he said.

His father nodded. "I'm fit."

They shook hands, looking at one another. They were in the dingy Hartford station and behind them Avery's train puffed like a worn-out runner. Avery picked up his bag and they walked down the platform.

"You look grand," his father said. "Have you been in the mountains?"

Avery shook his head. "I've been working on a farm," he said. "Pushing a tractor."

"Oh?" his father said. "Dairy farm?"

"No. Truck farm," Avery said. "Down on Long Island."

"Drought bad down there?" his father asked.

"Pretty bad," Avery nodded. "Pretty bad."

As they walked through the waiting room they passed a large plate-glass mirror set into the wall. Each of them chanced to be wearing a gray flannel suit of about the same shade and the resemblance between them was so striking that both paused for a moment, looking into the glass. Then they went on. It gave Avery an uncanny sensation to realize that in his father he saw himself as he would look in thirty years, and he remembered how he had hated his face in childhood, when he had looked more like his mother than his father.

His father backed the car and spun the wheel, making the tricky turn out of the station parking lot. It was the long new car that Avery had seen from the little window in the barn, an English car, a Jaguar, but with the wheel fitted on the American side. The sight of his father at the wheel of a car was so familiar that it brought back the past with a rush. "Nice car," he said. "How does she run?"

"Perfect," his father said. "You know I like a good car. Always have. This one cost too much, but I get something out of it."

"I guess," Avery said.

As they drove through downtown Hartford, his father said, "Did you, uh, enjoy the farm, Avery?"

"Yes, sir," Avery said. "Very much."

"Good. Good," his father said. "I'm glad you had a good summer."

They left the city and turned onto the highway, heading for Hull. Avery watched his father drive the long powerful car, carefully and expertly, as he had always driven. As he watched his father's face, intent on the road, he saw the age that had been added since his father had gone into the army. The face was a little less full and the lines around the eyes were deeper. He looked older than he had in his battle blouse the day Avery met him at the airport and drove him home to the tragic house. But he was still a vigorous and powerful man, with authority and animal command. He was fifty-three, Avery knew. He would live for twenty, maybe thirty years. He was nowhere near the end of life.

"I'm glad you're going into the service, Avery," he said, swinging out to pass a car then swinging back into his lane with a precision that expressed part of his character. "Too many young fellows seem to feel they have no duty to the country at all."

"I don't think it's my duty to go into the army," Avery said carefully. "As a matter of fact I have an idea that it's my duty to go back to the university and take my degree."

His father kept his eyes on the road. "Then why are you volunteering?" he asked.

"Because I want to," Avery said. "And because it's a luxury I think I can afford."

His father smiled. It was the first time he had smiled since they met in the station and Avery found himself smiling too.

"I don't think I'll comment on that one," his father said. "You have a right to your own reasons." He paused. "But I hope you don't mind my being pleased that you are going in?"

"No, sir," Avery said. "I'm glad you are."

After a while they reached the dirt road that led to the farm. Avery felt his chest tighten. He did not know how much of his emotion was aroused by the familiar scene and how much by the fact that in a few minutes he must come face to face with his father's wife.

He had underestimated her instinct for diplomacy.

She had not returned from her afternoon ride when he and his father reached the house and he did not see her until just before dinner, so that he had plenty of time to get over the first nervousness of homecoming.

"You go on in, Avery," his father said, on the driveway in front of the house. "I'll put the car away."

"All right, sir," Avery said.

He went into the house, and looked around. He felt that it was a kind of joke on himself that the downstairs rooms were furnished and arranged just as they had always been. In his resentments and imaginings he had sometimes been certain that the old house had been assaulted with God knows what decoratorish madness. Once in a dream he had envisioned the living room filled with straw-colored modern furniture, looking like the waiting room at an airport.

Nothing had been changed.

The room was exactly as it had been during his childhood and youth. Of course it made him sad and called up a flanking memory of his mother and brother and of his own used childhood. After all it was his mother's room and his grandmother's and his great-grandmother's. The blended accumulations of time were a reflection of his own past to a point long before his actual birth. As he stood in the center of the room, looking around, he felt an intense, imperative sense of proprietorship, of linkage with the generations, of shared, imprecise possession, possession by right, more complete than ownership and entailed to the future generations.

He was a Hollister in spite of it all, and he was at home. It was just that he was not at all the kind of Hollister his father was; he understood suddenly that when he had turned from the pattern, from the mold, that he had not changed the metal itself because it was an element and refused reduction. It was only the shape that could be changed. He could not be his father, as he had sometimes wanted to be when he was young. He could not be Breitbart, or Angus, or Dennis, or Dormaker, or his dead brother or his dead son. He could not be anyone on the face of the earth but himself: his father's son, enemy and ally.

What gave him a flash of understanding to which he was to return later was realization that his father in the end could not really have behaved much differently from the way he had behaved, given that pattern and that metal and that time of pouring.

He looked around the room and his eyes misted.

"The poor sonofabitch," he said half aloud. "The poor bastard."

He went upstairs to his own room, which had been prepared for him, and unpacked his bag. Then he cleaned up and put on a fresh shirt. There were outgrown clothes in the closet—suits he had worn at Colborn. They seemed related to another life.

When he went downstairs he found his father's wife in the living room. She was dressed in white breeches and black boots and wore a plain white shirt opened at the neck. She looked young and vivid and very attractive.

"Well, Avery."

She shook his hand.

"It's nice of you to let me come," he said.

"This is your home," she said. "You have more right here than I."

He let go of her hand and they stood looking at one another for a moment. Then she said, "We usually have dinner at seven, but we can put it up a little if you're hungry."

"Seven will be fine," he said.

She smiled. "I'll see you at dinner then," she said. "I've got to change."

She went across the room and through the door that led to the kitchen. He stood watching the door that had closed behind her, that he had passed through himself several thousand times, on the way to Annie's bailiwick with some pain or triumph that wanted attending to. He tried to recall what had been at the center of his hatred for this woman, toward whom at this moment he felt almost nothing at all. It astonished him that the passage of time and an altered context could blur into unrecognizability an emotion as consuming as that hatred had been. He did not understand it. He sat down in a comfortable chair with his legs stretched out, leafing through a magazine until it was time to go in to dinner.

The next day he drove into Hull to make arrangements with the draft board and found that he had ten days to himself before reporting to Fort Devens. It meant that his twenty-first birthday would occur before he left the house and he mentioned this to his father. They had a cake for him with twenty-one candles and he blew them out with one blow.

"That means you get your wish," his father said, handing him the broad-bladed silver knife.

"That's right," Avery said.

He made a single symbolic cut, then the cake was carried to the sideboard and cut into serving pieces. The Irish cook and the two maids came in from the kitchen and everyone sang "Happy Birthday" to him. He cried.

After dinner his father took him into the study for brandy and coffee. He offered him a cigar and Avery started to refuse, then changed his mind and took it. They sat in the familiar room, the two men, the air around them rich with the smells of coffee and good tobacco and rich fruity brandy. After a while his father leaned forward. It was an almost grotesquely familiar movement. Avery smiled.

"Have you, uh, anything you want to say to me, Avery?" his father asked. "Anything you'd like to discuss?"

Avery stared at the pattern of the Chinese rug on the study floor, a pattern burnt into his memory and that would remain there for life. He shook his head. What was there to discuss? And what language would you discuss it in?

"No, sir," he said. "I don't think so."

He looked across the desk at his father and felt both pity and love. He felt pity because he understood that his father was lost and must be bewildered. So many of the things that had given meaning to his life were gone, no longer true, and even the institutions in which he believed no longer existed in forms he understood: neither Yale College nor Colborn School, nor New England, nor the army, nor Britain, nor the United States of America. It was not so much that his father's world was imperfect or his ethic faulty, as the fact that the institutions and way of life to which these values and that ethic were complements no longer existed. Only the fact that he was cushioned by money, prestige, and the pattern of a familiar scene and milieu prevented the world from collapsing on his head.

But you could not tell a man these things. You would not be understood, and there would be no service or kindness in the telling.

Avery finished his brandy and said good night, leaving his father alone in the study. He went outdoors and crossed the lawn to the swimming pool, already drained of its water and bone-white in the starlight. The scene was at once familiar as breathing and strange as the surface of the moon. This was the home of half of him and he would never truly leave it. The other half had no home, and it was that second half that was forming him, around the core of the other. He was at once his father's son, and a changeling who might be expected to contradict the plan. He was unique.

Unique.

And this knowledge gave him a certain exhilarating awareness of power. He was unique and he was ambiguous, as, he had learnt, was all mankind, with the tragic fundamental ambiguity of every man, who is both object and subject, who lives and must die, and whose life is in its essence only a monologue addressed to death. Whatever meaning was to be found must be sought in the quality of each man's discourse and not in the antiseptic scientific heaven that only existed in the minds of men. He saw that the meaning of life for him was not fixed but had to be won all the time, each minute, each fraction of a second, and it seemed to him that there was no goal, no victory, but only, perhaps, a right direction. Old Dormaker once had told him, "Avery, you should understand. We cannot afford to be less than men."

He saw suddenly, under the stars, what Dormaker had meant.

There were no heroes. Only survivors. But the idea of the hero was one that was desperately needed. Art and science were important, for they were the fictions men lived by insofar as they were men, and not just animals a little shrewder than the others.

They must not be animals; he must not be.

The lonely crow had learned to count, but only up to four; Newton had made the leap of the mind and assumed that all of the numbers were counted and thus, acting as if all time were at his disposal, placed himself at the side of God. It was a dangerous, unprotected place and God would not put an arm around him, but it was the place for a man.

Avery shuddered, staring at the empty swimming pool that was like an enormous tomb in the night light. He sat on the edge of the pool, his legs dangling, and smoked a cigarette, comforted by the familiar taste and the reassuring glow of the cigarette end, larger to his eye than a star and red with warmth.

After a time he got to his feet and went back into the house. Through the open study door he saw his father, sitting as he had left him, engrossed in thought, the muscles of his face relaxed so that he looked older and more vulnerable. He stood in the doorway for a moment, looking at his father, then said, "Good night, Dad."

His father looked up, startled for a moment, then smiled and nodded. "Good night, son." He straightened up. "You off in the morning?"

"Yes, sir."

"I'll drive you to the city if you like."

Avery nodded. "Thanks," he said. "Thanks a lot."

He turned away and went upstairs to his own room, getting his bag out of the closet and packing the things he planned to take to Fort Devens with him. When the bag was packed, except for his shaving brush and razor that he would put in in the morning, he went to the window and looked out across the lawn, aware of a powerful feeling of serenity. He felt that he had made a step: that he was no longer merely an observer of himself but a participant in his own life. He felt like a man, more than just an animal with an intensely developed intelligence. There was a whole lifetime ahead and he had found out how to stand up, to stand erect, and the knowledge gave him something that was quite close to happiness.

www.ingramcontent.com/pod-product-compliance
Lightning Source LLC
Chambersburg PA
CBHW030845030726
47495CB00005B/1379